"THERE ARE NO MANNERS IN THE

BATTLE CIRCLE...

ONLY VICTORY AND DEFEAT."

In this stunningly imaginative trilogy, master science fiction writer Piers Anthony creates a brutal, unsparing vision of a return to savagery in a lawless postnuclear age. After the holocaust, tribes of barbaric warriors roam Earth's radioactive wasteland, where all disputes are settled in the "battle circle," and a man is known by the weapon he carries...

"Anthony's story of men fighting for mastery of wandering tribes, with sword, club, and rope in the ceremonial 'Great Circle,' has its own internal conviction—its own grandeur even...a rigorous masculine power, rare in any kind of novel nowadays."

The London Observer

BATTLE CIRCLE

A TRILOGY BY

PIERS ANTHONY

SOS THE ROPE
VAR THE STICK
NEQ THE SWORD

AVON BOOKS ◆ NEW YORK

AVON BOOKS
A division of
The Hearst Corporation
105 Madison Avenue
New York, New York 10016

Copyright © 1968 by Piers Anthony
Copyright © 1972 by Piers Anthony
Copyright © 1975 by Piers Anthony
Published by arrangement with the author
Library of Congress Catalog Card Number: 77-91015
ISBN: 0-380-01800-4

First Avon Books Printing: February 1978

AVON TRADEMARK REG. U.S. PAT. OFF. AND IN OTHER COUNTRIES, MARCA REGISTRADA, HECHO EN U.S.A.

Printed in Canada

UNV   15   14   13   12   11

Contents

Sos the Rope

CHAPTER ONE

The two itinerant warriors approached the hostel from opposite directions. Both were garbed conventionally: dark pantaloons cinched at waist and knee, loose white jacket reaching to hips and elbows and hanging open at the front, elastic sneakers. Both wore their hair medium: cropped above the eyebrows in front, above the ears on the sides, and above the jacket collar behind, uncombed. Both beards were short and scant.

The man from the east wore a standard straight sword, the plastic scabbard strapped across his broad back. He was young and large, if unhandsome, and his black brows and hair gave him a forbidding air that did not match his nature. He was well-muscled and carried his weight with the assurance of a practicing athlete.

The one from the west was shorter and more slender, but also in fine physical trim. His blue eyes and fair hair set off a countenance so finely molded that it would have been almost womanish without the beard, but there was nothing effeminate about his manner. He pushed before him a little one-wheeled cart, a barrow-bag, from which several feet of shining metal pole projected.

The dark-haired man arrived before the round building first and waited politely for the other to come up. They surveyed each other briefly before speaking. A young woman emerged, dressed in the attractive one-piece wrap-around of the available. She looked from one visitor to the other, her eyes fixing for a moment upon the handsome golden bracelet clasping the left wrist of each, but kept her silence.

The sworder glanced at her once as she approached,

appreciating the length of her glossy midnight tresses and the studied voluptuousness of her figure, then spoke to the man with the cart. "Will you share lodging with me tonight, friend? I seek mastery of other things than men."

"I seek mastery in the circle," the other replied, "but I will share lodging." They smiled and shook hands.

The blond man faced the girl. "I need no woman."

She dropped her eyes, disappointed, but flicked them up immediately to cover the sworder. He responded after an appropriate pause. "Will you try the night with me, then, damsel? I promise no more."

The girl flushed with pleasure. "I will try the night with you, sword, expecting no more."

He grinned and clapped his right hand to the bracelet, twisting it off. "I am Sol the sword, of philosophic bent. Can you cook?" She nodded, and he handed the bracelet to her. "You will cater to my friend also, for the evening meal, and clean his uniform."

The other man interrupted his smile. "Did I mishear your name, sir? *I* am Sol."

The larger warrior turned slowly, frowning. "I regret you did not. I have held this name since I took up my blade this spring. But perhaps you employ another weapon? There is no need for us to differ."

The girl's eyes went back and forth between them. "Surely your arm is the staff, warrior," she said anxiously, gesturing at the barrow.

"I am Sol," the man said firmly, "of the staff—and the sword. No one else may bear my name."

The sworder looked disgruntled. "Do you quarrel with me, then? I would have it otherwise."

"I quarrel only with your name. Take another, and there is no strife between us."

"I have earned this name by this blade. I can not give it up."

"Then I must deprive you of it in the circle, sir."

"Please," the girl protested. "Wait until morning. There is a television inside, and a bath, and I will fix a fine repast."

"Would you borrow the bracelet of a man whose name has been questioned?" the sworder inquired gently. "It must be now, pretty plaything. You may serve the winner."

She bit her red lip, chastened, and handed back the bracelet. "Then, will you permit me to stand witness?"

The men exchanged glances and shrugged. "Stand witness, girl, if you have the stomach for it," the blond man said. He led the way down a beaten side-trail marked in red.

A hundred yards below the cabin a fifteen-foot ring was laid out, marked by a flat plastic rim of bright yellow and an outer fringe of gravel. The center was flat, finely barbered turf, a perfect disk of green lawn. This was the battle circle, heart of this world's culture.

The black-haired man removed his harness and jacket to expose the physique of a giant, great sheaths of muscle overlaid shoulders, rib-cage and belly, and his neck and waist were thick. He drew his sword: a gleaming length of tempered steel with a beaten silver hilt. He flexed it in the air a few times and tested it on a nearby sapling. A single swing and the tree fell, cleanly severed at the base.

The other opened his barrow and drew forth a similar weapon from a compartment. Packed beside it were daggers, singlesticks, a club, the metal ball of a morningstar mace and the long quarterstaff. "You master *all* these weapons?" the girl inquired, astonished. He only nodded.

The two men approached the circle and faced each other across it, toes touching the outer rim. "I contest for the name," the blond declared, "by sword, staff, stick, star, knife and club. Select an alternate, and this is unnecessary."

"I will go nameless first," the dark one replied. "By the sword I claim the name, and if I ever take another weapon it will be only to preserve that name. Take your best instrument: I will match with my blade."

"For name *and* weapons, then," the blond said, beginning to show anger. "The victor will possess them all. But, since I wish you no personal harm, I will instead oppose you with the staff."

"Agreed!" It was the other's turn to glower. "The one who is defeated yields the name and these six weapons, nor will he ever lay claim to any of these again!"

The girl listened appalled, hearing the stakes magnify beyond reason, but did not dare protest.

They stepped inside the battle circle and became blurs of motion. The girl had expected a certain incongruity, since small men usually carried the lighter or sharper weapons while the heavy club and long staff were left to the large men. Both warriors were so skilled, however, that such notions became meaningless. She tried to follow thrust and counter, but soon became hopelessly confused. The figures whirled and struck, ducked and parried, metal blade rebounding from metal staff and, in turn, blocking defensively. Gradually, she made out the course of the fight.

The sword was actually a fairly massive weapon; though hard to stop, it was also slow to change its course, so there was generally time for the opposing party to counter an aggressive swing. The long staff, on the other hand, was more agile than it looked, since both hands exerted force upon it and made for good leverage—but it could deliver a punishing blow only against a properly exposed target. The sword was primarily offensive; the staff, defensive. Again and again the sword whistled savagely at neck or leg or torso, only to be blocked crosswise by some section of the staff.

At first, it had seemed as though the men were out to kill each other; then, it was evident that each expected his aggressive moves to be countered and was not trying for bloody victory so much as tactical initiative. Finally, it appeared to be a deadlock between two extraordinarily talented warriors.

Then the tempo changed. The blond Sol took the offensive, using the swift staff to force his opponents back and off balance by repeated blows at arms, legs and head. The sworder jumped out of the way often, rather than trying to parry the multiple blows with his single instrument; evidently the weight of his weapon was growing as the furious pace continued. Swords were not weapons of endurance. The staffer had conserved his strength and now had the advantage. Soon the tiring sword-arm would slow too much and leave the body vulnerable.

But not quite yet. Even she, an inexperienced observer, could guess that the large man was tiring too quickly for the amount of muscle he possessed. It was a ruse—and the staffer suspected it, too, for the more the motions slowed the more cautious he became. He refused to be lured into any risky commitment.

Then the sworder tried an astonishing strategem: as the end of the staff drove at his side in a fast horizontal swing, he neither blocked nor retreated. He threw himself to the ground, letting the staff pass over him. Then, rolling on his side, he slashed in a vicious backhand arc aimed at the ankles. The staffer jumped, surprised by this unconventional and dangerous maneuver; but even as his feet rose over the blade and came down again, it was swishing in a reverse arc.

The staffer was unable to leap again quickly enough, since he was just landing. But he was not so easily trapped. He had kept his balance and maintained control over his weapon with marvelous coordination. He jammed the end of the staff into the turf between his feet just as the sword struck. Blood spurted as the blade cut into one calf, but the metal of the staff bore the brunt and saved him from hamstringing or worse. He was wounded and partially crippled, but still able to fight.

The ploy had failed, and it was the end for the sworder. The staff lifted and struck him neatly across the side of the head as he tried to rise, sending him spinning out of the circle. He fell in the gravel, stunned, still gripping his weapon but no longer able to bring it into play. After a moment he realized where he was, gave one groan of dismay, and dropped the sword. He had lost.

Sol, now the sole owner of the name, hurled the staff into the ground beside his barrow and stepped over the plastic rim. He gripped the loser's arm and helped him to his feet. "Come—we must eat," he said.

The girl was jolted out of her reverie. "Yes—I will tend your wounds," she said. She led the way back to the cabin, prettier now that she was not trying to impress.

The building was a smooth cylinder, thirty feet in diameter and ten high, the outer wall a sheet of hard plastic seemingly wrapped around it with no more original effort than one might have applied to enclose a package. A transparent cone topped it, punctured at the apex to allow the chimney column to emerge. From a distance it was possible to see through the cone to the shiny machinery beneath it: paraphernalia that caught and tamed the light of the sun and provided regular power for the operation of the interior devices.

There were no windows, and the single door faced south: a rotating trio of glassy panels that admitted them singly without allowing any great flow of air. It was cool inside, and bright; the large central compartment was illuminated by the diffused incandescence of floor and ceiling.

The girl hauled down couch-bunks from the curving inner side of the wall and saw them seated upon the nylon upholstery. She dipped around the rack of assorted weapons, clothing and bracelets to run water in the sink set into the central column. In a moment she brought back a basin of warm water and set about sponging off Sol's bleeding leg and dressing it. She went on to care for the bruise on the loser's head, while the two men talked. There was no rancor between them, now that the controversy had been resolved.

"How did you come by that motion with the sword?" Sol inquired, not appearing to notice the ministrations of the girl though she gave him more than perfunctory attention. "It very nearly vanquished me."

"I am unsatisfied with conventional ways," the nameless one replied as the girl applied astringent medication. "I ask 'Why must this be?' and 'How can it be improved?' and 'Is there *meaning* in this act?' I study the writings of the ancients, and sometimes I come upon the answers, if I can not work them out for myself."

"I am impressed. I have met no warrior before who could read—and you fought well."

"Not well enough." The tone was flat. "Now I must seek the mountain."

"I am sorry this had to pass," Sol said sincerely.

The nameless one nodded curtly. No more was said for a time. They took turns in the shower compartment, also set in the central column, and dried and changed clothing, indifferent to the presence of the girl.

Bandaged on head and leg, they shared the supper the girl prepared. She had quietly folded down the dining table from the north face and set up stools, while she kept her feet and ferried dishes from range and refrigerator—the last of the fixtures of the column. They did not inquire the source of the spiced white meat or the delicate wine; such things were taken for granted, and even looked down upon, as was the hostel itself.

"What is your objective in life?" the nameless one inquired as they lingered over the ice cream, and the girl washed the dishes.

"I mean to fashion an empire."

"A tribe of your own? I have no doubt you can do it."

"An empire. Many tribes. I am a skilled warrior—better in the circle than any I have seen. Better than the masters of tribes. I will take what my arm brings me—but I have not encountered any I wish to keep, except yourself, and we did not contest for mastery. Had I known how good you were, I would have set different terms."

The other chose to ignore the compliment, but it pleased him. "To build a tribe you need honorable men, proficient in their specialties, who are capable of fighting for you and bringing others into your group. You need young ones, as young as yourself, who will listen to advice and profit from it. To build an empire you need more."

"More? I have not even found young warriors that are worthwhile. Only incompetent amateurs and feeble oldsters."

"I know. I saw few good fighters in the east, and had you found any in the west you would not have traveled alone. I never lost an engagement, before." He was silent a moment, remembering that he was no longer a warrior. To cover up the hurt that grew in him, he spoke again. "Haven't you noticed how old the masters are, and how careful? They will not fight at all unless they believe they can win, and they are shrewd at such judgments. All the best warriors are tied to them."

"Yes," Sol agreed, perturbed. "The good ones will not contend for mastership, only for sport. It makes me angry."

"Why should they? Why should an established master risk the work of a lifetime, while you risk only your service? You must have stature. You must have a tribe to match his; only then will any master meet you in the circle."

"How can I form a decent tribe when no decent men will fight?" Sol demanded, growing heated again. "Do your books answer that?"

"I never sought mastery. But if I were building a tribe, or an empire especially, I would search out promising youths and bind them to myself, even though they were not proficient in the circle yet. Then I would take them to some private place and teach them all I knew about combat, and make them practice against each other and me until they were fully competent. Then I would have a respectable tribe, and I would take it out to meet and conquer established tribes."

"What if the other masters still refused to enter the circle?" Sol was quite interested in this turn of the discussion.

"I would find some way to persuade them. Strategy would be required—the terms would have to appear even, or slightly in favor of the other party. I would show them men that they wanted, and bargain with them until they were ashamed not to meet me."

"I am not good at bargaining," Sol said.

"You could have some bright tribesmen bargain for you, just as you would have others to fight for you. The master doesn't have to do everything himself; he delegates the chores to others, while he governs over all."

Sol was thoughtful. "That never occurred to me. Fighters with the weapons and fighters with the mind." He pondered some more. "How long would it take to train such a tribe, once the men were taken?"

"That depends upon how good you are at training, and how good the men are that you have to work with. How well they get along. There are many factors."

"If you were doing it, with the men you have met in your travels."

"A year."

"A year!" Sol was dismayed.

"There is no substitute for careful preparation. A mediocre tribe could perhaps be formed in a few months, but not an organization fit to conquer an empire. That would have to be prepared for every contingency, and that takes times. Time and constant effort and patience."

"I do not have patience."

The girl finished her work and returned to listen. There were no compartments within the cabin, but she had gone around the column to the shower stall and changed. She now wore an alluring gown that accentuated a fine cleavage and a narrow waist.

Sol remained thoughtful, not seeming to notice the girl though she drew her stool close to him. "Where would there be a suitable place for such training, where others would not spy and interfere?"

"In the badlands."

"The badlands! No one goes there!"

"Precisely. No one would come across you there, or suspect what you were doing. Can you think of a better situation?"

"But it is death!" the girl said, forgetting her place.

"Not necessarily. I have learned that the kill-spirits of the Blast are retreating. The old books call it 'radiation,' and it fades in time. The intensity is measured in Roentgen, and it is strongest in the center. It should be possible to tell by the plants and animals whether a given area within the markers has become safe. You would have to be very careful about penetrating too far inside, but near the edge—"

"I would not have you go to the mountain," Sol broke in. "I have need of a man like you."

"Nameless and weaponless?" He laughed bitterly. "Go your way, fashion your empire, Sol of all instruments. I was merely conjecturing."

Sol persisted. "Serve me for a year, and I will give you back a portion of your name. It is your mind I require, for it is better than mine."

"My mind!" But the black-haired one was intrigued. He had spoken of the mountain, but did not really want to die. There were many curious things remaining to be fathomed, many books to be studied, many thoughts to be thought. He had employed his weapon in the circle because it was the established method of manhood, but despite his erstwhile prowess and physique he was a scholar and experimenter at heart.

Sol was watching him. "I offer—Sos."

"Sos—the weaponless," he said, mulling it over. He did not like the sound of it, but it was a reasonable alternative, close to his original name. "What would you want me to do, in return for the name?"

"The training, the camp, the building of empire you

described—I want you to do it for me. To be my fighter of the mind. My advisor."

"Sos the advisor." The notion grew on him, and the name sounded better. "The men would not listen to me. I would need complete authority, or it would come to nothing. If they argued, and I with no weapon—"

"Who argues, dies," Sol said with absolute conviction. "By my hand."

"For one year—and I keep the name?"

"Yes."

He thought of the challenge of it, the chance to test his theories in action. "I accept the offer."

They reached across the table and shook hands gravely. "Tomorrow we begin the empire," Sol said.

The girl looked up. "I would come with you," she said.

Sol smiled, not looking at her. "She wants your bracelet again, Sos."

"No." She was troubled, seeing her hints come to nothing. "Not without—"

"Girl," Sol reminded her sternly, "I want no woman. This man fought well; he is stronger than many who still bear weapons, and a scholar, which I am not. You would not be shamed to wear his emblem."

She thrust out her lip. "I would come—myself."

Sol shrugged. "As you wish. You will cook and wash for us, until you take a man. We will not be staying in a cabin always, though." He paused, thinking of something. "Sos, my advisor—is this wise?"

Sos studied the woman, now petulant but still lovely. He tried not to be moved by her cleavage. "I do not think so. She is excellently proportioned and a talented cook, but headstrong. She would be a disruptive influence, unattached."

She glared at him. "I want a name, as you do!" she snapped. "An *honorable* name."

Sol crashed his first against the table so hard the vinyl surface flexed. "You anger me, girl. Do you claim the name I give lacks honor?"

She retreated hastily. "No, man of all weapons. But you do not offer it to *me*."

"Take it, then!" He flung his golden bracelet at her. "But I need no woman."

Baffled but exultant, she picked up the heavy piece and squeezed it together to fit her wrist. Sos looked on, ill at ease.

CHAPTER TWO

Two weeks later they struck the red markers of warning in the open country to the north. The foliage did not change, but they knew there would be few animals and no men beyond the sinister line of demarcation. Even those who chose to die preferred the mountain, for that was a quick, honorable leavetaking, while the badlands were reputed to bring torture and horror.

Sol stopped, discommoded by the markers. "If it is safe, why are they still here?" he demanded. Sola nodded heartily, unashamed of her fear.

"Because the crazies haven't updated their maps in fifty years," Sos replied. "This area is overdue for resurvey, and one of these months they'll get around to it and set the markers back ten or fifteen miles. I told you radiation isn't a permanent thing; it fades away slowly."

Sol was not convinced, now that commitment was imminent. "You say this 'radiation' is something you can't see or hear or smell or feel, but it kills you just the same? I know you studied the books, but that just doesn't make sense to me."

"Maybe the books are lying," Sola put in, sitting down. The days of forced marching had tightened the muscles of her legs but diminished none of her femaleness. She was a good-looking woman and knew it.

"I've had doubts myself," Sos admitted. "There are many things I don't understand, and many books I've never had the chance to read. One text says that half the men will die when exposed to 450 Roentgen, while mosquitoes can survive over a hundred thousand—but I don't know how much radiation one Roentgen is, or how to spot it. The crazies have boxes that click when they get near radiation; that's how they know."

"One click to a Roent, maybe," she said, simplifying it. "*If* the books are honest."

"I think they are. A lot of it makes no sense at all, at first, but I've never caught them in an error. This radiation —as nearly as I can make it, it was put here by the Blast, and it's like fungus-light. You can't see the fungus glow in the daytime, but you know that light is still there. You can box it with your hands to shut out the sun, and the green—"

"Fungus-light," Sol said solemnly.

"Just imagine that it is poisonous, that it will make you sick if it touches your skin. At night you can avoid it, but in the day you're in trouble. You can't see it or feel it . . . that's what radiation is, except that it fills up everything where it exists. The ground, the trees, the air."

"Then how do we know it's gone?" Sola demanded. There was an edge to her voice which Sos put down to fear and fatigue. She had gradually lost the air of sweet naïveté she had affected the first evening at the hostel.

"Because it affects the plants and animals, too. They get at the fringe, and everything is dead at the center. As long as they *look* all right, we should be safe. There should be several miles clear of it beyond the markers now. It's a risk—but a worthwhile one, in the circumstances."

"And no cabins?" she asked a little forlornly.

"I doubt it. The crazies don't like radiation any better than we do, so they'd have no reason to build here until they survey it. We'll have to forage and sleep out."

"We'd better pick up bows and tents, then," Sol said.

They left Sola to watch Sol's barrow while they backtracked three miles to the last hostel. They entered its heat-pump interior comfort and selected two sturdy bows and arrow-packs from its armory. They donned camping gear: light plastic leggings, helmets and traveling packs. Each man placed three swift shots in the standing target near the battle circle, feeling out the instruments, then shouldered them and returned to the trail.

Sola was asleep against a tree, hiking skirt hitched up indecorously. Sos looked away; the sight of her body stirred him in spite of what he knew of her bad temper. He had always taken his women as they came and formed no lasting relationships; this continued proximity to another man's wife acted upon him in a way he did not like.

Sol kicked her. "Is this the way you guard my weapons, woman?"

She jumped up, embarrassed and angry. "It's the same way you take care of *mine*!" she retorted. Then, afraid, she bit her lip.

Sol ignored her. "Let's find a place quickly," he said, glancing at the nearest marker. Sos gave the woman the leggings and helmet he had brought for her; Sol hadn't thought of it. Sos wondered why they stayed together, when they evidently didn't get along. Could sex mean so much?

He forced his eyes away from her again, afraid to answer that.

They stepped across the line and moved slowly into the badlands. Sos repressed the nervous twinge he felt at the action, knowing that if *he* felt it, the others were struck much more forcefully. He was supposed to know; he had to prove he was right. Three lives depended on his alertness now.

Even so, the personal problem preoccupied him. Sol had said at the outset that he needed no woman. This had sounded like a courteous deferral to the other man, since no second woman was available. But then he had given the girl his bracelet, signifying their marriage. They had slept together two weeks, yet she now dared to express open dissatisfaction. Sos did not like the look of it.

The leaves and underbrush of the forest and field seemed healthy, but the rustle of wildlife faded out as they penetrated deeper. There were birds and numerous flying insects, but no deer, groundhogs or bear. Sos watched for the traces and found none. They would have trouble locating game for their arrows if this were typical. At least the presence of the birds seemed to indicate that the area was safe, so far; he did not know their tolerance, but assumed that one warm-blooded creature should be able to stand about as much as another. The birds would have to stay put while nesting, and would certainly have developed sickness if they were going to.

The trees gave way to a wide-open field leading down to

a meandering stream. They stopped to drink. Sos hesitated until he saw small fish in the water, quick to flee his descending hand. What fish could thrive in, man could drink.

Two birds shot across the field in a silent dance. Up and around they spun, the large one following the small. It was a hawk running down some kind of sparrow, and the chase was near its end. Obviously exhausted, the small bird barely avoided the outstretched claws and powerful beak. The men watched indifferently.

Suddenly the sparrow fluttered directly at them, as though imploring their protection. The hawk hovered uncertainly, then winged after it.

"Stop it!" Sola cried, moved by the fancied appeal. Surprised, Sol looked at her, then held up his hand to block off the hawk.

The predator sheered off, while the sparrow flopped to the ground almost at Sola's feet and hunched there, unable or afraid to rise again. Sos suspected that it was as much afraid of the people as the enemy. The hawk circled at a distance, then made up its mind. It was hungry.

Sol reached inside his barrow so quickly that his hand was a blur and whipped out a singlestick. As the hawk swooped low, intent on the grounded bird, he swung. Sos knew that the predator was out of reach and far too swift for such antics . . . but it gave a single sharp cry as the stick knocked it out of the air and hurled its broken body into the river.

Sos stared. It had been the quickest, most accurate motion with a weapon he had ever seen, yet the man had done it casually, in a fit of pique at a creature who disobeyed his warning. He had thought that it was merely the luck of the battle that had given Sol the victory in the circle, though the man was certainly able. Now he understood that there had been no luck about it; Sol had simply toyed with him until wounded, then finished it off quickly.

The little bird hopped on the ground, fluttering ineffectively. Sola retreated from it, perversely alarmed now that the action was over. Sos donned a gauntlet from his camping pack and reached down carefully to pinion the flapping wings and pick up the frightened creature.

It was not a sparrow after all, but some similar bird.

There were flecks of yellow and orange in the brown wings, and the bill was large and blunt. "Must be a mutant," he said. "I've never spotted one like this before."

Sol shrugged, not interested, and fished the body of the hawk out of the water. It would do for meat if they found nothing better.

Sos opened his glove and freed the bird. It lay in his palm, looking at him but too terrified to move. "Take off, stupid," he said, shaking it gently.

Its little claws found his thumb and clenched upon it.

He reached slowly with his bare hand, satisfied that the creature was not vicious, and pulled at a wing to see if it were broken. The feathers spread apart evenly. He checked the other wing, keeping his touch light so that the bird could slip free harmlessly if it decided to fly. Neither was damaged as far as he could tell. "Take off," he urged it again, flipping his hand in the air.

The bird hung tight, only spreading its wings momentarily to preserve its equilibrium.

"As you wish," he said. He brought the glove to the strap over his shoulder and jostled until the bird transferred its perch to the nylon. "Stupid," he repeated, not unkindly.

They resumed the march. Fields and brush alternated with islands of trees, and as dusk came the shrilling of insects became amplified, always loudest just a little distance away, but never from the ground. They crossed the spoor of no larger animals. At length they camped by the bank of the stream and netted several small fish. Sos struck a fire while Sola cleaned and prepared the flesh. The woman appeared to have had a good education; she could do things.

As the night advanced they opened the packs and set up the two nylon-mesh tents. Sos dug a pit downstream for offal while Sol did isometric exercises. Sola gathered a stock of dry branches for the fire, whose blaze seemed to give her comfort.

The bird remained with Sos all this time, moving from his shoulder when he had to get at the pack, but never straying far. It did not eat. "You can't live long that way, stupid," he reminded it affectionately. And that became its name: Stupid.

A white shape rose before him as he returned from the pit, spookily silent. One of the great hawk moths, he decided, and stepped toward it.

Stupid squawked unmelodiously and flew at it. There was a brief struggle in the air—the insect seemed as large as the bird, in this light—then the white collapsed and disappeared into the outsize avian mouth. Sos understood: his bird was a night feeder, at a disadvantage in full daylight. Probably the hawk had surprised it sleeping and run it down while in a befuddled state. All Stupid wanted was a safe place to perch and snooze by day.

In the morning they struck camp and advanced farther into the forbidden area. Still there was no animal life on the ground, mammal, reptile or amphibian, nor, he realized was there insect life there. Butterflies, bees, flies, winged beetles and the large nocturnal moths abounded— but the ground itself was clean. It was ordinarily the richest of nature's spawning habitats.

Radiation in the earth, lingering longer than that elsewhere? But most insects had a larval stage in ground or water . . . and the plants were unaffected. He squatted to dig into the humus with a stick.

They were there: grubs and earthworms and burrowing beetles, seemingly normal. Life existed *under* the ground and *above* it—but what had happened to the surface denizens?

"Looking for a friend?" Sola inquired acidly. He did not attempt to explain what was bothering him, since he was not sure himself.

In the afternoon they found it: a beautiful open valley, flat where a river had once flooded, and with a line of trees where the river remained. Upstream the valley narrowed into a cleft and waterfall, easy to guard, while downstream the river spread into a reedy swamp that neither foot nor boat could traverse handily. There were green passes through the rounded mountains on either side.

"A hundred men and their families could camp here!" Sol exclaimed. "Two, three hundred!" He had brightened considerably since discovering that the nemesis of the badlands had no teeth.

"It looks good," Sos admitted. "Provided there is no danger we don't know about." And was there?

"No game," Sol said seriously. "But there are fish and birds, and we can send out foraging parties. I have seen fruit trees, too." He had really taken this project to heart, Sos saw, and was alert for everything affecting its success. Yet there was danger in becoming prematurely positive, too.

"Fish and fruit!" Sola muttered, making a face, but she seemed glad that at least they would not be going deeper into the danger zone. Sos was glad, too; he felt the aura of the badlands, and knew that its mystery was more than what could be measured in Roentgens.

Stupid squawked again as the great white shapes of night appeared. There were several in sight on the plain, their color making them appear much larger than they were, and the bird flapped happily after them. Apparently the tremendous moths were its only diet—*his* diet, Sos thought, assigning a suitable sex—and he consumed them indefatigably. Did Stupid store them up in his crop for lean nights?

"Awful sound," Sola remarked, and he realized that she meant Stupid's harsh cry. Sos found no feasible retort. This woman both fascinated and infuriated him—but her opinion hardly made a difference to the bird.

One of the moths fluttered silently under Sol's nose on its way to their fire. Sol made that lightning motion and caught it in his hand, curious about it. Then he cursed and brushed it away as it stung him, and Stupid fetched it in.

"It *stung* you?" Sos inquired. "Let me see that hand." He drew Sol to the fire and studied the puncture.

There was a single red-rimmed spot in the flesh at the base of the thumb, with no other inflammation or swelling. "Probably nothing, just a defensive bite," Sos said. "I'm no doctor. But I don't like it. If I were you, I'd cut it open and suck out any venom there may be, just to be sure. I never heard of a moth with a sting."

"Injure my own right hand?" Sol laughed. "Worry over something else, advisor."

"You won't be fighting for at least a week—time enough for it to heal."

"No." And that was that.

They slept as they had before: the tents pitched side by side, the couple in one, Sos in the other. He lay tense and sleepless, not certain what it was that disturbed him so much. When he finally slept, it was to dream of mighty wings and enormous breasts, both images dead white, and he didn't know which frightened him more.

Sol did not awaken in the morning. He lay in his tent, fully clothed and burning with fever. His eyes were half open but staring, the lids fluttering sporadically. His respiration was fast and shallow, as though his chest were constricted—and it was, for the large muscles of limbs and torso were rigid.

"The kill-spirit has taken him!" Sola cried. "The—radiation."

Sos was checking over the laboring body, impressed by the solidity and power of it even in illness. He had thought the man was coordinated rather than strong, but another reassessment was in order. Sol usually moved so smoothly that the muscle was hardly apparent. But now he was in grave trouble, as some devastating toxin ravaged his system.

"No," he told her. "Radiation would have affected us as well."

"What *is* it then?" she demanded nervously.

"A harmless sting." But the irony was wasted on her. He had dreamed of death-white wings; she hadn't. "Grab his feet. I'm going to try dunking him in the water, to cool him off." He wished he had seen more medical texts, though he hardly understood what had been available. The body of a man generally knew what it was doing, and perhaps there was reason for the fever—to burn off the toxin?—but he was afraid to let it rampage amid the tissues of muscle and brain any longer.

Sola obeyed, and together they dragged the sturdy body to the river's edge. "Get his clothing off," Sos snapped. "He may swing into chills after this, and we'll have to keep him from strangling in wet garments."

She hesitated. "I never—"

"Hurry!" he shouted, startling her into action. "Your husband's life is at stake."

Sos ripped off the tough nylon jacket while Sola loosened

the waist cord and worked the pantaloons down. "Oh!" she cited.

He was about to rebuke her again. She had no cause to be sensitive about male exposure at this stage. Then he saw what she was looking at. Suddenly he understood what had been wrong between them.

Injury, birth defect or mutation—he could not be certain. Sol would never be a father. No wonder he sought success in his own lifetime. There would be no sons to follow him.

"He is still a man," Sos said. "Many women will envy his bracelet." But he was embarrassed to remember how similar Sol's own defence of him had been, after their encounter in the circle. "Tell no one."

"N-no," she said, shuddering. "No one." Two tears flowed down her cheeks. "Never." He knew she was thinking of fine children she might have had by this expert warrior, matchless in every respect except one.

They wrestled the body into the water, and Sos held the head up. He had hoped the cold shock would have a beneficial effect, but there was no change in the patient. Sol would live or die as the situation determined; there was nothing more they could do except watch.

After a few minutes he rolled Sol back onto the bank. Stupid perched on his head, upset by the commotion. The bird did not like deep water.

Sos took stock: "We'll have to stay here until his condition changes," he said, refraining from discussion of the likely direction of the change. "He has a powerful constitution. Possibly the crisis is over already. We don't dare get stung ourselves by those moths, though—chances are we'd die before the night was out. Best to sleep during the day and stand guard at night. Maybe we can all get into one tent, and let Stupid fly around outside. And gloves—keep them on all night."

"Yes," she said, no longer aggressive or snide.

He knew it was going to be a rough period. They would be terrified prisoners at night, confined in far too small a space and unable to step out for any reason, natural or temperamental, watching for white-winged terror while trying to care for a man who could die at any time.

And it did not help to remember that Sol, though he might regain complete health, could never bed his woman —the provocatively proportioned female Sos would now be jammed against, all night long.

CHAPTER THREE

"Look!" Sola cried, pointing to the hillside across the valley.

It was noon, and Sol was no better. They had tried to feed him, but his throat would not swallow and they were afraid water would choke him. Sos kept him in the tent and fenced out the sun and the boldly prying flies, furious in his uncertainty and inability to do anything more positive. He ignored the girl's silly distraction.

But their problems had only begun. "Sos, look!" she repeated, coming to grab at his arm.

"Get away from me," he growled, but he did look.

A gray carpet was spreading over the hill and sliding grandly toward the plain, as though some cosmic jug were spilling thick oil upon the landscape.

"What *is* it?" she asked him with the emphasis that was becoming annoying. He reminded himself that at least she no longer disdained his opinions. "The Roents?"

He cupped his eyes in a vain attempt to make out some detail. The stuff was not oil, obviously. "I'm afraid it's what abolished the game in this region." His nameless fears were being amply realized.

He went to Sol's barrow and drew out the two slim singlesticks: light polished rods two feet long and an inch and a half in diameter, rounded at the ends. They were made of simulated wood and were quite hard. "Take these, Sola. We're going to have to fight it off somehow, and these should come naturally to you."

She accepted the sticks, her eyes fixed on the approaching tide, though she showed no confidence in them as a weapon.

24

Sos brought out the club: the weapon no longer than the singlestick and fashioned of similar material, but far more hefty. From a comfortable, ribbed handle it bulged into a smooth teardrop eight inches in diameter at the thickest point, with the weight concentrated near the end, and it weighed six pounds. It took a powerful man to handle such an instrument with facility, and when it struck with full effect the impact was as damaging as that of a sledgehammer. The club was clumsy, compared to other weapons—but one solid blow usually sufficed to end the contest, and many men feared it.

He felt uneasy, taking up this thing, both because it was not his weapon and because he was bound by his battle path never to use it in the circle. But he repressed these sentiments as foolish; he was not taking the club as a weapon and had no intention of entering the circle with it. He required an effective mode of defence against a strange menace, and in that sense the club was no more a weapon of honor than the bow. It was the best thing at hand to beat back whatever approached.

"When it gets here, strike at the edge," he told her.

"Sos! It—it's *alive!*"

"That's what I was afraid of. Small animals, millions of them, ravaging the ground and consuming every flesh-bearing creature upon it. Like army ants."

"Ants!" she said, looking at the sticks in her hands.

"*Like* them—only worse."

The living tide had reached the plateau and was coming across in a monstrous ripple. Already some front-runners were near enough to make out separately. This close, the liquid effect was gone.

"Mice!" she exclaimed, relieved. "Tiny mice!"

"Maybe—because they're among the smallest mammals, and they reproduce fastest. Mammals are the most savage and versatile vertebrates on Earth. My guess is that these are carnivorous, whatever they are."

"*Mice*? But how—"

"Radiation. It affects the babies in some way, makes them mutants. Almost always harmful—but the few good ones survive and take over, stronger than before. The books claim that's how man himself evolved."

"But *mice!*"

The outriders were at their feet. Sos felt inane, holding the club aloft against such enemies. "Shrews, I'm afraid. Insectivores, originally. If the radiation killed off everything but the insects, these would be the first to move in again." He squatted and swept one up in his glove and held it for her to see. She didn't look, but Stupid did, and he wasn't happy. "The smallest but most vicious mammal of all. Two inches long, sharp teeth, deadly nerve poison—though there isn't enough of it in a shrew to kill a human being. This creature will attack anything that lives, and it eats twice its own weight in meat in a day."

Sola was dancing about, trying to avoid the charging midgets. She did not seem to be foolishly afraid of them, as some women were, but certainly did not want them on her body or under her feet. "Look!" she screamed. "They're—"

He had already seen it. A dozen of the tiny animals were scrambling into the tent, climbing over Sol, sniffing out the best places to bite.

Sos lunged at them, smacking the ground with the club while Sola struck with the sticks, but the horde had arrived in a mass. For every one they killed with clumsy blows a score were charging past, miniature teeth searching. The little bodies of the casualties were quickly torn apart by others and consumed.

The troops were small, but this was full-scale war.

"We can't fight them all!" Sos gasped. "Into the water!"

They opened the tent and hauled Sol out by his arms and splashed into the river. Sos waded to chest height, shaking off the determined tiny monsters. He discovered that his arms were bleeding from multiple scratches inflicted by the shrews. He hoped he was wrong about their poison; he and Sola must already have sustained more than enough bites to knock them out, if the effect were cumulative.

The little bundles of viciousness balked at the waterline, and for a moment he thought the maneuver had been successful. Then the hardier individuals plunged in and began swimming across, beady eyes fixed upon the target. More splashed in after them, until the surface of the river was covered with furry bodies.

"We've got to get away from them!" Sos shouted. "Swim for it!" Stupid had already flown to the opposite shore, and was perched anxiously upon a bush. No mystery any more why the surface of the land was clean!

"But the tents, the supplies—"

She was right. They had to have a tent, or nightfall would leave them exposed to the moths. Sheer numbers would protect the army of shrews, but all larger animals were vulnerable. "I'll go back for them!" he said, hooking his forearm under Sol's chin and striking out sidestroke for the bank. He had thrown aside the club somewhere; it was useless, anyway.

They outdistanced the animals and stumbled onto land. Sola bent down to give the patient what attention she could while Sos plunged back into the water for one of the most unpleasant tasks of his life. He swam across, stroking more strongly now that he had no burden—but at the far side he had to cut through the living layer of carnivores. His face was at their level.

He gulped a breath and ducked under, swimming as far as he could before coming up for air. Then he braced his feet against the bottom and launched himself upward at an angle. He broke water, spraying shrews in every direction, drew his breath through clenched teeth and dived again.

At the shore he lurched out, stepping on squealing struggling fur, swept up the nearest pack and ripped his standing tent loose from its moorings. If only they had folded them and put the things away . . . but Sol's illness had pre-empted everything.

The creatures were everywhere, wriggling over and inside the pack and through the folds of the bunched tent. Their pointed hairy snouts nuzzled at his face, the needle teeth seeking purchase, as he clasped the baggage to his chest. He shook the armful, not daring to stop running, but they clung tight, mocking him, and leaped for his eyes the moment he stopped.

He dived clumsily into the water, feeling the living layer he landed upon, and kicked violently with his feet. He could not submerge, this time; the pack had been constructed to float, the tent had trapped a volume of air and both arms were encumbered. Still the tiny devils danced upon the burden and clawed over his lips and nose, finding ready anchorage there. He screwed his eyes shut and continued kicking, hoping he was going in the right direction, while things scrambled through his hair and bit at his ears and tried to crawl inside earholes and nostrils. He heard Stupid's harsh cry, and knew that the bird had flown to meet him and been routed; at least he could stay clear by flying. Sos kept his teeth clenched, sucking air through them to prevent the attackers from entering there, too.

"Sos! Here!"

Sola was calling him. Blindly grateful, he drove for the sound—and then he was out of the lumpy soup and swimming through clear water. He had outdistanced them again!

The water had infiltrated the pack and tent, nullifying their buoyancy, and he was able to duck his head and open his eyes underwater, while the shrews got picked off by the current.

Her legs were before him, leading the way. He had never seen anything quite so lovely.

Soon he was sprawled upon the bank, and she was brushing things from him and stamping them into the muck. "Come *on!*" she cried into his ear. "They're halfway across!"

No rest, no rest, though he was abominably tired. He strove to his feet and shook himself like a great hairy dog. The scratches on his face stung and the muscles of his arms refused to loosen. Somehow he found Sol's body and picked it up and slung it over his shoulders in the fireman's carry and lumbered up the steep hillside. He was panting, although he was hardly moving.

"Come *on!*" her voice was screaming thinly, over and over. "Come on! Comeoncomeon!" He saw her ahead of him wearing the pack, the material of the tent jammed crudely inside and dripping onto her wet bottom. Fabulous bottom, he thought, and tried to fix his attention on that instead of the merciless weight upon his shoulders. It didn't work.

The retreat went on forever, a nightmare of exertion and fatigue. His legs pumped meaninglessly, numb stalks, stabbing into the ground but never conquering it. He fell, only to be roused by her pitiless screaming, and stumbled another futile thousand miles and fell again. And again. Furry snouts with glistening, blood-tinted teeth sped toward his eyes, his nostrils, his tongue; warm bodies crunched and squealed in agony under his colossal feet, so many bags of blood and cartilage; and stupendous, bone-white wings swirled like snowflakes wherever he looked.

And it was dark, and he was shivering on the soaking ground, a corpse beside him. He rolled over, wondering why death had not yet come—and there was a flutter of wings, brown wings flecked with yellow, and Stupid was sitting on his head.

"Bless you!" he whispered, knowing the moths would not get close tonight, and sank out of sight.

CHAPTER FOUR

Flickering light against his eyelids woke him again. Sol was lying next to him, living after all, and in the erratic glow from an outside fire he could see Sola sitting up, nude.

Then he realized that they were all naked. Sol had had minimal clothing since the dunking in the river, and the others—

"On a line by the fire," she said. "You were shaking so badly I had to get the sopping stuff off you. Mine was wet, too."

"You were right," he said. He had been quick enough to subordinate Sol's modesty to need; the same applied to himself. He wondered how she had gotten the clothing off him; he was certainly too heavy for her to lift. There must have been a real chore, there.

"I think they're dry now," she said. "But the moths—"

He saw the material of the tent enclosing them. She had situated the fire so that it radiated through the light netting in front, heating the interior without flooding it with smoke. She had placed the two men prone, heads near the heat, while she kneeled between their feet at the far end, leaning over so that the sloping nylon did not touch her back. It could hardly be a comfortable position, though from this angle it showed her unsupported bosom off to advantage.

He rebuked himself for his preoccupation with her body at such an inappropriate time. Yet it always came to this; he could not look at her without turning physical, any time. This was the other fear of his erstwhile dream: that he would covet his companion's wife and be led to dishonor. Sola had acted with eminent common sense and dispatch, even courage, and it was an insult to put a sexual meaning on it. She was naked and desirable . . . and wore another man's bracelet.

"Maybe I can fetch the clothing," he said.

"No. The moths are everywhere—much thicker than before. Stupid is gorging himself—but we can't put a hand outside."

"I'll have to stoke up the fire pretty soon." It was cold outside, and his feet could feel it despite the greenhouse effect of the closed tent. He could see her shivering, since she was more distant from the blaze.

"We can lie together," she said. "It will keep us all warm, if you can stand my weight."

Again, it made sense. The tent was not wide enough for three, but if she lay on top of the two men there would be both room and a prism of warmth. Both were in urgent demand. She was being supremely businesslike about it; could he be less?

Her thigh rubbed against his foot, a silken contact as she adjusted her weight. Intimate messages ran up his leg.

"I think his fever is broken," she said. "If we can keep him warm tonight, he may improve tomorrow."

"Maybe the shrew venom counteracted the moth poison," he said, glad to change the subject. "Where are we now? I don't remember getting here."

"Over the pass, the other side of the river. I don't think they can catch up to us here. Not tonight. Do they travel at night?"

"I wouldn't think so. Not if they travel by day. They must sleep sometime." He paused. "Straight in from the river? That means we're that much farther into the badlands."

"But you said the radiation is gone."

"I said it is *retreating*. I don't know how far or fast. We could be in it now."

"I don't feel anything," she said nervously.

"You can't feel it." But it was a pointless discussion. They had no way to escape it, if they were in the fringe zone. "If the plants haven't changed, it must be all right. It kills everything." But insects were a hundred times as tolerant as man, and there were more moths than ever. . . .

The conversation lapsed. He knew what the problem was: though they had agreed on the necessity to conserve heat, and knew what was called for, it was awkward initiating the action. He could not boldly invite her to lay her generous breasts against his naked body, and she could not stretch upon him without some specific pretext. What was intellectually sensible remained socially awkward—the more so because the prospect of such contact excited him, practical as its purpose might be, and he was sure it would show. Perhaps it interested her as well, since they both knew that Sol would never embrace her.

"That was the bravest thing I ever saw," she said. "Going back for the tent like that."

"It had to be done. I don't remember much about it, except your screaming at me 'Come on! Come on!' " He realized that sounded ungracious. "You were right, of course. You kept me going. I didn't know what I was doing."

"I only yelled once."

So it had been in his head, along with the other phantasms. "But you guided me away from the shrews."

"I was afraid of them. You picked up Sol and ran after me. On and on. I don't know how you did it. I thought you were done when you tripped, but you kept getting up again."

"The books call it hysterical strength."

"Yes, you are very strong," she agreed, not understanding him. "Maybe not so quick with your hands as he is, but much stronger."

"Still, you carried the gear," he reminded her. "And you set all this up." He looked about the tent, knowing that she must have carved pegs to replace the ones lost when he uprooted the works amid the shrew invasion, and that she must have hammered them into the ground with a stone. The tent was not mounted evenly, and she had forgotten to dig a drainage trench around it, but the props were firm and the flaps tight. It was proof against the moths, with luck and vigilance, which was what counted, and could probably withstand rough use. The placement of the fire was a stroke of genius. "An excellent job, too. You have a lot more ability than I gave you credit for."

"Thank you," she said, looking down. "It had to be done."

There was silence again. The fire was sinking, and all he could see were the highlights of her face and the rounded upper contours of her breasts, all lovely. It was time to lie down together, but still they held back.

"Sometimes we camped out, when I was with my family," she said. "That's how I knew to pitch the tent on a rise, in case it rained." So she *had* been aware of the necessity for drainage. "We used to sing songs around the fire, my brothers and I, trying to see how late we could stay awake."

"So did we," he said reminiscently. "But I can only remember one song now."

"Sing it for me."

"I can't," he protested, embarrassed. "My notes are all off-key."

"So are mine. What's the song?"

" 'Greensleeves.' "

"I don't know it. Sing it."

"I can't sing lying on my side."

"Sit up, then. There's room."

He floundered into an upright posture, facing her across the length of the tent, Sol's still form stretched out diagonally between them. He was glad, now, that it was dark.

"It isn't suitable," he said.

"A folk song?" Her tone made the notion ridiculous.

He took a breath and tried, having run out of objections:

> Alas, my love, you do me wrong
> To cast me out discourteously
> When I have loved you so long
> Delighting in your company.

"Why that's beautiful!" she exclaimed. "A love ballad."

"I don't remember the other verses. Just the refrain."

"Go ahead."

> Greensleeves was my delight
> Greensleeves was all my joy
> Greensleeves was my heart of gold
> And who but my lady Greensleeves?

"Does a man really love a woman like that?" she inquired meditatively. "I mean, just thinking about her and being delighted in her company?"

"Sometimes. It depends on the man. And the woman, I suppose."

"It must be nice," she said sadly. "Nobody ever loaned me his bracelet, just for company. That kind, I mean. Except—"

He saw her eyes move to Sol, or thought he did, and spoke to cut off the awkward thought. "What do you look for in a man?"

"Leadership, mostly. My father was second-ranked in the tribe, but never the master, and it wasn't much of a tribe. He finally got wounded too bad and retired to the crazies, and I was so ashamed I struck out on my own. I want a name everyone will admire. More than anything else, I want that."

"You may have it already. He is a remarkable warrior, and he wants an empire." He refrained again from reminding her what that name could not provide.

"Yes." She did not sound happy.

"What is your song?"

" 'Red River Valley.' I think there *was* such a place, before the Blast."

"There was. In Texas, I believe."

Without further urging she began singing. Her voice, untrained, was better than his.

> Come and sit by my side if you love me
> Do not hasten to bid me adieu
> But remember the Red River Valley
> And the girl who has loved you so true.

"How did you get to be a scholar?" she asked him then, as though retreating from the intimacy of the song.

"The crazies run a school in the east," he explained. "I was always curious about things. I kept asking questions nobody could answer, like what was the cause of the Blast, and finally my folks turned me over to the crazies for service, provided they educated me. So I carried their slops and cleaned their equipment, and they taught me to read and figure."

"It must have been awful."

"It was wonderful. I had a strong back, so the work didn't bother me, and when they saw that I really wanted to learn they put me in school full time. The old books—they contained incredible things. There was a whole history of the world, before the Blast, going back thousands of years. There used to be nations, and empires, much bigger than any of the tribes today, and so many people there wasn't enough food to feed them. They were even building ships to go into space, to the other planets we see in the sky—"

"Oh," she said, uninterested. "Mythology."

He gave it up as a bad job. Almost nobody, apart from the crazies, cared about the old times. To the average person the world began with the Blast, and that was as far as curiosity extended. Two groups existed upon the globe: the warriors and the crazies, and nothing else that mattered. The former were nomad families and tribes, travelling from cabin to cabin and camp to camp, achieving individual status and rearing children. The latter were thinkers and builders who were said to draw their numbers from retired or unsuccessful warriors; they employed great pre-Blast machines to assemble cabins and clear paths through the forests. They distributed the weapons and clothing and other supplies, but did not produce them, they claimed; no one knew where such things came from, or worried particularly about it. People cared only for the immediacies; so long as the system functioned, no one worried about it. Those who involved themselves with studies of the past and similarly useless pursuits were crazy. Hence the "crazies"—men and women very like the nomads, if the truth were known, and not at all demented.

Sos had come to respect them sincerely. The past lay with the crazies—and, he suspected, the future, too. They alone led a productive existence. The present situation was bound to be temporary. Civilization always displaced anarchy, in time, as the histories had clearly shown.

"Why aren't you a—" she cut herself off. The last light from the fire had gone and only her voice betrayed her location. He realized that his sitting posture cut off even more of the heat from her, though she had not complained.

"A crazy?" He had often wondered about that matter

himself. Yet the nomad life had its rough appeal and tender moments. It was good to train the body, too, and to trust in warrior honor. The books contained marvels—but so did the present world. He wanted both. "I suppose I find it natural to fight with a man when I choose, and to love a woman the same way. To do what I want, when I want, and be beholden to no one else, only to the power of my right arm in the circle."

But that wasn't true any more. He had been deprived of his rights in the circle, and the woman he would have clasped had given herself to another man. His own foolishness had led him to frustration.

"We'd better sleep," he said gruffly, lying down again.

She waited for him to get settled, then crawled upon him without a word. She placed herself face down upon the backs of the two men. Sos felt her head with its soft hair nestling upon his right shoulder, ticklish tresses brushing down between his arm and body suggestively, though he knew this aspect of her repose was accidental. Women were not always aware of the sexual properties of long hair. Her warm left breast flattened against his back, and her smooth fleshy thigh fell inside his knee. Her belly expanded as she breathed, pressing rhythmically against his buttock.

In the dark he clenched his fist.

CHAPTER FIVE

"Next time, advisor, if you tell me to smash my own hand to pulp with the club, I will do it gladly," Sol said, acknowledging his error about the moth sting. His features were pale, but he had recovered. They had dressed him in new trunks from the pack before he woke, and let him guess what he might about the loss of the other clothing. He did not inquire.

Sola had found small green fruit on a wild apple tree, and they made a distasteful meal of it. Sos explained about their flight from the shrews, skimping on certain details, while the woman nodded.

"So we can't use the valley," Sol said, dismissing the rest of it.

"On the contrary—it is a fine training ground."

Sola squinted at him. "With the *shrews*?"

Sos turned seriously to Sol. "Give me twenty good men and a month to work, and I'll have it secure the year around."

Sol shrugged. "All right."

"How are we going to get out of here?" Sola wanted to know.

"The same way we came in. Those shrews are defeated by their appetites. They can't wait around very long in any one place, and there was hardly anything for them to eat in that valley. They must have moved on to fresher pastures already, and soon they'll die off. Their life cycle is short. They probably only swarm every third or fourth generation, though that would still be several times a year."

"Where did they come from?" Sol asked.

"Must have been mutated from the fringe radiation."

He began his description of evolution, but Sol yawned. "At any rate they must have been changed in some way to give them the competitive edge, here, and now they are wiping out almost every form of ground life. They'll have to range farther and farther, or starve; they can't go on indefinitely like this."

"And you can keep them clear of the valley?"

"Yes, after preparations."

"Let's move."

The valley was empty again. No trace of the tiny mammals remained, except for the matted grass flattened by their myriad feet and brown earth showing where they had burrowed for fat grubs. They had evidently climbed every stalk in search of food, bearing it down by the weight of numbers and chewing experimentally. Strange scourge!

Sol eyed the waste. "Twenty men?"

"And a month."

They went on.

Sol seemed to gain strength as he marched, little worse for wear. The other two exchanged glances occasionally and shook their heads. The man might make a good show of it, but he had been very near death and had to be feeling the residual effects now.

They set a swift pace, anxious to get out of the badlands before dusk. Travel was much more rapid now that they knew where they were going, and by nightfall they were near the markers. Stupid remained with Sos, perched on his shoulder, and this protection encouraged them to keep moving through the dusk toward the hostel.

There they collapsed for a night and a day, basking in its controlled temperature, safe sleeping and ample food. Sola slept beside her man, no longer complaining. It was as though their experience of the last night in the badlands meant nothing to her—until Sos heard her humming "Greensleeves." Then he knew that no victor stood in this circle yet. She had to make her choice between opposing desires, and when she came to her decision she would either give back Sol's bracelet—or keep it.

Stupid seemed to have no problem adapting to a diet of lesser insects. The white moths were a phenomenon of the badlands only, but the bird elected to stick with the empire even at the sacrifice of his favorite victual.

They traveled again. Two days out they met a single warrior carrying a staff. He was young and fair, like Sol, and seemed to smile perpetually. "I am Sav the Staffer," he said, "in quest of adventure. Who will meet me in the circle?"

"I fight for service," Sol replied. "I am forming a tribe."

"Oh? What is your weapon?"

"The staff, if you prefer."

"You use more than one weapon?"

"All of them."

"Will you take the club against me?"

"Yes."

"I'm very good against the club."

Sol opened his barrow and drew out the club.

Sav eyed him amiably. "But I'm not forming any tribe myself. Don't misunderstand, friend—I'm willing to join yours if you beat me, but I don't want your service if I beat you. Do you have anything else to put up?"

Sol looked at him baffled. He turned to Sos.

"He's thinking of your woman," Sos said, keeping it carefully neutral. "If she will accept his bracelet for a few nights, as forfeit—"

"One night is enough," Sav said. "I like to keep moving."

Sol turned to her uncertainly. He had spoken truly when he said he was a good bargainer. Standard terms were fine, but a variable or three-person arrangement left him hanging.

"If you beat my husband," Sola said to the staffer, "I will accept your bracelet for as many nights as you desire." And Sos understood her nostalgia for attentions other than sexual; this commitment was routine. She paid a penalty for her beauty.

"One night," Sav repeated. "No offense, miss. I never visit the same place twice."

Sos said nothing more. The staffer was disarmingly frank, and whatever Sola was, she was no hypocrite. She went to the best man, wanting his name. If she had to put herself on the line to promote a settlement, she would. There was little room in her philosophy for a loser, as he had learned.

Or did she have such confidence in Sol that she knew she risked nothing?

"Agreed then," Sol said. They trekked as a party to the nearest hostel, several miles down the trail.

Sos had his private doubts as the two men stepped up to the circle. Sol was exceedingly swift, but the club was basically a power tool, not given to clever maneuvering. Even if it didn't show in ordinary travel, Sol's recent illness was bound to have its effect upon his strength and endurance in battle. The staff was a defensive weapon, well suited to a prolonged encounter, while the club rapidly sapped the strength of the wielder. Sol had committed himself foolishly and given himself the very worst chance.

Yet what did it matter to him? If Sol won, the tribe had its first real member. If he lost, Sola would take another bracelet and become Sava, and likely be free shortly thereafter. Sos could not be certain which alternative would benefit him personally, if either did. Best to let the circle decide.

No! He had agreed to serve Sol, in exchange for a name. He should have seen to it that Sol's chances were good. As it was, he had already let the man down, when he should have been alert. Now he could only hope that his lapse did not cost Sol the victory.

The two men entered the ring, and the contest began immediately. There were no manners in the battle circle, only victory and defeat.

Sav sparred, expecting a fierce attack. It did not come. The staff was about six and a half feet long and the same diameter as a singlestick, with square-cut ends; it flexed slightly when put under strain, but otherwise was nothing more or less than a rigid pole. It was one of the easiest weapons to use, though it seldom led to a quick decision. It readily blocked any other instrument, but was as easily blocked itself.

Sol feinted four times with the heavy club, watching the defensive posture of his opponent, then shrugged and lashed out with a backhand blow to the chest that neatly bypassed the horizontal shaft.

Sav looked surprised, fighting for the wind and steam that had been knocked out of him. Sol placed his club gently against the staff and pushed. The man fell backwards out of the circle.

Sos was amazed. It had looked so simple, as though a

lucky blow, but he knew it was not. Sol had expertly tested his opponent's reflexes, then struck with such quick precision that no parry had been feasible. It was a remarkable feat with the crude club—and no accident. Sol, nothing special outside the circle, was a tactical genius within it. A man had been added to the group, efficiently and virtually uninjured.

It appeared Sol needed no advice on terms of combat.

Sav took it philosophically. "I looked pretty foolish, didn't I, after all my talk," he said, and that was all. He didn't mope and he made no further overtures to Sola.

The law of averages Sos had read about indicated that it would be a couple of weeks before they encountered any really able warrior. That afternoon, notwithstanding, they met two men with swords, Tor and Tyl. The first was swarthy and greatbearded, the second slim and clean-shaven. Sworders often shaved, as did daggers; it was an unofficial mark of their specialty, since it subtly hinted their skill with the blade. Sos had tried to shave with his sword once and had sliced his face severely; after that he stuck to the shears and did not try for closeness. There were electric razors in the cabins, though few men condescended to use them. He had never understood why it should be considered degrading to use the crazies' razors, while all right to eat their food, but that was the way convention had it.

Both sworders were married, and Tor had a little girl. They were friends, but it turned out that Tyl was the master of the group of two. Both agreed to fight, Tor first, with the stipulation that what he won belonged to Tyl. That was the way of a tribe of any size.

Against Tor, Sol took a matching sword. These were straight, flat, slashing instruments twenty inches long, pointed but seldom used for stabbing. Sword contests were usually dramatic and swift. Unfortunately, wounds were frequent, too, and deaths not uncommon. That was why Sol had taken the staff against Sos, weeks ago; he had really been sure of his skill and had not wanted to risk injuring his opponent seriously.

"His wife and daughter are watching," Sola murmured beside him. "Why does he match weapons?"

Sos understood her question to mean Tora and Tori as

spectators and Sol's matching sword to sword. "Because Tyl is also watching," he told her.

Tor was powerful and launched a vigorous attack, while Sol merely fended him off. Then Sol took his turn on the offense, hardly seeming to make an effort yet pressing the other man closely. After that there was a pause in the circle as neither attacked.

"Yield," Tyl said to his man.

Tor stepped out and it was over, bloodlessly after all. The little girl gaped, not understanding, and Sola shared this confusion, but Sos had learned two important things. First, he had seen that Tor was an expert sworder who might very well have defeated Sos himself in combat. Second, he knew Tyl was even better. This was a rare pair to come upon so casually, after going so long without meeting anyone of caliber—except that that was the way the averages worked.

Sola had thought that sword against sword meant inevitable bloodshed, but in this situation the truth was opposite. Tor had felt out Sol, and been felt out in turn, neither really trying for a crippling blow. Tyl had watched, not his own man whose capabilities he knew, but Sol, and made his judgment. He had seen what Sos had seen: that Sol possessed a clear advantage in technique and would almost certainly prevail in the end. Tyl had been sensible: he had yielded his man before the end came, accepting the odds. Perhaps the little girl was disappointed, thinking her father invulnerable—but her education in this respect would have been rude indeed.

"I see," Sola said, keeping her voice low. "But suppose they had been just about even?"

Sos didn't bother to answer.

As it was, Sol had won painlessly again, and added a good man to his roster. Only by employing a weapon Tyl knew well could he have made his point so clearly.

Sos had maintained a wait-and-see attitude on Sol's plans for empire, knowing how much more than speed and versatility in the circle was required. His doubts were rapidly evaporating. If Sol could perform like this in the time of his weakness, there seemed to be no practical limit to his capabilities as he regained strength. He had now demonstrated superlative proficiency with staff, club and sword, and had never been close to defeat. There seemed to be no barrier to continued additions to his tribe.

Tyl stood up and presented a surprise of his own: he set aside his sword and brought out a pair of singlesticks. He was a man of two weapons and had decided not to tackle Sol with the one just demonstrated.

Sol only smiled and drew out his own sticks.

The fight was swift and decisive, as Sos had expected after witnessing the skill of Sol's wrist. The four sticks flashed and spun, striking, thrusting and blocking, acting both as dull swords and light staffs. This was a special art, for two implements had to be controlled and parried simultaneously, and excellent coordination was required. It was hardly possible for those outside the circle to tell which man had the advantage—until one stick flew out of the circle, and Tyl backed out, half disarmed and defeated. There was blood on the knuckles of his left hand where the skin had been broken by Sol's connection.

Yet bruises were appearing upon Sol's body, too, and blood dripped from a tear over his eye. The battle had not been one-sided.

Three men now belonged to his group, and two were not beginners.

Two weeks later Sos had his twenty men. He led them back toward the badlands, while Sol went on alone except for Sola.

CHAPTER SIX

"Pitch your tents well up on the hillside, two men or one family to a unit, with a spare pack stacked across the river," Sos directed the group when they arrived in the valley. "Two men will walk guard day and night around the perimeter; the rest will work by day and be confined to their tents by night, without exception. The night guards will be entirely covered with mesh at all times and will scrupulously avoid any contact with the flying white moths. There will be a four-man hunting party and a similar carrying party each day. The rest will dig our trench."

"Why?" one man demanded. "What's the point of all this foolishness?" It was Nar, a blustering dagger who did not accept orders readily.

Sos told them why.

"You expect us to believe such fantastic stories by a man without a weapon?" Nar shouted indignantly. "A man who raises birds instead of fighting?"

Sos held his temper. He had known that something like this would come up. There was always some boor who thought that honor and courtesy did not extend beyond the circle. "You will stand guard tonight. If you don't choose to believe me, open your face and arms to the moths." He made the other assignments, and the men got busy setting up the camp.

Tyl approached him. "If there is trouble with the men ..." he murmured.

Sos understood him. "Thanks," he said gruffly.

There was time that afternoon to mark off the trench he had in mind. Sos took a crew of men and laid out light cord, tying it to pegs hammered into the ground at suitable

44

intervals. In this fashion, they marked off a wide semi-circle enclosing the packs stored beside the river with a radius of about a quarter mile.

They ate from stored rations well before dusk, and Sos made a personal inspection of all tents, insisting that any defects be corrected immediately. The object was to have each unit tight: no space open large enough for a moth to crawl through. There were grumbles, but it was done. As night filled the valley, all but the two marching guards retired to their tents, there to stay sealed in until daylight.

Sos turned in, satisfied. It was a good beginning. He wondered where the moths hid during the day, where neither sun nor shrew could find them.

Sav, who shared his tent, was not so optimistic. "There's going to be trouble in Red River Valley," he remarked in his forthright manner.

"Red River Valley?"

"From that song you hum all the time. I know 'em all. 'Won't you think of the valley you're leaving, Oh, how lonely and sad it will be; Oh, think of the fond heart you're breaking, and the grief—' "

"All *right!*" Sos exclaimed, embarrassed.

"Well, they aren't going to like digging and carrying," Sav continued, his usually amiable face serious. "And the kids'll be hard to keep in at night. They don't pay much attention to regulations, you know. If any of them get stung and die—"

"Their parents will blame *me*. I know." Discipline was mandatory. It would be necessary to make a convincing demonstration before things got out of hand.

The opportunity came sooner than he liked. In the morning Nar was discovered in his tent. He had not been stung by the moths. He was sound asleep.

Sos called an immediate assembly. He pointed out three men at random. "You are official witnesses. Take note of everything you see this morning and remember it." They nodded, perplexed.

"Take away the children," he said next. Now the mothers were upset, knowing that they were about to miss something important; but in a few minutes only the men and about half the women remained.

He summoned Nar. "You are accused of dereliction in

the performance of your duty. You were assigned to mount guard, but you slept in the tent instead. Have you any defense to make?"

Nar was vexed at being caught but decided to bluster it out. "What are you going to do about it, bird-man?"

This was the awkward point. Sos could not take up his sword and remain true to his oath, though he had no doubt of his ability to handle this man in the circle. He could not afford to wait the weeks until Sol would show up again. He had to take action now.

"Children might have died through your neglect," he said. "A tent might have been torn unnoticed, or the shrews might have come after all by night. Until we have security from these dangers, I can not allow one man's laziness to endanger the group."

"*What* danger? How come none of *us* have seen this terrible horde of itty-bitty critters?" Nar exclaimed, laughing. There were a few smiles around the group. Sos saw that Sav was not smiling; he had predicted this.

"I'm granting you a trial, however," Sos said evenly. "By combat."

Nar drew his two daggers, still laughing. "I'm gonna carve me a big bird!"

"Take care of the matter, Tyl," Sos said, turning away. He forced his muscles to relax so that he would not show his tension, knowing that he would be branded a coward.

Tyl stepped forward, drawing his sword. "Make a circle," he said.

"Now just a minute!" Nar protested, alarmed. "It's *him* I got the fight with. Bird-brain, there."

Stupid perched on Sos's shoulder, and for once he wished the bird's loyalty lay elsewhere.

"You owe service to Sol," Tyl said, "and the forfeit is your life, as it is for all of us. He appointed Sos leader of this party, and Sos has appointed me to settle matters of discipline."

"All *right*!" Nar shouted, brazen through his fear. "Try one of *these* in your gut!"

Sos continued to face away as the sounds of battle commenced. He was not proud of himself or of what he had to do, but he had seen no alternative. If this action served to prevent recurrences, it was worth it. It had to be.

There was a scream and a gurgle, followed by the thud of a body hitting the ground. Tyl came up to stand beside him, wiping the bright life blood from his sword. "He was found guilty," he said gently.

Why, then, was it Sos who felt guilty?

In a week the trench was complete, and the crews were working on the ramp just inside it. Sos insisted that the bottom of the trench be level and that the water be diverted to flow through it steadily. "Little dribble like that won't stop the beasties," Sav remarked dubiously. "Anyhow, didn't you say they could swim?"

"Right." Sos went on to supervise the installation of mounted fire-strikers, set in the inner edge of the trench and spaced every hundred yards.

Meanwhile the bearers were hauling drums of alcohol from all cabins in range—but not for drinking. They were stored at intervals along the ramp.

Another week passed, and still the shrews did not come. A row of battle circles was set up, and a huge central tent fashioned of sewn family-tent sheets—but the group continued to camp at night in the tight little tents across the river. The hunting parties reported that game was moving into the area: deer and wild goats, followed by wolves and large cats and a few fierce pigs, as well as more numerous rodents. There was fresh meat for all.

Tyl went on enforcing discipline, usually with the sticks; one execution, though of doubtful validity, had been enough. But the seeming pointlessness of the labor made the men surly; they were accustomed to honorable fighting, not menial construction, and they did not like taking orders from a coward who bore no weapon.

"It would be better if you did it yourself," Sav said, commenting on one of Tyl's measures. "It needs to be done—we all know that—but when he does it it makes *him* the leader. No one respects you—and that bird doesn't help much, either."

Sav was such a harmless, easygoing sort that it was impossible to take offense at what he said. It was true: Sos was accomplishing his purpose at the expense of his reputation, which had not been good to begin with. None of these people knew the circumstances of his deprivation of weapons or his bond to Sol, and he did not care to publicize it.

Tyl was the *de facto* leader of the valley group—and if Sol did not return, Tyl would surely take over. He had had aspirations for a tribe of his own, and he was a highly skilled warrior. Like Sol, he had spurned inept opponents, and so had accumulated only one tribesman in his travels; but also like Sol, he was quick enough to appreciate what could be done with ordinary men once the way was shown. Was he being genuinely helpful—or was he biding his time while he consolidated the group around himself?

Sos could not carry a weapon. He was dependent upon Tyl's good will and his own intellectual abilities. He had a year of service to give, and he meant to complete it honorably. After that—

At night it was Sola's face he saw, and Sola's body he felt touching his, her hair upon his shoulder. Here, too, he would never prevail without a weapon. The truth was that *he* was as dangerous to Sol's ambitions as was Tyl, because he wanted what only complete leadership would bring. Sola would not accept the bracelet of the second warrior of the tribe, or the third or fourth. She had been candid about that.

Yet even if he carried a weapon, he could not defeat Sol in the circle, or even Tyl. It would be fatally unrealistic ever to assume otherwise. To that extent his disarmed state was his protection.

Finally the shrews struck. They boiled over the hillside in mid-afternoon and steamed toward the camp defenses. He was almost glad to see them; at least this would vindicate his elaborate precautions. They had been gone a long time, as the resurgence of game proved; it would have destroyed his program, paradoxically, if they had not come at all.

"Dump the barrels!" he shouted, and the men assigned to this task and drilled for it repetitively knocked open the containers of alcohol and began pouring them carefully into that shallow moat.

"Women and children to the tents!" Protesting shrilly, now that the excitment had come, the families forded the river and mounted the hillside.

"Stand by with weapons!" And all those not otherwise

occupied took up the defensive formation, somewhat shamefaced as they saw the size of their adversaries. There were fifteen men and several of the older boys present; the hunting party happened to be out.

The barrel-dumpers finished their job, not without regretful glances at the good intoxicant going to waste, and stood by the extended wooden handles of the fire-strikers. Sos held off, hoping that the hunters would appear, but there was no sign of them.

The shrews surged up to the moat and milled about, mistrusting the smell of it. Then, as before, the bolder ones plunged in, and the mass crossing commenced. Sos wondered whether the animals could become intoxicated in the same fashion as men.

"Fire!" he yelled. The assigned drummer beat a slow, regular cadence, and in absolute unison the men struck the igniters and leaped back. This had been one of the really sore spots of the training: grown men dancing to a musical rhythm.

A sheet of flame shot up from the moat, and the stench and smoke of improperly combusted alcohol filled the air. They were fenced in by a rising semicircle of fire. Watching it, the "dancers" shielded their eyes and gaped; now they understood what could have happened to the late man.

Sos had worked this out carefully. He knew from his readings that alcohol in its various forms would float on water and, if ignited, would burn more readily there than on land, where dirt or wood would absorb it. The layer of water in the moat offered a perfect surface for it, and the current would carry it along the entire perimeter. He was glad to have the proof; even he had had his doubts, since common sense encouraged him to believe that water quenched all fires. Why hadn't he thought to spill a few drops of the stuff into a basin of water and experiment?

Some animals had gotten through. The men were busy already beating the ground with sticks and clubs, trying to flatten the savage but elusive creatures. Several warriors cursed as they were bitten. There was no longer any reason to disparage the ferocity of the tiny enemies.

The burning vapors sank; the alcohol volatized too rapidly to last long. At Sos's signal the men rolled up more barrels from the big central tent. Here they stopped—they could not dump more alcohol until the blaze died entirely, or they would be trapped in the midst of the rising fire and possibly blown apart by ignition of the barrels themselves. This was a problem Sos had not anticipated; the main conflagration had subsided, but individual flames would remain for some time at the canal banks where fuel had seeped into the ground.

Tor the sworder came up, his black beard singed. "The upper end is clear," he gasped. "If you dump there—"

Sos cursed himself for not thinking of that before. The current had swept the upriver section of the moat clean, and the shrews were already swarming across to consume their roasted vanguard and climb the breastwork. Alcohol could be dumped there a barrel at a time, and the current would feed it through the entire retrenchment at a reduced rate and enable them to maintain a controlled fire. "Take care of it!" he told Tor, and the man ran off, shouting to those nearby for help.

Everyone was occupied, stamping and striking at the endless supply of miniature appetites. The swarm beyond the moat reminded Sos again of a division of invading ants, except that the mammals lacked the organization of the insects. The flames came up again as Tor put his plan into operation, but somehow the numbers of the enemy did not seem to diminish. Where were they coming from?

He found out. The shrews were swimming out into the river and recurving to land within the protected semicircle! Most of them did not make it, since there was no coherent organization to their advance; they either got caught in the fringe fire or went straight across to land on the opposite shore. Many drowned in the center current, and more died fighting in the water for the corpses, but the supply was such that even five or ten per cent drifting back into the open area behind the parapet was enough to overrun the area.

Would alcohol dumped directly into the river stop them? Sos ruled it out quickly. There was not enough left, and if it did *not* do the job the entire human party could be trapped by the lingering fires of its own defense, while the animals inundated the base.

He decided to cut his losses. The shrews had won this battle. "Evacuate!"

The men, once contemptuous of the enemy, had had enough. Shrews decorated arms and legs and wriggled in pantaloons and carpeted the ground, teeth everywhere. Warriors dived into the river and swam for safety, ducking under the surface whenever they could, in full retreat. Sos made a quick check to see that no wounded remained, and followed.

It was now late afternoon. Was there time to move the tents back before nightfall? Or would the shrews stop before reaching the present encampment? He had to decide in a hurry.

He could not take the risk. "Pick up tents and move back as far as you can before dusk," he shouted. "Single men may camp here and stand guard." He had stored the duplicate packs within the enclosure in case the shrews attacked from the unexpected side of the river, and those reserves were now inaccessible. Another error in judgment—yet until he was sure of the route and timing of the hordes, such losses would occur.

The shrews did not ascend the hill that night. This species, at least, was a daytime marauder. Perhaps the moths saw to that. In the morning the main body, gorged on its casualties and still numberless, crossed the river and marched downstream. Only a few hardy climbers on the outskirts reached the tents.

Sos looked about. He could not assume that this was a safe location, and it was certainly not as convenient as the valley plain. There was no more wildlife here than below. It might merely mean that the shrews' route was random; obviously they could overrun the hill if they chose to. Most likely they followed the general contours of the land, ascending where there was smoother going, and came *down* at this point when they came this way.

At least he had learned one thing: the shrews traveled only in the group, and thus were governed by group dynamics. He strained to remember the commentary in a complex text on the subject, that he had not suspected would ever have meaningful application to his life. Groups were shaped by leaders and reflected the personalities and drives of those leaders; divert the key individuals, and you diverted the pack. He would have to think about that, and apply it to this situation.

It would also be wise to spy on the continuing progress of the horde and learn for certain what finally happened to it. And to trace its origin—there might be a restricted breeding ground that could be put to the fire before the next swarm became a menace. He had been preoccupied with defense, and he saw now that that wouldn't work.

By noon the enemy was gone, and the men were able to recover their campsite. It was a ruin; even nylon was marked by the bite of myriad teeth and fouled by layers of dung.

A committee plunged eagerly into the problem of shrew tracing and diversion, while women and children moved into the main semicircle to clean up and pitch new tents. It seemed as safe a place as any, since the following horde would starve if it followed the identical route of this one. The next shrew foray was more likely to come down the opposite bank. Besides, there was a great deal of laundry to do in the river.

The bones and gear of the missing hunting party were discovered three miles upriver. Suddenly everyone appreciated the menace properly, and no more grumbles about the work were heard. Sos, too, was treated with somewhat more respect than hitherto. He had proved his point.

CHAPTER SEVEN

Sol arrived two weeks later with another group of fifty men. He now had a fair-sized tribe of sixty-five warriors, though the majority of these were inexperienced and untrained youths. The best men were still tied up in established tribes, as Sos had pointed out in their discussion— but that situation would change in due course.

Sos trotted out the witnesses to the execution of Nar and had them describe to Sol what they had observed. There were only two; the third had been a hunter on the day of warfare. Sos was not certain how the master of the tribe would take it, since his management of the valley group had cost five men. That was a full quarter of the complement put in his charge.

"There were two guards?" Sol inquired.

The witnesses nodded. "Always."

"And the other that night did not report that the first was sleeping?"

Sos clapped his palm to his forehead. For a man who fancied his brain, he had blundered ridiculously. *Two* had been guilty, not one.

In the end Tyl had another job with the sticks, while Sos and Sol retired for a private consultation. Sos described in detail the events of the past five weeks, and this time Sol's attention never wandered. He had little patience with history or biology, but the practical matters of empire building were of prime interest to him. Sos wondered whether the man had also had some intervening experience with the problems of discipline. It seemed likely.

"And you can form these new men into a group that

will conquer other tribes?" Sol inquired, wanting the reassurance.

"I think I can, in six months, now that we have plenty of men and good grounds. Provided they will obey me implicitly."

"They obey Tyl."

Sos looked at him, disturbed. He had expected to have Sol's direct backing for this longer haul. "Aren't you going to stay here?"

"I go out tomorrow to recruit more men. I leave their training to you."

"But sixty-five warriors! There is bound to be trouble."

"With Tyl, you mean? Does he want to be the leader?" Sol was perceptive enough, where his empire was concerned.

"He has never said so, and he has stood by me steadily," Sos admitted, wanting to be fair. "But he would not be human if he did not think in such terms."

"What is your advice?"

Now it was in his own lap again. At times Sol's faith in him was awkward. He could not demand that the master stay with his tribe; Sol evidently liked recruiting. He could ask him to take Tyl with him—but that would only require his replacement as disciplinary leader, and the next man would present much the same problem. "I have no evidence that Tyl lacks honor," he said. "I think it would be best to give him good reason to stay with your tribe. That is, show him that he stands to profit more by remaining with you than by striking out on his own, with or without any of the present group."

"He stands to profit the loss of his *head* if he moves against me!"

"Still—you could designate him first warrior, in your absence, and put him in charge of his own group. Give him a title to sport, so to speak."

"But I want *you* to train my men."

"Put him over me and give him the orders. It will amount to the same thing."

Sol thought it over. "All right," he said. "And what must I give *you*?"

"Me?" Sos was taken aback. "I agreed to serve you one year, to earn my name. There is nothing else you need to give me." But he saw Sol's point. If Tyl's loyalty required buttressing, what about his own? Sol was well aware that the training was, in the long run, more important than the discipline of the moment, and he had less hold on Sos than on the others. Theoretically Sos could renounce the name and leave at any time.

"I like your bird," Sol said surprisingly. "Will you give him to me?"

Sos peered sidewise at the little fellow snoozing on his shoulder. The bird had become so much a part of his life that he hardly thought about the matter any more. "No one owns Stupid. Certainly you have as much claim on him as I do—you were the one who cut down the hawk and saved him. The bird just happened to fix on me, for some reason nobody understands, even though I did nothing for him and tried to shoo him away. I can't give him to you."

"I lost my bracelet in similar fashion," Sol said, touching his bare wrist.

Sos looked away uncomfortably.

"Yet if I borrowed your bird, and he mated and fathered an egg, I would return that egg to you," Sol murmured.

Sos stomped away, too angry to speak.

No further words passed between them—but the next morning Sol set out again, alone, and Sola stayed at the camp.

Tyl seemed quite satisfied with his promotion. He summoned Sos as soon as the master was out of sight. "I want you to fashion this bunch into the finest fighting force in the area," he said. "Anyone who malingers will answer to me."

Sos nodded and proceeded with his original plan.

First he watched each man practice in the circle, and assessed his style and strengths and weaknesses, making notes on a pad of paper in the script of the ancient texts. Then he ranked the warriors in order, by weapon: first sword, second sword, first staff, and so on. There were twenty swords in the collection; it was the most popular instrument, though the injury and death rate was high. There were sixteen clubs, twelve staffs, ten sticks (he had never discovered why the misnomer "singlestick" should apply to the pair), five daggers and a solitary star.

The first month consisted entirely of drill within the

individual groups, and continual exercise. There was much more of both than the warriors had ever had before, because contestants were readily available and there was no delay or traveling between encounters. Each practiced with his weapon until fatigued, then ran laps around the inner perimeter of the camp and returned for more practice. The best man in each weapon class was appointed leader and told to instruct the others in the fine points of his trade. The original rankings could be altered by challenge from below, so that those whose skill increased could achieve higher standing. There was vigorous competition as they fell into the spirit of it, with spectators from other weapons applauding, jeering and watching to prevent injurious tactics.

The star, in a group of one, practiced with the clubs. The morningstar weapon was an oddity: a short, stout handle with a heavy spiked ball attached by a length of chain. It was a particularly dangerous device; since it lacked control, it was impossible to deliver a gentle blow. The devastating star-ball either struck its target, the points gouging out flesh and bone, or it didn't; it could not be used defensively. The loser of a star vs. star match was often killed or grievously wounded, even in "friendly" matches, and not always by his opponent's strike. Even experienced warriors hesitated to meet an angry starrer in the circle; internecine casualties were too likely.

So it went. The men were hardly aware of general improvement, but Sos saw it and knew that a number of them were turning into very fine artists of battle.

By twos and threes, new men and their families arrived to join the group, sent hither by Sol. They were integrated into the specialty companies and ranked as their skills warranted; the old-timers remarked that the quality of recruits seemed to be descending. By the end of that first month the tribe had swelled to over a hundred fighting men.

At first there were many gawky youngsters, taken only because they were available. Sos had cautioned Sol not to judge by initial skill or appearance. As the training and exercise continued, these youngsters began to fill out and learn the vital nuances of position and pacing, and soon were rising up their respective ladders. Some of the best, Sos suspected, would never have lived long enough to have become really proficient in the normal course; their incorporation into Sol's tribe was their greatest fortune.

Gradually the dissimilar and sometimes surly individuals thrown together by the luck of conquest caught the spirit of the group. A general atmosphere of expectancy developed. It was evident that this was a tribe destined for greater things. Sos picked out the most intelligent men and began instructing them in group tactics: when to fight and when *not* to fight, and how to come out ahead when the sides seemed even.

"If your group has six good men ranked in order, and you meet a group with six men, each of whom is just a little better than yours, how should you arrange your battle order?" he asked them one day.

"How much better?" Tun wanted to know. He was a clubber, low-ranked because he was too heavy to move quickly.

"Their first man can take your first. Their second can take your second but not your first. Their third can take your third, but not your second or first, and so on down the line."

"I have no one who can beat their first?"

"No one—and he insists on fighting, as do the rest."

"But their first will certainly not stand by and let my first overcome a lesser weapon. He will challenge my first, and take him from me. Then their second will do the same to my second . . ."

"Right."

Tun pondered the matter. "The luck of the circle should give me one victory, perhaps two—but I should do best not to meet this tribe."

Tor, the black-bearded sworder, brightened. "I can take five of their men, and lose only my poorest."

"How?" Tun demanded. "Theirs are all better than—"

"I will send my sixth man against their leader, as though he were my best, and keep the rest of my order the same."

"But your first would never agree to fight below your sixth!"

"*My* first will take my orders, even if he thinks they insult him," Tor said. "He will meet their second, and defeat him, and then my second will take their third, and finally my fifth will take their sixth."

57

"But their first—"

"Will conquer only my sixth—who would have likely lost to any other man. I do not need him."

"And you will have ten men, while he is left with only two," Sos finished. "Yet his team was better than yours, before you fought."

Tun gaped, then laughed, seeing it, for he was not a stupid man. "I will remember that!" he exclaimed. Then he sobered. "Only—what if their best refused to fight any but my best?"

"How is he to know?" Tor demanded.

"How do you know *his* rankings?"

They agreed that the strategy would be effective only with advance scouting, preferably by some experienced but retired warrior. Before long they were all eagerly inventing similar problems and challenging each other for solutions. They fetched dominoes from the game-compartment of the hostel and set them up against each other as tactical situations, the higher values indicating greater proficiency. Tor soon proved to be cleverest at this, and got so that he could parlay almost any random deal into a winning effort. Sos had started this type of competition, but he lost ground to his pupils.

He had shown them how to win with their intelligence when they could not do it by brute force, and he was well satisfied.

The second month, with the physical rankings firmly established, the tribe began inter-weapon competition. The advisors rejoined their own ranks and conspired to overcome all enemies by means of their more subtle skills. Each subgroup now had *esprit de corps* and was eager to demonstrate its superiority over its fellows.

Sos trained men to keep tally: a point for each victory, nothing for each loss. Some laughed to see grown men carrying pencil and pad, emulating scribes among the crazies, and soon the women moved in to take over this task. They prevailed upon Sos to teach them how to write identifications for each group, so that competitive scores could be posted on a public board. Instead he suggested that they learn to make symbols: simplified swords, clubs and other weapons, to be followed by lines slashed in bunches of five for ready comparison. Every day men were to be seen trekking to that board and exclaiming over their victories or bemoaning their losses of rank. As the fives grew too cumbersome with the cumulative totals, the women mastered the more versatile Arabic numerals, and, after them, the men. This was a dividend Sos had not anticipated; the tribe was learning to figure. He walked by one day and spied a little girl adding up her group's daily total on her fingers. Then she took the pencil and posted "56" beside the sword-symbol.

That was when he realized how simple it would be to set up a training course in basic mathematics, and even in full-fledged writing. The nomads were illiterate because they had no reason to read or write. Given that need, the situation could quickly change. But he was too busy to make anything of it at the time.

The daggers, being the smallest group, were at a disadvantage. Their leader complained to Sos that, even if all five of them won every encounter, they could hardly keep up with the swords, who could lose more than they won and still finish the day with more points. Sos decided that this was a valid objection, so he showed them how to figure on index: the number of points *per man*. Then he did have to start his class in maths, to teach the women how to compute the averages. Sola joined it; she was not the smartest woman available but, since she was alone, she had more time and was able to master the procedures well enough to instruct them. Sos appreciated the help, but her proximity disturbed him. She was too beautiful, and she came too close when he was explaining something.

Strange things happened in the circle. It was discovered that the ranking swords were not necessarily the most effective against the crude clubs, and that those who *could* master clubs might be weak against the staffs. The advisors who first caught on to the need to shift rankings as the type of opposition shifted gained many points for their groups.

Tyl came upon Tor setting out his dominoes in his tent and laughed. Then he saw Tor make notes and call off a marvelously effective battle strategy, and stopped laughing. Tyl, also aloof at first because of the deference he felt due his position, watched the individual progress being made and decided to participate. No one could afford to stand still, and already there were sworders rivaling his prowess. The time even came when he was seen pondering dominoes.

The third month they began doubles drill. Two men had to take the circle against two opponents and defeat them as a team.

"Four men in the circle?" Tyl demanded, shocked. "What charade is this?"

"Ever hear of the tribe of Pit?"

"No."

"A very powerful organization in the far east. They put up their swords by pairs, and their clubs and staffs. They will not enter the circle singly. Do you want them to claim a victory over us by default?"

"No!" And the drill went on.

The daggers and sticks had little trouble, but the staffs could entangle each other and the free-swinging clubs and swords were as likely to injure their partners as their targets. The first day's doubles practice was costly. Again the rankings were shuffled, as the teamed first and second swords found themselves ignominiously defeated by the tenth and fifteenth duo. Why? Because the top-rankers were individualists, while the lower numbers had wisely paired complementary styles: the aggressive but foolhardy offense supported by the staid but certain defense. While the two top sworders lurched against each other and held back strokes because they could not separate friend from foe, the smooth teamwork of the lesser warriors prevailed.

Then inter-group competition again, with reshuffled rankings, and finally mixed doubles: sword paired with club, dagger with staff, until every man could pair with any other weapon against any combination and fight effectively. The scoring had to be revised to match; the women learned fractions and apportioned the sections of the victories where due. Months passed unnoticed as the endless combinations were explored, and an experienced cadre developed to break in the newcomers, naturally bewildered, and show how to improve and ascend the rankings.

The leaves fell, then snow, and the moths and shrews disappeared, though group vigilance and action had long since reduced these menaces to comparative impotence. As a matter of fact, shrew stew had become a staple in the diet, and it was awkward to replace this bountiful source of meat when winter came.

The rings were swept clean each day and the interminable drill went on, in shine or snow. Additional warriors appeared steadily, but still Sol did not return.

CHAPTER EIGHT

With the cold weather, Sav elected to move into the main tent, which was heated by a perpetual fire. It had been subdivided into numerous smaller compartments, for a certain amount of privacy between families. Increasingly, eligible young women were showing up in search of bracelets. Sav was candid about passing his around.

Sos stayed in the small tent, unwilling to mix freely with those who bore weapons. His impotence in the circle was a matter of increasing distress, though he could not admit it openly. He had not appreciated the extent of his compulsion to assert himself and solve problems by force of arms until denied this privilege. He had to have a weapon again—but was barred from employing any of the six that the crazies distributed to the cabins. These were mass-produced somewhere, standardized and stocked freely in the hostels, and alternates such as the bow and arrows were not useful in the circle.

He had wondered often about this entire state of affairs. Why did the crazies take so much trouble to provide these things, making the nomad existence possible, then affect complete lack of concern for the use men made of them? Sometime he meant to have the answer. Meanwhile he was a member of the battle society, and it was necessary for him to assert himself in its terms.

If he were able.

He stripped his clothing and climbed naked into the warm sleeping bag. This was another item the crazies obligingly stocked in wintertime, and many more than the normal number had been provided at the local cabin, in response to the increased drain on its facilities. They almost certainly knew about this camp, but didn't seem to care. Where the men were, they sent supplies and sought no other controls.

He had a small gas lamp now, which enabled him to read the occasional books the crazies left behind. Even in this regard they were helpful; when he started taking books from the hostel, more appeared, and on the subjects he seemed to favor. He lit the lamp and opened his present volume: a text on farming, pre-Blast style. He tried to read it, but it was complicated and his mind could not concentrate. Type and quantity of fertilizer for specified acreage; crop rotation; pesticide, applications of and cautions concerning . . . such incomprehensible statistifying, when all he wanted to know was how to grow peanuts and carrots. He put the book aside and turned off the light.

It was lonely, now that Sav was gone, and sleep did not come readily. He kept thinking of Sav, passing his bracelet around, embracing yielding and willing flesh, there in the main tent. Sos could have done likewise; there were women who had eyed his own clasp suggestively even though he carried no weapon. He had told himself that his position required that he remain unattached, even for isolated nights. He knew that he deceived himself. Possession of a woman was the other half of manhood, and a warrior could bolster his reputation in that manner as readily as in the circle. The truth was that he refused to take a woman because he was ashamed to do so while weaponless.

Someone was approaching his tent. Possibly Tor, wanting to make a private suggestion. The beard had a good mind and had taken such serious interest in group organization and tactics that he outstripped Sos in this regard. They had become good friends, as far as their special circumstances permitted. Sometimes Sos had eaten with Tor's family, though the contact with plump good-natured Tora and precocious Tori only served to remind him how much he had wanted a family of his own.

Had wanted? It was the other way around. He had never been conscious of the need until recently.

"Sos?"

It was a woman's voice—one he knew too well. "What do you want, Sola?"

Her hooded head showed before the entrance, black against the background snow. "May I come in? It's cold out here."

"It is cold here, too, Sola. Perhaps you should return to your own tent." She, like him, had maintained her own residence, pitched near Tyl's. She had developed an acquaintance with Tyla. She still wore Sol's bracelet, and the men stayed scrupulously clear of her.

"Let me in," she said.

He pulled open the mesh with one bare arm. He had forgotten to let down the solid covering after shutting off the lamp. Sola scrambled in on hands and knees, almost knocking over the lamp, and lay down beside his bag. Sos now dropped the nylon panel, cutting off most of the outside light and, he hoped, heat loss from inside.

"I get so tired, sleeping alone," she said.

"You came here to sleep?"

"Yes."

He had intended the question facetiously and was set back by her answer. A sudden, fierce hope set his pulses thudding, seeming more powerful for its surprise. He had deceived himself doubly: it was neither his position nor his lack of a weapon that inhibited him, but his obsession with one particular woman. This one.

"You want my bracelet?"

"No."

The disappointment was fiercer. "Get out."

"No."

"I will not dishoner another man's bracelet. Or adulterate my own. If you will not leave yourself, I will have you out by force."

"And what if I scream and bring the whole camp running?" Her voice was low.

He remembered encountering a similar situation in his diverse readings, and knew that a man who succumbed to that ploy the first time could never recover his independence of decision. Time would only make it worse. "Scream if you must. You will not stay."

"You would not lay your hands on me," she said smugly, not moving.

He sat up and gripped her furry parka, furious with her and with his guilty longing. The material fell open immediately, wrapped but not fastened. His hand and the filtered light still reflecting in from the snow told him quickly that she wore nothing underneath. No wonder she had been cold!

"It would not look very nice, a naked man struggling in his tent with a naked woman," she said.

"It happens all the time."

"Not when she objects."

"In *my* tent? They would ask why she came naked to it, and did not scream before entering."

"She came dressed, to inquire about a difficult problem. An error in fractions." She fumbled in the pocket and drew out a pad with figures scrawled upon it—he could not see them, but was sure she had done her homework in this respect. Even to the error, one worthy of his attention. "He drew her inside—no, *tricked* her there—then tore off her clothing."

He had fallen rather neatly into her trap after all. She was too well versed. His usefulness to the group would be over, if the alarm were given now. "What do you want?"

"I want to get warm. There is room in your bag for two."

"This will gain you nothing. Are you trying to drive me out?"

"No." She found the zipper and opened the bag, letting the cold air in. In a moment she was lying against him, bare and warm, her parka outside and the zipper refastened.

"Sleep, then." He tried to turn away from her, but the movement only brought them closer together.

She attempted to bring his head over to hers, catching at his hair with one hand, but he was rigid. "Oh, Sos, I did not come to torment you!"

He refused to answer that.

She lay still for a little while, and the burning muliebrity of her laid siege to his resistance. Everything he desired, so close. Available—in the name of dishonor.

Why did she choose this way? She had only to put aside Sol's emblem for a little while. . . .

Another figure detached itself from the shadow of the main tent and trod through the packed snow. Sos could see it, though his eyes were closed, for he recognized the tread. Tor.

"You have your wish. Tor is coming."

Then her bluff stood exposed, for she shrank into the bag and tired to hide. "Send him away!" she whispered.

Sos grabbed the parka and tossed it to the foot of the tent. He drew the lip of the bag over her head, hoping the closure wouldn't suffocate her. He waited.

Tor's feet came up to the tent and stopped. No word was spoken. Then Tor wheeled and departed, evidently deciding that the dark, closed tent meant that his friend was already asleep.

Sola's head emerged when it was safe. "You *do* want me," she said. "You could have embarrassed me. . . ."

"Certainly I want you. Remove his bracelet and take mine, if you want the proof."

"Do you remember when we lay against each other before?" she murmured, this time evading the direct refusal.

" 'Greensleeves.' "

"And 'Red River Valley.' And you asked me what I wanted in a man, and I told you leadership."

"You made your choice." He heard the bitterness in his tone.

"But I did not know then what *he* wanted." She shifted position, placing her free arm under his and around his back and Sos was unable to control the heat of his reaction and knew she knew it.

"You are the leader of this camp," she said. "Everybody knows it, even Tyl. Even Sol. He knew it first of all."

"If you believe that, why do you keep his bracelet?"

"Because I am not a selfish woman!" she flared, amazing him. "He gave me his name when he didn't want to, and I must give him something in return, even if *I* don't want to. I can't leave him until we are even."

"I don't understand."

It was her turn for bitterness. "You understand!"

"You have a strange system of accounting."

"It is *his* system, not mine. It doesn't fit into your numbers."

"Why not pick on some other man for your purpose?"

"Because he trusts you—and I love you."

He could offer no rebuttal to that statement. Sol had made the original offer, not her.

"I will leave now, if you ask me," she whispered. "No screaming, no trouble, and I will not come again."

She could not afford the gesture. She had already won. Wordlessly he clasped her and sought her lips and body.

And now she held back. "You know the price?"

"I know the price."

Then she was as eager as he.

CHAPTER NINE

In the spring Sol reappeared, lean and scarred and solemn, toting his barrow. More than two hundred men were there to greet him, tough and eager to the last. They knew his return meant action for them all.

He listened to Tyl's report and nodded matter-of-factly. "We march tomorrow," he said.

That night Sav came to share his tent again. It occurred to Sos that the staffer's departure and return had been remarkably convenient, but he did not comment directly. "Your bracelet got tired?"

"I like to keep moving. 'Bout run out of ground."

"Can't raise much of a family that way."

"Sure can't!" Sav agreed. "Anyway, I need my strength. I'm second staff now."

Yes, he thought forlornly. The first had become second, and there was nothing to do but abide by it. The winter had been warmer than the spring.

The tribe marched. The swords, fifty strong, moved out first, claiming their privilege as eventual winners of the point-score tournament. The daggers followed, winners on index, and then the sticks, staffs and clubs. The lone morningstar brought up the rear, low scorer but not put out. "My weapon is not for games," he said, with some justice.

Sol no longer fought. He stayed with Sola, showing unusual concern for her welfare, and let the fine military machine Sos had fashioned operate with little overt direction. Did he know what his wife had been doing all winter? He had to, for Sola was pregnant.

Tyl ran the tribe. When they encountered a single man who was willing to come to terms, Tyl gave the assignment to the group corresponding to the man's weapon and let the leader of that group select a representative to enter the circle. The advantage of the extended training quickly showed: the appointed warriors were generally in better physical shape than their opponents and superior strategists, and almost always won. When they lost, more often than not the victor, perceiving the size and power of the tribe, challenged the group leader in order to be incorporated into it. Tyl allowed no one to travel with the tribe who was not bound to it.

Only Sos was independent—and he wished he were not.

A week out they caught up to another tribe. It contained about forty men, and its leader was typical of the crafty oldsters Sos had anticipated. The man met Tyl and surveyed the situation—and agreed to put up just four warriors for the circle: sword, staff, sticks and club. He refused to risk more.

Disgruntled, Tyl retired for a conference with Sos. "It's a small tribe, but he has many good men. I can tell they are experienced and capable by the way they move and the nature of their scars."

"And perhaps also by the report of our advance scouts," Sos murmured.

"He won't even send his best against us!" Tyl said indignantly.

"Put up fifty men and challenge him yourself for his entire group. Let him inspect the men and satisfy himself that they are worth his trouble."

Tyl smiled and went to obtain Sol's official approval, a formality only. In due course he had forty-five assorted warriors assembled.

"Won't work," Tor muttered.

The wily tribemaster looked over the offerings, grunting with approval. "Good men," he agreed. Then he contemplated Tyl. "Aren't you the man of two weapons?"

"Sword and stick."

"You used to travel alone—and now you are second in command to a tribe of two hundred."

"That's right."

"I will not fight you."

"You insist upon meeting our master Sol?"

"Certainly not!"

Tyl controlled his temper with obvious difficulty and turned to Sos. "What now, advisor?" he demanded with irony.

"Now you take Tor's advice." Sos didn't know what the beard had in mind, but suspected it would work.

"I think his weak spot is his pride," Tor said conspiratorily. "He won't fight if he thinks he might lose, and he won't put up more than a few men at a time, so he can quit as soon as the wind blows against him. No profit for us there. But if we can make him look ridiculous——"

"Marvelous!" Sos exclaimed, catching on. "We'll pick up four jokers and shame him into a serious entry!"

"And we'll assign a core of chucklers. The loudest mouths we have."

"And we have plenty," Sos agreed, remembering the quality of heckling that had developed during the intense intergroup competition.

Tyl shrugged dubiously. "You handle it. I want no part of this." He went to his tent.

"He really wanted to fight himself," Tor remarked. "But he's out. He never laughs."

They compared notes and decided upon a suitable quartet for the circle. After that they rounded up an even more special group of front-row spectators.

The first match began at noon. The opposing sworder strode up to the circle, a tall, serious man somewhat beyond the first flush of youth. From Sol's ranks came Dal, the second dagger: a round-faced, short-bodied man whose frequent laugh sounded more like a giggle. He was not a very good fighter overall, but the intense practice had shown up his good point: he had never been defeated by the sword. No one quite fathomed this oddity, since a stout man was generally most vulnerable to sharp instruments, but it had been verified many times over.

The sworder stared dourly at his opponent, then stepped into the circle and stood on-guard. Dal drew one of his knives and faced him—precociously imitating with the eight-inch blade the formal stance of the other. The picked watchers laughed.

More perplexed than angry, the sworder feinted experimentally. Dal countered with the diminutive knife as though it were a full-sized sword. Again the audience laughed, more boisterously than strictly necessary.

Sos aimed a surreptitious glance at the other tribe's master. The man was not at all amused.

Now the sworder attacked in earnest, and Dal was obliged to draw his second dagger—daintily—and hold off the heavier weapon with quick feints and maneuvers. A pair of daggers were generally considered to be no match for a sword unless the wielder were extremely agile. Dal looked quite *un*agile—but his round body always happened to be just a hair out of the sword's path, and he was quick to take advantage of the openings created by the sword's inertia. No one who faced the twin blades in the circle could afford to forget that there were *two*, and that the bearer had to be held at a safe distance at all times. It was useless to block a single knife if the second were on its way to a vulnerable target.

Had the sworder been a better man, the tactics would have been foolhardy; but again and again Dal was able to send his opponent lumbering awkwardly past, wide open for a crippling stab. Dal didn't stab. Instead he flicked off a lock of the sworder's hair and waved it about like a tassel while the picked audience roared. He slit the back of the sworder's pantaloons, forcing him to grab them hastily, while Sol's men rolled on the ground, yanked up their own trunks and slapped each other on shoulders and backs.

Finally the man tripped over Dal's artful foot and fell out of the circle, ignominiously defeated. But Dal didn't leave the circle. He kept on feinting and flipping his knives as though unaware that his opponent was gone.

The opposite master watched with frozen face.

Their next was the staffer. Against him Tor had sent the sticks, and the performance was a virtual duplicate of the first. Kin the Sticker fenced ludicrously with one hand while carrying the alternate singlestick under his arm, in his teeth or between his legs, to the lewd glees of the scoffers. He managed to make the staffer look inept and untrained, though the man was neither. Kin beat a tattoo against the staff, as though playing music, and bent down to pepper the man's feet painfully. By this time even some of the warriors of the other tribe were chuckling . . . but not their chief.

The third match was the reverse: Sav met the sticks. He hummed a merry folksong as he poked the slightly bulky belly of his opposite with the end of his staff, preventing him from getting close. "Swing low, sweet chariot!" he sang as he jabbed. The man had to take both sticks in one hand in order to make a grab for the staff with the other. "Oh, no John, no John, no John, no!" Sav caroled as he wrapped that double hand and sent both sticks flying.

It was not his name, but that man was ever after to be known in the tribe as Jon.

Against their club went Mok the Morningstar. He charged into the circle whirling the terrible spiked ball over his head so that the wind sang through the spikes, and when the club blocked it the chain wrapped around the hand until the orbiting ball came up tight against the clubber's hand and crushed it painfully. Mok yanked, and the club came away, while the man looked at his bleeding fingers. As the star had claimed; his was not a weapon for games.

Mok caught the club, reversed it, and offered the handle to his opponent with a bow. "You have another hand," he said courteously. "Why waste it while good bones remain?" The man stared at him and backed out of the circle, utterly humbled. The last fight was over.

The other master was almost incoherent. "Never have I seen such—such—"

"What did you expect from the buffoons you sent against us?" a slim, baby-faced youngster replied, leaning against his sword. He had been foremost among the scoffers, though he hardly looked big enough to heft his weapon. "*We* came to fight, but your cavorting clowns—"

"You!" the master cried out furiously. "*You* meet my first sword, then!"

The boy looked frightened. "But you said only four—"

"No! All my men will fight. But first I want you—and that foul beard next to you. And those two loudmouthed clubbers!"

"Done!" the boy cried, standing up and running to the circle. It was Neq, despite his youth and diminutive stature the fourth sword of fifty.

The beard, of course, was clever Tor himself, now third sword. The two clubbers were first and second in their group of thirty-seven.

At the end of the day Sol's tribe was richer by some thirty men.

Sol pondered the matter for a day. He talked with Tyl and thought some more. Finally he summoned Sos and Tor: "This dishonors the circle," he said. "We fight to win or lose, not to laugh."

Then he sent Sos after the other master to apologize and offer a serious return match, but the man had had enough. "Were you not weaponless, I would split your head in the circle!" he said.

So it went. The group's months in the badlands camp had honed it to a superb fighting force, and the precise multiweapon ranking system placed the warriors exactly where they could win. There were some losses—but these were overwhelmingly compensated by the gains. Upon occasion Tyl had the opportunity to take the circle against a master, matching a selected subtribe equivalent to the other tribe, as he had wanted to do the first time. Twice he won, bringing a total of seventy warriors into Sol's group, much to his pride . . . and once he lost.

That was when Sol came out of his apparent retirement to place his entire tribe of over three hundred men against the fifty—now one hundred—belonging to the victor and challenged for it all. He took the sword and killed the other master in as ruthless and businesslike an attack as Sos had ever seen. Tor made notes on the technique, so as to call them out as pointers for the sword group. Tyl kept his ranking—and if he had ever dreamed of replacing Sol, it was certain that the vision perished utterly that day.

Only once was the tribe seriously balked, and not by another tribe. One day an enormous, spectacularly muscled man came ambling down the trail swinging his club as though it were a singlestick. Sos was actually one of the largest men in the group, but the stranger was substantially taller and broader through the shoulders than he. This was Bog, whose disposition was pleasant, whose intellect was scant, and whose chiefest joy was pulverising men in the circle.

Fight? "Good, good!" he exclaimed, smiling broadly. "One, two, three a'time! Okay!" And he bounded into the circle and awaited all comers. Sos had the impression that the main reason the man had failed to specify more at a time was that he could count no higher.

Tyl, his curiosity provoked, sent in the first club to meet him. Bog launched into battle with no apparent science. He simply swept the club back forth with such ferocity that his opponent was helpless against it. Hit or miss, Bog continued unabated, fairly bashing the other out of the circle before the man could catch his footing.

Victorious, Bog grinned. "More!" he cried.

Tyl looked at the tribe's erstwhile first clubber, a man who had won several times in the circle. He frowned, not quite believing it. He sent in the second club.

The same thing happened. Two men lay stunned on the ground, thoroughly beaten.

Likewise the two ranking swords and a staff, in quick order. "More!" Bog exclaimed happily, but Tyl had had enough. Five top men were shaken and lost, in the course of only ten minutes, and the victor hardly seemed to be tired.

"Tomorrow," he said to the big clubber.

"Okay!" Bog agreed, disappointed, and accepted the hospitality of the tribe for the evening. He polished off two full-sized meals and three willing women before he retired for the night. Male and female alike gaped at his respective appetites, hardly able to credit either department, but these were not subject to refutation. Bog conquered everything —one, two or three at a time.

Next day he was as good as ever. Sol was on hand this time to watch while Bog bashed club, sticks and daggers with equal facility, and even flattened the terrible star. When struck, he paid no attention, though some blows were cruel; when cut, he licked the blood like a tiger and laughed. Blocking him was no good; he had such power that no really effective inhibition was practical. "More!" he cried after each debacle, and he never tired.

"We must have that man," Sol said.

"We have no one to take him," Tyl objected. "He has already wiped out nine of our best, and hasn't even felt the competition. I might kill him with the sword—but I

couldn't defeat him bloodlessly. We'd have no use for him dead."

"He must be met with the club," Sos said. "That's the only thing with the mass to slow him. A powerful, agile, durable club."

Tyl stared meaningfully at the three excellent clubbers seated by Bog's side of the circle. All wore large bandages where flesh and bone had succumbed to the giant's attack. "If those were our ranked instruments, we need an unranked warrior," he observed.

"Yes," Sol said. He stood up.

"Wait a minute!" both men cried. "Don't chance it yourself," Sos added. "You have too much to risk."

"The day any man conquers me with any weapon," Sol said seriously, "is the day I go to the mountain." He took up his club and walked to the circle.

"The master!" Bog cried, recognizing him. "Good fight?"

"He didn't even settle terms," Tyl groaned. "This is nothing more than man-to-man."

"Good fight," Sol agreed, and stepped inside.

Sos concurred. In the headlong drive for empire, it seemed a culpable waste to chance Sol in the circle for anything less than a full tribe. Accidents were always possible. But they had already learned that their leader had other things on his mind these days than his empire. Sol proved his manhood by his battle prowess, and he could allow no slightest question there, even in his own mind. He had continued his exercises regularly, keeping his body toned.

Perhaps it took a man without a weapon to appreciate just how deeply the scars of the other kind of deprivation went.

Bog launched into his typical windmill attack, and Sol parried and ducked expertly. Bog was far larger, but Sol was faster and cut off the ferocious arcs before they gained full momentum. He ducked under one swing and caught Bog on the side of the head with the short, precise flick Sos had seen him demonstrate before. The club was not clumsy or slow in Sol's hand.

The giant absorbed the blow and didn't seem to notice. He bashed away without hesitation, smiling. Sol had to back away and dodge cleverly to avoid being driven out of the circle, but Bog followed him without letup.

Sol's strategy was plain. He was conserving his strength, letting the other expend his energies uselessly. Whenever there was an opening, he sneaked his own club in to bruise head, shoulder or stomach, weakening the man further. It was a good policy—except that Bog refused to be weakened. "Good!" he grunted when Sol scored—and swung again.

Half an hour passed while the entire tribe massed around the arena, amazed. They all knew Sol's competence; what they couldn't understand was Bog's indefatigable power. The club was a solid weapon, heavier with every swing, and prolonged exercise with it inevitably deadened the arm, yet Bog never slowed or showed strain. Where did he get such stamina?

Sol had had enough of the waiting artifice. He took the offense. Now he laid about him with swings like Bog's, actually forcing the bigger man to take defensive measures. It was the first time they had seen it; for all they had known until that point, Bog *had* no defense, since he had never needed it. As it was, he was not good at it, and soon got smashed full force across the side of the neck.

Sos rubbed his own neck with sympathetic pain, seeing the man's hair flop out and spittle fly from his open mouth. The blow should have laid him out for the rest of the day. It didn't. Bog hesitated momentarily, shook his head, then grinned. "Good!" he said—and smote mightily with his own weapon.

Sol was sweating profusely, and now took the defensive stance from necessity. Again he fended Bog off with astute maneuvers, while the giant pressed the attack as vigorously as before. Sol had not yet been whacked upon head or torso; his defense was too skilled for the other to penetrate. But neither could he shake his opponent or wear him down.

After another half hour he tried again, with no better effect. Bog seemed to be impervious to physical damage. After that Sol was satisfied to wait.

"What's the record for club-club?" someone asked.

"Thirty-four minutes," another replied.

The timer Tor had borrowed from the hostel indicated a hundred and four minutes. "It isn't possible to keep that pace indefinitely," he said.

The shadows lengthened. The contest continued.

Sos, Tyl and Tor huddled with the other advisors. "They're going on until dark!" Tun exclaimed incredulously. "Sol won't quit, and Bog doesn't know how."

"We have to break this up before they *both* drop dead," Sos said.

"*How?*"

That was the crux. They were sure neither participant would quit voluntarily, and the end was not in view. Bog's strength seemed boundless, and Sol's determination and skill matched it. Yet the onset of night would multiply the chances for a fatal culmination, that nobody wanted. The battle would have to be stopped.

It was a situation no one had imagined, and they could think of no ethical way to handle it. In the end, they decided to stretch the circle code a bit.

The staff squad took the job. A phalanx of them charged into the circle, walling off the combatants and carrying them away. "Draw!" Sav yelled. "Tie! Impasse! Even! No decision!"

Bog picked himself up, confused.

"Supper!" Sos yelled at him. "Sleep! Women!"

That did it. "Okay!" the monster clubber agreed.

Sol thought about it, contemplating the extended shadows. "All right," he said at last.

Bog went over to shake hands. "You pretty good, for little guy," he said graciously. "Next time we start in morning, okay? More day."

"Okay!" Sol agreed, and everyone laughed.

That night Sola rubbed liniment into Sol's arms and legs and back and put him away for a good twelve hours' exhaustion. Bog was satisfied with one oversized meal and one sturdy well-upholstered lass. He disdained medication for his purpling bruises. "Good fight!" he said, contented.

The following day he went his way, leaving behind the warriors he had conquered. "Only for fun!" he explained. "Good, good."

They watched him disappear down the trail, singing tunelessly and flipping his club end-over-end in the air.

CHAPTER TEN

"My year is up," Sos said.

"I would have you stay," Sol replied slowly. "You have given good service."

"You have five-hundred men and an elite corp of advisors. You don't need me."

Sol looked up and Sos was shocked to see tears in his eyes. "I do need you," he said. "I have no other friend."

Sos did not know what to say.

Sola joined them, hugely pregnant. Soon she would travel to a crazy hospital for delivery. "Perhaps you have a son," Sos said.

"When you find what you need, come back," Sol told him, accepting the inevitable.

"I will." That was all they could say to each other.

He left the camp that afternoon, travelling east. Day by day the landscape became more familiar as he approached the region of his childhood. He skirted the marked badlands near the coast, wondering what mighty cities had stood where the silent death radiated now, and whether there would ever be such massive assemblages of people again. The books claimed that nothing green had grown in the centers of these encampments, that concrete and asphalt covered the ground between buildings and made the landscape as flat as the surface of a lake, that machines like those the crazies used today had been everywhere, doing everything. Yet all had vanished in the Blast. Why? There were many unanswered questions.

A month of hiking brought him to the school he had attended before beginning his travels as a warrior. Only a

year and a half had elapsed, but already it had become an entirely different facet of his existence, one now unfamiliar to him and strange to see again. Still, he knew his way around.

He entered the arched front doorway and walked down the familiar, foreign hall to the door at the end marked "Principal." A girl he did not remember sat at the desk. He decided she was a recent graduate, pretty, but very young. "I'd like to see Mr. Jones," he said, pronouncing the obscure name carefully.

"And who is calling?" She stared at Stupid, perched as ever upon his shoulder.

"Sos," he said, then realized that the name would mean nothing here. "A former student. He knows me."

She spoke softly into an intercom and listened for the reply. "Doctor Jones will see you now," she said, and smiled at him as though he were not a ragged-bearded, dirt-encrusted pagan with a mottled bird on his shoulder.

He returned the gesture, appreciating her attention though he knew it was professional, and went on through the inner door.

The principal rose immediately and came around his desk to greet him. "Yes of course I remember you! Class of '107, and you stayed to practice with the—the sword, wasn't it? What do you call yourself now?"

"Sos." He knew Jones knew it already, and was simply offering him the chance to explain the change. He didn't take it immediately, and the principal, experienced in such matters, came to his rescue again.

"Sos. Beautiful thing, that three-letter convention. Wish I knew how it originated. Well, sit down, Sos, and tell me everything. Where did you acquire your pet? That's a genuine mock-sparrow, if I haven't lost my eye for bad-lands fauna." A very gentle fatherly inflection came into his voice. "You have been poking into dangerous regions, warrior. Are you back to stay?"

"I don't know. I don't think so. I—I don't know where my loyalties lie, now." How rapidly he resumed the mood of adolescence, in this man's presence.

"Can't make up your mind whether you're sane or crazy, eh?" Jones said, and laughed in his harmless way. "I know

it's a hard decision. Sometimes I still wish I could chuck it all and take up one of those glamorous weapons and—you didn't kill anybody, I hope?"

"No. Not directly, anyway," he said, thinking of the recalcitrant dagger Nar and Tyl's execution of him. "I only fought a few times, and always for little things. The last time was for my name."

"Ah, I see. No more than that?"

"And perhaps for a woman, too."

"Yes. Life isn't always so simple in the simple world, is it? If you care to amplify—"

Sos recounted the entire experience he had had, the emotional barriers overcome at last, while Jones listened sympathetically. "I see," the principal said at the end. "You do have a problem." He cogitated for a moment—"thought" seemed too simple a word to apply to him—then touched the intercom. "Miss Smith, will you check the file on one 'Sol,' please? S-O-L. Probably last year, no, two years ago, west coast. Thank you."

"Did he go to school?" Sos had never thought of this.

"Not here, certainly. But we have other training schools, and he sounds as though he's had instruction. Miss Smith will check it out with the computer. There just might be something on the name."

They waited for several minutes, Sos increasingly uncomfortable as he reminded himself that he should have cleaned up before coming here. The crazies had something of a fetish about dirt: they never went long without removing it. Perhaps it was because they tended to stay within their buildings and machines, where aromas could concentrate.

"The girl," he said, filling time, "Miss Smith—is she a student?"

Jones smiled tolerantly. "No longer. I believe she is actually a year older than you are. We can't be certain because she was picked up running wild near one of the radioactive areas a number of years ago and we never did manage to trace her parentage. She was trained at another unit, but you can be sure there was a change in her, er, etiquette. Underneath, I daresay, there is nomad yet, but she's quite competent."

It was hard to imagine that such a polished product was

forest-born, even though he had been through it himself. "Do you really get all your people from——"

"From the real world? Very nearly, Sos. I was a sword-bearer myself, thirty years ago."

"A sworder? You?"

"I'll assume that your astonishment is complimentary. Yes, I fought in the circle. You see——"

"I have it, Dr. Jones," the intercom said. "S.O.L. Would you like me to read it off?"

"Please."

"Sol—adopted code name for mutilated foundling, testes transplant, insulin therapy, comprehensive manual training, discharged from San Francisco orphanage B107. Do you want the details on that, Dr. Jones?"

"No thanks. That will do nicely, Miss Smith." He returned to Sos. "That may not be entirely clear to you. It seems your friend was an orphan. There was some trouble, I remember, about fifteen years ago on the west coast and, well, we had to pick up the pieces. Families wiped out, children tortured—this type of thing will happen occasionally when you're dealing with primitives. Your Sol was castrated at the age of five and left to bleed to death . . . well, he was one of the ones we happened to catch in time. A transplant operation took care of the testosterone, and insulin shock therapy helped eradicate the traumatic memories, but—well, there's only so much we can do. Evidently he wasn't suited to intellectual stimulation, as you were, so he received manual instead. From what you told me, it was exceptionally effective. He seems to have adjusted well."

"Yes." Sos was beginning to understand things about Sol that had baffled him before. Orphaned at a vulnerable age by tribal savagery, he would naturally strive to protect himself most efficiently and to abolish all men and all tribes that might pose a personal threat. Raised in an orphanage, he would seek friendship—and not know how to recognize it or what to do with it. And he would want a family of his own, that he would protect fanatically. How much more precious a child—to the man who could never father one!

Couple this background with a physical dexterity and endurance amounting to genius, and there was—Sol.

"Why do you do all this?" Sos asked. "I mean, building hostels and stocking them, training children, marking off the badlands, projecting television programs. You get no thanks for it. You know what they call you."

"Those who desire nonproductive danger and glory are welcome to it," Jones said. "Some of us prefer to live safer, more useful lives. It's all a matter of temperament, and that can change with age."

"But you could have it all for yourselves! If—if you did not feed and clothe the warriors, they would perish."

"That's good enough reason to continue service, then, don't you think?"

Sos shook his head. "You aren't answering my question."

"I can't answer it. In time you will answer it for yourself. Then perhaps you will join us. Meanwhile, we're always ready to help in whatever capacity we are able."

"How can you help a man who wants a weapon when he has sworn to carry none, and who loves a woman who is pledged to another man?"

Jones smiled again. "Forgive me, Sos, if these problems appear transistory to me. If you look at it objectively, I think you'll see that there *are* alternatives."

"Other women, you mean? I know that 'Miss' you put on your receptionist's name means she is looking for a husband, but I just don't find it in me to be reasonable in quite that way. I was willing to give any girl a fair trial by the bracelet, just as I gave any man fair battle in that circle, but somehow all my preferences have been shaped to Sola's image. And she loves me, too."

"That seems to be the way love is," Jones agreed regretfully. "But if I understand the situation correctly, she will go with you, after her commitment to Sol is finished. I would call this a rather mature outlook on her part."

"She *won't* just 'go' with me! She wants a name with prestige, and I don't even carry a weapon."

"Yet she recognized your true importance in the tribe. Are you sure it isn't your own desire, more than hers? To win a battle reputation, that is?"

"I'm not sure at all," Sos admitted. His position, once stated openly, sounded much less reasonable than before.

"So it all comes down to the weapon. But you did not swear to quit all weapons—only the six standard ones."

"Same thing, isn't it?"

"By no means. There have been hundreds of weapons in the course of Earth's history. We standardized on six for convenience, but we can also provide prototype non-standard items, and if any ever became popular we could negotiate for mass production. For example, you employed the straight sword with basket hilt, patterned after medieval models, though of superior grade, of course. But there is also the scimitar—the curved blade—and the rapier, for fencing. The rapier doesn't look as impressive as the broadsword, but it is probably a more deadly weapon in confined quarters, such as your battle circle. We could—"

"I gave up the sword in *all* its forms. I don't care to temporize or quibble about definitions."

"I suspected you would feel that way. So you rule out any variation of blade, club or stick?"

"Yes."

"And *we* rule out pistols, blowguns and boomerangs—anything that acts at a distance or employs a motive power other than the arm of the wielder. We allow the bow and arrow for hunting—but that wouldn't be much good in the circle anyway."

"Which pretty well covers the field."

"Oh, no, Sos. Man is more inventive than that, particularly when it comes to modes of destruction. Take the whip, for example—usually thought of as a punitive instrument, but potent as a weapon too. That's a long fine thong attached to a short handle. It is possible to stand back and slash the shirt off a man's back with mere flicks of the wrist, or to pinion his arm and jerk him off balance, or snap out an eye. Very nasty item, in the experienced hand."

"How does it defend against the smash of the club?"

"Much as the daggers do, I'm afraid. The whipper just has to stay out of the club's way."

"I would like to defend myself as well as to attack." But Sos was gaining confidence that some suitable weapon for him did exist. He had not realized that Jones knew so much about the practical side of life. Wasn't it really for some such miracle he had found his way here?

"Perhaps we shall have to improvise." Jones tugged a piece of string between his fingers. "A net would be fine

defensively, but—" His eyes continued to focus on the string as his expression became intent. "That may well be it!"

"String?"

"The garrote. A length of cord used to strangle a man. Quite effective, I assure you."

"But how would I get close enough to a dagger to strangle him, without getting disemboweled? And it still wouldn't stop a sword or club."

"A long enough length of it would. Actually, I am visualizing something more like a chain—flexible, but hard enough to foil a blade and heavy enough to entangle a club. A—a metal rope, perhaps. Good either offensively or defensively, I'm sure."

"A hope." Sos tried to imagine it as a weapon, but failed.

"Or a bolas," Jones said, carried away by his line of thought. "Except that you would not be allowed to throw the entire thing, of course. Still, weighted ends—come down to the shop and we'll see what we can work up."

Miss Smith smiled at him again as they passed her, but Sos pretended not to notice. She had a very nice smile, and her hair was set in smooth light waves, but she was nothing like Sola.

That day Sos gained a weapon—but it was five months before he felt proficient enough with it to undertake the trail again.

Miss Smith did not speak to him at the termination, but Jones bid him farewell sadly. "It was good to have you back with us, if only for these few months, Sos. If things don't work out—"

"I don't know," Sos said, still unable to give him a commitment. Stupid chirped.

CHAPTER ELEVEN

As he had begun two years before, Sos set out to find his fortune. Then he had become Sol the Sword, not suspecting what his alliteratively chosen name would bring him to; now he was Sos the Rope. Then he had fought in the circle for pleasure and reputation and minor differences; now he fought to perfect his technique. Then he had taken his women as they came; now he dreamed of only one.

Yet there were things about the blonde Miss Smith that could have intrigued him, in other circumstances. She was literate, for one thing, and that was something he seldom encountered in the nomad world. True, she was of the crazies' establishment—but she would have left it, had he asked her to; that much had become apparent. He had not asked . . . and now, briefly, he wondered whether he had made a mistake.

He thought of Sola and that wiped out all other fancies.

Where was Sol's tribe now? He had no idea. He could only wander until he got word of it, then follow until he caught up, sharpening his skill in that period. He had a weapon now, and with it he meant to win his bride.

The season was early spring, and the leaf-buds were just beginning to form. As always at this time of year, the men brought their families to the cabins, not anxious to pitch small tents against the highly variable nights. The young single girls came, too, seeking their special conquests. Sos merged with these groups in crowded camaraderie, sleeping on the floor when necessary, declining to share a bunk if it meant parting with his bracelet, and conversing with others on sundry subjects. Sol's tribe? No—no one knew

its present whereabouts, though some had heard of it. Big tribe—a thousand warriors, wasn't it? Maybe he should ask one of the masters; they generally kept track of such things.

The second day out Sos engaged in a status match with a sticker. The man had questioned whether a simple length of rope could be seriously considered a weapon, and Sos had offered to demonstrate, in friendly fashion. Curious bystanders gathered around as the two men entered the circle.

Sos's intensive practice had left his body in better condition than ever before. He had thought he had attained his full growth two years ago, but the organs and flesh of his body had continued to change, slowly. Indeed, he seemed to be running more and more to muscle, and today was a flat solid man of considerable power. He wondered sometimes whether he *had* been touched by radiation, and whether it could act in this fashion.

He was ready, physically—but it had been a long time since he took the circle with a weapon. His hands became sweaty, and he suddenly felt unsure of himself, a stranger in this ring of physical decision. Could he still fight? He had to; all his hopes depended upon this.

His rope was a slender metallic cord twenty-five feet long, capped and weighted at either end. He wore it coiled about his shoulders when traveling, and it weighed several pounds.

Stupid had learned to watch the rope. Sos loosened several feet of it and held a slack loop in one hand as he faced the other man, and Stupid quickly made for a nearby tree. The two sticks glinted as the other attacked, the right beating at his head while the left maintained a defensive guard. Sos jumped clear, bounding to the far side of the circle. His nervousness vanished as the action began, and he knew he was all right. His rope shot out as the man advanced again, entangling the offensive wrist. A yank, and the sticker was pulled forward, stumbling.

Sos jerked expertly and the cord fell free, just as he had practiced it, and snapped back to his waiting hand. The man was on him again, directing quick blows with both sticks so that a single throw could not interfere with the pair. Sos flipped a central loop over the sticker's neck, ducked under his arm and leaped for the far side of the

ring again. The loop tightened, choking the man and pulling him helplessly backward.

Another jerk and the rope fell free again. Sos could have kept it taut and finished the fight immediately, but he preferred to make a point. He wanted to prove, to others and to himself, that the rope could win in a number of guises—and to discover any weaknesses in it before he had a serious encounter.

The sticker approached more cautiously the third time, keeping one arm high to ward off the snaking rope. The man knew now that the coil was an oddity but no toy; a weapon to be wary of. He jumped in suddenly, thinking to score a blow by surprise—and Sos smacked him blindingly across the forehead with the end.

The man reeled back, grasping the fact of defeat. A red welt appeared just above his eyes, and it was obvious that the rope could have struck an inch lower and done terrible damage, had Sos chosen so. As it was, his eyes watered profusely, and the sticker had to strike out almost randomly.

Sos let down his guard, looking for a kind way to finish the encounter—and the man happened to connect with a hard rap to the side of his head. The singlestick was no club, but still could easily knock out a man, and Sos was momentarily shaken. His opponent followed up with the other stick immediately, raining blows upon head and shoulders before Sos could plunge away.

He *had* been away from the circle too long! He should never have eased his own attack. He was fortunate that the other was operating on reflex rather than calculated skill, and had struck without proper aim. He had his lesson, and he would not forget it.

Sos stayed away until his head was clear, then set about finishing it. He wrapped the rope about the man's legs, lassoing them, and yanked the feet from under. He bent over the sticker, this time hunching his shoulders to absorb the ineffective blows, and pinioned both arms with a second loop. He gripped the coils with both hands strategically placed, lifted, and heaved.

The man came up, hogtied and helpless. Sos whirled him around in a complete arc and let go. The body flew out of the ring and landed on the lawn beyond the gravel. He had not been seriously hurt, but was completely humiliated.

The rope had proven itself in combat.

The following weeks established Sos as a reputable fighter against other weapons as well. His educated rope quickly snared the hand that wielded sword or club, defending by incapacitating the offense, and the throttle-coil kept the flashing hands of the dagger away. Only against the staff did he have serious trouble. The long pole effectively prevented him from looping the hands, since it extended the necessary range for a lasso enormously and tended to tangle his rope and slow alternate attacks. Wherever he flung, there was the length of rigid metal, blocking him. But the staff was mainly a defensive weapon, which gave him time to search out an opening and prevail. He made a mental note, however: never tackle the quarterstaff when in a hurry.

Still there was no positive word on Sol's tribe. It was as though it had disappeared, though he was certain this was not the case. Finally he took the advice offered the first night and sought the nearest major tribe.

This happened to be the Pit doubles. He was not at all sure that their leader would give information to an isolated warrior merely because he asked for it. The Pit master had a reputation for being surly and secretive. But Sos had no partner to make a doubles challenge for information, and none of the men he had met were ones he cared to trust his life to in the circle.

He gave a mental shrug and set course for the Pit encampment. He would dodge that obstacle when he came to it.

Three days later he met a huge clubber ambling in the opposite direction, tossing his weapon into the air and humming tunelessly. Sos stopped, surprised, but there was no doubt.

It was Bog, the indefatigable swinger who had battered Sol for half a day, for the sheer joy of fighting.

"Bog!" he cried.

The giant stopped, not recognizing him. "Who you?" he demanded, pointing the club.

Sos explained where they had met. "Good fight!" Bog exclaimed, remembering Sol. But he did not know or care where Sol's tribe had gone.

"Why not travel with me?" Sos asked him, thinking of

the Pit doubles. To team with such a man—! "I'm looking for Sol. Maybe we can find him together. Maybe another good fight."

"Okay!" Bog agreed heartily. "You come with me."

"But I want to inquire at the Pit's. You're going the wrong way."

Bog did not follow the reasoning. "My way," he said firmly, hefting the club.

Sos could think of only one way to budge him—a dangerous way. "I'll fight you for it. I win, we go my way. Okay?"

"Okay!" he agreed with frightening enthusiasm. The prospect of a fight always swayed Bog.

Sos had to backtrack two hours' journey to reach the nearest circle, and by that time it was late afternoon. The giant was eager to do battle, however.

"All right—but we quit at dusk."

"Okay!" And they entered the circle as people rushed up to witness the entertainment. Some had seen Bog fight before, or heard of him, and others had encountered Sos. There was considerable speculation about the outcome of this unusual match. Most of it consisted of estimates of the number of minutes or seconds it would require for Bog to take the victory.

It was fully as bad as he had feared. Bog blasted away with his club, heedless of obstructions. Sos ducked and weaved and backpedaled, feeling naked without a solid weapon, knowing that sooner or later the ferocious club would catch up to him. Bog didn't seem to realize that his blows hurt his opponents; to him, it was all sport.

Sos looped the arm with a quick throw—and Bog swung without change of pace, yanking the rope and Sos after him. The man had incredible power! Sos dropped the garrote over his head and tightened it behind the tremendous neck—and Bog kept swinging, unheeding, the muscles lining that column so powerful that he could not be choked.

The spectators gaped, but Bog was not even aware of them. Sos saw a couple of them touch their necks and knew they were marveling at Bog's invulnerability. Sos gave up the choke and concentrated on Bog's feet, looping them together when he had the chance and yanking. The big man

simply stood there, legs spread, balanced by the backlash of his own swings, and caught the taut rope with a mash that ripped the other end from Sos's hands painfully.

By the time he recovered it, Bog was free, still swinging gleefully. Sos has managed to avoid anything more serious than grazing blows—but these were savage enough. It was only a matter of time, unless he retreated from the circle before getting tagged.

He could not give up! He needed this man's assistance, and he had to ascertain that his weapon was effective against a top warrior as well as the mediocre ones. He decided upon one desperate stratagem.

Sos looped, not Bog's arm, but the club itself, catching it just above the handle. Instead of tightening the coil, however, he let it ride, keeping the rope slack as he ducked under the motion. As he did so, he dropped the rest of the rope to the ground, placed both feet upon it, and shifted his full weight to rest there.

As the club completed its journey the rope snapped taut. Sos was jerked off his feet by the yank—but the club received an equal shock, right at the moment least expected by the wielder. It twisted in Bog's hand as the head flipped over—and flew out of the circle.

Bog stared at the distant weapon openmouthed. He did not understand what had happened. Sos got to his feet and hefted his rope—but he still wasn't sure he could make the giant concede defeat.

Bog started to go after his club, but halted as he realized that he could not leave the circle without being adjudged the loser. He was baffled.

"Draw!" Sos shouted in a fit of inspiration. "Tie! Food! Quit!"

"Okay!" Bog replied automatically. Then, before the man could figure out what it meant, Sos took his arm in a friendly grasp and guided him out of the arena.

"It was a draw," Sos told him. "As with Sol. That means nobody won, nobody lost. We're even. So we have to fight together next time. A team."

Bog thought about it. He grinned. "Okay!" He was nothing if not agreeable, once the logic was properly presented.

That night no women happened to be available for a

bracelet. Bog looked around the cabin, circled the center column once in perplexity, and finally turned on the television. For the rest of the evening he was absorbed by the silent figures gesticulating there, smiling with pleasure at the occasional cartoons. He was the first person Sos had seen actually watch television for any length of time.

Two days later they found the large Pit tribe. Twin spokesmen came out to meet them. Sos's suspicions had been correct: the master would not even talk to him.

"Very well. I challenge the master to combat in the circle."

"You," the left spokesman said dryly, "and who else?"

"And Bog the club, here."

"As you wish. You will meet one of our lesser teams first!"

"One, two, three a'time!" Bog exclaimed. "Good, good!"

"What my partner means," Sos said smoothly, "is that we will meet your first, second and third teams—consecutively." He put a handsome sneer into his voice. "Then we will sell them back to your master for suitable information. They will not be able to travel, in their condition."

"We shall see," the man said coolly.

The Pit's first team was a pair of swords. The two men were of even height and build, perhaps brothers, and seemed to know each other's location and posture without looking. This was a highly polished team that had fought together for many years, he was sure. A highly dangerous team, better than any he had trained in the badlands camp . . . and he and Bog had never fought together before. As a matter of fact, neither of them had fought in any team before, and Bog hardly understood what it was all about.

But Sos was counting on the fact that the rope weapon would be strange to these men—and Bog was Bog. "Now remember," Sos cautioned him, "I'm on *your* side. Don't hit *me*."

"Okay!" Bog agreed, a little dubiously. To him, anything in the circle with him was fair game, and he still wasn't entirely clear on the details of this special arrangement.

The two sworders functioned beautifully. Both were expert. While one slashed, the other parried, and while the first recovered, his partner took the offense. Every so

often with no apparent signal they lunged together, twin blades swinging with synchronized precision just inches apart.

This, at any rate, was the way it was during the brief practice they engaged in prior to the formal battle. The situation changed somewhat when Bog and Sos took the circle against them.

Bog, turned on by the circle in the usual fashion, blasted away at both opponents simultaneously, while Sos stood back and twirled the end of his rope and watched, only cautioning his partner when Bog began to forget who was on which side. The devastating club knocked both swords aside, then swept back to knock them again, to the consternation of the Pit team. They didn't know what to make of it and couldn't quite believe that it was happening.

But they were neither cowardly nor stupid. Very soon they split apart, one attempting to engage Bog defensively from the front while the other edged to the side for an angled cut.

That was when Sos's rope snaked out and caught his wrist. It was the only move Sos made, but it sufficed. Bog smashed them out of opposite sides of the circle, and Sos was right: they were not in fit condition to travel.

The second team consisted of two clubs. A good idea, Sos thought, giving the Pit director due credit, but not good enough. Bog mowed them both down zestfully while Sos continued to stay out of harm's way. The contest was over even more quickly than the first.

The Pit strategist, however, learned from experience. The third team consisted of a staffer and a netter.

Sos knew immediately that it meant trouble. He had only learned of the existence of non-standard weapons after returning to gain the advice of his mentor, Principal Jones. The very fact that a man had a net and knew how to use it in the circle meant that he had had crazy training—and that was dangerous.

It was. The moment the four were in the circle, the netter made his cast—and Bog was hopelessly entangled. He tried to swing, but the pliant nylon strands held him in. He tried to punch the net away, but did not know how. Meanwhile the netter drew the fine but exceedingly strong

mesh closer and closer about him, until Bog tripped and crashed to the ground, a giant cocoon.

All this time Sos was trying savagely to reach and help his partner—but the staff held him at bay. The man made no aggressive moves; he only blocked Sos off, and at that simple task he was most effective. The staffer never looked behind him, having full confidence in his partner; and so long as he concentrated on Sos and refused to be drawn out, Sos could not hurt him.

The netter finished his job of wrapping and began rolling the hapless Bog out of the circle, net and all. Sos could guess what was coming next: the netter deprived of his own weapon, would grab for the rope, taking whatever punishment he had to to get a grip on it. Then he would keep pulling while his partner took the offensive. All the netter needed was an opening, with the staffer's distractions and two men against one. The netter would naturally be good with his bare hands on anything flexible.

"Roll, Bog, roll!" Sos shouted. "Back in the circle! Roll!"

For once in his life Bog understood immediately. His wrapped body flexed like a huge grub, then countered the netter's efforts to maneuver him over the rim. Bog was a hefty hunk of man and could hardly be moved against his will. Bog grunted, the staffer looked—and that was his mistake.

Sos's rope whipped around the man's neck and brought him down choking, while the Pit spectators groaned. Sos hurdled his hunching body and landed on the back of the straining netter. He clasped the man in his arms, picked him up and threw him down on top of his rising partner. A quick series of loops, and both men were bound together, the staff crosswise between them. Sos did not foolishly approach them again. They could still maneuver together, or grab him and hang on. Instead he bent to the net, searching out the convolutions and ripping them away from Bog's body. "Lie still!" he yelled in Bog's ear as the cocoon continued to struggle. "It's me! Sos!"

Untended, the two Pit men rapidly fought free. Now they had possession of both staff and rope, while only Bog's legs were loose from the complicated, tenacious net. Sos had lost his play for time.

"Roll, Bog, roll!" he shouted again, and gave his partner a vigorous urge in the right direction. Bog kicked his legs and tried, but the motion was clumsy. The two opponents hurdled him easily—and were caught at waist height by Sos's flying tackle.

All four men landed in a heap, entangled by rope and net. But the net was spoken for while the rope was loose. Sos quickly wrapped it around all three men and knotted it securely about the striving bundle. Bog, finding the netter similarly bound, grinned through the mesh and heaved his bulk about, trying to crush the man.

Sos extracted the staff and aimed its blunt tip at the head of its owner. "Stop!" the Pit spokesman cried. "We yield! We yield!"

Sos smiled. He had not really intended to deliver such an unfair blow.

"Tomorrow the Pits will speak with you," the spokesman said, no longer so distant. He watched the three men work their way out of the involuntary embrace. "Our hospitality, tonight."

It was good hospitality. After a full meal, Sos and Bog retired to the nearest hostel, that the Pit tribe had vacated for their use. Two pretty girls showed up to claim their bracelets. "Not for me," Sos said, thinking of Sola. "No offense."

"I take both!" Bog cried. Sos left him to his pleasures; it was the rope's turn to watch television.

In the morning Sos learned why the Pits were so secretive about their persons—and why they had formed the doubles tribe. They were Siamese twins: two men joined together by a supple band of flesh at the waist. Both were swords, and Sos was certain that their teamwork, when they fought, was unexcelled.

"Yes, we know of Sol's tribe," the left one said. "Tribes, rather. Two months ago he split his group into ten subtribes of a hundred warriors each, and they are roving about the country, expanding again. One of them is coming to meet us in the circle soon."

"Oh? Who governs it?"

"Tor the Sword. He is reputed to be an able leader."

"So I can believe."

"May we inquire your business with Sol? If you seek to

join a tribe yourself, we can offer you and your partner an advantageous situation—"

Sos politely declined. "My business is of a private nature. But I am sure Bog will be happy to remain for a few days by himself to give your teams practice, so long as your men, women and food hold out . . ."

CHAPTER TWELVE

"Is this the tribe of Sol of all weapons?" Sos inquired. He had not waited for the arrival of Tor's subtribe at the Pit camp, much as he would have enjoyed being on hand for the contest of wits between Tor and the perceptive Pit strategist. It would probably be a standoff. It was Sol he was after, and now that he knew where to find him no further delay was tolerable.

As it happened, he had met Tor on the way, and obtained updating and redirection—but it was hard to believe, even so, that this was the proper camp.

Warriors were practicing everywhere, none of them familiar. Yet this was the only major group in the arena, so the directions had not been mistaken. Had he traveled a month only to encounter Sol's conqueror? He hoped not. The camp was well disciplined, but he did not like its atmosphere.

"Speak to Vit the Sword," the nearest man told him.

Sos searched out the main tent and asked for Vit. "Who are you?" the tent guard, a swarthy dagger, demanded, eying the bird on his shoulder.

"Step into the circle and I will show you who I am!" Sos said angrily. He had had enough of such bureaucracy.

The guard whistled and a man detached himself from practice and trotted over. "This intruder wishes to make himself known in the circle," the dagger said contemptuously, "Oblige him."

The man turned to study Sos.

"Mok the Morningstar!" Sos cried.

Mok started. "Sos! You have come back—and Stupid, too! I did not recognize you, in all that muscle!"

"You know this man?" the guard inquired.

"Know him! This is Sos—the man who built this tribe! Sol's friend!"

The guard shrugged indifferently. "Let him prove it in the circle."

"You nuts? He doesn't carry a—" Mok paused. "Or *do* you, now?"

Sos had his rope about him, but the man had not recognized it as a weapon. "I do. Come, I'll demonstrate."

"Why not try it against the staff or sticks?" Mok suggested diplomatically. "My weapon is—"

"Is dangerous? You seem to lack faith in my prowess."

"Oh, no," Mok protested, obviously insincere. "But you know how it is with the star. One accident—"

Sos laughed. "You force me to vindicate myself. Come—I'll make a believer out of you."

Mok accompanied him to the circle, ill at ease. "If anything happens—"

"This is my weapon," Sos said, hefting a coil of rope. "If you are afraid to face it, summon a better man."

Several neighboring men chuckled, and Mok had to take the circle. Sos knew the jibe had been unfair; the man had wanted to spare him from possible mutilation. Mok was no coward, and since he was still with the tribe, his skill was sufficient too. But it was important that the rope prove itself as a real weapon; men like Mok would not believe in Sos's new status as a warrior otherwise.

Friendship ended in the circle, always. Mok lifted his morningstar and whirled the spiked ball in an overhead spiral. He had to attack, since the weapon could not be used defensively. Sos had never faced the star before and discovered that it was a peculiarly frightening experience. Even the faint tune of air passing the circling spikes was ominous.

Sos backed away, treating the flying ball with utmost respect. He fired a length of rope at it, caught the metal chain, fouled it, and yanked ball, chain and handle out of Mok's hand. Mok stood there staring, as Bog had done before him. The spectators laughed.

"If any of you think you can do better, step inside," Sos invited.

A sticker was quick to accept the challenge—and as

quick to fall to the throttle-loop. This time it was Mok who laughed. "Come—you must see Vit now!"

A group of men continued to stand around the vacated circle, murmuring as Sos left. They had never witnessed such a performance.

"I'm glad you're back," Mok confided as they came to the tent. "Things aren't the same around here since—" he broke off as they approached the guard.

This time there was no trouble about entry. Mok ushered him into the leader's presence.

"Yes?" Vit was a tall slender, dour man of middle years who looked familiar. The name, also, jogged an image. Then Sos placed him: the sworder that Dal the Dagger had humiliated, back in the first full-fledged tribal encounter. Times had certainly changed!

"I am Sos the Rope. I have come to talk to Sol."

"By what right?"

Mok started to explain, but Sos had had enough. He knew Vit recognized him and was simply placing difficulties in his way. "By the right of my weapon! Challenge me in the circle before you attempt to balk me!" It was good to be able to assume this posture again; the weapon made all the difference. Sos realized that he was being less than reasonable, and enjoyed the feeling.

Vit merely looked at him. "Are you that rope who disarmed Bog the club, five weeks ago in the east?"

"I am." Sos was beginning to appreciate why Vit had risen to such a position of power so rapidly: he had complete command of his temper and knew his business. Apparently supremacy in the circle was no longer a requirement for leadership.

"Sol will see you tomorrow."

"Tomorrow!"

"He is absent on business today. Accept our hospitality tonight."

Sol away on business? He did not like the smell of that. Sol should have no reason to recruit warriors alone, any more—not with ten tribes to manage, the nucleus of his empire. He could not be inspecting any of those tribes, either; the nearest was at least a week away.

A woman emerged from a compartment and walked

slowly toward them. She was dressed in a breathtakingly snug sarong and wore very long, very black hair.

It was Sola.

Sos started toward her, only to be blocked by Vit. "Eyes off that woman! She belongs to the master!"

Sola looked up and recognized him. "Sos!" she cried, then checked herself. "I know this man," she said formally to Vit. "I will speak to him."

"You will *not* speak to him." Vit stood firmly between them.

Sos gripped his rope, furious, but Sola backed away and retreated into her compartment. Mok tugged his arm, and he controlled himself and wheeled about. Something was certainly wrong, but this was not the moment for action. It would not be wise to betray his former intimacy with Sola.

"All the old stalwarts are gone," Mok said sadly as they emerged. "Tyl, Tor, Sav, Tun—hardly any of the ones we built the badlands camp with are here today."

"What happened to them?" He knew already, but wanted more information. The more he saw of this tribe, the less he liked it. *Was* Sol still in control, or had he become a figurehead? Had there been some private treachery to incapacitate him?

"They command the other tribes. Sol trusts no one you did not train. We need you again, Sos. I wish we were back in the badlands, the way it was before."

"Sol seems to trust Vit."

"Not to command. This is Sol's own tribe, and he runs it himself, with advisors. Vit just handles the details."

"Such as keeping Sola penned up?"

"Sol makes him do it. She is allowed to see no one while he is away. Sol would kill Vit if—but I told you, everything is different."

Sos agreed, profoundly disturbed. The camp was efficient, but the men were strangers to him. He recognized no more than half a dozen of the hundred or so he saw. It was a strange pass when the closest companion he could find in Sol's tribe was Mok—whose dealing with him had always been brief, before. This was not, in fact, a tribe at all; it was a military camp, of the type he had read about,

with a military martinet in charge. The *esprit de corps* he had fostered was gone.

He accepted a small tent on the outskirts, alone, for the night. He was troubled, but still did not want to act until he understood the ramifications of what he had observed. Evidently the dour Vit had been put in charge because he followed orders without imagination and was probably completely trustworthy in that respect. But why the need? Something had gone drastically wrong, and he could not believe that his own absence could account for it. Tor's tribe was hardly like this. What had taken the spirit out of Sol's drive for empire?

A woman came quietly to the tent. "Bracelet?" she inquired, her voice muffled, her face hidden in the dusk.

"No!" he snapped, turning his eyes from the hourglass figure that showed in provocative silhouette against the distant evening fires.

She tugged open the mesh and kneeled to show her face. "Would you shame me, Sos?"

"I asked for no woman," he said, not looking at her. "Go away. No offense."

She did not move. "Greensleeves," she murmured.

His head jerked up. "Sola!"

"It was never your habit to make me wait so long for recognition," she said with wry reproof. "Let me in before someone sees." She scrambled inside and refastened the mesh. "I changed places with the girl assigned, so I think we're safe. But still—"

"What are you doing here? I thought you weren't—"

She stripped and crawled into his bedroll. "You must have been exercising!"

"Not any more."

"Oh, but you have! I never felt such a muscular body."

"I mean we're not lovers any more. If you won't meet me by day, I won't meet you by night."

"Why did you come, then?" she inquired, placing against him a body that had become magnificent. Her pregnancy of the year before had enhanced her physical attributes.

"I came to claim you honorably."

"Claim me, then! No man but you has touched me since we first met."

"Tomorrow. Give back his bracelet and take mine, publicly."

"I will," she said. "Now——"

"No!"

She drew back and tried to see his face in the dark. "You mean it."

"I love you. I came for you. But I will have you honorably."

She sighed. "Honor is not quite that simple, Sos." But she got up and began putting on her clothing.

"What has happened here? Where is Sol? Why are you hiding from people?"

"You left us, Sos. That's what happened. You were the heart of us."

"That doesn't make sense. I had to leave. You were having——the baby. *His* son."

"No."

"That was the price of you. I will not pay it again. This time it has to be *my* son, conceived upon *my* bracelet."

"You don't understand *anything!*" she cried in frustration.

He paused, knowing the mystery to be yet unfathomed. "Did it——die?"

"No! That's not the point. That——oh, you stupid, stupid clubhead! You——" She choked over her own emotion and faced away from him, sobbing.

She was more artful, too, than she had been, he thought. He did not yield. He let her run down, unmoving.

Finally she wiped her face and crawled out of the tent. He was alone.

CHAPTER THIRTEEN

Sol was a little leaner, a little more serious, but retained the uncanny grace his coordination provided. "You came!" he exclaimed, grasping Sos's hand in an unusual display of pleasure.

"Yesterday," Sos said, somewhat embarrassed. "I saw Vit, but he wouldn't let me talk to your wife, and I hardly know the others here." How much should he say?

"She should have come to you anyway. Vit knows nothing." He paused reflectively. "We do not get along. She keeps to herself."

So Sol still didn't care about Sola. He had protected her for the sake of the coming heir and no longer even bothered with pretense. But why, then, had he kept her isolated? It had never been Sol's way to be pointlessly selfish.

"I have a weapon now," Sos said. Then, as the other looked at him: "The rope."

"I am glad of it."

There did not seem to be much else to say. Their reunion, like their parting, was an awkward thing.

"Come," Sol said abruptly. "I will show her to you."

Sos followed him into the main tent, uncomfortably off-balance. He should have admitted that he *had* talked with Sola and prevented this spurious introduction. He had come on a matter of honor, yet he was making himself a liar.

Nothing was falling out quite the way he had expected— but the differences were intangible. The subtle wrongnesses were entangling him, as though he had fallen prey in the circle to the net.

They stopped before a homemade crib in a small compartment. Sol leaned down to pick up a chuckling baby. "This is my daughter," he said. "Six months, this week."

Sos stood with one hand on his rope, speechless gazing at the black-haired infant. A daughter! Somehow that possibility had never occurred to him.

"She will be as beautiful as her mother," Sol said proudly. "See her smile."

"Yes," Sos agreed, feeling every bit as stupid as Sola had called him. The name should not have gone to his bird.

"Come," Sol repeated. "We will take her for a walk." He hefted the baby upon his shoulder and led the way. Sos followed numbly, realizing that *this* was the female they had come to see, not the mother. If he had only known, or guessed, or allowed himself to hear, last night. . . .

Sola met them at the entrance. "I would come," she said.

Sol sounded annoyed. "Come, then, woman. We only walk."

The little party threaded its way out of the camp and into the nearby forest. It was like old times, when they had journeyed to the badlands—yet completely different. What incredible things had grown from the early coincidence of names!

This was all wrong. He had come to claim the woman he loved, to challenge Sol for her in the circle if he had to, yet he could not get the words out. He loved her and she loved him and her nominal husband admitted the marriage was futile—but Sos felt like a terrible intruder.

Stupid flew ahead, happy to sport among the forest shadows; or perhaps there were insects there.

This could not go on. "I came for Sola," he said baldly.

Sol did not even hesitate. "Take her." It was as though the woman were not present.

"My bracelet on her wrist," Sos said, wondering whether he had been understood. "My children by her. She shall be Sosa."

"Certainly."

This was beyond credence. "You have no conditions?"

"Only your friendship."

Sos spluttered, "This is not a friendly matter!"

"Why not? I have preserved her only for you."

"You—Vit—?" This elaborate guardianship had been for his, Sos's benefit? "Why—?"

"I would have her take no lesser name," Sol said.

Why not, indeed? There seemed to be no barrier to an amicable changeover—but it was wrong. It couldn't work. He could not put his finger on the flaw, but knew there was something.

"Give me Soli," Sola said.

Sol handed the baby over. She opened her dress and held Soli to her breast to nurse as they walked.

And that was it. The baby! "Can she leave her mother?" Sos asked.

"No," Sola replied.

"You will not take my daughter," Sol said, raising his voice for the first time.

"No—of course not. But until she is weaned—"

"Until, nothing," Sola said firmly. "She's my daughter, too. She stays with me."

"Soli is mine!" Sol said with utter conviction. "You woman—stay or go as you will, wear whose clasp you will—but Soli is mine."

The baby looked up and began to cry. Sol reached over and took the little girl, and she fell contentedly silent. Sola made a face but said nothing.

"I make no claim upon your daughter," Sos said carefully. "But if she cannot leave her mother—"

Sol found a fallen tree and sat down upon it, balancing Soli upon his knee. "Sorrow fell upon our camp when you departed. Now you are back, and with your weapon. Govern my tribe, my empire, as you did before. I would have you by my side again."

"But I came to take Sola away with me! She cannot stay here after she exchanges bracelets. It would bring shame upon us both."

"Why?"

"Sosa nursing Sol's child?"

Sol thought about it. "Let her wear my bracelet, then. She will still be yours."

"You would wear the horns?"

Sol jiggled Soli on his knee. He began to hum a tune: then, catching the range, he sang the words in a fine clear tenor:

From this valley they say you are going
We shall miss your bright eyes and sweet smile
For they say you are taking the sunshine
That brightens our pathway a while.
Come sit by my—

Sos interrupted him, appalled. "You heard!"

"I heard who my true friend was, when I was in fever and could not move my body or save myself from injury. I heard who carried me when I would have died. If I must wear the horns, these are the horns I would wear, for all to see."

"No!" Sos cried, shocked.

"Only leave me my daughter; the rest is yours."

"Not dishonor!" Yet it seemed late for this protest. "I will not accept dishonor—yours or mine."

"Nor I," Sola said quietly. "Not now."

"How can there be dishonour among us!" Sol said fervently. "There is only friendship."

They faced each other in silence then, searching for the solution. Sos ran over the alternatives in his mind, again and again, but nothing changed. He could leave—and give up all his dreams of union with the woman he loved, while she remained with a man she did *not* love and who cared nothing for her. Could he take comfort in such as blonde Miss Smith, while that situation existed? Or he could stay—and accept the dishonorable liaison that would surely emerge, knowing himself to be unworthy of his position and his weapon.

Or he could fight—for a woman *and* honor. Everything or nothing.

Sol met his gaze. He had come to the same conclusion. "Make a circle," he said.

"No!" Sola cried, realizing what was happening. "It is wrong either way!"

"That is why it must be settled in the circle," Sos told her regretfully. "You and your daughter must be together. You *shall* be—either way."

"I will leave Soli," she said with difficulty. "Do not fight again."

Sol still sat holding the baby, looking very little like the master of an empire. "No—for a mother to leave her child

is worse than for the leader to leave his tribe. I did not think of that before, but I know it now."

"But you brought no weapon," she said, trying to stave it off.

Sol ignored her and looked at Sos. "I would not kill you. You may serve me if you wish, and do what you wish—but never again will you bear weapon against me," he finished with some force.

"I would not kill you either. You may keep your weapons and your empire—but child and mother go with me."

And that defined it. If Sol won, Sos would be deprived of any honorable means to advance his case, which would mean that he was helpless. If Sos won, Sol would have to give up the baby, leaving Sola free to go with the rope. The winner would have his desire; the loser, what remained.

What remained, despite the theoretical generosity of the terms, was the mountain. Sos would not remain to adulterate the bracelet Sola wore or return in shame to the crazies' establishment. Sol would spurn his empire, once mastered in combat; that had always been clear. It was not a pretty situation, and the victor would have his sorrows, but it was a fair solution. Trial by combat.

"Make the circle," Sol said again.

"But your weapon——" They were repeating themselves. Neither really wanted to fight. Was there some other way out?

Sol handed the baby to Sola and peered through the trees. He located a suitable sapling and stripped the branches and leaves by hand. Seeing his intent, Sos proceeded to clear a place on the forest floor to form a roughly level disk of earth the proper size. The arrangements were crude, but this was not a matter either man cared to advertise in front of the tribe.

They met, standing on opposite sides of the makeshift arena, Sola standing anxiously near. The scene reminded Sos of their first encounter, except for the baby in Sola's arms.

Sos now far outweighed his opponent, and held a weapon he was sure Sol had never seen before. Sol, on the other hand, held a makeshift implement—but he was the finest

warrior ever seen in the area, and the weapon he had fashioned was a staff.

The one thing the rope was weak against.

Had Sol's barrow been available, he might have taken the sword or the club or one of the other standardized instruments of battle; but in his self-reliance he had procured what could be had from nature, and with it, though he could not know it yet, the victory.

"After this we shall be friends," Sol said.

"We shall be friends." And somehow that was more important than all the rest of it.

They stepped into the circle.

The baby cried.

CHAPTER FOURTEEN

It was midsummer by the time he stood at the foot of the mountain. This was a strange heap of lava and slag towering above the twisted landscape, sculptured in some manner by the Blast but free of radiation. Shrubs and stunted trees approached the base, but only weeds and lichen ascended the mountain itself.

Sos peered up but could not see the top. A few hundred yards ahead, great projections of metallic material obscured the view, asymmetrical and ugly. Gliding birds of prey circled high in the haze overhead, watching him.

There was wind upon the mountain, not fierce, but howling dismally around the brutal serrations. The sky above it was overcast and yellowish.

This was surely the mountain of death. No one could mistake it.

He touched his fingers to his shoulder and lifted Stupid. The bird had never been handsome; his mottled brown feathers always seemed to have been recently ruffled, and the distribution of colors remained haphazard—but Sos had become accustomed to every avian mannerism in the time they had had their association. "This is about as far as you go, little friend," he said. "I go up, never to come down again—but it is not your turn. Those vultures aren't after *you*."

He flicked the bird into the air, but Stupid spread his wings, circled, and came to roost again upon his shoulder.

Sos shrugged. "I give you your freedom, but you do not take it. Stupid." It was meaningless, but he was touched. How could the bird know what was ahead?

For that matter, how could *anyone* know? How much of human loyalty and love was simply ignorance of destiny?

He still wore the rope, but no longer as a weapon. He caught a languishing sapling and stripped it as Sol had done, making himself a crude staff for balance during the climb. He adjusted his heavy pack and moved out.

The projections *were* metal—enormous sheets and beams melted at the edges and corners, securely embedded in the main mass, the crevices filled with pebbles and dirt. It was as though a thousand men had shoved it together and set fire to it all—assuming that metal would burn. Perhaps they had poured alcohol upon it? Of course not; this was the handiwork of the Blast.

Even at this terminal stage of his life, Sos retained his curiosity about the phenomenon of the Blast. What was its nature, and how had it wrought such divers, diverse things as the invisibly dangerous badlands and the mountain of death? If it had been unleashed somehow by man himself, as the crazies claimed, why had the ancients chosen to do it?

It was the riddle of all things, unanswerable as ever. The modern world began with the Blast; what preceded it was largely conjecture. The crazies claimed that there had been a strange other society before it, a world of incredible machines and luxury and knowledge, little of which survived. But while he half believed them, and the venerable texts made convincing evidence, the practical side of him set it all aside as unproven. He had described past history to others as though it were fact, but it was as realistic to believe that the books themselves, along with the men and landscape, had been created in one moment from the void, by the Blast.

He was delaying the climb unnecessarily. If he meant to do it, now was the time. If fear turned him back, he should admit it, rather than pretending to philosophize. One way or the other: action.

He roped a beam and hauled himself up, staff jammed down between his back and the pack. There was probably an easier way to ascend, since the many men who had gone before him would not have had ropes or known how to use them, but he had not come to expire the easy way. Stupid, dislodged, flew up and perched on the beam, peek-

ing down at him. The bird never criticized, never got in the way; he winged himself to safety when there was action in the circle or in the tent at night, but always came back. He waited only for the conquest of this particular hazard, before joining his companion. Was this the definition of true friendship?

Sos scrambled to the upper surface of the beam and dislodged the rope. Sure enough, Stupid swooped in, brushing the tip of a wing against his right ear. Always the right shoulder, never the left! But not for long—the out-cropping was merely the first of many, vertical and horizontal and angled, large and small and indefinite, straight and looped and twisted. It would be a tedious, grueling climb.

As evening came, he unlimbered warmer clothing from the pack and ate the solid bread he had found stocked for the mountaineers at the nearest cabin. How considerate of the crazies, to make available the stuff of life for those bent on dying!

He had looked at everything in that hostel, knowing that he would not have another chance . . . even the television. It was the same silent meaningless pantomime as ever; men and women garbed like exaggerated crazies, fighting and kissing in brazen openness but never using proper weapons or making proper love. It was possible, with concentration, to make out portions of some kind of story—but every time it seemed to be making sense the scene would change and different characters would appear holding up glasses of liquid that foamed or putting slender cylinders in their mouths and burning them. No wonder no one watched it! He had once asked Jones about the television, but the principal had only smiled and said that the maintenance of that type of technology was not in his department. It was all broadcast from pre-Blast tapes, anyway, Jones explained.

Sos put such foolishness aside. There were practical problems to be considered. He had loaded the pack carefully, knowing that a man could starve anywhere if he ventured without adequate preparation. The mountain was a special demise, not to be demeaned by common hunger or thirst. He had already consumed the quart bottle of fortified water, knowing that there would be edible snow

at the height to take its place. Whatever lurked, it was not malnutrition.

What *did* lurk? No one had been able to tell him, since it was a one-way journey, and the books were strangely reticent. The books all seemed to stop just *before* the Blast; only scattered manuals used by the crazies were dated after it. That could be a sign that the books *were* pre-Blast—or it could discredit them entirely, since not one of them related to the *real* world. They and the television were parts of the elaborate and mystifying myth-world framework whose existence he believed one day and denied the next. The mountain could be yet another aspect of it.

Well, since he couldn't turn his mind off, there was a very practical way to find out. He would mount the mountain and see for himself. Death, at least, could not be secondhand.

Stupid fluttered about, searching out flying insects, but there did not seem to be many. "Go back down, birdbrain," Sos advised him. "This is no place for you." It seemed that the bird obeyed, for he disappeared from sight, and Sos yielded himself to the turbulence of semiconsciousness: television and iron beams and Sola's somber face and nebulous uncertainties about the nature of the extinction he sought. But in the cold morning Stupid was back, as Sos had known he would be.

The second day of the climb was easier than the first, and he covered three times the distance. The tangled metal gave way to packed rubble clogged by weeds: huge sections of dissolving rubber in the shape of a torus, oblong sheets of metal a few inches long, sections of ancient boots, baked clay fragments, plastic cups and hundreds of bronze and silver coins. These were the artifacts of pre-Blast civilization, according to the books; he could not imagine what the monstrous rubber doughnuts were for, but the rest appeared to be implements similar to those stocked in the hostels. The coins were supposed to have been symbols of status; to possess many of them had been like victory in the circle.

If the books could be believed.

Late in the afternoon, it rained. Sos dug one of the cups

out of the ground, knocked out the caked dirt and held it up to trap the water. He was thirsty, and the snow was farther away than he had expected. Stupid sat hunched on his shoulder, hating the drenching; Sos finally propped up a flap of the pack to shield the little bird.

But in the evening there were more insects abroad, as though the soaking had forced them out, and that was good. He applied repellant against the mosquitoes while Stupid zoomed vigorously, making up for lean times.

Sos had kept his mind on his task, but now that the mountain had lost its novelty his thoughts returned to the most emotional episodes of his life. He remembered the first meeting with Sol, both of them comparatively new to the circle, still exploring the world and feeling their way cautiously in protocol and battle. Evidently Sol had tried all his weapons out in sport encounters until sure of himself; then, with their evening's discussion, that first night, Sol had seen the possible mechanisms of advancement. Play had stopped for them both, that day and night, and already their feet had been treading out the destinies leading to power for the one, and for the other——the mountain.

He remembered Sola, then an innocent girl, lovely and anxious to prove herself by the bracelet. She had proven herself——but not by the bracelet she wore. That, more than anything else, had led him here.

Strange, that the three should meet like that. Had it been just the two men, the empire might even now be uniting them. Had the girl appeared before or after, he might have taken her for a night and gone on, never missing her. But it had been a triple union, and the male empire had been sown with the female seed of destruction even as it sprouted. It was not the particular girl who mattered, but the presence at the inception. Why had she come *then!*

He closed his eyes and saw the staff, blindingly swift, blocking him, striking him, meeting him everywhere he turned, no instrument of defense but savage offense; the length of it across his body, the end of it flying at his face, fouling his rope, outmaneuvering him, beating down his offense and his defense. . . .

And now the mountain, the only honorable alternative. He had lost to the better man.

He slept, knowing that even victory would not have been the solution. He had been in the wrong—not totally, but wrong on balance.

On the third day the snows began. He wrapped the last of the protective clothing around him and kept moving. Stupid clung to him, seemingly not too uncomfortable. Sos scooped up handfuls of the white powder and crammed them into his mouth for water, though the stuff numbed his cheeks and tongue and melted grudgingly down into almost nothing. By nightfall he was ploughing through drifts several inches deep and had to step carefully to avoid treacherous pitfalls that did not show in the leveled surface.

There was no shelter. He lay on his side, facing away from the wind, comfortable enough in the protective wrappings. Stupid settled down beside his face, shivering, and suddenly he realized that the bird had no way to forage anymore. Not in the snow. There would be no living insects here.

He dug a handful of bread out of the pack and held a crumb to Stupid's beak; but there was no response. "You'll starve," he said with concern, but did not know what to do about it. He saw the feathers shaking, and finally took off his left glove, cupped the bird in his bare warm palm, and held his gloved right hand to the back of the exposed one. He would have to make sure he didn't roll or move his hands while sleeping, or he would crush the fragile body.

He woke several times in the night as gusts of cold snow slapped his face and pried into his collar, but his left hand never moved. He felt the bird shivering from time to time and cupped it close to his chest, hoping for a suitable compromise between warmth and safety. He had too much strength and Stupid was too small; better to allow some shivering than to. . . .

Stupid seemed all right in the morning, but Sos knew this could not last. The bird was not adapted to snow; even his coloration was wrong. "Go back down," he urged. "Down. Where it is warm. Insects." He threw the tiny body into the air, downhill, but to no avail; Stupid spread his wings and struggled valiantly with the cold, harsh air, uphill, and would not leave.

Yet, Sos asked himself as he took the bird in hand again and continued climbing, was this misplaced loyalty any more foolish than Sol's determination to retain a daughter he had not sired? A *daughter*? Or Sos's own adherence to a code of honor already severely violated? Men were irrational creatures; why not birds too? If separation were so difficult, they would die together.

A storm came up that fourth day. Sos drove onward, his face numbed in the slashing wind. He had goggles, tinted to protect his eyes, and he put them on now, but the nose and mouth were still exposed. When he put his hand up he discovered a beard of ice superimposed upon his natural one. He tried to knock it off, but knew it would form again.

Stupid flew up as he stumbled and waved his hands. Sos guided the bird to his shoulder, where at least there was some stability. Another slip like that and the bird would be smashed, if he continued to carry it in his hand.

The wind stabbed into his clothing. Earlier he had been sweating, finding the wrappings cumbersome; now the moisture seemed to be caking into ice against his body. That had been a mistake; he should have governed his dress and pace so that he never perspired. There was nowhere for the moisture to go, so of course it eventually froze. He had learned this lesson too late.

This, then, was the death of the mountain. Freezing in the blizzardly upper regions or falling into some concealed crevasse . . . he had been watching the lay of the land, but already he had slipped and fallen several times, and only luck had made his errors harmless. The cold crept in through his garments, draining his visibility, and the eventual result was clear. No person had ever returned from the mountain, if the stories were true, and no bodies had ever been discovered or recovered. No wonder!

Yet this was not the kind of mountain he had heard about elsewhere. After the metal jumble near the base—how many days ago?—there had been no extreme irregularities, no jagged edges, sheer cliffs or preposterous ice bridges. He had seen no alternate ranges or major passes when the sky was clear. The side of this mountain tilted up fairly steadily, fairly safely, like that of an inverted bowl. Only the cold presented a genuine hazard.

Surely there was no impediment to those who elected to

descend again. Not all, or even most, but *some* must have given it up and returned to the foot, either choosing a less strenuous way to die or deciding to live after all. He could still turn about himself. . . .

He picked the quiet bird from his shoulder, disengaging the claws with difficulty. "How about it, Stupid? Have we had enough?"

There was no response. The little body was stiff.

He brought it close to his face, not wanting to believe it. He spread one wing gently with his fingers, but it was rigid. Stupid had died rather than desert his companion, and Sos had not even known the moment of his passing.

True friendship. . . .

He laid the feathered corpse upon the snow and covered it over, a lump in his throat. "I'm sorry, little friend," he said. "I guess a man takes more dying than a bird." Nothing utterable came to mind beyond that, inadequate as it was.

He faced up the mountain and tramped ahead.

The world was a bleak place now. He had taken the bird pretty much for granted, but the sudden, silent loss was staggering. Now there was nothing he could do, but go through with it. He had killed a faithful friend, and there was a raw place in his breast that would not ease.

Yet it was not the first time his folly had damaged another. All Sol had asked was friendship—and, rather than grant him that, Sos had forced him into the circle. What had been so damned urgent about his own definition of honor? Why had he resisted Sol's ultimate offer with such determination? Was it because he had used a limited concept of honor to promote his own selfish objectives ruthlessly, no matter who else was sacrificed? And, failing in these, bringing further pain by wiping out whatever else might have been salvaged?

He thought again of Stupid, so recently dead upon his shoulder, and had his answer.

The mountain steepened. The storm intensified. Let it come! he thought; it was what he had come for. He could no longer tell whether it was day or night. Ice rimmed his goggles, if they were still on. He wasn't sure and didn't care. Everywhere was whirling whiteness. He was panting, his lungs were burning and he wasn't getting enough air.

The steep snowscape before him went on and on; there was no end to it.

He did not realize that he had fallen until he choked on the snow. He tried to stand up, but his limbs did not respond properly. "Come *on!*" he heard Sola calling him, and he listened though he knew it for illusion. He did go on, but more securely: on hands and knees.

Then he was crawling on his belly, numb everywhere except for the heartache.

At last the pleasant lassitude obliterated even that.

CHAPTER FIFTEEN

"Up muscles. It's better if you walk around, get the system functioning again and all that."

Sos recovered unwillingly. He tried to open his eyes, but the darkness remained.

"Uh-uh! Leave that bandage alone! Even if you aren't snowblind, you're frostbit. Here, take my hand." A firm man's hand thrust itself against his arm.

"Did I die?" Sos asked, bracing against the proffered palm as he stood.

"Yes. In a manner of speaking. You will never be seen on the surface again."

"And—Stupid?"

"What?"

"My bird, Stupid. Did he come here too?"

The man paused. "Either there's a misunderstanding, or you are insolent as hell."

Sos constricted his fingers on the man's arm, bringing an exclamation of pain. He caught at the bandage on his head with his free hand and ripped it off. There was bright pain as packed gauze came away from his eye-balls, but he could see again.

He was in a hostel room, standing before a standard bunk surrounded by unstandard equipment. He wore his pantaloons but nothing else. A thin man in an effeminate white smock winced with the continuing pressure of his grip. Sos released him, looking for the exit.

Not a hostel room, for this room was square. The standard furnishings had given him the impression. He had never seen a cabin this shape, however.

"I must say, that's an unusual recovery!" the man re-

marked, rubbing his arm. He was of middle age with sparse hair and pale features: obviously long parted from sun and circle.

"Are you a crazy?"

"Most people in your situation are content to inquire 'Where am I?' or something mundane like that. You're certainly original."

"I did not come to the mountain to be mocked," Sos said, advancing on him.

The man touched a button in the wall. "We have a live one," he said.

"So I see," a feminine voice replied from nowhere. An intercom, Sos realized. So they *were* crazies. "Put him in the rec room. I'll handle it."

The man touched a second button. A door slid open beside him. "Straight to the end. All your questions will be answered."

Sos rushed by him, more anxious to find the way out than to question an uncooperative stranger. But the hall did not lead out; it continued interminably, closed doors on either side. This was certainly no hostel, nor was it a building like the school run by the crazies. It was too big.

He tried a door, finding it locked. He thought about breaking it down, but was afraid that would take too much time. He had a headache, his muscles were stiff and flaccid at once, his stomach queasy. He felt quite sick, physically, and just wanted to get out before any more annoying strangers came along.

The end door was open. He stepped into a very large room filled with angular structures: horizontal bars, vertical rods, enormous boxes seemingly formed of staffs tied together at right angles. He had no idea what it all signified and was too dizzy and ill to care.

A light hand fell across his arm, making him jump. He grabbed for his rope and whirled to face the enemy.

The rope was gone, of course, and the one who touched him was a girl. Her head did not even reach to his shoulder. She wore a baggy coverall, and her hair was bound in a close-fitting headcap, making her look boyish. Her tiny feet were bare.

Sos relaxed, embarrassed, though his head still throbbed and the place still disturbed him by its confinement. He had

never been this tense before, yet inadequate. If only he could get out into the open forest . . .

"Let me have this," the little girl said. Her feather-gentle fingers slid across his forearm and fastened upon the bracelet. In a moment she had it off.

He grabbed for it angrily, but she eluded him. "What are you doing?" he demanded.

She fitted the golden clasp over her own wrist and squeezed it snug. "Very nice. I always wanted one of these," she said pertly. She lifted a pixie eyebrow at him. "What's your name?"

"Sos the—Sos," he said, remembering his defeat in the circle and considering himself, therefore, weaponless. He reached for it again, but she danced nimbly away. "I did not give that to you!"

"Take it back, then," she said, holding out her wrist. Her arm was slender but aesthetically rounded, and he wondered just how young she was. Certainly not old enough to be playing such games with a grown man.

Once more he reached . . . and grasped air. "Girl, you anger me."

"If you are as slow to anger as you are to move, I have nothing to worry about, monster."

This time he leaped for her, slow neither to anger nor to motion—and missed her again.

"Come on, baby," she cooed, wriggling her upraised wrist so that the metal band glittered enticingly. "You don't like being mocked, you say, so don't let a woman get away with anything. Catch me."

He saw that she wanted him to chase her, and knew that he should not oblige; but the pain in his head and body cut short his caution and substituted naked fury. He ran after her.

She skipped fleetly beside the wall, looking back at him and giggling. She was so small and light that agility was natural to her; her body could not have weighed more than a hundred pounds including the shapeless garment. As he gained on her, she dodged to the side and swung around a vertical bar, making him stumble cumbersomely.

"Lucky you aren't in the cir-cle!" she trilled. "You can't even keep your feet!"

By the time he got on her trail once more, she was in among the poles, weaving around them with a facility obviously stemming from long experience.

Sos followed, grasping the uprights and swinging his body past them with increasing dexterity. Now that he was exerting himself he felt better, as though he were throwing off the lethargy of the freezing mountains. Again he gained —and again she surprised him.

She leaped into the air and caught the bottom rung of a ladder suspended from the high ceiling. She flipped athletically and hooked it with her feet, then ascended as though she had no weight at all. In moments she was far out of reach.

Sos took hold of the lowest rung, just within his range, and discovered that it was made of flexible plastic, as were the two vertical columns. He jerked experimentally. A ripple ran up the ropes, jarring the girl. Ropes? He smiled and shook harder, forcing her to cling tightly in order not to be shaken off. Then, certain he had her trapped, he gradually hauled down until his entire weight was suspended.

It would hold him. He hoisted himself to the rung, unused to this type of exercise but able to adapt. He could handle a rope.

She peeked down, alarmed, but he climbed steadily, watching her. In a few seconds he knew he would be able to grab her foot and haul her down with him.

She threaded her legs through the top of the ladder and leaned out upside down, twisting her body and touching it with her freed hands. The coverall came away from her shoulders and to her hips—up or down, depending upon perspective—then she caught one arm in the ladder and stripped herself the rest of the way. She wore a slight, snug two-piece suit underneath that decorated little more than her bosom and buttocks. Sos revised his estimate of her age sharply upward; she was as well rounded a woman as he had seen.

She contemplated him with that elfin expression, spread out the coveralls, and dropped them neatly upon his raised face.

He cursed and pawed it away, almost losing his grip on the ladder. She was shaking it now, perhaps in belief she

could dislodge him while he was blinded, and he felt her strike his clutching hand.

By the time he had secured his position and cast off the clinging, faintly scented cloth, she was standing on the floor below him, giggling merrily. She had gone right by him! "Don't you want your bracelet, clumsy?" she teased.

Sos handed himself down and dropped to the floor, but she was gone again. This time she mounted the boxlike structure, wriggling over and under the bars as though she were a flying snake. He ran to the base, but she was amidst it all and he could not get at her from any direction without climbing into it himself. He knew by this time that he could never catch her that way; she was a gymnast whose size and weight made her entirely at home here.

"All right," he said, disgruntled but no longer angry. He took the time to admire her lithe and healthy body. Who would have suspected such rondure in so brief a package? "Keep it."

A moment and several gyrations and she stood beside him. "Give up!"

He snapped his fingers over her upper arm, using the trick of his rope throw to make the motion too quick to elude. "No."

She did not even wince at the cruel pressure. She sliced her free hand sidewise into his stomach, just below the rib cage and angling up, fingers flat and stiff.

He was astonished at the force of the blow, coming as it did with so little warning, and he was momentarily paralyzed. Still, he maintained his grip and tightened it until her firm young flesh was crushed against the bone.

Even so, she did not shrink or exclaim. She struck him again with that peculiar flat of the hand, this time across the throat. Incredible agony blossomed there. His stomach drove its content up into his mouth and he could not even catch his breath or cry out. He let go, gagging and choking.

When he became aware of his surroundings again he was sitting on the floor and she was kneeling astride his legs and resting her hands upon his shoulders. "I'm sorry I did that, Sos. But you are very strong."

He stared dully at her, realizing that she was somewhat more talented than he had guessed. She was a woman, but her blows had been sure.

"I really *would* like to keep your bracelet, Sos. I know what it means."

He thought about the way Sol had given his bracelet to Sola. The initial carelessness of the act had not signified any corresponding laxity in the relationship, though its terms were strange. Was he now to present his own bracelet even more capriciously, simply because a woman asked for it? He tried to speak, but his larynx, still constricted from the knock, did not permit it.

She held out her wrist to him and did not retreat. He reached up slowly and circled it with his fingers. He remembered that he had fought for Sola and lost, while this woman had, in more than a manner of speaking challenged him for the bracelet and won.

Perhaps it *had* to be taken from him. Had he been ready to give it away, he should have given it to blonde Miss Smith, knowing that she wanted it. Sola, too, had forced her love upon him and made him respond. He did not like what this seemed to indicate about his nature, but it was better to accept it than to try to deny it.

He squeezed the bracelet gently and dropped his hand.

"Thank you, Sos," she murmured, and leaned over to kiss him on the neck.

CHAPTER SIXTEEN

When he woke again, he suspected that it had been a fantasy, like the oddities visible on the silent television, except that his bracelet was gone and his left wrist was pale where it had rested. This time he was gone, in another squared-off cabin, and feeling fit. Somehow he had been taken from the mountain and revived and left here, while his little friend Stupid had died. He could not guess the reason.

He got up and dressed, finding his clothing clean and whole, beside the bunk. If this were death, he thought, it was not unlike life. But that was foolishness; this was *not* death.

No food had been stocked, and there were no weapons upon the rack. As a matter of fact, the rack itself was absent. Sos opened the door, hoping to see familiar forest or landscape or even the base of the mountain—and found only a blank wall similar to the one he had traveled down in the vision. No vision after all, but reality.

"I'll be right with you, Sos." It was the voice of the little girl—the tiny woman who had teased him and outmaneuvered him and finally struck him down. His throat still ached, now that he thought of it, though not obtrusively. He looked at his bare wrist again.

Well, she had claimed to know what the bracelet meant.

She trotted down the hall, as small as ever, wearing a more shapely smock and smiling. Her hair, now visible, was brown and curly, and it contributed considerably to her femininity. The bracelet on her arm glittered; evidently she had polished it to make the gold return to life. He saw that it reached all the way around her wrist and over-

lapped slightly, while the mark it left on his own wrist left a good quarter of the circle open. Had this tiny creature actually prevailed over him?

"Feeling better, Sos?" she inquired solicitously. "I know we gave you a rough time yesterday, but the doc says a period of exercise is best to saturate the system. So I saw that you got it."

He looked uncomprehendingly at her.

"Oh, that's right—you don't understand about our world yet." She smiled engagingly and took his arm. "You see, you were almost frozen in the snow, and we had to bring you around before permanent damage was done. Sometimes a full recovery takes weeks, but you were so healthy we gave you the energizer immediately. It's some kind of drug—I don't know much about these things—it scours out the system somehow and removes the damaged tissue. But it has to reach everywhere, the fingers and toes and things—well, I don't really understand it. But some good, strenuous calisthenics circulate it nicely. Then you sleep and the next thing you know you're better."

"I don't remember—"

"I put you to sleep, Sos. After I kissed you. It's just a matter of touching the right pressure points. I can show you, if—"

He declined hastily. She must have gotten him to the cabin room, too—or more likely had a man haul him there. Had she also undressed him and cleaned his clothing, as Sola had done so long ago? The similarities were disturbing.

"It's all right, Sos. I have your bracelet, remember? I didn't stay with you last night because I knew you'd be out for the duration, but I'll be with you from now on." She hesitated. "Unless you changed your mind?"

She was so little, more like a doll than a woman. Her concern was quite touching, but it was hard to know what to say. She was hardly half his weight. What could she know of the way of men and women?

"Oh, is that so!" she exclaimed, flashing, though he had not spoken. "Well, let's go back to your room right now and I'll show you I don't just climb ladders!"

He smiled at her vehemence. "No, keep it. I guess you

know what you're doing." And he guessed he liked being chased, too.

She had guided him through right-angled corridors illuminated by overhead tubes of incandescence and on to another large room. These seemed to be no end to this odd enclosed world. He had yet to see honest daylight since coming here. "This is our cafeteria. We're just in time for mess."

There was a long counter with plates of food set upon it—thin slices of bacon, steaming oatmeal, poached eggs, sausage, toasted bread and other items he did not recognize. Farther down he saw cups of fruit juice, milk and hot drinks, as well as assorted jellies and spreads. It was as though someone had emptied the entire larder of a hostel and spread it out for a single feast. There was more than anyone could eat.

"Silly. You just take anything you want and put it on your tray," she said. "Here." She lifted a plastic tray from a stack at the end and handed it to him. She took one herself and preceded him down the aisle, selecting plates as she moved. He followed, taking one of each.

He ran out of tray space long before the end of the counter. "Here," she said, unconcerned. "Put some on mine."

The terminus opened into an extended dining area, square tables draped with overlapping white cloths. People were seated at several, finishing their meals. Both men and women wore coveralls and smocks similar to what he had seen already, making him feel out of place though he was normally dressed. Sosa led him to a vacant table and set the array of food and beverage upon it.

"I could introduce you to everyone, but we like to keep meals more or less private. If you want company, you leave the other chairs open; if you want to be left alone, tilt them up, like this." She leaned the two unused chairs forward against the sides of the table. "No one will bother us."

She viewed his array. "One thing, Sos—we don't waste anything. You eat everything you take."

He nodded. He was ravenous.

"We call this the underworld," she said as he ate, "but

we don't consider ourselves criminals." She paused, but he didn't understand the allusion. "Anyway, we're all dead here. I mean, we all would have been dead if we hadn't— well, the same way you came. Climbing the mountain. I came last year. Just about every week there's someone— someone who makes it. Who doesn't turn back. So our population stays pretty steady."

Sos looked up over a mouthful. "Some turn back?"

"*Most* do. They get tired, or they change their minds, or something, and they go down again."

"But no one ever returns from the mountain!"

"That's right," she said uncomfortably.

He didn't press the matter, though he filed it away for future investigation.

"So we're really dead, because none of us will ever be seen in the world again. But we aren't idle. We work very hard, all of us. As soon as we're finished eating, I'll show you."

She did. She took him on a tour of the kitchen, where sweaty cooks worked full time preparing the plates of food and helpers ran the soiled dishes and trays through a puffing cleaning machine. She showed him the offices where accounts were kept. He did not grasp the purpose of such figuring, except that it was essential in some way to keep mining, manufacturing and exporting in balance. This made sense; he remembered the computations he had had to perform when training Sol's warriors, and this underworld was a far more complex community.

She took him to the observation deck, where men watched television screens and listened to odd sounds. The pictures were not those of the ordinary sets in the cabins, however, and this attracted his immediate interest.

"This is Sos," she said to the man in charge. "He arrived forty-eight hours ago. I—took him in charge."

"Sure—Sosa," the man replied, glancing at the bracelet. He shook Sos's hand. "I'm Tom. Glad to know you. Matter of fact, I recognize you. I brought you in. You certainly gave it a try!"

"Brought me in?" There was something strange and not altogether likeable about this man with the unusual name, despite his easy courtesy.

"I'll show you." Tom walked over to one of the screens

that was blank. "This is a closed-circuit teevee covering the east slope of Helicon, down below the snowline." He turned it on, and Sos recognized the jumbled terrain he had navigated with the help of his rope. He had never seen a real picture on the television before—that is, one that applied to the present world, he corrected himself, and it fascinated him.

"Helicon—the mountain?" he asked, straining to remember where he had read of something by that name. "The home of . . . the muses?"

Tom faced him, and again there was a strangeness in his pale eyes. "Now how would you know that? Yes—since we remember the things of the old world here, we named it after—" He caught a signal from one of the others and turned quickly to the set. "There's one coming down now. Here, I'll switch to him."

That reminded Sos. "The ones that come down—where do they go?" He saw that Sosa had withdrawn from their conversation and was now showing off her bracelet to the other workers.

"I'm afraid you're about to find out, though you may not like it much," Tom said, watching him with a peculiar eagerness. Sos was careful not to react; these people obviously did not contest in the circle, but had their methods of trial. He was about to be subjected to something unpleasant.

Tom found his picture and brought the individual into focus. It was a middle-aged staffer, somewhat flabby. "He probably lost his woman to a younger warrior and decided to make the big play," Tom remarked without sympathy. "A lot are like that. There's something about a broken romance that sends a man to the mountain." Sos's stomach tightened, but the man wasn't looking at him. "This one ascended to the snowline, then turned about when his feet got cold. Unless he changes his mind again pretty soon—"

"They do that?"

"Oh yes. Some waver half a dozen times. The thing is, the mountain is real. Death looks honorable from a distance, but the height and snow make it a matter of determination. Unless a man is really serious about dying, that climb will make him reconsider. He wonders whether

things back home are quite so bad as he thought, whether he couldn't return and try again. If he's weak, he vacillates, and of course we don't want the quitters. It's natural selection, really, not that that would mean anything to you."

Sos refused to be drawn out by the condescending tone and assumptions of ignorance. It occurred to him that his general knowledge could be a hidden asset, in case things got ugly here.

"A man who carries his conviction all the way to the end is a man worth saving," Tom continued as the picture, evidently controlled by the motions of his fingers on the knobs, followed the staffer unerringly. "We want to be sure that he really has renounced life, and won't try to run back at the first opportunity. The ordeal of the mountain makes it clear. You were a good example—you charged right on up and never hesitated at all. You and that bird—too bad we couldn't save it, but it wouldn't have been happy here anyway. We saw you try to scare it away, and then it froze. I thought for a moment you were going to turn back then, but you didn't. Just as well, I liked your looks."

So all the agonies of his private demise had been observed by this cynical voyeur? Sos maintained the slightly stupid expression he had adopted since becoming suspicious, and watched the staffer pick his way along the upper margin of the projecting metal beams. There would be some later occasion, perhaps, to repay this mockery. "How did you—fetch me?"

"Put on a snowsuit and dragged you into the nearest hatch. Took three of us to haul the harness. You're a bull of a man, you know. After that—well, I guess you're already familiar with the revival procedure. We had to wait until you were all the way under; sometimes people make a last-minute effort to start down again. We don't bring them in if they're facing the wrong way, even if they freeze to death. It's the intent that counts. You know, you almost made it to the top. That's quite something, for an inexperienced climber."

"How did you know I wouldn't kill myself when I woke up?"

"Well, we can never be sure. But generally speaking, a person doesn't choose the mountain if he's the suicidal type. That sounds funny, I know, but it's the case. Anyone

can kill himself, but only the mountain offers complete and official oblivion. When you ascend Helicon, you never come back. There is no news and no body. It's as though you have entered another world—perhaps a better one. You're not giving up, you're making an honorable departure. At least, that's the way I see it. The coward kills himself; the brave or devout man takes the mountain."

Much of this made sense to Sos, but he didn't care to admit it yet. "But you said some turn back."

"*Most* turn back. They're the ones who are doing it for bravado, or as a play for pity, or just plain foolishness. We don't need that kind here."

"What about that staffer out there now? If you don't take him in, where will he go?"

Tom frowned. "Yes, I'm afraid he really means to give up." He raised his voice. "Bill, you agree?"

" 'Fraid so," the man addressed called back. "Better finish it; there's another at the base. No sense having him see it."

"This is not a pleasant business," Tom said, licking his lips with an anticipation that seemed to be, if not pleasure, a reasonable facsimile. "But you can't maintain a legend on nothing. So—" He activated another panel, and wavy cross-hairs appeared on the screen. As he adjusted the dials the cross moved to center on the body of the staffer. He pulled a red handle.

A column of fire shot out from somewhere offscreen and engulfed the man. Sos jumped, but realized that he could do nothing. For a full minute the terrible blaze seared on the screen; then Tom lifted the handle and it stopped.

A blackened mound of material was all that remained.

"Flamethrower," Tom explained pleasantly.

Sos had seen death before, but this appalled him. The killing had been contrary to all his notions of honor; no warning, no circle, no sorrow. "You mean—if I had?—?"

Tom faced him, the light from the screen reflecting from the whites of his eyes in miniature skull-shapes. This was the question he had been waiting for. "Yes."

Sosa was tugging at his arm. "That's enough," she said. "Come on, Sos. We had to show you. It isn't all bad."

"What if I decide to leave this place?" he demanded, sickened by such calculated murder.

She pulled him on. "Don't talk like that. Please."

So that was the way it stood, he thought. They had not been joking when they named this the land of the dead. Some were dead figuratively, and some dead inside. But what had he expected when he ventured upon the mountain? Life and pleasure?

"Where are the women?" he inquired as they traveled the long passages.

"There aren't many. The mountain is not a woman's way. The few we have are—shared."

"Then why did you take my bracelet?"

She increased her pace. "I'll tell you, Sos, really I will—but not right now, all right?"

They entered a monstrous workshop. Sos had been impressed by the crazies' "shop," but this dwarfed it as the underworld complex dwarfed an isolated hostel. Men were laboring with machines in long lines, stamping and shaping metal objects. "Why," he exclaimed, "those are weapons!"

"Well, *someone* has to make them, I suppose. Where did you think they came from?

"The crazies always—"

"The truth is we mine some metals and salvage some, and turn out the implements. The crazies distribute them and send us much of our food in return. I thought you understood about that when I showed you the accounting section. We also exchange information. They're what you call the service part of the economy, and we're the manufacturing part. The nomads are the consumers. It's all very nicely balanced, you see."

"But *why*?" It was the same question he had asked at the school.

"That's something each person has to work out for himself."

And the same answer. "You sound like Jones."

"Jones?"

"My crazy instructor. He taught me how to read."

She halted, surprised. "Sos! You can *read*?"

"I was always curious about things." He hadn't meant to reveal his literacy. Still, he could hardly have concealed it indefinitely.

"Would you show me how? We have so many books here—"

"It isn't that simple. It takes years to learn."

"We have years, Sos. Come, I want to start right away." She fairly dragged him in a new direction, despite the disparity in their sizes. She had delightful energy.

It was easy to recognize the library. In many respects the underworld resembled the crazies' building. "Jim, this is Sos. He can read!"

The spectacled man jumped up, smiling. "Marvelous!" He looked Sos up and down, then, a trifle dubiously. "You look more like a warrior than a scholar. No offense."

"Can't a warrior read?"

Jim fetched a book. "A formality, Sos—but would you read from this? Just a sample passage, please."

Sos took the volume and opened it at random. "BRUTUS: Our course will seem too bloody, Caius Cassius, To cut the head off and then to hack the limbs, Like wrath in death and envy afterwards; for Anthony is but a limb of Caesar; Let us be sacrificers, but not butchers, Caius. We all stand up against the spirit of Caesar; And in the spirit of men there is no blood; O! that we then—"

"Enough! Enough!" Jim cried. "You can read, you **can** read, you certainly can. Have you been assigned yet? We must have you in the library! There is so much to—"

"You can give classes in reading," Sosa added excitedly. "We all want to learn, but so few know how—"

"I'll call Bob immediately. What a discovery!" The librarian fumbled for the intercom on his desk.

"Let's get out of here," Sos said, embarrassed by the commotion. He had always considered reading a private pursuit, except in the school, and found this eagerness upsetting.

It was a long day in the perpetual artificiality of the underworld, and he was glad to retire at the end of it. He was hardly certain he wanted to spend the rest of his life under the mountain, extraordinary as this world might be.

"But it really isn't a bad life, Sos," she said. "You get used to it—and the things we do are really important. We're the manufacturers for the continent; we make all the weapons, all the basic furnishings for the hostels, the prefabricated walls and floors, the appliances and electronic equipment—"

"Why did you take my bracelet?"

The question brought her up short. "Well, as I said, there aren't many women here. They have it scheduled so that each man has a—a night with someone each week. It isn't quite like a full-time relationship, but on the other hand there is variety. It works out pretty well."

The game of traveling bracelets. Yes, he could imagine how certain people would enjoy that, though he had noticed that most men did not use the golden signals here. "Why am I excluded?"

"Well you *can*, if you want. I thought—"

"I'm not objecting, girl. I just want to know *why*. Why do I rate a full-time partner when there aren't enough to go around?"

Her lip trembled, "Do—do you want it back?" She touched the bracelet.

He grabbed her, unresisting, and pressed her down upon the bunk. She met his kiss eagerly. "No I *don't* want it back. I—oh, get that smock off, then!" What use to demand reason of a woman?

She divested herself of her clothing, all of it, with alacrity. Then, womanlike, she seemed to change her mind. "Sos—"

He had expected something like this. "Go ahead."

"I'm barren."

He watched her silently.

"I tried—many bracelets. Finally I had the crazies check me. I can never have a baby of my own, Sos. That's why I came to the mountain . . . but babies are even more important here. So—"

"So you went after the first man they hauled off the mountain."

"Oh, no, Sos. I took my turn on the list. But when there isn't any love *or* any chance for—well, some complained I was unresponsive, and there really didn't seem to be much point in it. So Bob put me on the revival crew, where I could meet new people. The one who is on duty when someone is brought in is, well, responsible. To explain everything and make him feel at home and get him suitably situated. You know. You're the nineteenth person I've handled—seventeen men and two women. Some of

them were old, or bitter. You're the first I really—that sounds even worse, doesn't it!"

Young, strong, pliable: the answer to a lonely woman's dreams, he thought. Yet why not? He had no inclination to embrace assorted women in weekly servicings. Better to stick to one, one who might understand if his heart were elsewhere.

"Suppose I happen to want a child of my own?"

"Then you—take back your bracelet."

He studied her, sitting beside him, halfway hiding behind the balled smock as though afraid to expose herself while the relationship was in doubt. She was very small and very woman-shaped. He thought about what it meant to be denied a child, and began to understand as he had not understood before what had driven Sol.

"I came to the mountain because I could not have the woman I loved," he said. "I know all that is gone, now—but my heart doesn't. I can offer you only—friendship."

"Then give me that," she said, dropping the smock.

He took her into the bed with him, holding her as carefully as he had held Stupid, afraid of crushing her. He held her passively at first, thinking that that would be the extent of it. He was wrong.

But it was Sola his mind embraced.

CHAPTER SEVENTEEN

Bob was a tall, aggressive man, the manifest leader of the mountain group. "I understand you can read," he said at once. "How come?"

Sos explained about his schooling.

"Too bad."

Sos waited for him to make his point.

"Too bad it wasn't the next one. We could have used your talent here."

Sos still waited. This was like taking the circle against an unknown weapon. Bob did not have the peculiar aura of the death-dealing Tom, but he was named as strangely and struck Sos as thoroughly ruthless. He wondered how common this stamp was among those who had renounced life. It probably was typical; he had seen for himself how the manner, the personality of the leader, transmitted itself to the group. Sos had shaped Sol's empire with tight organization and a touch of humor, letting the men enjoy their competition for points as they improved their skills. When he left, Tyl had ruled, and the discipline remained without the humor. The camps had become grim places. Strange that he only saw this now!

"We have a special and rather remarkable assignment for you," Bob was saying. "A unique endeavour."

Seeing that Sos was not going to commit himself, Bob got down to specifics. "We are not entirely ignorant of affairs on the surface, can't afford to be. Our information is largely second hand, of course—our teevee perceptors don't extend far beyond the Helicon environs—but we have a much better overall view than you primitives have.

There's an empire building up there. We have to break it up in a hurry."

Evidently that excellent overall view did not reveal Sos's own place in the scheme. He suspected more strongly now that it would be best if it never were known. The flame-thrower undoubtedly pointed in the direction of the organizer of such an empire, while an ignorant, if literate, primitive was safe. "How do you know?"

"You have not heard of it?" The contempt was veiled and perhaps unconscious; it had not occurred to Bob that a newcomer could know more than he. The question had lulled any suspicions he might have had and strengthened his preconceptions. "It's run by one Sol, and it's been expanding enormously this past year. Several of our recent arrivals have had news of it, and there's even been word from the South American unit. Very wide notoriety."

"South America?" Sos had read about this, the continent of pre-Blast years, along with Africa and Asia, but had no evidence it still existed.

"Did you think we were the only such outfit in the world? There's one or more Helicons on every continent. We have lines connecting us to all of them, and once in a while we exchange personnel, though there is a language barrier. South America is more advanced than we are; they weren't hit so hard in the war. We have a Spanish-speaking operator, and quite a few of theirs speak English, so there's no trouble there. But that's a long ways away; when *they* get wind of an empire here, it's time to do something about it."

"Why."

"Why do you think? What would happen to the status quo if the primitives started really organizing? Producing their own food and weapons, say? There'd be no control over them at all!"

Sos decided that further questions along this line would be dangerous. "Why me?"

"Because you're the biggest, toughest savage to descend upon us in a long time. You bounced back from your exposure on the mountain in record time. If anyone can take it, you can. We need a strong body now, and you're it."

It occurred to Sos that it had been a long time since this man had practiced diplomacy, if ever. "It for *what*?"

"It to return to life. To take over that empire."

If Bob had intended to shock him, he had succeeded. To return to life! To go back . . . "I'm not your man. I have sworn never to bear a weapon again." That was not precisely true, but if they expected him to face Sol again, it certainly applied. He had agreed never to bring a weapon against Sol again—and regardless of other circumstances, he meant to abide by the terms of their last encounter. It was a matter of honor, in life or death.

"You take such an oath seriously?" But Bob's sneer faded as he looked at Sos. "Well, what if we train you to fight without weapons?"

"Without a weapon—in the *circle*?"

"With the bare hands. The way your little girl does. That doesn't violate any of your precious vows, does it? Why are you so reluctant? Don't you realize what this means to you? You will have an empire!"

Sos was infuriated by the tone and implications, but realized that he could not protest further without betraying himself. This was big; the moment Bob caught on—

"What if I refuse? I came to the mountain to die."

"I think you know that there is no refusal here. But if personal pressure or pain doesn't faze you, as I hope it doesn't, there may be things that will. This won't mean much to you right now, but if you think about it for a while you'll come around, I suspect." And Bob told him some things that vindicated Sos's original impression of him utterly.

Not for the reason the underground master thought—but Sos was committed.

"To *life*?" Sosa demanded incredulously, when he told her later. "But no one ever goes back!"

"I will be the first—but I will do it anonymously."

"But if you want to return, why did you come to the mountain? I mean—"

"I don't want to return. I have to."

"But—" She was at a loss for words for a moment. "Did Bob threaten you? You shouldn't let him—"

"It was not a chance I could afford to take."

She looked at him, concerned. "Was it to—to harm *her*? The one you—"

"Something like that."

"And if you go, you'll get her back."

After his experience in the observation deck, Sos was aware that anything he said or did might be observed in this region. He could not tell Sosa anything more than Bob thought he knew. "There is an empire forming out there. I have to go and eliminate its leader. But it won't be for a year or more, Sosa. It will take me that long to get ready. I have a lot to learn first."

Bob thought he had been swayed, among other things, by the dream of owning an empire. Bob must never know where his real loyalty lay. If someone were sent to meet Sol, it was best that it be a friend. . . .

"May I keep your bracelet—that year?"

"Keep it forever, Sosa. You will be training me."

She contemplated him sadly. "Then it wasn't really an accident, our meeting. Bob knew what you would be doing before we brought you in. He set it up."

"Yes." Again, it was close enough.

"Damn him!" she cried. "That was cruel!"

"It was necessary, according to his reasoning. He took the most practical way to do what had to be done. You and I merely happen to be the handiest tools. I'm sorry."

"*You're* sorry!" she muttered. Then she smiled, making the best of it. "At least we know where we stand."

She trained him. She taught him the blows and the holds she knew, laboriously learned in childhood from a tribe that taught its women self-defense—and cast out the barren ones. Men, of course, disdained the weaponless techniques—but they also disdained to accept any woman who was an easy mark, and so the secret knowledge passed from mother to daughter how to destroy a man.

Sos did not know what inducement Bob had used to make Sosa reveal these tactics to a man, and did not care to inquire.

She showed him how to strike with his hands with such power as to sunder wooden beams, and how to smash them with his bare feet, and his elbow, and his head. She made him understand the vulnerable points of the human body, the places where a single blow could stun or maim or kill. She had him run at her as though in a rage, and she brought him down again and again, feet and arms tangled uselessly. She let him try to choke her, and she broke that hold in

half a dozen painful and embarrassing ways, though there was more strength in his two thumbs than in her two hands. She showed him the pressure points that were open to pain, the nerve centers where pressure induced paralysis or unconsciousness. She demonstrated submission holds that she could place on him with a single slender arm, that held him in such agony he could neither break nor fight. She brought out the natural weapons of the body, so basic they were almost forgotten by men: the teeth, the nails, the extended fingers, the bone of the skull, even the voice.

And when he had mastered these things and learned to avoid and block the blows and break or nullify the holds and counter the devious strategies of weaponless combat, she showed him how to fight when portions of his body were incapacitated: one arm, two arms, the legs, the eyes. He stalked her blindfolded, with feet tied together, with weights tied to his limbs, with medicine to make him dizzy. He climbed the hanging ladder with arms bound in a straitjacket; he swung through the elevated bars with one arm shackled to one foot. He stood still while she delivered the blows that had brought him down during their first encounter, only twisting almost imperceptibly to take them harmlessly.

Then he set it all aside. He went to the operating room and exposed himself to the anaesthetics and the scalpels. The surgeon placed flexible plastic panels under the skin of his belly and lower back, tough enough to halt the driven blade of knife or sword. He placed a collar upon Sos's neck that locked with a key, and braced the long bones of arms and legs with metallic rods, and embedded steel mesh in the crotch. He mutilated the face, rebuilding the nose with stronger stuff and filling the cheeks with nylon weave. He ground and capped the teeth. He peeled back the forehead and resodded with shaped metal.

Sundry other things occurred in successive operations before they turned him loose to start again. No part of him was recognizable as the man once known as Sos; instead he walked slowly, as a juggernaut rolls, fighting against the pain of an ugly rebirth.

He resumed training. He worked on the devices in the rec room, now more familiar to him than his new body. He climbed the ladder, swung on the bars, lifted the weights.

He walked up and down the hallways, balancing his suddenly heavier torso and increasing his pace gradually until he was able to run without agony. He hardened his healing hands and feet by smashing the boards; in time he developed monstrously thick calluses. He stood still, this time not moving at all, while Sosa struck his stomach, neck and head with all her strength—with a staff—and he laughed.

Then with a steeltrap motion he caught the weapon from her inexpert grasp and bent it into an S shape by a single exertion of his two trunklike wrists. He pinioned her own wrists, both together, with the fingers and thumb of one hand and lifted her gently off the floor, smiling.

Sosa jackknifed and drove both heels against his exposed chin. "Ouch!" she screamed. "That's like landing on a chunk of stone!"

He chuckled and draped her unceremoniously across his right shoulder while hefting his weight and hers upon the bottom rung of the ladder with that same right arm. She writhed and jammed stiffened fingers into his left shoulder just inside the collarbone. "You damned gorilla," she complained. "You've got calluses over your pressure points!"

"Nylon calluses," he said matter-of-factly. "I could break a gorilla in two." His voice was harsh; the collar constricting his throat destroyed any dulcet utterances he attempted.

"You're still a great ugly beast!" she said, clamping her teeth hard upon the lobe of his ear and chewing.

"Ugly as hell," he agreed, turning his head so that she was compelled to release her bite or have her neck stretched painfully.

"Awful taste," she whispered as she let go. "I love you."

He reversed rotation, and she jammed her lips against his face and kissed him furiously. "Take me back to our room, Sos," she said. "I want to feel needed."

He obliged, but the aftermath was not entirely harmonious. "You're still thinking of *her*," she accused him. "Even when we're—"

"That's all over," he said, but the words lacked conviction.

"It's *not* over! It hasn't even begun yet. You still love her —and you're going back!"

"It's an assignment. You know that."

"*She* isn't the assignment. It's almost time for you to go, and I'll never see you again, and you can't even tell me you love me."

"I do love you."

"But not as much as you love her."

"Sosa, she is hardly fit to be compared to you. You're a warm, wonderful girl, and I would love you much more, in time. I'm going back, but I want you to keep my bracelet. How else can I convince you?"

She wrapped herself blissfully about him. "I know it, Sos. I'm a demented jealous bitch. It's just that I'm losing you forever, and I can't stand it. The rest of my life without you—"

"Maybe I'll send a replacement." But it ceased to be funny as he said it.

After a moment she brightened slightly. "Let's do it again, Sos. Every minute counts."

"Hold on, woman! I'm not *that* sort of a superman!"

"Yes you are," she said. And she proved him wrong again.

CHAPTER EIGHTEEN

Nameless and weaponless, he marched. It was spring, almost two years after he had journeyed dejectedly toward the mountain. Sos had gone to oblivion; the body that clothed his brain today was a different one, his face a creation of the laboratory, his voice a croak. Plastic contacts made his eyes stare out invulnerably, and his hair sprouted without pigment.

Sos was gone—but secret memories remained within the nameless one, surging irrepressibly when evoked by familiar sights. He was anonymous but not feelingless. It was almost possible to forget, as he traveled alone, missing the little bird on his shoulder, that he came as a machine of destruction. He could savor the forest trails and friendly cabins just as the young sworder had four years ago. A life and death ago!

He stood beside the circle: the one where Sol the sword had fought Sol of all weapons for name and armament and, as it turned out, woman. What a different world it would have been, had that encounter never taken place!

He entered the cabin, recognizing the underworld manufacture and the crazy maintenance. Strange how his perceptions had changed! He had never really wondered before where the supplies had come from; he, like most nomads, had taken such things for granted. How had such naïveté been possible?

He broke out supplies and prepared a Gargantuan meal for himself. He had to eat enormously to maintain this massive body, but food was not much of a pleasure. Taste had been one of the many things that had suffered in the cause of increased power. He wondered whether, in the

past, the surgeons had been able to perform their miracles without attendant demolition of peripheral sensitivity. Or had their machines taken the place of warriors?

A girl showed up at dusk, young enough and pretty enough, but when she saw his bare wrist she kept to herself. Hostels had always been excellent places to hunt for bracelets. He wondered whether the crazies knew about this particular aspect of their service.

He slept in one bunk, the girl courteously taking the one adjacent though she could have claimed privacy by establishing herself on the far side of the column. She glanced askance when she perceived that he was after all alone, but she was not concerned. His readings had also told him that before the Blast women had had to watch out for men, and seldom dared to sleep in the presence of a stranger. If that were true—though it was hardly creditable in a civilization more advanced than the present one—things had certainly improved. It was unthinkable that a man require favors not freely proffered—or that a woman should withhold them capriciously. Yet Sosa had described the perils of her childhood, where tribes viewed women differently; not all the badness had been expunged by the fire.

The girl could contain her curiosity no longer. "Sir, if I may ask—where is your woman?"

He thought of Sosa, pert little Sosa, almost too small to carry a full-sized bracelet, but big in performance and spirit. He missed her. "She is in the world of the dead," he said.

"I'm sorry," she said, misunderstanding as he had meant her to. A man buried his bracelet with his wife, if he loved her, and did not take another until mourning was over. How was he to explain that it was not Sosa's death, but his own return to life that had parted them forever?

The girl sat up in her bed, touching her nightied breast and showing her embarrassment. Her hair was pale. "It was wrong of me to ask," she said.

"It was wrong of me not to explain," he said graciously, knowing how ugly he would appear to this innocent.

"If you desire to—"

"No offense," he said with finality.

"None," she agreed, relieved.

Would this ordinary, attractive, artless girl sharing his

cabin but not his bed—would she ever generate the violence of passion and sorrow he had known? Would some stout naïve warrior hand her his bracelet tomorrow and travel to the mountain when he lost her?

It was possible, for that was the great modern dream of life and love. There was in the least of people, male and female, the capacity to arouse tumultuous emotion. That was the marvel and the glory of it all.

She fixed his breakfast in the morning, another courteous gesture that showed she had been well brought up. She tried not to stare as he stepped out of the shower. He blessed her and went his way, and she hers. These set customs were good, and had they met four years ago and she been of age then—

It took him only a week to cover the distance two men and a girl traveled before. Some of the cabins were occupied, others not, but he kept to himself and was left alone. It surprised him a little that common manners had not changed; this was another quality of the nomad society that he had never properly appreciated until he learned how blunt things could be elsewhere.

But there were some changes. The markers were gone; evidently the crazies, perhaps prompted by his report to Jones, had brought their Geiger clickers (manufactured in the underworld electronics shop) and resurveyed the area at last. That could mean that the moths and shrews were gone, too, or at least brought into better harmony with the rest of the ecology. He saw the tracks of hoofed animals and was certain of it.

The old camp remained, replete with its memories—and was still occupied! Men exercised in the several circles, and the big tent had been maintained beside the river. The firetrench, however, had been filled in, the retrenchment leveled; this was the decisive evidence that the shrews no longer swarmed. They had finally given way to the stronger species: man.

But back nearer the fringe of the live radiation, where man could not go—who ruled there? And if there should ever be another Blast. . . .

Why was he surprised to find men here? He had known this would be the case; that was why he had come first to this spot. This had been the birthing place of the empire.

He approached the camp and was promptly challenged. "Halt! Which tribe are you bound to?" a hefty staffer demanded, eyeing his tunic as though trying to identify his weapon.

"No tribe. Let me see your leader."

"What's your name?"

"I am nameless. Let me see your leader."

The staffer scowled. "Stranger, you're overdue for a lesson in manners."

Sos reached out slowly and put one hand under the staff. He lifted.

"Hey, what are you——!" But the man had either to let go or to follow; he could not overcome. In a moment he was reaching for the sky, as Sos's single arm forced the staff and both the man's hands up.

Sos twisted with contemptuous gravity, and the staffer was wrenched around helplessly. "If you do not take me to your master, I will carry you there myself." He brought the weapon down suddenly and the man fell, still clinging to it.

Others had collected by this time to stare. Sos brought up his other hand, shifted his grip to the two ends of the rod, while the staffer foolishly hung on, bent it into a spendid half-circle. He let go, leaving the useless instrument in the hands of its owner.

Very shortly, he was ushered into the leader's presence. It was Sav.

"What can I do for you, strongster?" Sav inquired, not recognizing him under the mauled features and albino hair. "Things are pretty busy right now, but if you come to enlist——"

"What you can do for me is to identify yourself and your tribe and turn both over to me." For once he was glad of the harshness inherent in his voice.

Sav laughed good-naturedly. "I'm Sav the Staff, in charge of staff-training for Sol, master of empire. Unless you come from Sol, I'm turning nothing over to you."

"I do not come from Sol. I come to vanquish him and rule in his stead."

"Just like that, huh? Well, mister nameless, you can start here. We'll put up a man against you in the circle,

and you'll either take him or join our tribe. What's your weapon?"

"I have no weapon but my hands."

Sav studied him with interest. "Now let me get this straight. You don't have a name, you don't have a tribe and you don't have a weapon—but you figure to take over this camp?"

"Yes."

"Well, maybe I'm a little slow today, but I don't quite follow how you plan to do that."

"I will break you in the circle."

Sav burst out laughing. "Without a weapon?"

"Are you afraid to meet me?"

"Mister, I wouldn't meet you if you *had* a weapon. Not unless you had a tribe the size of this one to put up against it. Don't you know the rules?"

"I had hoped to save time."

Sav looked at him more carefully. "You know, you remind me of someone. Not your face, not your voice . . . You—"

"Select some man to meet me, then, and I will take him and all that follow him from you, until the tribe is mine."

Sav's look was pitying now. "You really want to tackle a trained staffer in the circle? With your bare hands?"

Sos nodded.

"This goes against the grain, but all right then." He summoned one of his men and showed the way to a central circle.

The selected staffer was embarrassed. "But he has no weapon!" he exclaimed.

"Just knock him down a couple of times," Sav advised. "He insists on doing it." Men were gathering; word had spread of Sos's feat with the guard's staff.

Sos removed his tunic and stood in short trunks and bare feet.

The bystanders gasped. The tunic had covered him from chin to knee and elbow, exposing little more than the hands and feet. The others had assumed that he was a large chubby man, old because of the color of his hair and the leathery texture of his face. They had been curious about the strength he had shown, but not really convinced it had not been a fluke effort.

"Biceps like clubheads!" someone exclaimed. "Look at that neck!" Sos no longer wore the metal collar; now his neck was a solid mass of horny callus and scar tissue.

The staffer assigned to meet him stood openmouthed.

Sav pulled the man back. "Gom, take the circle," he said tersely.

A much larger staffer came forward, his body scarred and discolored by many encounters: a veteran. He held his weapon ready and stepped into the circle without hesitation.

Sos entered and stood with hands on hips.

Gom had no foolish scruples. He feinted several times to see what the nameless one would do, then landed a vicious blow to the side of the neck.

Sos stood unmoved.

The staffer looked at his weapon, shrugged, and struck again.

After standing for a full minute, Sos moved. He advanced on Gom, reached out almost casually for the staff, and spun it away with a sharp twist of one wrist. He hurled it out of the circle.

Sos had never touched the man physically, but the staffer was out of business. He had tried to hold on to his weapon. Gom's fingers were broken.

"I have one man, and myself," Sos announced. "My man is not ready to fight again, so I will fight next for two."

Shaken, Sav sent in another warrior, designating a third as collateral. Sos caught the two ends of the staff and held them while the man tried vainly to free it. Finally Sos twisted and the weapon buckled. He let go and stepped back.

The man stood holding the S-shaped instrument, dazed. Sos only had to touch him with a finger, and the staffer stumbled out of the circle.

"I have four men, counting myself. I will match for four."

By this time the entire camp was packed around the circle. "You have already made your point," Sav said. "I will meet you."

"Yourself and your entire tribe against what I have here?" Sos inquired, mocking him.

"My skill against your skill," Sav said, refusing to be ruffled. "My group—against your service and complete information about yourself. Who you are, where you came from, how you learned to fight like that, who sent you here."

"My service you may have, if you win it, or my life— but I am sworn to secrecy about the rest. Name other terms."

Sav picked up his staff. "Are you afraid to meet me?"

The men chuckled. Sav had nicely turned the dialogue on him. Who mocked whom?

"I cannot commit that information to the terms of the circle. I have no right."

"You have shown us your strength. We are curious. You ask me to put up my entire camp—but you won't even agree to put up your history. I don't think you really want to fight, stranger." The gathered men agreed vociferously, enjoying the exchange.

Sos appreciated certain qualities of leadership he had never recognized in Sav before. Sav had surely seen that he must lose if he entered the circle, and be shamed if he didn't. Yet he was forcing *Sos* to back off. Sav could refuse to do battle unless his terms were met, and do so with honor—and the word would quickly spread to Sol's other tribal leaders. It was a tactical masterstroke.

He would have to compromise. "All right," he said. "But I will tell only you. No one else."

"But *I* will tell whom I please!" Sav specified.

Sos did not challenge that. He had to hope that, if by some mischance he lost, he could still convince Sav in private of the necessity for secrecy. Sav was a sensible, easygoing individual; he would certainly listen and think before acting.

It was too bad that the smiling staffer had to be hurt by his friend.

Sav entered the circle. He had improved; his staff was blindingly swift and unerringly placed. Sos tried to catch the weapon and could not. The man had profited from observation of the two lesser warriors, and never let his staff stand still long enough to be grabbed. He also wasted no effort striking the column of gristle. He maneuvered

instead for face shots, hoping to blind his antagonist, and rapped at elbows and wrists and feet. He also kept moving, as though certain that so solid a body would tire soon.

It was useless. Sos sparred a few minutes so that the staffer would not lose face before his men, then blocked the flying shaft and caught Sav's forearm. He yanked it to him and brought his other hand to bear.

There was a crack.

Sos let go and shoved the man out of the circle. No warrior present could mistake the finality of a dripping compound fracture. Men took hold of Sav as he staggered, hauled at his arm and set the exposed bone in place and bound the terrible wound in gauze, while Sos watched impassively from the circle.

It had not been strictly necessary. He could have won in a hundred kinder ways. But he had needed a victory that was serious and totally convincing. Had Sav lost indecisively, or by some trick blow that made him stumble from the circle like an intoxicated person, unmarked, the gathered witnesses would have been quick to doubt his capability or desire to fight, and the job would be unfinished. The break was tangible; Sav's men knew immediately that no one could have succeeded where their leader had failed, and that there had been no collusion and no cowardice.

Sos had inflicted dreadful pain, knowing that his erstwhile friend could bear it, in order to preserve what was more important: the loser's reputation.

"Put your second-in-command in charge of this camp," Sos snapped at Sav, showing no softness. "You and I take the trail—tomorrow morning, alone."

CHAPTER NINETEEN

Two men moved out, one with his arm in cast and sling.
They marched as far as the broken arm and loss of blood
permitted, and settled into a hostel for the evening, without company.

"Why?" Sav inquired as Sos fixed supper.

"Why the arm?"

"No. I understand that. Why you?"

"I have been assigned to take over Sol's empire. He will
hardly meet me in the circle until I bring down his chief
lieutenants."

Sav leaned back carefully, favoring the arm. "I mean
why *you*—Sos?"

First man, second day. He had betrayed himself already.

"You can trust me," Sav said. "I never told anyone
about your nights with Sola, and I wasn't bound by the
circle code then, not to you, I mean. I won't tell anyone
now. The information belonged to me only if I won it from
you, and I didn't."

"How did you know?"

"Well, I did room with you quite a spell, remember. I
got to know you pretty well, and not just by sight. I know
how you think and how you smell. I was awake some last
night—little ache in my arm—and I walked by your tent."

"How did you know me sleeping when you did not
know me awake?"

Sav smiled. "I recognized your snore."

"My—" He hadn't even known he snored.

"And one or two other things fit into place," Sav continued. "Like the way you stared at the spot on the ground
where our little tent used to be—and I know you weren't

149

remembering me! And the way you hummed 'Red River Valley' today while we marched, same way Sola used to hum 'Greensleeves,' even if you do carry a tune even worse than you did before. And the way you took care to make me look good in the circle, make me lose like a man. You didn't have to do that. You were taking care of me, same way I took care of you before."

"You took care of me?"

"You know——keeping the gals away from your tent all winter, even if I had to service 'em myself. Sending a man to bring Sol back when it was time. Stuff like that."

Sol had stayed away . . . until Sola was pregnant!

"You knew about Sol?"

"I'm just naturally nosy, I guess. But I can keep my mouth shut."

"You certainly can!" Sos took a moment to adjust himself to the changed situation. The staffer was a lot more knowledgeable and discreet than he had ever suspected. "All right, Sav. I'll tell you everything——and you can tell me how to keep my secrets so that nobody *else* catches on. Fair enough?"

"Deal! Except——"

"No exceptions. I can't tell anyone else."

"Except a couple are going to know anyway, no way to stop it. You get within a hundred feet of Sol, he'll know you. He's that way. And you won't fool Sola long, either. The others——well, if we can fake out Tor, no problem."

Sav was probably right. Somehow the thought did not disturb Sos; if he did his honest best to conceal his identity, but was known by those closest to him anyway, he could hardly be blamed. The word would not spread.

"You asked 'why me?' That's the same question I asked myself. They put pressure on me, but it wouldn't have been enough if I hadn't had internal doubts. Why me? The answer is, because I built the empire, though they didn't know that. I started it, I organized it, I trained it, I left men after me who could keep it rolling. If it is wrong, then I have a moral obligation to dismantle it——and I may be the only one who can do it without calamitous bloodshed. I am the only one who really understands its nature and the key individuals within it——and who can defeat Sol in the circle."

"Maybe you better start at the beginning," Sav said. "You went away, then I heard you came back with the rope, and Sol beat you and you went to the mountain—"

It was late at night by the time the complete story had been told.

Tyl's camp was much larger than Sav's had been. This was an acquisition tribe, contrasted to the training tribe, and by itself numbered almost five-hundred warriors. This time there was no stupidity at the entrance; Sav was a ranking member of the hierarchy, and there was the unmistakable ring of command in his normally gentle voice as he cut through obstacles. Ten minutes after they entered the camp they stood before Tyl himself.

"What brings you here unattended, comrade?" Tyl inquired cautiously, not commenting on the mending arm. He looked older, but no less certain of himself.

"I serve a new master. This is the nameless one, who sought me out and defeated me in the circle. Now he offers me and my tribe against you and yours."

Tyl contemplated Sos's tunic, trying to penetrate to the body beneath it. "With all due respect, ex-comrade, my tribe is more powerful than yours. He will have to meet my subchiefs first."

"Of course. Post a third of your tribe to correspond to mine. After the nameless one defeats your man, he will match both sections against the remainder. You can study him today and meet him tomorrow."

"You seem to have confidence in him," Tyl observed.

Sav turned to Sos. "Master, if you would remove your dress—"

Sos obliged, finding it easy to let Sav handle things. The man certainly had talent for it. This early acquisition had been most fortunate.

Tyl looked. "I see," he said, impressed. "And what is his weapon?" Then, "I see," again.

That afternoon Sos knocked out the subchief sworder with a single hammerblow of one fist to the mid-section. He had the sword by the blade, having simply caught it in midthrust and held it. A slight crease showed along the callus covering the metallic mesh embedded in his palm where the edge had cut; that was all. He had closed upon the blade carefully, but the witnesses had not been aware

of that. They had assumed that he had actually halted the full thrust with an unprotected hand.

Tyl, like Sav, was quick to learn. He, too, employed the sword, and he fenced with Sos's hands as though they were daggers, and with his head as though it were a club, and he kept his distance. It was wise strategy. The singing blade maintained an expert defense, and Tyl never took a chance.

But he forgot one thing: Sos had feet as well as hands and head. A sharp kick to the kneecap brought temporary paralysis there, interfering with mobility. Tyl knew he had lost, then, for even a narrow advantage inevitably grew, but he fought on, no coward. Not until both knees were dislocated did he attempt the suicide plunge.

Sos left the blade sticking in his upper arm and touched his fingers to the base of Tyl's exposed neck, and it was over.

Then he withdrew the blade and bound the wound together himself. It had been a stab, not a slash, and the metal reinforcement within the bone had stopped the point. The arm would heal.

When Tyl could walk, Sos added him to the party. They set out for the next major tribe, getting closer to Sol's own camp. Tyl traveled with his family, since Sos had not guaranteed any prompt return to the tribe, and Tyla took over household chores. The children stared at the man who had defeated their father, hardly able to accept it. They were too young yet to appreciate all the facts of battle, and had not understood that Tyl had been defeated at the time he joined Sol's nascent group. There were no frank conversations along the way. Tyl did not recognize the nameless one, and Sav cleverly nullified dangerous remarks.

They caught up to Tor's tribe after three weeks. Sos had determined that he needed one more leader in his retinue before he had enough to force Sol into the circle. He now had authority over more than six-hundred men—but eight tribes remained, some very large. Sol could still preserve his empire by refusing to let these tribes accept the challenge and by refraining from circle combat himself. But acquisition of a third tribe should make Sos's chunk of empire too big to let go. . . .

Tor's tribe was smaller than Tyl's and more loosely

organized, but still a formidable spread. A certain number of doubles teams were practicing, as though the encounter with the Pits had come out about even. Sos expected competent preparations for his coming, and was not disappointed. Tor met him promptly and took him into private conference, leaving Sav and Tyl out of it.

"I see you are a family man," he said.

Sos glanced at his bare wrist. "I was once a family man."

"Oh, I see." Tor, searching for weakness, had missed. "Well, I understand you came out of nowhere, defeated Sav and Tyl and mean to challenge Sol for his empire—and that you actually enter the circle without a weapon."

"Yes."

"It would seem foolish for me to meet you personally, since Tyl is a better fighter than I."

Sos did not comment.

"Yet it is not in my nature to avoid a challenge. Suppose we do this: I will put my tribe up against yours—if you will meet my representative."

"One of your subchiefs? I will not put up six-hundred men against a minor." But Sos's real concern was whether Tor recognized him.

"I did not say that. I said my representative, who is not a member of my group, against you, alone. If he beats you, you will release your men and go your way; Sol will reconquer them in time. If you overcome him, I will turn over my group to you, but I will remain in the service of Sol. I do not care to serve any other master at this time."

"This is a curious proposition." There had to be a hidden aspect to it, since Tor was always clever.

"Friend, *you* are a curious proposition."

Sos considered it, but discovered nothing inherently unfair about the terms. If he won, he had the tribe. If he lost, he was still free to try for Sol at a later date. It did not matter whom he fought; he would have to defeat the man sooner or later anyway, to prevent resurgence of the empire under some new master.

And it seemed that Tor did *not* recognize him, which was a private satisfaction. Perhaps he had worried too much about that.

"Very well. I will meet this man."

"He will be here in a couple of days. I have already sent

a runner to fetch him. Accept our hospitality in the interim."

Sos got up to leave. "One thing," he said, remembering. "Who is this man?"

"His name is Bog. Bog the club."

Trust wily Tor to think of that! The one warrior not even Sol had been able to defeat.

It was three days before Bog showed up, as big and happy as ever. He had not changed a bit in two years. Sos wanted to rush out and shake the giant's hand and hear him exclaim "Okay!" again, but he could not; he was a nameless stranger now and would have to meet and overcome the man anonymously.

This selection made clear why Tor had arranged the terms as they were. Bog was entirely indifferent to power in the tribal sense. He fought for the sheer joy of action and made no claims upon the vanquished. The messenger had only to whisper "Good fight!" and Bog was on his way.

And Tor had chosen well in another respect, for Bog was the only man Sos knew of who shared virtual physical invulnerability. Others had tried to prevail over the nameless one by skill and had only been vanquished. Bog employed no skill, just inexhaustible power.

The day was waning, and Tor prevailed upon Bog to postpone the battle until morning. "Tough man, long fight," he explained. "Need all day."

Bog's grin widened. "Okay!"

Sos watched the huge man put away food for three and lick his lips in anticipation as several lovely girls clustered solicitously around him and touched the bracelet upon his wrist. Sos felt nostalgia. Here was a man who had an absolute formula for perpetual joy: enormous power, driving appetites and no concern for the future. What a pleasure it would be to travel with him again and bask in the reflected light of his happiness! The reality might have been troubling for others, but never for Bog.

Yet it was to preserve the goodness in the system that he fought now. By defeating Bog he would guarantee that there would always be free warriors for such as Bog to fight. The empire would never swallow them all.

They waited only long enough for the sun to rise to a reasonable height before approaching the circle in the

morning. The men of the camp were packed so tightly Tor had to clear a path to the arena. Everyone knew what the stakes were, except possibly Bog himself, who didn't care; but the primary interest was in the combat itself. Only twice, legend said, had Bog been stopped—once by the onset of night and once by a fluke loss of his weapon. No one had ever actually defeated him.

It was also said, however, that he never entered the circle against the net or other unfamiliar weapon.

Bog jumped in, already swinging his club enthusiastically, while Sos remained outside the ring and stripped to his trunks. He folded the long tunic carefully and stood up straight. The two men looked at each other while the audience studied them.

"They're the same size!" a man exclaimed, awed.

Sos started. He, the same size as the giant? Impossible!

Nonetheless, fact. Bog was taller and broader across the shoulders, but Sos was now more solidly constructed. The doctors had given him injections, in the underworld operatory to stimulate muscular development, and the inserted protective materials added to his mass. He was larger than he had been, and none of the added mass was fat. He probably weighed almost twice what he had when he first set out in search of adventure.

Each man had enormously overmuscled shoulders and arms and a neck sheathed in scars; but where Bog slimmed down to small hips and comparatively puny legs, Sos had a midriff bulging with protective muscles and thighs so thick he found it awkward to run.

Now he carried no weapon: he *was* a weapon.

He stepped into the circle.

Bog proceeded as usual, swinging with indifferent aim at head and body. Sos ducked and took other evasive action. He had stood still to accept the blows of the staff, as a matter of demonstration, but the club was a different matter. A solid hit on the head by such as Bog could knock his senseless. The metal in his skull would not dent, but the brain within would smash itself against the barrier like so much jelly. The reinforced bones of arms and legs would not break, but even the toughened gristle and muscle would suffer if pinched between that bone and the full force of the club. Bog could hurt him.

Sos avoided the moving club and shot an arm up behind Bog's hand to block the return swing. He leaped inside and drove the other fist into Bog's stomach so hard the man was pushed backward. It was the rock-cracking blow.

Bog shifted hands and brought the weapon savagely down to smash Sos's hip. He stepped back to regain balance and continued the attack. He hadn't noticed the blow.

Sos circled again, exercising the bruised hip and marveling. The man was not exactly flabby in the stomach; that blow could have ruptured the intestines of an ordinary warrior. The way he had shifted grips on his club showed that there was more finesse to his attack than men had given him credit for. As a matter of fact, Bog's swings were not wild at all, now. They shifted angles regularly and the arcs were not wide. There was no time for a sword to cut in between them, or a staff, and lesser weapons would have no chance at all. Bog had an excellent all-purpose defense concealed within his showy offense.

Strange that he had never noticed this before. Was Bog's manifest stupidity an act? Had Sos, who should certainly have known better, assumed that a man as big and strong as Bog must be lacking in mental qualities? Or was Bog a —natural fighter, like Sol, who did what he did unconsciously and who won because his instincts were good?

Still, there would be weak points. There had to be. Sos kicked at an exposed knee, hardly having time to set up for the proper angle for dislocation—and had his own leg clipped by a seemingly accidental descent of the club. He parried the club arm again, leading it out of the way, and leaped to embrace Bog in a bear-hug, catching his two hands together behind the man's back. Bog held his breath and raised the club high in the air and brought it down. Sos let go and shoved him away barely in time to avoid a head blow that would have finished the fight.

Yes, Bog knew how to defend himself.

Next time, Sos blocked the arm and caught it in both hands to apply the breaking pressure. It was no use; Bog tensed his muscles and was too strong. Bog flipped the club to the alternate hand again and blasted away at Sos's back, forcing another hasty retreat. Sos tried once more, pounding his reinforced knuckles into the arm just above the

elbow, digging for nerves, but had to let go; the club was too dangerous to ignore. He could do a certain amount of weakening damage to Bog's arms that would, in time, incapacitate the man, but in the meanwhile he would be subjected to a similar amount of battery by the club, which would hardly leave him in fit condition to fight again soon.

It was apparent that simple measures would not do the job. While consciousness remained, Bog would keep fighting—and he was so constructed that he could not be knocked out easily. A stranglehold from behind? Bog's club could whip over the back or around the side to pulverize the opponent long before consciousness departed—and how could a forearm do what the rope could not? A hammer-blow to the base of the skull? It was as likely to kill the man as to slow him down. Bog being what he was.

But he was vulnerable. The kick to the crotch, the stiffened finger to the eyeball . . . any rapid blow to a surface organ would surely bring him down.

Sos continued to dodge and parry, forearm against forearm. Should he do it? Did any need justify the deliberate and permanent maiming of a friend?

He didn't argue it. He simply decided to fight as he had to: fairly.

Just as the club would knock him out once it connected, so one of his own blows or grips would bring down Bog, when properly executed. Since Bog didn't know the meaning of defeat, and would never give in to numbing blows or simple pain, there was no point in such tactics. He would have to end the contest swiftly and decisively—which meant accepting at least one full smash from the club as he set up his position. It was a necessary risk.

Sos timed the next pass, spun away from it, ducked his head and thrust out in the high stamping kick aimed for Bog's chin. The club caught him at the thigh, stunning the muscle and knocking him sidewise, but his heel landed.

Too high. It caught Bog's forehead and snapped his head back with force abetted by the impact of the club upon his leg. A much more dangerous blow than the one intended. Sos dropped to the ground, rolled over to get his good leg under him, and leaped up again, ready to follow up with a sustained knuckle-beat to the back of the neck. Bog

could not swing effectively so long as he was pinned to the ground, and even he could not withstand more than a few seconds of—

Sos halted. Suddenly he knew what had happened.

The slight misplacement of the kick, providing added leverage against the head; the forward thrust of Bog's large body as he swung; the feedback effect of the club blow upon the leg; the very musculature constricting the clubber's neck—these things had combined to make the very special connection Sos had sought to avoid.

Bog's neck was broken.

He was not dead—but the damage was irreparable, here. If he survived, it would be as a paralytic. Bog would never fight again.

Sos looked up, becoming aware of the audience he had completely forgotten, and met Tor's eyes. Tor nodded gravely.

Sos picked up Bog's club and smashed it with all his force against the staring head.

CHAPTER TWENTY

"Come with me," Sav said.

Sos followed him into the forest, paying no attention to the direction. He felt as he had when Stupid perished in the snow. Here was a great, perhaps slow-witted but happy fellow—abruptly dead in a manner no one had wanted or expected, least of all Sos himself. Sos had liked the hearty clubber; he had fought by his side. By the definition of the circle, Bog had been his friend.

There were many ways he could have killed the man, had that been his intent, or maimed him, despite his power. Sos's efforts to avoid doing any real damage had been largely responsible for the prolongation of the encounter— yet had led to nothing. Perhaps there had been no way to defeat Bog without killing him. Perhaps in time Sos could convince himself of that, anyway.

At least he had seen to it that the man died as he might have wished: by a swift blow from the club. Small comfort.

Sav stopped and gestured. They were in a forest glade, a circular mound with a small, crude pyramid of stones at the apex. It was one of the places of burial and worship maintained by volunteer tribesmen who did not choose to turn over the bodies of their friends to the crazies for cremation.

"In the underworld—could they have saved him?" Sav inquired.

"I think so."

"But if you tried to take him there—"

"They would have blasted us both with the flame-thrower before we got within hailing distance of the entrance. I am forbidden ever to return."

"Then, this is best," Sav said.

They stood looking at the mound, knowing that Bog would soon lie within it.

"Sol comes to these churches every few days, alone," Sav said. "I thought you'd like to know."

Then it seemed that no time passed, but it had been a month of travel and healing, and he was standing beside another timeless mound and Sol was coming to pray.

Sol kneeled at the foot of the pyramid and raised his eyes to it. Sos dropped to his own knees beside him. They stayed there in silence for some time.

"I had a friend," Sos said at last. "I had to meet him in the circle, though I would not have chosen it. Now he is buried here."

"I, too," Sol said. "He went to the mountain."

"Now I must challenge for an empire I do not want, and perhaps kill again, when all that I desire is friendship."

"I prayed here all day for friendship," Sol said, speaking of all the mounds in the world as one, and all times as one, as Sos had done. "When I returned to my camp I thought my prayer was answered—but he required what I could not give." He paused. "I would give my empire to have that friend again."

"Why can't we two talk away from here, never to enter the circle again?"

"I would take only my daughter." He looked at Sos, for the first time since staff and rope had parted, and if he recognized him as anything more than the heralded nameless challenger, or found this unheralded mode of contact strange, he did not say. "I would give you her mother, since your bracelet is dead."

"I would accept her, in the name of friendship."

"In the name of friendship."

They stood up and shook hands. It was as close as they could come to acknowledging recognition.

The camp was monstrous. Five of the remaining tribes had migrated to rejoin their master, anticipating the arrival of the challenger. Two-thousand men spread across plain and forest with their families, sleeping in communal tents and eating at communal hearths. Literate men supervised distribution of supplies and gave daily instruction in reading and figuring to groups of apprentices. Parties trekked

into the mountains, digging for the ore that the books said was there, while others cultivated the ground to grow the nutritive plants that other books said could be raised. Women practiced weaving and knitting in groups, and one party had a crude native loom. The empire was now too large to feed itself from the isolated cabins of a single area, too independent to depend upon any external source for clothing or weapons.

"This is Sola," Sol said, introducing the elegant, sultry high lady. He spoke to her: "I would give you to the nameless one. He is a powerful warrior, though he carries no weapon."

"As you wish," she said indifferently. She glanced at Sos, and through him. "Where is his bracelet? What should I call myself?"

"Keep the clasp I gave you. I will find another."

"Keep the name you bear. I have none better."

"You're crazy," she said, addressing both.

"This is Soli," Sol said as the little girl entered the compartment. He picked her up and held her at head height. She grasped a tiny staff and waved it dangerously.

"I'm a Amazon!" she said, poking the stick at Sos. "I'm fighting in circle."

They moved on to the place where the chieftains gathered: Sav and Tyl together, Tor and Tun and Neq and three others Sos did not recognize in another group. They spread out to form a standing circle as Sol and Sos approached.

"We have reached a tentative agreement on terms," Sav said. "Subject to approval by the two masters, of course."

"The terms are these," Sol said, not giving him a chance to continue. "The empire will be disbanded. Each of you will command the tribe you now govern in our names, and Tor his old tribe, but you will never meet each other in the circle."

They stared at him uncomprehendingly. "You fought already?" Tun inquired.

"I have quit the circle."

"Then we must serve the nameless one."

"I have quit the circle too," Sos said.

"But the empire will fall apart without one of you as master. No one else is strong enough!"

Sol turned his back on them. "It is done," he said. "Let's take our things and go."

"Wait a minute!" Tyl exclaimed, running stiff-legged after them. "You owe us an explanation."

Sol shrugged, offering none. Sos turned about and spoke. "Four years ago you all served small tribes or traveled alone. You slept in cabins or in private tents, and you did not need anything that was not provided. You were free to go and to do as you chose.

"Now you travel in large tribes and you fight for other men when they tell you to. You till the land, working as the crazies do, because your numbers are too great for the resources of any one area. You mine for metals, because you no longer trust the crazies to do it for you, though they have never broken trust. You study from books, because you want the things civilization can offer. But this is not the way it should be. We know what civilization leads to. It brings destruction of all the values of the circle. It brings competition for material things you do not need. Before long you will overpopulate the Earth and become a scourge upon it, like shrews who have overrun their feeding grounds.

"The records show that the end result of empire is—the Blast."

But he hadn't said it well.

All but Sav peered incredulously at him. "You claim," Tor said slowly, "that unless we remain primitive nomads, dependent upon the crazies, ignorant of finer things, there will be a second Blast?"

"In time, yes. That is what happened before. It is our duty to see that it never happens again."

"And you believe that the answer is to keep things as they are, disorganized?"

"Yes."

"So more men like Bog can die in the circle?"

Sos stood as if stricken. Was he on the right side, after all?

"Better that, than that we all die in the Blast," Sol put in surprisingly. "There are not enough of us, now, to recover again."

Unwittingly, he had undercut Sos's argument, since overpopulation was the problem of empire.

Neq turned on Sol. "Yet you preserve the circle by deserting it!"

Sav, who understood both sides, finally spoke. "Sometimes you have to give up something you love, something you value, so as not to destroy it. I'd call that sensible enough."

"I'd call it cowardice!" Tyl said.

Both Sol and Sos jumped toward him angrily.

Tyl stood firm. "Each of you defeated me in the circle. I will serve either. But if you fear to face each other for supremacy, I must call you what you are."

"You have no right to build an empire and throw it away like that," Tor said. "Leadership means responsibility."

"Where did you learn all this 'history'?" Neq demanded. "I don't believe it."

"We're just beginning to cooperate like men, instead of playing like children," Tun said.

Sol looked at Sos. "They have no power over us. Let them talk."

Sos stood indecisively. What these suddenly assertive men were saying made distressing sense. How could he be sure that what the master of the underworld had told him was true? There were so many obvious advantages of civilization—and it had taken thousands of years for the Blast to come, before. Had it really been the fault of civilization, or had there been factors he didn't know about? Factors that might no longer exist. . . .

Little Soli appeared and ran toward Sol. "Are you going to fight now, Daddy?"

Tyl stepped ahead of him and managed to intercept her, squatting with difficulty since his knees were still healing. "Soli, what would you do if your daddy decided not to fight?"

She presented him with the round-eyed stare. "Not fight?"

No one else spoke.

"If he said he wouldn't go in the circle any more," Tyl prompted her. "If he went away and never fought again."

Soli burst out crying.

Tyl let her go. She ran to Sol. "You go in the circle, Daddy!" she exclaimed. "Show him!"

It had happened again. Sol faced him, defeated. "I must fight for my daughter."

Sos struggled with himself, but knew that the peaceful settlement had flown. He saw, in a terrible revelation, that this, not name, woman or empire, had been the root of each of their encounters: the child. The child called Soli had been there throughout; the circle had determined which man would claim the name and privilege of fatherhood.

Sol could not back down, and neither could Sos. Bob, of the underworld, had made clear what would happen if Sos allowed the empire to stand.

"Tomorrow, then," Sos said, also defeated.

"Tomorrow—friend."

"And the winner rules the empire—all of it!" Tyl shouted, and the others agreed.

Why did their smiles look lupine?

They ate together, the two masters with Sola and Soli. "You will take care of my daughter," Sol said. He did not need to define the circumstance further.

Sos only nodded.

Sola was more direct. "Do you want me tonight?"

Was this the woman he had longed for? Sos studied her, noting the voluptuous figure, the lovely features. She did not recognize him, he was certain—yet she had accepted an insulting alliance with complacency.

"She—loved another," Sol said. "Now nothing matters to her, except power. It is not her fault."

"I still love him," she said. "If his body is dead, his memory is not. My own body does not matter."

Sos continued to look at her—but the image he saw was of little Sosa of the underworld, the girl who wore his bracelet. The girl Bob had threatened to send in his place, should Sos refuse to undertake the mission . . . to work her way into Sol's camp as anybody's woman and to stab Sol with a poisoned dart and then herself, leaving the master of empire dead and disgraced. The girl who would still be *sent*, if Sos failed.

At first it had been Sol's fate that had concerned him, though Bob never suspected this. Only by agreeing to the mission could Sos arrange to turn aside its treachery. But as the time of training passed, Sosa's own peril had become

as important. If he betrayed the underworld now, she would pay the penalty.

Sol and Sosa: the two had never met, yet they controlled his destiny. He had to act to protect them both—and he dared tell neither why.

"In the name of friendship, take her!" Sol exclaimed. "I have nothing left to offer."

"In the name of friendship," Sos whispered. He was sickened by the whole affair, so riddled with sacrifice and dishonor. He knew that the man Sola embraced in her mind would be the one who had gone to the mountain. She might never know the truth.

And the woman *he* embraced would be Sosa. *She* would never know, either. He had not realized until he left her that he loved her more.

At noon the next day they met at the circle. Sos wished there were some way he could lose, but he knew at the same moment that this was no solution. Sol's victory would mean his death; the underworld had pronounced it.

Twice he had met Sol in battle, striving to win and failing. This time he would strive in his heart to lose, but had to win. Better the humiliation of one, than the death of two.

Sol had chosen the daggers. His handsome body glistened in the sunlight—but Sos imagined with sadness the way that body would look after the terrible hands of the nameless one closed upon it. He looked for some pretext to delay the onset, but found none. The watchers were massed and waiting, and the commitment had been made. The masters had to meet, and there was no friendship in the circle. Sos would spare his friend if he were able—but he had to win.

They entered the circle together and faced each other for a moment, each respecting the other's capabilities. Perhaps each still hoped for some way to stop it, even now. There was no way. It had been unrealistic to imagine that this final encounter could be reneged. They were the masters: no longer, paradoxically, their own masters.

Sos made the first move. He jumped close and drove a sledgehammer fist at Sol's stomach—and caught his balance as the effort came to nothing. Sol had stepped aside, as he had to, moving more swiftly than seemed possible, as he always did—and a shallow slash ran the length of

the challenger's forearm. The fist had missed, the knife had not wounded seriously, and the first testing of skill had been accomplished.

Sos had known better than to follow up with a second blow in the moment Sol appeared to be off-balance. Sol was never caught unaware. Sol had refrained from committing the other knife, knowing that the seeming ponderosity of Sos's hands was illusory. Tactics and strategy at this level of skill looked crude only because so many simple ploys were useless or suicidal; finesse seemed like bluff only to the uninitiate.

They circled each other, watching the placements of feet and balance of torso rather than face or hands. The expression in a face could lie, but not the attitude of the body; the motion of a hand could switch abruptly, but not that of a foot. No major commitment could be made without preparation and reaction. Thus Sol seemed to hold the twin blades lightly while Sos hardly glanced at them.

Sol moved, sweeping both points in toward the body, one high, the other low. Sos's hands were there, closing about the two wrists as the knives were balked by protected shoulder and belly, and Sol pinioned. He applied pressure slowly, knowing that the real ploy had not yet been executed.

Sol was strong, but he could not hope to compete with his opponent's power. Gradually his arms bent down as the vice-like grip intensified, and the fingers on the knives loosened. Then Sol flexed both wrists—and they spun about within the grip! No wonder his body shone: he had greased it.

Now the daggers took on life of their own, flipping over together to center on the imprisoning manacles. The points dug in, braced against clamped hands, feeling for the vulnerable tendons, and they were feather-sharp.

Sos had to let go. His hardened skin could deflect lightning slashes, but not the anchored probing he was exposed to here. He released one wrist only, yanking tremendously at the other trying to break it while his foot lashed against the man's inner thigh. But Sol's free blade whipped across unerringly, to bury itself in the flesh of Sos's other forearm, and it was not the thigh but the hard bone of hip that met

the moving foot. It was far more dangerous to break with Sol than to close with him.

They parted, the one with white marks showing the crushing pressure exerted against him, the other with spot punctures and streaming blood from one arm. The second testing had passed. It was known that if the nameless one could catch the daggers, he could not hold them, and the experienced witnesses nodded gravely. The one was stronger, the other faster, and the advantage of the moment lay with Sol.

The battle continued. Bruises appeared upon Sol's body, and countless cuts blossomed on Sos's, but neither scored definitely. It had become a contest of attrition.

This could go on for a long time, and no one wanted that. A definite decision was required, not a suspect draw. One master had to prevail or the other. By a certain unvoiced mutual consent they cut short the careful sparring and played for the ultimate stakes.

Sol dived, in a motion similar to the one Sos had used against him during their first encounter, going not for the almost invulnerable torso but the surface muscles and tendons of the legs. Sol's success would cripple Sos, and put him at a fatal disadvantage. He leaped aside, but the two blades followed as Sol twisted like a serpent. He was on his back now, feet in the air, ready to smite the attacked. He had been so adept at nullifying prior attacks that Sos was sure the man was at least partially familiar with weaponless techniques. This might also explain Sol's phenomenal success as a warrior. The only real advantage Sos had was brute strength.

He used it. He hunched his shoulders and fell upon Sol, pinning him by the weight of his body and closing both hands about his throat. Sol's two knives came up, their motion restricted but not blocked, and stabbed into the gristle on either side of Sos's own neck. The force of each blow was not great, since the position was quite awkward, but the blades drove again and again into the widening wounds. The neck was the best protected part of his body, but it could not sustain this attack for long.

Sos lifted himself and hurled the lighter man from side to side, never relinquishing the cruel constriction, but his

position, too, was improper for full effect. Then, as his head took fire with the exposure of vital nerves, he knew that he was losing this phase; the blades would bring him down before Sol finally relinquished that tenacious consciousness.

It would not be possible to finish it gently.

He broke, catching Sol's hair to hold his head down, and hammered his horny knuckle into the exposed windpipe.

Sol could not breathe and was in excruciating pain. His throat had been crushed. Still the awful daggers searched for Sos's face, seeking, if not victory, mutual defeat. It was not in Sol to lose in the circle.

Sos used his strength once more. He caught one blade in his hand, knowing that the edge could not slip free from his flesh. With the other hand he grabbed again for the hair. He stood up, carrying Sol's body with him. He whirled about—and flung his friend out of the circle.

As quickly as he had possession of the circle, he abdicated it, diving after his fallen antagonist. Sol lay on the ground, eyes bulging, hands clasping futilely at his throat. Sos ripped them away and dug his fingers into the sides of the neck, massaging it roughly. His own blood dripped upon Sol's chest as he squatted above him.

"It's over!" someone screamed. "You're out of the circle! Stop!"

Sos did not stop. He picked one dagger from the ground and cut into the base of Sol's throat, using the knowledge his training in destruction had provided.

A body fell upon him, but he was braced against it. He lifted one great arm and flung the person away without looking. He widened the incision until a small hole opened in Sol's trachea; then he put his mouth to the wound.

More men fell upon him, yanking at his arms and legs, but he clung fast. Air rushed into the unconscious man's lungs as Sos exhaled, and his friend was breathing again, precariously.

"Sav! It's me, Sav," a voice bellowed in his ear, "Red River! Let go! I'll take over!"

Only then did Sos lift bloodflecked lips and surrender to unconsciousness.

He woke to pain shooting along his neck. His hand found bandages there. Sola leaned over him, soft of expression,

and mopped the streaming sweat from his face with a cool sponge. "I know you," she murmured as she saw his eyes open. "I'll never leave you—nameless one."

Sos tried to speak, but not even the croak came out. "Yes, you saved him," she said. "Again. He can't talk any more, but he's in better shape than you are. Even though you won." She leaned down to kiss him lightly. "It was brave of you to rescue him like that—but nothing is changed."

Sos sat up. His neck exploded into agony as he put stress upon it, and he could not turn his head, but he kept on grimly. He was in the main tent, in what was evidently Sola's compartment. He looked about by swiveling his body. No one else was present.

Sola took his arm gently. "I'll wake you before he goes. I promise. Now lie down before you kill yourself—again."

Everything seemed to be repeating. She had cared for him like this once long ago, and he had fallen in love with her. When he needed help, she was—

Then it was another day. "It's time," she said, waking him with a kiss. She had donned her most elegant clothing and was as beautiful as he had ever seen her. It had been premature to discount his love for her; it had not died.

Sol was standing outside with his daughter, a bandage on his throat and discoloration remaining on his body, but otherwise fit and strong. He smiled when he saw Sos and came over to shake hands. No words were necessary. Then he placed Soli's little hand in Sos's and turned away.

The men of the camp stood in silence as Sol walked past them, away from the tent. He wore a pack but carried no weapon.

"Daddy!" Soli cried, wrenching away from Sos and running after him.

Sav jumped out and caught her. "He goes to the mountain," he explained gently. "You must stay with your mother and your new father."

Soli struggled free again and caught up to Sol. "Daddy!"

Sol turned, kneeled, kissed her and turned her to face the way she had come. He stood up quickly and resumed his walk. Sos remembered the time he had tried to send Stupid down the mountain.

"Daddy!" she cried once more, refusing to leave him. "I

go with you!" Then, to show she understood: "I die with you."

Sol turned again and looked beseechingly at the assembled men.

No one moved.

Finally he picked Soli up and walked out of the camp.

Sola put her face to Sos's shoulder and sobbed silently, refusing to go after her daughter. "She belongs to him," she said through her tears. "She always did."

As he watched the lonely figures depart, Sos saw what was in store for them. Sol would ascend the mountain, carrying the little girl. He would not be daunted by the snow or the death that waited him. He would drive on until overwhelmed by the cold, and fall at last with his face toward the top, shielding his daughter's body with his own until the end.

Sos knew what would happen then, and who would be waiting to adopt a gallant husband and a darling daughter. There would be the chase in the recreation room, perhaps, and special exercise for Soli. It had to be, for Sosa would recognize the child. The child she had longed to bear herself . . .

Take her! he thought. Take her—in the name of love.

While Sos remained to be the architect of the empire's quiet destruction, never certain whether he was doing the right thing. He had built it in the name of another man; now he would bring it down at the behest of a selfish power clique whose purpose was to prevent civilization from arising on the surface. To prevent *power* from arising . . .

Sos had always been directed in key decisions by the action of other men, just as his romancing had been directed by those women who reached for it. Sol had given him his name and first mission; Dr. Jones had given him his weapon; Sol had sent him to the mountain and Bob had sent him back. Sol's lieutenants had forced the mastership upon him, not realizing that he was the enemy of the empire.

Would the time ever come when he made his own decisions? The threat that had existed against Sol now applied against Sos: if he did not dismantle the empire, someone would come for him, someone he would have no way to

recognize or guard against, and hostages would die. Three of them, one a child . . .

He looked at Sola, lovely in her sorrow, and knew that the woman he loved more would belong to Sol. Nothing had changed. Dear little Sosa—

Sos faced the men of his empire, thousands strong. They thought him master now—but was he the hero, or the villain?

Var
the
Stick

CHAPTER ONE

Tyl of Two Weapons waited in the night cornfield. He had one singlestick in his hand and the other tucked in his waist band, ready to draw. He had waited two hours in silence.

Tyl was a handsome man, sleek but muscular. His face was set in a habitual frown stemming from years of less than ideal command. The empire spanned a thousand miles, and he was second only to the Master in its hierarchy, and first in most practical matters. He set interim policy within the general guidelines laid down by the Master, and established the rankings and placement of the major subchiefs. Tyl had power—but it chafed at him.

Then he heard it: a rustle to the north that was not typical of the local animals.

Carefully he stood, shielded from the intruder by the tall plants. There was no moon, for the beast never came in the light. Tyl traced its progress toward the fence by the subtle sounds. The wind was from the north; otherwise the thing would have caught his scent and stayed clear.

There was no doubt about it. This was his quarry. Now it was mounting the sturdy split-rail fence, scrambling over, landing with a faint thump within the corn. And now it was quiet for a time, waiting to see whether it had been discovered. A cunning animal—one that avoided deadfalls, ignored poison and fought savagely when trapped. In the past month three of Tyl's men had been wounded in night encounters with this creature. Already it was becoming known as a hex upon the camp, an omen of ill, and skilled warriors were evincing an unseemly fear of the dark.

And so it was up to the chief to resolve the matter. Tyl,

long bored by the routine of maintaining a tribe that was not engaged in conquest, was more than satisfied by the challenge. He had no awe of the supernatural. He intended to capture the thing and display it before the tribe: here is the spook that made cowards of lesser men!

Capture, not death, for this quarry. This was the reason he had brought his sticks instead of his sword.

Slight noise again. Now it was foraging, stripping the ripening corn from the stalk and consuming it on the spot. This alone set it apart from ordinary carnivores, for they would never have touched the corn. But it could not be an ordinary herbivore either, for they did not harvest and chew the cobs like that. And its footprints, visible in daylight following a raid, were not those of any animal he knew. Broad and round, with the marks of four squat claws or slender hoofs—not a bear, not anything natural.

It was time. Tyl advanced on the creature, holding one stick aloft, using his free hand to part the corn stalks quietly. He knew he could not come upon it completely by surprise, but he hoped to get close enough to take it with a sudden charge. Tyl knew himself to be the best fighter in the world, with the sticks. The only man who could beat him, stick to stick, was dead, gone to the mountain. There was nothing Tyl feared when so armed.

He recalled that lone defeat with nostalgia, as he made the tedious approach. Four years ago, when he had been young. Sol had done it—Sol of All Weapons, creator of the empire—the finest warrior of all time. Sol had set out to conquer the world, with Tyl as his chief lieutenant. And they had been doing it, too—until the Nameless One had come.

He was close now, and abruptly the foraging noises ceased. The thing had heard him!

Tyl did not wait for the animal to make up its crafty mind. He launched himself at it, heedless of the shocks of corn he damaged in his mad passage. Now he had both sticks ready, batting stalks aside as he ran.

The creature bolted. Tyl saw a hairy hump rise in the darkness, heard its weird grunt. He was tempted to use his flash, but knew it would destroy the night vision he had built up in the silent wait and put his mission in peril. The animal was at the fence now, but the fence was strong

and high, and Tyl knew he could catch it before it got over.

The creature knew it too. Its back to the course rails, it came to bay, its breath rasping. Tyl saw the dim glint of its eye, the vague outline of its body, shaggy and warped and menacing. Tyl laid into it with both sticks, seeking a quick head-blow that would reduce it to impotence.

But the thing was as canny about weapons as about traps. It dived, passing under his defense in the obscurity, and fastened its teeth on Tyl's knee. He clubbed it on the head once, twice, feeling the give of the tangled fur, and it let go. The wound was not serious, as the thing's snout was recessed and its teeth blunt, but his knees had been tricky since the Nameless One had smashed them a year before. And he was angry at his defensive negligence; nothing should have penetrated his guard like that, by day or night.

It drew back, snarling, and Tyl was chilled by that sound. No wolf, no wildcat articulated like that. And now, as it tasted blood, its mewling became hungry as well as defiant.

It pounced, not smoothly but with force. This time it went for his throat, as he had known it would. He rapped its head again with the stick, but again it anticipated him, hunching so that the blow skidded glancingly off the skull. It struck Tyl's chest, bearing him down, and its foreclaws raked his neck while its hindclaws dug for his groin.

Tyl, dismayed by its ferocity, beat it off blindly, and it jumped away. Before he could recover it was up again, scrambling over the fence while he hobbled behind, too late.

Now he cursed aloud in fury at its escape—but the expletives were tinged with a certain brute respect. He had chosen the locale of combat, and the marauder had bested him in this context. But there was a use he could make of this situation—perhaps a better one than he had had in mind before.

The creature dropped outside the fence and loped off into the forest. It was bleeding from a wound reopened by the blows of the attacker, and it was partially lame on flat ground because of malformed bones in its feet. But it made

rapid progress, its armored toes finding good purchase in the wilder turf.

And it was clever. It had seen Tyl clearly and smelled him. Only its pressing hunger had dulled its alertness prior to the encounter. It had recognized the singlesticks as weapons and had avoided them. Still, blows had landed, and they had hurt. The creature thought about it, turning the problem over in its mind as it angled toward the badlands. Then menfolk were getting more difficult about their crops. Now they lay in wait, ambushed, attacked, pursued. This last had been quite effective; if the hunger were not so strong, the area would be best avoided entirely. As it was, better protection would have to be devised.

It entered the badlands where no man could follow and slowed to catch its breath. It picked up a branch, curling stubby mottled digits around it tightly. The forelimb was angular, the claws wide and flat—less effective as a weapon than as supplementary protection for the tips of the calloused fingers. It wrestled the stick around, finding comfortable purchase, imitating the stance of the man in the cornfield. It banged the wood against a tree, liking the feel of the impact. It banged harder, and the dry, rotted branch shattered, releasing a stunned grub. The creature quickly pounced on this, squashing it dead and licking the squirting juices with gusto, forgetting the useless stick. But it had learned something.

Next time it foraged, it would take along a stick.

CHAPTER TWO

The Master of Empire pondered the message from Tyl of Two Weapons. Tyl had not written the note himself, of course, for he like most of the nomadic leaders was illiterate. But his smart wife Tyla, like many of the empire women, had taken up the art with enthusiasm, and was now a fair hand at the written language.

The Master was literate, and he believed in literacy, yet he had not encouraged the women's classes in reading and figuring. The Master knew the advantages of farming, too, yet he ignored the farms. And he comprehended the dynamics of empire, for he, in other guise, had fashioned this same empire and brought it from formless ambition to a mighty force. Yet he now let it drift and stagnate and atrophy.

This message was deferentially worded, but it constituted a clever challenge to his authority and policy. Tyl was an activist, impatient to resume conquest. Tyl wanted either to goose the Master into action, or to ease him out of power so that new leadership might bring a new policy. Because Tyl himself was bonded to this regime, he could do nothing directly. He would not go against the man who had bested him in the circle. This was not cowardice but honor.

If the Master declined to deal with this mysterious menace to the local crops, he would be admitting either timidity or treason to the purpose of the empire. For farming was vital to growth; the organized nomads could not afford to remain dependent on the largesse of the crazies. If he did not support the farm program the resultant unrest would throw him into disrepute, and lead to

solidification of resistance around some other figure. He could not afford that, for he would then soon be spending all his time defeating such weedlike pretenders in the circle. No—he had to rule the empire, and keep it quiescent.

So there was nothing to do but tackle this artfully posed problem. He could be sure it was not an easy one, for this wild beast had wounded Tyl himself and escaped. That suggested that no lesser man than the Master could subdue it.

Of course he could organize a large hunting party—but this would violate the precepts of single combat, and it went against the grain, even when an animal was involved. In fact, it would be another implication of cowardice.

It was necessary that the Master prove himself against this beast. That was what Tyl wanted, for failure would certainly damage his image. He did not appreciate being maneuvered, but the alternatives were worse—and he did privately admire the manner Tyl had set this up. The man would be a valuable ally, at such time as certain things changed.

So it was the Nameless One, the Man of No Weapon, Master of Empire—this leader took leave of the wife he had usurped from the former master, put routine affairs in the hands of competent subordinates, and set out on foot alone for Tyl's encampment. He wore a cloak over his grotesque and mighty body, but all who saw him in that region knew him and feared him. His hair was white, his visage ugly, and there was no man to match him in the circle.

In fifteen days he arrived. A young staffer who had never seen the Master challenged him at the border of the camp. The Nameless One took that staff and tied a knot in it and handed it back. "Show this to Tyl of Two Weapons," he said.

And Tyl came hurriedly with his entourage. He ordered the guard with the pretzel-staff to the fields to work among the women, as penalty for not recognizing the visitor. But the Weaponless said, "He was right to challenge when in doubt; let the man who straightens that weapon chastise him, no other." So he was not punished, for no one except

a smithy could have unbent that metal rod. And no other man of that camp failed to know the Nameless One by sight thereafter.

Next morning the Master took up a bow and a length of rope, for these were not weapons of the circle, and set off on the trail of the raider. He took along a hound and a pack of supplies doubly loaded, but would tolerate the company of no other man. "I will bring the creature back," he said.

Tyl made no comment, thinking his own thoughts.

The trail passed from the open fields of corn and buck-wheat to the birches fringing the forestland, and on toward the dwindling region of local badland. The Master observed the markers that the crazies placed and periodically re-surveyed. Unlike the average person, he had no supersti-tions, no fear of these. He knew that it was radiation that made these areas deadly—Roentgen left from the fabled Blast. Every year there was less of it, and the country at the fringe of the badlands became habitable for plant, animal and man. He knew that so long as the native life was healthy, there was little danger—from radiation.

But there were other terrors in the fringe. Tiny shrews swarmed periodically, consuming all animals in their path and devouring each other when nothing else offered. Large white moths came out at night, their stings deadly. And there were wild tales told by firelight, of strange haunted buildings, armored bones, and living machines. The Master did not credit much of this and sought some reasonable explanation for what he did credit. But he did know the badlands were dangerous, and he entered them with caution.

The traces skirted the heart of the radioactive area, stay-ing a mile or so within the crazy boundary. This told the Master something else important: that the creature he hunted was not some supernatural spook from the deep horror-region, but an animal of the fringe, leary of radia-tion. That meant he could run it down in time.

For two days he followed the trail the cheerful hound sniffed out. He fed the dog and himself from his pack, occasionally bringing down a rabbit with an arrow and cooking it whole as a mutual treat. He slept on the open

ground, well covered. This was late summer, and the warm crazy sleeping-bag sufficed. He had a spare, in case. He rather enjoyed the trek, and did not push the pace.

On the evening of the second day he found it. The hound bayed and raced ahead—then yelped and ran back, frightened.

The thing stood under a large oak: about four feet tall, bipedal, hunched. Wild hair radiated from its head and curled about its muzzle. Mats of shaggy fur hung over its shoulders. Its skin, where it showed on head and limbs and torso, was mottled gray and yellow, and encrusted with dirt.

But it was no animal. It was a mutant human boy.

The boy had made a crude club. He made as though to attack his pursuer, having naturally been aware of the Master for some time. But the sheer size of the man daunted him, and he fled, running on the balls of his blunted, callused feet.

The Nameless One made camp there. He had suspected that the raider was human or human-derived, for no animal had the degree of cunning and dexterity this prowler had shown. But now that he had made the confirmation, he needed to reconsider means. It would not do to kill the boy—yet it would hardly be kind to bring him back prisoner for the torment the angry farmer-warriors would inflict. Civilization grew very thin in such a case. But one or the other had to be accomplished, for the Master had his own political expedience to consider.

He thought it out, slowly, powerfully. He decided to take the boy to his own camp, so that the lad could join human society without compelling prejudice. This would mean months, perhaps years of demanding attention.

The white moths were coming out. He covered his head with netting, sealed his bag, and settled for sleep. He knew of no reliable way to protect the dog, for the animal would not comprehend the necessity for confinement in the spare bag. He hoped the animal would not snap at a moth and get stung. He wondered how the boy survived in this region. He thought about Sola, the woman he once had loved, the wife he now pretended to love. He thought of Sol, the friend he had sent to the mountain—the man for whom he would trade all his empire, just to travel to-

gether again and converse without trial of strength. And he thought lingeringly of the woman of Helicon, his true wife and the woman he really loved, but would never see again. Great thoughts, petty thoughts. He suffered. He slept.

Next morning the chase resumed. The dog was well; it seemed that the moths did not attack wantonly. Perhaps they died when delivered of their toxin, in the manner of bees. Probably a man could expose himself safely, if he only treated them deferentially. That might explain the boy's survival.

The trail led deeper into the badlands. Now they would discover who had more courage and determination: pursuer or fugitive.

The boy had obviously haunted this area for some time. If there were lethal radiation he should have died already. In any event, the Master could probably withstand any dosage the boy could. So if the lad hoped to escape by hiding in the hot region, he would be disappointed.

Still, the Master could not entirely repress his apprehension as the trail led into a landscape of stunted and deformed trees. Surely these had been touched. And game was scarce, tokening the irregular ravages of the fringe-shrews. If radiation were not present now, it had not departed long since.

He caught up to the boy again. The hunched condition of the youngster's body was more evident by full daylight, and his piebald skin more striking. And the way he ran—heels high, knees bent, so that the whole foot never touched the ground—forelimbs dropping down periodically for support—this was uncanny. Had this boy ever shared a human home?

"Come!" the Weaponless called. "Yield to me and I will spare your life and give you food."

But as he had expected, the fugitive paid no attention. Probably this wilderness denizen had never learned to speak.

The trees became mere shrubs, scabbed with discolored woodrinds and sap-bleeding abrasions, and their leaves were limp, sticky, asymmetric efforts. Then only shriveled sticks protruded from the burned soil, twisted grotesquely. Finally all life was gone, leaving caked ashes and greenish

glass. The hound whined, afraid of the dead bare terrain, and the Master felt rather like whining himself, for this was grim.

But still the boy ran ahead, bounding circuitously around invisible obstacles. At first the Nameless One thought it was strategy, to confuse the pursuit. Then, as he perceived the maneuvering to take forms that were by no means evasive or concealing, he pondered dementia. Radiation might indeed make mad before it destroyed. Finally he realized that the boy was actually skirting pockets of radiation. *He could tell where the roentgen remained!*

Dangerous terrain indeed! The Nameless One followed the trail exactly, and kept the hound to it, knowing that shortcuts would expose him to invisible misery. He was risking his health and his life, but he would not relent.

"Are you ashamed because you are ugly?" he called. He took off his great cloak and showed his own massive, scarred torso, and his neck so laced with gristle that it resembled the trunk of an aged yellow birch. "You are not more ugly than I!"

But the boy ran on.

Then the Master paused, for ahead he saw a building.

Buildings were scarce in the nomad culture. There were hostels that the crazies maintained, where wandering warriors and their families might stay for a night or a fortnight without obligation except to take due care with the premises. There were the houses of the crazies themselves, and the school buildings and offices they maintained. And of course there were the subterranean fortifications of the underworld, wherein were manufactured the weapons and clothing the nomads used—though only the crazies and the Master himself knew this. But the great expanse of land was field and fern and forest, cleared by the Blast that had destroyed the marvelous, warlike culture of the Ancients. The wilderness had returned in the wake of the radiation, open and clean.

This building was tremendous and misshapen. He counted seven distinct levels within it, one layered atop another, and above the last fiber-clothed story metal rods projected like the ribs of a dead cow. Behind it was another structure, of similar configuration, and beyond that a third.

He contemplated these, amazed. He had read about such a thing in the old books, but he had half believed it was a myth. This was a "city."

Before the Blast, the texts had claimed, mankind had grown phenomenally numerous and strong, and had resided in cities where every conceivable (and inconceivable) comfort of life was available. Then these fabulously prosperous peoples had destroyed it all in a rain of fire, a smash of intolerable radiation, leaving only the scattered nomads and crazies and underworlders, and the extensive badlands.

He could poke a thousand logical holes in that fable. For one thing, it was obvious that no culture approaching the technological level described would be at the same time so primitive as to throw it away so pointlessly. And such a radically different culture as that of the nomads could not have sprung full-blown from ashes. But he was sure the ultimate truth did lie hidden somewhere within the badlands, for their very presence seemed to vindicate the reality of the Blast, whatever its true cause.

Now, astonishingly, these badlands were ready to yield some of their secrets. For the century since the cataclysm no man had penetrated far into the posted regions and lived—but always the proscribed area declined. He knew the time would come, though not in his lifetime, when the entire territory would be open once more to man. Meanwhile the fever of discovery was on him; he was so eager to learn the truth that he gladly risked the roentgen.

The boy's tracks were clear in the dirt, that had been freshened by recent rainfall. The glass had broken up and disappeared, here; sprouts of pale grass rimmed the path. Nothing, not even the radiation, was consistent about the badlands.

The boy had gone into the building. Most nomads were in awe of solid structures of any size, and avoided even the comparatively modest buildings of the crazies. But the Master had traveled widely and experienced as much as any man of his time, and he knew that there was nothing supernatural about a giant edifice. There could be danger, yes—but the natural hazards of falling timbers and deep pits and radiation and crazed animals, nothing more sinister.

Still, he hesitated before entering that ancient temple.

It would be easy to become trapped inside, and perhaps the wily boy had something of the sort in mind. He had been known to place deadfalls for unwary trackers, laboriously scraped out of the Earth by hand and nail and artfully covered. That was one of the things he had evidently learned from the measures applied against *him*. Too smart for an animal—adding to the terror surrounding him—and not bad for a human.

The Master looked about. Within the shelter of the window arches there were fragments of dry wood. Most had rotted, but not all. There was bound to be more wood inside. He could fire it and drive the boy out. This seemed to be the safest course.

Yet there could be invaluable artifacts within— machines, books, supplies. Was he to destroy it all so wantonly? Better to preserve the building intact, and assemble a task force to explore it thoroughly at a later date.

So deciding, the Master entered at the widest portal and began his final search for the boy. The hound whined and stayed so close that it was tricky to avoid tripping over it, but the animal did sniff out the trail.

There were stone steps leading down, an avenue of splendid and wasteful breadth, and this was where the boy had gone. And, so easily that it was suspicious, they had tracked the marauder to his lair. There did not seem to be another exit apart from the stair. The boy had to be waiting below.

Would it be wise to check the upper floors first? The boy might actually be leading him into the final trap, while his real residence was above. No—best to follow closely, for otherwise he ran too strong a risk of encountering radiation. Had he realized that the chase would end so deep in the badlands, he would have arranged to obtain a crazy geiger. As it was, he had to proceed with exceeding caution. That meant, in this case, to dispense with much of his caution in the pursuit. Physical attack by the boy was much less to be feared than the radiation that might be lurking on either side of the boy's trail.

As the Nameless One approached the final chamber an object flew out. The boy, unable to flee again, was pelting his tormentor with any objects available.

The Master paused, contemplating the thing that had

been thrown. He squatted to pick it up, watching the door so that he would not be taken by surprise. Then he turned the object over in his hands, studying it closely.

It was metal, but not a can or tool. A weapon, but no sword or staff or dagger. One end was solid and curved around at right angles to the rest; the other end was hollow. The thing had a good solid heft to it, and there were assorted minor mechanisms attached.

The Master's hands shook as he recognized it. This, too, had been described in the books; this, too, was an artifact of the old times.

It was a gun.

CHAPTER THREE

The boy stood astride the boxes and made ready to throw another metal rock, for the tremendous man and the tame animal had trapped him here. Never before had pursuit been so relentless; never before had he had to defend his lair. Had he anticipated this, he would have hidden elsewhere.

But there were so many places here that burned his skin and drove him back! This building was the only one completely safe.

The giant appeared again in the doorway. The boy threw his rock and reached for another. But this time the man jerked aside, letting the missile glance off his bulging thigh, and heaved a length of rope forward. The boy found himself entangled and, in a moment, helpless. It was as though that rope were alive, the way it twisted and coiled and jerked.

The man bound him and slung him over one tremendous shoulder and carried him out of the room and up the stairs and from the building. The man's brute strength was appalling. The boy tried to squirm and bite, but his teeth met flesh like baked leather.

His skin burned as the man passed through a hot region. Was the monster invulnerable to this too? He had charged through several similar areas on the way in—areas the boy had meticulously avoided. How could one fight such a force?

In the forest the man set him down and loosed the rope, making man-sounds that were only dimly familiar. The boy bolted as soon as he was free.

The rope sailed out like a striking snake and wrapped itself about his waist, hauling him back. He was captive again. "No," the man said, and that sound was a clear negation.

The giant removed the rope again, and immediately the boy dashed away. Once more he was lassoed.

"No!" the man repeated, and this time his huge hand came across in a blow that seemed nearly to cave in the boy's chest. The boy fell to the ground, conscious of nothing but his pain and the need for air.

A third time the man unwound the rope. This time the boy remained where he was. Lessons of this nature were readily learned.

They walked on toward the main camp, still far distant. The boy led, for the eyes of the man never left him. The boy avoided the diminishing patches of radiation, and man and animal followed. By evening they had come to the place they had seen each other the previous day.

The man opened his pack and brought out chunks of material that smelled good. He bit off some, chewing with gusto, and passed some along to the boy. The invitation did not have to be repeated, for this was food.

After eating, the man urinated against a tree and covered his body again. The boy followed the example, even imitating the upright stance. He had learned long ago to control his eliminations, for carelessly deposited traces could interfere with hunting, but it had never occurred to him to direct the flow with his hand.

"Here," the man said. He threw the boy down gently and shoved him feet-first into a constraining sack. The boy struggled as some kind of mesh covered his head. "Stay there tonight, or . . ." And the ponderous fist came down, to tap only lightly at the bruised chest. Another warning.

Then the man went apart a certain distance and climbed into another bag, and the dog settled down under the tree.

The boy lay there, needing to escape but hesitant to brace the dangers of the night, this close to the hot region. He could see well enough, and usually foraged in the dark—but not *here*. He had been stung once by a white moth and had nearly perished. It was possible to avoid

them, but never with certainty, for they rested under leaves and sometimes on the ground. Here beneath the netting he was at least protected.

But if he did not flee by night, he would not have the chance by day. The rope was too swift and clever, the giant too strong.

He heard the man sleeping, and decided. He sat up and began to claw his way out.

The man woke at the first sound. "No!" he called.

It was hazardous to defy the giant, who might run him down again anyway. The boy lay back, resigned. And slept.

In the morning they ate again. It had been a long time since the boy had two such easy meals in succession. It was a condition he could learn to like.

The man then conveyed him to a stream and washed them both. He applied ointments from his pack to the assorted bruises and scratches on the boy's body, and replaced the uncured animal skins with an oversize shirt and pantaloons. After this disgusting process they resumed the journey toward the mancamp.

The boy shrugged and chafed under the awful clothing. He thought once more of bolting for freedom, before being taken entirely out of his home territory, but a grunted warning changed his mind. And the fact was that the man, apart from his peculiarities of dress and urination, was not a harsh captor. He did not punish without provocation, and even showed gruff kindness.

About the middle of the day the man's pace slowed. He seemed weary or sleepy, despite his enormous muscles and stamina. He began to stagger. He stopped and disgorged his breakfast, and the boy wondered whether this was another civilized ritual. Then he sat down on the ground and looked unhappy.

The boy watched for a time. When the man did not rise, the boy began to walk away. Unchallenged, he ran swiftly back the way they had come. He was free!

About a mile away he stopped and threw off the fettering man-clothing. Then he paused. He knew what was wrong with the giant. The man was not immune to the hot places; he simply hadn't been aware of them, so had exposed himself recklessly. Now he was coming down with the sickness.

The boy had learned about this, too, the hard way. He had been burned, and had become weak, and vomited, and felt like dying. But he had survived, and after that his skin had been sensitized, and whenever he approached a hot area he felt the burn immediately. His brothers, lacking the skin patches that set him apart, had had no such ability, and died gruesomely. He had also discovered certain leaves that cooled his skin somewhat, and the juices of certain fringe-plant stems eased his stomach of such sickness. But he never ventured voluntarily into the hot sections. His skin always warned him off in time, and he took the other medicines purely as precautionary procedure.

The giant man would be very sick, and probably he would die. At night the moths would come, and later the shrews, while he lay helpless. The man had been stupid to enter the badlands' heart.

Stupid—yet brave and kind. No other stranger had ever extended a helping hand to the boy or fed him since his parents died, and he was oddly moved by it. Somewhere deep in his memory he found a basic instruction: kindness must be met with kindness. It was all that remained of the teaching of his long lost parents, whose skulls were whitening in a burn.

This giant man was like his dead father: strong, quiet, fierce in anger but gentle when unprovoked. The boy had appreciated both the attention and the savage discipline. It was possible to trust a man like that.

He gathered select herbs and came back, his motives uncertain but his actions sure. The man was lying where he had originally settled to the ground, his body flushed. The boy placed a compress of leaves against the fever-ridden torso and limbs and squeezed drops of stem-juice into the grimacing mouth, but could do little else. The giant was too heavy for him to move, and the boy's clubbed hands could not grasp him properly for such an effort. Not without bruising the flesh.

But as the coolness of night came, the man revived somewhat.

He cleaned himself up with agonized motions but did not eat. He climbed into his bag and lost consciousness.

In the morning the man seemed alert, but stumbled when

he attempted to stand. He could not walk. The boy gave him a stem to chew on, and he chewed, not seeming to be aware of his action.

The food in the pack ran out on the following day, and the boy went foraging. Certain fruits were ripening, certain wild tubers swelling. He plucked and dug these and bound them in the jacket he no longer wore and loped with the bundle back to their enforced camp. In this manner he sustained them both.

On the fourth day the man began bleeding from the skin. Some parts of his body were as hard as wood and did not bleed; but where the skin was natural, it hemorrhaged. The man touched himself with dismay, but could not hold on to consciousness.

The boy took cloth from the pack and soaked it in water and bathed the blood away. But when more blood came, appearing as if magically on the surface though there was no abrasion, he let it collect and cake. This slowed the flow. He knew that blood had to be kept inside the body, for he had bled copiously once when wounded and had felt very weak for many days. And when animals bled too much, they died.

Whenever the man revived, the boy gave him fruit and the special stems to eat, and whatever water he could accept without choking. When he sank again into stupor, the boy packed the moist leaves tightly about him. When it grew cold, he covered the man with the bag he slept in, and lay beside him, shielding him from the worst of the night wind.

The dog crawled away and died.

Days passed. The sick man burned up his own flesh, becoming gaunt, and the contours of his body were bizarre. It was as though he wore stones and boards under the skin, so that no point could penetrate; but with the supportive flesh melting away, the armor hung loosely. It hampered his breathing, his elimination. But perhaps it had also stopped some of the radiation, for the boy knew that physical substance could do this to a certain extent.

The man was near death, but he refused to die. The boy watched, aware that he was spectator to a greater courage battling a more horrible antagonist than any man could hope to conquer. The boy's own father and brothers had

yielded up their lives far more readily. Blood and sweat and urine matted the leaves, and dirt and debris covered the man, but still he fought.

And finally he began to mend. His fever passed, the bleeding stopped, some of his strength returned and he ate—at first tentatively, then with huge appetite. He looked at the boy with renewed comprehension, and he smiled.

There was a bond between them now. Man and boy were friends.

CHAPTER FOUR

The warriors gathered around the central circle. Tyl of Two Weapons supervised the ceremony. "Who is there would claim the honor of manhood and take a name this day?" he inquired somewhat perfunctorily. He had been doing this every month for eight years, and it bored him.

Several youths stepped up: gangling adolescents who seemed hardly to know how to hang on to their weapons. Every year the crop seemed younger and gawkier. Tyl longed for the old days, when he had first served Sol of All Weapons. Then men had been men, and the leader had been a leader, and great things had been in the making. Now—weaklings and inertia.

It was no effort to put the ritual scorn into his voice. "You will fight each other," he told them. "I will pair you off, man to man in the circle. He who retains the circle shall be deemed warrior, and be entitled to name and band and weapon with honor. The other . . ."

He did not bother to finish. No one could be called a warrior unless he won at least once in the circle. Some hopefuls failed again and again, and some eventually gave up and went to the crazies or the mountain. Most went to other tribes and tried again.

"You, club," Tyl said, picking out a chubby would-be-clubber. "You, staff," selecting an angular hopeful staffer.

The two youths, visibly nervous, stepped gingerly into the circle. They began to fight, the clubber making huge clumsy swings, the staffer countering ineptly. By and by the club smashed one of the staffer's misplaced hands, and the staff fell to the ground.

That was enough for the staffer. He bounced out of the circle. It made Tyl sick—not for the fact of victory and defeat, but for the sheer incompetence of it. How could such dolts ever become proper warriors? What good would a winner such as this clubber be for the tribe, whose decisive blow had been sheer fortune?

But it was never possible to be certain, he reflected. Some of the very poorest prospects that he sent along to Sav the Staff's training camp emerged as formidable warriors. The real mark of a man was how he responded to training. That had been the lesson that earlier weaponless man had taught, the one that never fought in the circle. What was his name—Sos. Sos had stayed with the tribe a year and established the system, then departed for ever. Except for some brief thing about a rope. Not much of a man, but a good mind. Yes—it was best to incorporate the clubber into the tribe and send him to Sav; good might even come of it. If not—no loss.

Next were a pair of daggers. This fight was bloody, but at least the victor looked like a potential man.

Then a sworder took on a sticker. Tyl watched this contest with interest, for his own two weapons were sword and sticks, and he wished he had more of each in his tribe. The sticks were useful for discipline, the sword for conquest.

The sticker-novice seemed to have some promise. His hands were swift, his aim sure. The sworder was strong but slow; he laid about himself crudely.

The sticker caught his opponent on the side of the head, and followed up the telling blow with a series to the neck and shoulders. So doing, he let slip his guard—and the keen blade-edge caught him at the throat, and he was dead.

Tyl closed his eyes in pain. Such folly! The one youngster with token promise had let his enthusiasm run away with him, and had walked into a slash that any idiot could have avoided. Was there any hope for this generation?

One youth remained—a rare Morningstar. It took courage to select such a weapon, and a certain morbidity, for it was devastating and unstable. Tyl had left him until last because he wanted to match him against an experienced warrior. That would greatly decrease the star's chance of success, but would correspondingly increase his

chance of survival. If he looked good, Tyl would arrange to match him next month with an easy mark, and take him into the tribe as soon as he had his band and name.

One of the perimeter sentries came up. "Strangers, Chief—man and woman. He's ugly as hell; she must be, too."

Still irritated by the loss of the promising sticker, Tyl snapped back: "Is your bracelet so worn you can't tell an ugly woman by sight?"

"She's veiled."

Tyl became interested. "What woman would cover her face?"

The sentry shrugged. "Do you want me to bring them here?"

Tyl nodded.

As the man departed, he returned to the problem of the star. A veteran staffer would be best, for the Morningstar could maim or kill the wielders of other weapons, even in the hands of a novice. He summoned a man who had had experience with the star in the circle, and began giving him instructions.

Before the test commenced, the strangers arrived. The man was indeed ugly: somewhat hunchbacked, with hands grossly gnarled, and large patches of discolored skin on limbs and torso. Because of his stoop, his eyes peered out from below shaggy brows, oddly impressive. He moved gracefully despite some peculiarity of gait; there was something wrong with his feet. His aspect was feral.

The woman was shrouded in a long cloak that concealed her figure as the veil concealed her face. But he could tell from the way she stepped that she was neither young nor fat. That, unless she gave him some pretext to have her stripped, was as much as he was likely to know.

"I am Tyl, chief of this camp in the name of the Nameless One," he said to the man. "What is your business here?"

The man displayed his left wrist. It was naked.

"You came to earn a bracelet?" Tyl was surprised that a man as muscular and scarred and altogether formidable as this one should not already be a warrior. But another look at the almost useless hands seemed to clarify that. How could he fight well, unless he could grasp his weapon?

Or could he be another weaponless warrior? Tyl knew of only one in the empire—but that one was *the* Weaponless, the Master. It could, indeed, be done; Tyl himself had gone down to defeat in the circle before that juggernaut.

"What is your chosen weapon?" he asked.

The man reached to his belt and revealed, hanging beneath the loose folds of his jacket, a pair of singlesticks.

Tyl was both relieved and disappointed. A novice weaponless warrior would have been intriguing. Then he had another notion. "Will you go against the star?"

The man, still not speaking, nodded.

Tyl gestured to the circle. "Star, here is your match," he called.

The size of the audience seemed to double as he spoke. This contest promised to be interesting!

The star stepped into the circle, hefting his spiked ball. The stranger removed his jacket and leggings to stand in conventional pantaloons that still looked odd on him. His chest, though turned under by his posture, was massive. Across it the flesh was yellowish. The legs were extremely stout, ridged with muscle, and the short feet were bare. The toenails curled around the toes thickly, almost like hoofs. Strange man!

The arms were not proportionately developed, though on a man with lighter chest and shoulders they would have been impressive enough. But the hands, as they closed about the sticks, resembled pincers. The grip was square, unsophisticated, awkward—but tight. This novice was either very bad or very good.

The veiled woman settled near the circle to watch. She was as strange in her concealment as the young hunchback was in his physique.

The sticker entered the circle circumspectly, like an animal skirting a deadfall, but his guard was up. The star whirled his chained mace above his head so that the spokes whistled in the air. For a moment the two faced each other at the ready. Then the star advanced, the wheel of his revolving sledge coming to intersect the body of his opponent.

The sticker ducked, as he had to; no flesh could withstand the strike of that armored ball. His powerful legs carried him along bent over, and his natural hunch facili-

tated this; half his normal height, he raced across the circle and came up behind the star.

That one ploy told half the story. Tyl knew that if the sticker could jump as well as he could stoop, the star would never catch him. And the star had to catch him soon, for the whirling ball was quickly fatiguing to the elevated arm.

But it never came to that. Before the star could reorient, the sticks had clipped him about the business arm, and he was unable to maintain his pose. The motion of the ball slowed; the man staggered.

Seeing that he was too stupid to realize he had already lost and to step out of the circle, Tyl spoke for the man: "Star yields."

The star looked about, confused. "But I'm still in the circle!"

Tyl had no patience with folly. "Stay, then."

The man started to wheel his ball again, unsteadily. The sticker stepped close and rapped him on the skull. As man and ball fell, the sticker put one of his sticks between his own teeth and used that hand to clamp on to the chain. This was an interesting maneuver, because the typical star chain was spiked against just such contact—tiny, needle-pointed barbs. But the sticker seemed not to notice. He dragged the unconscious man to the edge of the ring, then let go and bent to roll him out.

With something akin to genuine pleasure, Tyl presented the grotesque sticker with the golden band of manhood. He noticed that the man's hands were enormously callused. No wonder he did not fear barbs! "Henceforth, warrior, be called——" Tyl paused. "What name have you chosen?"

The man tried to speak, but his voice was rasping. It was as though he had calluses in his larynx, too. The word that came out sounded like a growl.

Tyl took it in stride. "Henceforth be called Var—Var the Stick." Then: "Who is your companion?"

Var shook his shaggy leaning head, not answering. But the woman came forth of her own accord, removing her veil and cloak.

"Sola!" Tyl exclaimed, recognizing the wife of the Master. She was still a handsome woman, though it had been almost ten years since he had first seen her. She had

stayed about four years with Sol, then gone to the new Master of Empire. Because the conqueror was weaponless and wore no bracelet and used no name, she had kept the band and name she had. This was tantamount to adultery, openly advertised—but the Master had won her fairly. He was the mightiest man ever to enter the circle, armed or not. If *he* didn't care about appearances, no one else could afford to comment.

But Sola had at least been faithful to her chosen husbands, except for a little funny business at the very beginning with that Sos fellow. What was she doing now, wandering about with a (hitherto) nameless youth?

"The Master trained him," she said. "He wanted him to take his name by himself, without prejudice."

A protégé of the Weaponless! That made several things fall into place. Well-trained—naturally; the Master knew all weapons as adversaries. Strong—yes, that followed. Ugly—of course. This was exactly the sort of man the Nameless One would like. Perhaps this was what the Master himself had been like as a youth.

And then he made another connection. "That wild boy that ravaged the crops, five years ago———"

"Yes. A man, now."

Tyl's hands went to his own sticks. "He bit me, then. I will have vengeance on him now."

"No," she said. "That is why I came. You shall not take Var to the circle."

"Is he afraid to meet me by day? I will waive terms."

"Var is afraid of nothing. But he is novice yet, and you the second ranked of the empire. He returns with me."

"He requires a woman to protect him? I should have named him Var the Schtick!"

She stood up straight, her figure blooming like that of a freshly nubile girl. "Do you wish to answer to my husband?"

And Tyl, because he was bonded to the man she termed her husband, and was himself a man of honor, had to stifle his fury and answer, "No."

She turned to Var. "We'll stay the night here, then begin the journey back tomorrow. You will want to take your bracelet to the main tent."

Tyl smiled to himself. The new warrior, with his grotesqueries, would find no takers for his band. Let him celebrate alone!

And perhaps one day, one year, they would meet again, when the protection of the Nameless One did not apply. . . .

CHAPTER FIVE

Var knew well enough the significance of the golden bracelet. It was the product of crazy workmanship and distribution, costing the wearer nothing, indistinguishable physically from thousands of others. But not only did it identify him as a man, it served as a license to have a woman—for a night or a year or a lifetime. He had but to put the bracelet on the slender wrist of the girl of his choice and she was his, provided she agreed. Most girls were said to be flattered to be offered such attention, and sought to retain the bracelet as long as possible. They were particularly pleased to bear sons by the bracelet, for as a man proved himself in the circle, so a woman proved herself in fertility. The land always needed more people.

The big tent was standard. Each camp had one, where the unattached warriors resided, and where single girls made themselves available. In winter a great fire heated the central chamber, while the couples occupying the fringe compartments trusted to sleepingbags and mutual warmth for their comfort.

Var was sure he would get by nicely on the latter system. In any event, it was summer.

Dusk, and the lamps were already lighted inside. The collective banquet was just finishing. Var, flush with his achievement of a name, had not been hungry, so that was no loss.

The girls were there, lounging on home-made furniture. The crazies provided everything a warrior might need, but it was considered gauche to use such unearned merchandise. The nomads preferred, generally, to do for themselves.

He walked up to the nearest girl. She wore a lovely one-piece wrap-around fastened in front with a silver brooch—the costume signifying her availability. Her hair was a languorous waving brown. Her figure was excellent: high-breasted, low-thighed. Yes, she would do.

He looked the question at her, putting his right hand on the bracelet and beginning to twist it off. This was approved technique; he had seen warriors do it at the Master's camp.

"No," she said.

Var stopped, hand on wrist. Had he misunderstood? He was tempted to query her again, but preferred not to speak. Words were not supposed to be necessary. He had only learned, or perhaps relearned, the language since joining the Master and though he understood it well enough, his mouth and tongue did not form the syllables well.

He went on to the next, somewhat disgruntled. He had not considered refusal, and didn't know how to handle it. This adjacent girl was slightly younger, fair-haired and in pink. Now that he thought about it, she really looked better than the first. He tapped his bracelet.

She looked at him casually. "Can't you talk?"

Embarrassed, he grunted the word. "Brach-rit." Bracelet. It was clear in his mind.

"Get lost, stupid."

Var did not know how to deal with this either, so he nodded and went on.

None of the girls were interested. Some showed their contempt with disconcerting candor.

Finally an older woman, wearing a bracelet, came up to him.

"You obviously don't understand, Warrior, so I'll explain it to you. I saw you fight today, so don't think I'm trying to insult you."

Var was glad to have anyone treat him with respect. Gratefully, he listened to her.

"These girls are young," she said. "They have never had to work, they have never borne children, they have little experience. They're out for a good time. You—well, you're a stranger, so they're cautious. And you're a fledgling warrior, so they're contemptuous. Unjustly so. But as I

said, they're young. And—I have to tell you—you're not pretty to look at. That doesn't matter in the circle, but it does here. An experienced woman might understand—but not these good-time juniors. Don't blame them. They need tempering by time, just as a warrior does. They make mistakes too."

Var nodded, frustrated but thankful for her advice, though he did not completely understand it. "Who———"

"I'm Tyla, the chief's wife. I just wanted you to understand."

He had meant to ask what girl to solicit next, but was glad to know the identity of this helpful woman.

"Go back to your home-camp, where they know you," she said. "Tyl doesn't like you, and that also prejudices your case here. I'm sorry to spoil your big night, but that's the way it is."

Now he understood. He wasn't wanted here. "Thanks," he said.

"Good luck, Warrior. You'll find one who's right for you, and she'll be worth the wait. You have lost nothing here."

Var walked out of the tent.

Only as the cooling night air brushed him did the reaction come. *He was not wanted.* At the Master's camp he had been kindly treated, and no one had told him he was ugly. He had seemed to fit in with human life, despite his childhood in the wilderness. Now he knew that he had been sheltered—not physically, but socially. Today, with his formal achievement of manhood, he was also exposed to the truth. He was still a wild boy, unfit to mingle with human beings.

First he was embarrassed, so that his head was hot, his hands shaking. He had been blithely offering his shiny virgin bracelet. . . .

Then he was furious. Why had he been subjected to this? What right had these tame pretty people to pass judgment on him? He tried to accommodate himself to their rules, and they rejected him. None of them would survive in the badlands!

He took out his shiny metal sticks and hefted them fondly. He was good with these. He was a warrior now. He needed to accept insults from no one. He stepped into

the circle, the same one in which he had won his manhood earlier in the day. He waved his weapon.

"Come fight me!" he cried, knowing the words came out as gibberish but not caring. "I challenge you all!"

A man emerged from a small tent. "What's the noise?" he demanded. It was Tyl, the camp chief, dressed in a rough woollen nightshirt. The man who, for some reason, did not like Var. Var had never seen him before, that he recalled—though the man could have been among the crowds of people that had gawked at him when the Master first brought him from the badlands.

"What are you doing?" Tyl demanded, coming close. A yellow topknot dangled against the side of his head.

"Come fight me!" Var shouted, waving his sticks threateningly. His words might be incoherent, but his meaning could not be mistaken.

Tyl looked angry, but he did not enter the circle. "There is no fighting after dark," he said. "And if there were, I would not meet you, much as it would give me pleasure to bloody your ugly head and send you howling back through the cornfields. Stop making a fool of yourself."

Cornfields? Almost, Var made a connection.

Other people gathered, men and women and excited children. They peered through the gloom at Var, and he realized that he was now a far more ludicrous figure than he had been in the tent.

"Leave him alone," Tyl said, and returned to his residence with an almost comical flirt of his topknot. The others dispersed, and soon Var was standing by himself again. He had only made things worse by his belligerence.

Dejected, he went to the only place he knew where he could find some understanding, however cynical. The isolated tent of his traveling companion: the Master's wife.

"I was afraid it would come to this," Sola said, her voice oddly soft. "I will go to Tyl and have him fetch you a damsel. You shall not be deprived, this night."

"No!" Var cried, horrified that he should have to be satisfied by the intercession of a woman going to his enemy. Human mores were not natural to him, but this was too obviously a thing of shame.

"That, too, I anticipated," she said philosophically.

"That's why I had my tent set up away from the main camp."

Var did not understand.

"Come in, lie down," she said. "It's not as bad as you think. A man doesn't prove himself in one day or one night; it's the years that show the truth."

Var crawled into the tent and lay down beside her. He really did not know this woman well. She had remained aloof all the years the Master trained him, only instructing him curtly in computations. Thanks to her, he could count to one hundred, and tell whether six handfuls of four ears of corn were more than two baskets with fifteen ears each. (They were not.) Such calculations were difficult and pointless, and he had not enjoyed the lessons, and Sola had made him feel particularly stupid, but the Master had insisted. Thus his chief association with her had been negative.

He had been surprised when she was delegated—or had volunteered—to accompany him here for his manhood test. A woman! But as it had turned out, she was quite competent. She walked well, so that they made good distance each day and knew the route, and when they encountered strangers she had done the talking. They had spent the nights in the hostels, she in one bunk, he in another, though he would have preferred even now to sleep in a familiar tree. Aloof she remained—but she did not entirely conceal her body as she showered and changed for the night, and the glimpses he had had, had given him painful erections. His nature was animal; *any* female, even one as old as this, provoked him. And she did know his origin and understand his limitations.

Now, in this strange unfriendly camp, hurt by his own failures, he had come to her—his only contact with his only friend, the Master.

"So you asked the young girls, and they ridiculed you," she said. "I had hoped better for you—but I was young once myself, and just as narrow. I thought power was most important—to marry a chief. And so I lost the man I loved, and now I am sorry."

She had never talked like this before. Var lay silent, satisfied for the moment to listen. It was better than think-

ing of his own humiliations. She referred, of course, to her former husband—Sol of All Weapons, who had lost his empire to the Master, and had gone to the mountain with his baby girl. The episode had become legend already; everyone knew of that momentous transfer of power and that tragic father-daughter suicide.

If Sola had loved power so much that she had given up the man she loved and the daughter she had borne to him, and taken the victor to her bed—no wonder she suffered!

"Would you understand," she asked, "if I told you that when I thought I'd lost my love for ever, he returned to me—and I found that it was only his body, not his heart, that was mine, and even that body maimed and unfamiliar?"

"No," Var said honestly. It was easier to voice the words for her, for she understood him whether or not his wilderness mouth cooperated.

"Not everything is what it seems," she murmured. "You, too, will find that friendship can make hard requirements of you, and those you might deem enemy are men to be trusted. Life is like that. Come, let's get this done with."

He recognized a dismissal and began to crawl out of the tent.

"No," she said gently, holding him back. "This is your night, and you shall have it in full measure. I will be your woman."

Var made a guttural sound, dumbfounded. Could he have understood her correctly?

"Sorry, Var," she said. "I hit you with that too abruptly. Lie down."

He lay down again.

"Wild boy," she continued, "you are not a man until you have taken a woman. So it is written in our unwritten code. I came to make sure you accomplished it all. I have"—here she paused—"done this before. Long ago. My husband knows. Believe me, Var, though this appears to be a violation of the standards we have taught you, this is the way it must be. I cannot explain it further. But you must understand one thing, and promise me another."

He had to speak. "The Master——"

"Var, *he knows!*" she whispered fiercely. "But he will never speak of it. This was decided almost ten years ago.

And you must know this, too: I am older than you, but I am not past bearing age. The Nameless One is sterile. Tonight, and the nights that follow—it ends when we reach home camp. If you should beget a child on me, it will be the child of the Weaponless. I will never wear your bracelet. I will never touch you again, after this journey. I will never speak of what happened here between us, and neither will you. If I am pregnant, you will be sent away. You have no claim upon me. It will be as though it never happened—except that you will be a man. Do you understand!"

"No, no———" he mumbled, already sick with lust for her.

"You understand." She reached out suddenly and put her hand upon his loin. "You understand."

He understood that she was offering her body to him, and that he had no stamina to refuse. He was wilderness bred; the willingness of the female was the male's command.

"But you must promise," she said, as she took his clubbed hand, only recently capable of any gentleness, and brought it to her tender breast. She was already nude within her bag. "You must promise———"

The heat was rising in him, abolishing any scruples he might have had. Var knew he would do it. Perhaps the Master would kill him, but tonight———

"You must promise—*to kill the man who harms my child*."

Var went chill. "You have no child!" he blurted. "None that can be harmed———" And became aware again of his crudity and cruelty of word and concept. He was still wild.

"Promise."

"How can I promise when your child is long dead?"

She silenced him with the first fully female kiss he had ever experienced. His body accelerated in response, knowing what to do despite his confusion and what seemed like madness on her part. She talked of her dead child while preparing to make love, but her breasts remained soft, her legs open. "If ever the situation arises, you will know," she said.

"I promise." What else could he do?

She said no more, but her body spoke for her. This

supposedly aloof, cold woman—novice that he was, Var still recognized in her a sexual fury of unprecedented proportion. She was hot, she was lithe, she was savage. She was at least twenty-five years old, but in the dark she seemed a buxom, eager fifteen. It was not hard to forget for the moment that she was in fact middle-aged.

As the connection was made and the explosion formed within him, he realized that it might be his own future child he had just sworn to avenge . . . anonymously.

CHAPTER SIX

The Master was waiting for them. He used one of the crazy hostels as a business office, and had entire drawers of papers with writing on them. Var had never comprehended the reason for such records, but did not question the wisdom of his mentor. The Master was literate: he was able to look at the things called books and repeat speeches that men long dead had said. This was an awesome yet useless ability.

"Here is your warrior," Sola said. "Var the Stick—a man in every sense of the word." And with an obscure smile she departed for her own tent.

The Master stood in the glassy rotating door of the cylindrical hostel and studied Var for a long moment. "Yes, you are changed. Do you know now what it is to keep a secret? To know and not speak?"

Var nodded affirmatively, thinking of what had passed between him and the Master's phenomenal wife on the way home. Even if he had not been forbidden to talk of that, he would have balked at this point.

"I have another secret for you. Come." And with no further question or explanation the Nameless One led the way away from the cabin, letting the door spin about behind him. Var glanced once more at the sparkling transparent cone that topped the hostel and its mysterious mechanisms, and turned to follow.

They walked a mile, passing warriors and their families busy at sundry tasks—practising with weapons, mending clothing, cleaning meat—and exchanged routine greetings. The Master seemed to be in no hurry. "Sometimes," he said, "a man can find himself in a situation not of his

making or choosing, where he must keep silence even though he prefers to speak, and though others may deem him a coward. But his preference is not always wise, and the opinion of others does not make a supposition true. There is courage of other types than that of the circle."

Var realized that his friend was telling him something important, but he wasn't sure how it applied. He sensed the Master's secret was going to be as important to his life as Sola's had been to his manhood. Strange things seemed to be developing; the situation was changed from his prior experience.

When they were well beyond the sight or hearing of any other person, the Master cut away from the beaten trail and began to run. He galloped ponderously, shaking the ground, and his breath emerged noisily, but he maintained a good pace. Var ran with him, far more easily, mystified. The Master, as he well knew, was tireless—but where was he going?

Their route led toward the local badlands markers, then along them, then through them. Var had thought the Weaponless was afraid of such regions, since his severe radiation sickness of the time the two had met. It had taken the man months to regain his full strength; and from time to time, in the privacy of tent or office, he had bled again or been sick or reeled from surges of weakness. Var knew this well, and Sola was aware of it, but it had been hidden from others of the empire. Much of the early battle training Var had received had been as much to exercise the Master gradually as to profit the wild boy. And it had been common knowledge that the Master avoided the badlands with almost cowardly care.

Obviously he was *not* afraid. Why had he let men think he was? Was this what he had referred to just now—that other kind of courage? But what reason could there be for it?

Deep in the badlands, but in a place where there was no radiation, there was a camp. Strange warriors manned it—men Var had never seen before. They wore funny green clothing riddled with knobs and pockets, and on their heads were inverted pots. They carried metal rocks.

The leader of this odd tribe came up promptly. He was short, stout, old, and had curly yellow hair. Obviously

unfit to fight in the circle. "This is Jim," the Master said. "Var the Stick," he added, completing the introduction.

The two men eyed each other suspiciously.

"Jim and Var," the Master said, smiling grimly, "you don't know each other, but I want you to accept my word on this: you can trust each other. You both have had similar misfortunes—Jim whose brother of the same name went to the mountain twenty years ago, Var whose whole family was lost in the badlands."

Var still was not impressed, and the other man seemed to share his sentiment. To be without family was no signal of merit.

"Var is a warrior I have personally trained. His skin is immediately sensitive to radiation, so that he cannot accidentally be burned, no matter where he goes."

Jim became intensely interested.

"And Jim—Jim the Gun, if you want his weapon—is literate. He and I made contact by letter years ago, when the—the need developed. He has studied the old texts, and knows as much as any man among the nomads about explosive weapons. He is training this group in the ancient techniques of warfare."

Var recognized the man's weapon now. It was one of the metal stones that were stored in certain badlands buildings. But it hardly seemed suitable for use in the circle. It had no cutting edge, and was far too small and clumsy to serve as a club. And once thrown, it would be lost.

"Var will be liaison man between this group and the outside," the Master said. "Assuming he is willing. Later he'll be an advance scout. But I want him to know how to shoot, too."

Jim and Var still merely looked at each other. "I'll break the ice," the Master said. "Then I'll have to go back before someone misses me. Var, fetch that jug over there, if you please." He pointed across a field to a brown ceramic jar perched on an old stump.

Jim started to say something, but the Master held up his hand. Var loped toward it. About half the way he skidded to a stop. His skin was burning. He retreated a few paces and circled to the side, looking for a way around the radiation.

It took him several minutes, but finally he found a

channel and reached the jug. He brought it back, retracing his devious route. The Master and Jim had been joined by a dozen other men, all watching silently.

Var handed over the jug.

"It's true! A living geiger!" Jim exclaimed, amazed. "We can use him, all right."

The Master returned the jug to Var. "Set it on the ground about fifty feet away, if you please."

Var complied.

"Demonstrate your shotgun," the Master said to Jim.

The man went into a tent and brought out an object like a sheathed sword. He held it up, pointing the narrow end toward the jug.

"There will be noise," the Master warned Var. "It will not harm you. I suggest you watch the jug."

Var did so. Suddenly a blast of thunder occurred beside him, making him jump and grab for his weapon. The distant jug shattered as though smashed by a club. No one had touched it or thrown anything at it.

"Pieces of metal from this long gun did that," the Master said. "Jim will show you how it works. Stay with him, as you choose; I will return another day." And he left, cantering as before.

Jim turned to Var. "How is it that you are not bonded, since he trained you himself and trusts you with this secret?"

Var did not answer immediately. He had not realized it before, but it was true he was not bonded. He was not a member of the Nameless One's empire or any of its subject tribes, for he had never been defeated in the circle. His only battle had been the formal achievement of his manhood. Ordinarily a warrior joined a tribe of his choosing by ritually challenging its chief. When he lost—as was inevitable, for no novice could match a chief—he was according to nomad convention bonded, subject to the will of that leader, or the leader's leader. If he fought a man from another tribe and lost, his allegiance changed; if he won, the other man joined his own tribe. Once Var had taken name and bracelet, he had become a free agent— until such time as he lost that freedom in the circle.

Why had the Weaponless never made arrangement for Var? And how had Jim known about this omission?

"He was scrupulous about saying 'if you please' to you," Jim said. "That meant he could not order you."

"I—don't know why," Var said. Then, seeing the perplexity on the man's face, he repeated it more carefully, forcing his tongue to get it right. "Don't—know."

"Well, it's none of my business," Jim said easily, affecting not to notice Var's clumsiness with the language. "I won't bother with the formality of address; if I tell you to do something, it's not an order, only advice. OK?"

"OK," Var said, able to pronounce these syllables well enough.

"And I'll have to tell you a lot, because guns are dangerous. They can kill just as readily as a sword can, and do it from a distance. You saw the jug."

Var had seen the jug. What could shatter it at fifty feet should be able to hurt a man at the same distance.

Jim put his hand on the metal at his hip. "Here—first lesson. This is a pistol—a small handgun. One of the hundreds we found stored in boxes in a badlands building. We had to use the click-boxes to chart a route in; I don't know how the boss knew about it. I've been running this camp for the past three years, training the men he sends . . . but that's beside the point." He did something and the metal opened. "It's hollow, see. This is the barrel. And this is a bullet. You put the bullet in here, close it up, and when you press this trigger—blam! The bullet explodes, and part of it shoots out here, very fast. It's like a thrown dagger. Watch."

He set up a piece of wood, pointed the hollow end of the pistol at it and shoved his forefinger against the spike he called the trigger. "Noise," he warned, and there was a burst of sound. Smoke shot out of the gun and the wood jumped.

Jim broke open the weapon, that now seemed to be hot, and showed Var the interior. "See—bullet's gone. And if you'll look at the target—that piece of wood—you'll see where it hit." He offered the weapon to Var. "Now you try it."

Var accepted the gun, and after some struggle got a bullet in. But his hand would not fit around the base properly, and his finger was too thick and warped to maneuver the trigger. Jim, perceiving the difficulty as quickly as Var

did, quickly produced a larger gun. This one he managed to fire.

The shock traveled up his arm, but it was slight compared to the tap of a stick in the circle. His bullet plowed into the ground. "We'll show you how to aim," Jim said. "Remember, the gun *is* a weapon, but unlike the instruments you are familiar with, it can kill by accident. Treat it as you would a sword in motion. With respect."

Var learned a great deal in the following days. He had thought there was little more to discover, after Sola had shown him the marvelous social intricacies of generating life. Now he wondered that anything at all remained, as Jim showed him the devastating unsocial devices for terminating life.

The Master came for him. "Now you know part of my secret," he said. "And I will tell you another part. This is an invasion force—and we shall invade the mountain."

"The mountain!"

"The mountain of death, yes. It is not what you have supposed—what all nomads suppose. Not every man who goes there dies. There are people living beneath it—similar to the crazies, but with guns. They hold hostages——" But here he changed his mind. "We must storm that mountain and drive out these men. Only then will the empire be secure."

"I don't understand." Actually, it was a questioning grunt.

"I have held the empire in check for six years, because I feared the power of the underworld. Now I am ready to move against it. I do not say that these are evil men, but they must be displaced. Once the enemy is gone, the empire will expand rapidly, and we shall bring civilization to all the continent."

So the murmurings of discontent had been wrong there too! The Weaponless was *not* stifling the empire—not permanently.

"I have a dangerous assignment for you. I have left you a free agent so that you may choose for yourself. It will require working alone, going into extremely unpleasant places, and telling no one of your mission or your adventures except me. I told Jim you were to be liaison man and scout, but this is dangerous scouting he doesn't know

about. You may die violently, but not in the circle. You may be tortured. You may be trapped in lethal radiation. You may have to violate the code of the circle in order to succeed, for we are dealing with unscrupulous men. The leader of the underworld has only contempt for our mores and our honor."

The Master waited, but Var did not reply.

"You may ask what you want in return. I mean to deal fairly with you."

"After I do this," Var enunciated carefully, "then can I join the empire?"

The Nameless One looked at him, astonished. Then he began to laugh. Var laughed too, not certain what was funny.

CHAPTER SEVEN

The beginning was only a hole in a pit in a cavity in the ground, where water disappeared during storms. But underneath it expanded into a cavern he could almost stand in. Var remained there for a time, motionless, getting his full night vision and absorbing the smells.

He knew in which direction the mountain lay. This sense, like that of smell and his sharp night sight and his ability to run almost doubled over, had remained with him after he left the wild life. He was still quite at home in the wilderness.

He shook off his shoes. He had never been comfortable in them, and for this work his hooflike toes were best.

Some water still seeped down, but the main section of the cave was clear. The base was caked with gravel; the sides were slimy with mosslike fungus. On a hunch abetted by observation, Var took a singlestick and scraped the wall. As the plant life and grime gave way, metal touched metal.

This cave was not completely natural. The Master had suggested that this might be the case. The entire mountain, he had said, was unnatural—though he did not know how it had come about.

The chances of an unnatural cave connecting to an unnatural mountain seemed good.

Var, eye, ear and nose now adjusted to this environment, moved on. His mission was to chart a route into the dread mountain—a route that bypassed the surface defenses, and that men could follow. If he found the route, and kept it secret from the underworlders, the empire could have an almost bloodless victory.

If there were no route, there would be a much worse battle on the surface. Lives depended on his mission—perhaps the life of the Master himself.

The tunnel branched. The pipe going toward the mountain was clogged with rubble; the other was wide and clear. Var knew why: when rainfall was heavy, water coursed this way, removing all obstructions. He would have to follow the water, to be sure of getting anywhere—but he would also have to pay close attention to the weather, lest the water follow *him*. Was it possible to anticipate a storm . . . underground?

The passage widened as it descended. Its walls were almost vertical and metallic; overhead, metal beams now showed regularly. It debouched into an extremely large concourse with a long pit down the center. He peered down, noting how the delta of rubble tipped into that chasm. He did not venture into it himself. The bottom was packed with slick-looking mud, and there were dark motions within that mud: worms, maggots or worse. There had been a time when he had eaten such with gusto, but civilization had affected his appetite.

He tapped the level surface of the upper platform. Under the crusted grime there was tile very like that of a hostel. The footing was sound.

The Master had told him that there were many artifacts in this region remaining from the time before the Blast. The Ancients had made buildings and tunnels and miraculous machines, and some of these remained, though no one knew their function. Certainly Var could not fathom the use of such a large, long compartment with a tiled floor and a pit dividing it completely.

He followed it down, listening to distant rustles and sniffing the stale drifts of air. Though his eyes were fully adapted to the gloom, he could not see clearly for any distance. There was not enough light for any proper human vision, this deep in the bowel.

Soon the platform narrowed, and finally the wall slanted into the pit, and there was nowhere to go but down. The Ancients could not have used this for walking, then, since it went nowhere. They had been, the Master said, like the crazies and like the underworlders, only more so; there was

no fathoming their motives. This passage proved it. To put such astonishing labors into so useless a structure. . . .

He climbed down carefully. The drop was only a few feet, not hazardous in itself. It was the life in that lower muck that he was wary of. Familiar, it might be harmless, as familiar poison-berries were harmless—no one would eat them. Unfamiliar, it was potentially deadly.

But the mud was harder than he had supposed; the gloom had changed its seeming properties. Rising from it were two narrow metal rails, side by side but several feet apart. They were quite firm, refusing to bend or move no matter what pressure he applied, and they extended as far as he could discern along the pit. He found that by balancing on one, he could walk along without touching the mud at all, and that was worthwhile.

He moved. His hoof-toes, softened some by the shoes he had had to wear among men but still sturdy, pounded rapidly on the metal as he got the feel of it, and his balance became sure despite the darkness and the slender support. The pit-tunnel was interminable, and did not go toward the mountain. He hesitated to go too far, lest a rainstorm develop above and send its savage waters down to drown him before he could escape. Then he realized that this tunnel was too large to fill readily, and saw the dusky watermarks on its cold walls: only two or three feet above the level of the rails. He could wade or swim, if it came to that.

Even so, it was pointless to follow this passage indefinitely. It was now curving farther away from the mountain, so could hardly serve the Master's purpose.

He would follow it another five minutes or so, then turn back.

But in one minute he was stopped. The tunnel ended. Rather, something was blocking it. A tremendous metal plug, with spurs and gaps and rungs.

Var tapped it with his stick. The thing was hollow, but firm. It seemed to rest on the rails, humping up somewhat between them so as not to touch the floor.

Could there be a branching or turning beyond this obstacle? Var grabbed hold and hauled himself up the face of the plug, curling his fingers stiffly around what offered.

He was searching to learn whether there were a way through it.

There was. He poked his head into the musty interior, inhaling the stale air. He knocked on the side of the square aperture and it clanged. He could tell the surrounding configuration of metal by the sound and echo. He climbed inside.

The floor here was higher than outside. It was mired in a thick layer of dirt and droppings. This was like a badlands building, with places that could be seats, and other places that could be windows, except that there was only a brief space between the apertures and the blank tunnel wall. And all of it was dark. Eyes useless, ears becoming confused by the confinement of sound, Var finally had to use the crazy flashlight the Master had given him. For there was life here.

Something stirred. Var suppressed a reflexive jump and put the beam of light on it, shielding his eyes somewhat from the intolerable glare. Then he got smart and clapped his hand over the plastic lens, holding in the light so that only red welts glowed through. He aimed, let digits relax, let the beam shove out to spear its prey.

It was a rat—a blotched, small-eyed creature that shied away from the brilliance with a squeal of pain.

This Var knew: rats did not travel alone. Where one could live, a hundred could live. And where rats resided, so did predators. Probably small ones—weasels, mink, mongoose—but possibly numerous. And the rats themselves could be vicious, and sometimes rabid, as he knew from badlands buildings.

He walked quickly down the long, narrow room, seeing a doorway at its end outlined by the finger-modulated beam. He had to move along before too many creatures gathered. Rats did not stay frightened long without reason.

Beyond the door was a kind of chamber and another door. More mysterious construction by the Ancients!

Coming down the hall beyond that was a snake. A large one, several feet long. Not poisonous, he judged—but unfamiliar and possibly mutant. He retreated.

The rats were already massed in the other room. Var strode through them, shining his light where he intended

to step, and they skittered back. But they closed in behind, little teeth showing threateningly. Too aggressive for his comfort. He had stirred up an ugly nest, and they were bold in their own territory.

He scrambled out the window and dropped to the dank floor of the tunnel. His feet sank in the mud; it was softer here, or he had broken through a crust. He turned off the flash, waited a moment to recover sight, and found a rail to follow back down the tunnel.

Some other way would have to be found. It was not that the rats and snakes stopped him—but there were sure to be other animals, and a troop of men would stir them all up. In any event, the direction was wrong.

But he could not escape the angry stir so easily. Something silent came down the tunnel. He felt the moving air and ducked nervously. It was a bat—the first of many.

What did all these creatures feed on? There seemed to be no green plants, only mold and fungus.

And insects. Now he heard them stirring, rising into the foul air from their myriad burrows.

Apprehensively, he flashed his light.

Some were white moths.

Var's heart thudded. There was no way he could be sure of avoiding these deadly stingers here except by standing still—and that had its own dangers. He had to move, and if he brushed into one—well, he would have a couple of hours to reach the surface and seek help before the poison brought him to a full and possibly fatal coma. Certainly fatal if he succumbed to it here in the tunnels, where men would never find him. Even if he received only a minor sting, that weakened him, and then it rained . . . or if the rats and snakes became more bold, and ventured along the rail. . . .

But not all white moths were badlands mutants. These seemed smaller. Maybe they were innocuous.

If these were of the deadly variety, this route was doomed. Men could not use it, however directly it might lead to the mountain. That would make further exploration useless.

Best to know immediately. Var ran along the track until he saw the high platforms. He climbed up and oriented himself, identifying his original point of entry. Then

he ran after a white moth and swooped with his two hands, trapping it. It was his fingers that were awkward, not his wrists or hands.

He held the insect cupped clumsily between his palms, terrified yet determined. For thirty seconds he stood there, controlling his quivering, sweating digits.

The moth fluttered in its prison, but Var felt no sting. He squeezed it gently and it struggled softly.

At last he opened his hands and let the creature go. It was harmless.

Then he rested for five minutes, regaining his equilibrium. He would much rather have stepped into the circle with lame hands against a master sworder, than against a badlands moth like this. But he had made the trial and won. The way was still clear.

He crossed the double-rail pit and mounted to the far platform. There were tunnels leading away in the proper direction. He chided himself for not observing them before. He selected one and ran down it.

And halted. His skin was burning.

There was radiation here. Intense.

He backed off and tried another branch. Even sooner he encountered it. Impassable.

He tried a third. This went farther, but eventually ran into the same wall of radiation. It was as though the mountain were ringed by roentgen. . . .

That left the railed tunnel, going in the other direction. This might circle around the flesh-rotting rays. He had to know.

Var dropped down and ran along the track. He went faster than before, because time had been consumed in the prior explorations, and he had greater confidence in the narrow footing. Probably a man with normal, soft, wide feet could not have stayed on the track so readily. Or have felt its continuing solidity by the tap of nail on metal—an important reassurance, in this gloom.

On and on it went, for miles. He passed another series of platforms, and felt the barest tinge of radiation; just before he stopped on the track, it faded, and he went on. Such a level of the invisible death was not good to stay in, but was harmless for a rapid passage.

The rubble between the tracks became greater, the walls

more ragged, as though some tremendous pressure had pressed and shaken this region. He had seen such collapsed structures during his wild-boy years; now he wondered whether the rubble and the radiation could be connected in any way. But this was idle speculation.

He was very near the mountain now. He came to a third widening of the tunnel and platform—but this one was in very bad condition. Tumbled stone was everywhere, and some radiation. He ran on by, nervous about the durability of this section. A badlands building in such disrepair was prone to collapse on small provocation, and here the falling rock would be devastating.

But the track stopped. It twisted about, unsettling him unexpectedly (he should have paid attention to its changing beat under his toes!), and terminated in a ragged spire, and beyond that the rubble filled in the tunnel until there was no room to pass.

Var went back to the third set of platforms. He crawled up on the mountain-side, avoiding rubble and alert to any sensation in his skin. When he felt the radiation, even so slight as to be harmless, he shied away. The Master had stressed that a route entirely clear must be found, for ordinary men might be more sensitive to the rays than Var, despite their inability to detect it without click-boxes.

Two passages were invisibly sealed off. The third was clear, barely. There were large droppings in it, showing that the animals had already discovered its availability. This in turn suggested that it went somewhere—perhaps to the surface—for the animals would not travel so frequently in and out of a dead end.

It branched—the Ancients must have had trouble making up their minds!—and again he took the fork leading toward the mountain. And again he ran into trouble.

For this was the lair of an animal—a large one. The droppings here were ponderous and fresh—the fruit of a carnivore. Now he smelled its rank body effusions, and now he heard its tread.

But the tunnel was high and clear and he could run swiftly along it. It was narrow enough so that any creature could come at him only from front or back. So he waited for it impelled by curiosity. If it were something that

could be killed to clear the passage for human infiltration of the mountain, he would make the report. He cupped the light and aimed it ahead.

Rats scuttled around a bend, squinted in the glare, and milled in confusion. Then a gross head appeared: frog-like, large-eyed, horny-beaked. The mouth opened tooth-lessly. There was a flash of pink. A rat squealed and bounced up—then was drawn by a pink strand into that orifice. It was an extensive, sticky tongue that did the hauling.

The beam played over one bulging eye, and the creature blinked and twisted aside. It seemed to be a monstrous salamander. As Var stepped back, some fifteen feet of its body came into sight. The skin was flexible, glistening; the legs were squat, the tail was stout.

Var wasn't certain he could kill it with his sticks, but he was sure he could hurt it and drive it back. This was an amphibian mutant. The moist skin and flipper-like extremities suggested that it spent much time in water. And his skin reacted to its presence: the creature was slightly radio-active.

That meant that there was water—probably a flooded tunnel. Water that extended into radiation, and was contaminated by it. And there would be other such mutants, for no creature existed alone. This was not a suitable route for man.

Var turned and ran, not fearing the creature but not caring to stay near it either. It was a rat eater, and probably beneficial to man in that sense. He had no reason to fight it.

That left the other fork of the passage. He turned into it and trotted along, feeling the press of time more acutely. He was hungry, too. He wished he could unroll his tongue and spear something tasty, many feet away, and suck it in. Man didn't have all the advantages.

There was another cave-in, but he was able to scramble through. And on the far side there was light.

Not daylight. The yellow glow of an electric bulb. He had reached the mountain.

The passage was clean here, and wide. Solid boxes were stacked in piles, providing cover. This had to be a store-room.

Near the opening through which he had entered there was food: several chunks of bread, a dish of water.

Poison! his mind screamed. He had avoided such traps many times in the wild state. Anything set out so invitingly and inexplicably was suspect. This would be how the under-worlders kept the rats down.

He had accomplished his mission. He could return and lead the troops here, with their guns. This chamber surely opened into the main areas of the mountain, and there was room here for the men to mass before attacking.

Still—he had better make quite sure, for it would be very bad if by some fluke the route were closed beyond this point. He moved deeper into the room, hiding behind the boxes though there was no one to see him. At the far end he discovered a closed door. He approached it cautiously. He touched the strange knob——

And heard footsteps.

Var started for the tunnel, but realized almost immediately that he could not get through the small aperture unobserved in the time he had. He ducked behind the boxes again as the knob rotated and the door opened. He could wait, and if discovered he could kill the man and be on his way. He hefted his two sticks, afraid to peek around lest he expose himself.

The steps came toward him, oddly light and quick. To check the poison, he realized suddenly. The food would have to be replaced every few hours, or the rats would foul it and ignore it. As the person passed him, Var poked his head over between shielding flaps and looked.

It was a woman.

His grip tightened on the sticks. How could he kill a woman? Only men fought in the circle. Women were not barred from it, specifically; they merely lacked the intelligence and skill required for such activity, and of course their basic function was to support and entertain the men. And if he did kill her—what would he do with the body? A corpse was hard to conceal for long, because it began to smell. It would betray his presence, if not immediately certainly within hours. Far too soon for the nomads to enter secretly.

She was middle-aged, though of smaller build than the similarly advanced woman he had known, Sola. Her hair

was short, brown and curly, but her face retained an elfin quality and she moved with grace. She wore a smock that concealed her figure; had her face and poise not given her away, Var might have mistaken her for a child because of her diminutive stature. Was this what all underworlders were like? Small and old and smocked? No need to worry about the conquest, then.

She glanced at the bread, then beyond—and stopped.

There, in the scant dust, was Var's footprint. The round, callused ball, the substantial, protective, curled-under toe-nails. She might not recognize it as human, but she had to realize that something much larger than a rat had passed.

Var charged her, both sticks lifted. He had no choice now.

She whirled to face him, raising her small hands. Somehow his sticks missed her head . . . and he was wrenched about, half-lifted, stumbling into the wall, twisting, falling.

He caught his footing again and oriented on her. He saw her fling off her smock and stand waiting for him, hands poised, body balanced, expression alert. She wore a brief skirt and briefer halter and was astonishingly feminine in contour for her age. Again—like Sola.

He had seen that wary, competent attitude before. When the Master had captured him in the badlands. When men faced each other in the circle. It was incredible that a woman, one past her prime and hardly larger than a child, should show such readiness. But he had learned to deal with oddities, and to read the portents rapidly and accurately.

He turned again and scrambled into the tunnel.

On the dark side he rolled over and waited with the sticks for her head to poke through the narrow aperture. But she was clever: she did not follow him. He risked one look back through—and saw her standing still, watching.

Quickly he retreated. When he deemed it safe, he began to run, retracing his route. He had a report to make.

CHAPTER EIGHT

The Master listened with complete passivity to the report. Var was afraid he had failed, but did not know quite how, for he *had* found a route into the mountain. "So if she tells the mountain master, they will seal up the passage. But we could reopen it——"

"Not against a flamethrower," the Nameless One said morosely. Then, amazingly, he bent his head into his hands. "Had I known! Had I known! *She,* of all people! I would have gone myself!"

Var stared at him, not comprehending. "You recognize the woman?"

"Sosa."

He waited, but the Master did not clarify the matter. The name meant nothing to Var.

After a long time, the Weaponless spoke: "We shall have to mount a direct frontal attack. Bring Tyl to me."

Var left without replying. Tyl was no friend of his, and Tyl was in his own camp several hundred miles away, and Var did not *have* to follow any empire directive. But he would go for Tyl.

Jim the Gun intercepted him as he departed. "Show him this," he said. "No one else."

And he gave Var a handgun and a box of ammunition. And a written note.

Tyl was impressed by power and therefore fascinated by the gun. In some fashion Var did not follow, but which he suspected was influenced by the note Tyl's wife read, the chief set aside his standing grudge and cultivated Var for his knowledge of firearms.

Var had good memory for any person who had ever threatened his well-being, and he had not at all forgotten his embarrassments of the first meeting with this man. But Tyl was one of those who, though maddening when antipathetic, could be absolutely charming when friendly. As surely as he might have courted a lovely girl, Tyl courted Var.

And by the time Tyl and his vast tribe reached the mountain, he and Var were friends. They entered the circle together many times, but never for terms or blood, and under Tyl's expert guidance Var became far more proficient with the sticks. He saw that he had been a preposterous fool ever to challenge Tyl with this weapon; the man had never had cause to fear him in the circle. A dozen times in practice Tyl disarmed him, each time showing him the mistake he had made and drilling him in the proper countermoves.

Tyl named him a score of names, stickers of the empire, that were his marks to excel, and warned him of the other warriors to be wary of. "You are strong and tough," he said, "and courageous—but you still lack sufficient experience. In a year, two years——"

Var, in those evenings when the tribe settled for the night and went about the processes even a travelling tribe must go about, also had a regular practise against other weapons. The Master had instructed him in the basic techniques, but that was not at all the same as actual combat. The stick had to learn to blunt the sword, thwart the club, and to navigate the staff—or the stick was useless. Here with Tyl's disciplined, combat-ready tribe, Var's stick mastered these things.

More of a warrior than he had been, he returned to the Nameless One's hidden camp near the mountain. Now he understood why Tyl was second in command. The man was honorable and sensible and capable and an expert warrior—and not given to letting minor grudges override his judgment. The feud between them had been a momentary thing that Var had mistaken once for malice. The Master must have known, and shown him the truth by sending him on this mission.

Var was present when the Weaponless conferred with the Two Weapons.

"You have seen the gun," the Master said. "What it can do."

Tyl nodded. The truth was that he had fired it many times and become fairly proficient. He had even brought down a rabbit with it—something Var, with his clumsy grip, could not do.

"The men we face have guns—and worse weapons. They do not honor the code of the circle."

Tyl nodded again. Var knew he was fascinated by the tactical problems inherent in gun-combat.

"For six years I have held the empire in check—for fear of the killers of the underworld. Their guns—when we had none."

Tyl looked surprised, realizing that this was not just a staging area. "The men who travel to the mountain——"

"Do not always die there."

Var did not comprehend the expression that crossed Tyl's face. "Sol of All Weapons——"

"There—alive. Hostage."

"And you——"

"I came from the mountain. I returned."

Now Tyl's mouth fell open. "Sos! Sos the Rope! And the bird——"

"Nameless, weaponless, helpless. Stupid dead. Bound to dismantle the empire."

Tyl looked as though something astonishing and profound and not entirely pleasing had passed between them, more than the information about the mountain. Var could not quite grasp what, though he did recognize the name "Sos" as connected to "Sosa." He suspected that Tyl's most basic loyalty lay with Sol of All Weapons, the former Master of the empire; perhaps the knowledge that that man lived made Tyl excited.

"Now——?" Tyl inquired.

"Now we also have guns."

"The empire——"

"Will expand. Perhaps under Sol, as before. After this conquest of the mountain."

"But these—guns—are not circle weapons," Tyl protested. Var could see how eager he was.

"This is not a circle matter. It is war."

Var was shocked. He knew what war was. The Master had told him many times. War was the cause of the Blast.

The Master glanced at him, fathoming his disturbance.

"I have told you war is evil, that it must never come to our society. It very nearly destroyed the world, once. But we are faced here with a problem that cannot be allowed to stand. The mountain must be reduced. This is the war to end wars."

What the Master said seemed reasonable, but Var knew that something was wrong. There was evil in this project, and not the evil of war itself. For the first time he questioned the wisdom of the Weaponless. But he could not decide what it was that bothered him, so he said nothing.

Tyl did not look comfortable either, but he did not argue. "How are we to accomplish this?"

The Master brought out a sketch he must have made during the months of his encampment here. "This is what the crazies call a contour map. I have made sightings of the mountain from all sides, and the land about it. See— here is our present camp, well beyond its defensive perimeter. Here is the hostel where the suicides stop before making the ascent. Here is the subway tunnel Var explored."

"Subway?" Evidently the word was as new to Tyl as it was to Var.

"The Ancients used it for travelling. Metal vehicles something like crazy tractors, except that they rolled on tracks and moved much faster. The ones on the ground were called 'trains' and the ones below, 'subways.' Var tells me he discovered an actual train down there, too."

Var had told him no such thing. He had only reported on what he found—tunnels, platforms, rails, a plug, a cave-in, radiation, a monster. He had seen nothing like a crazy tractor. Why should the Master lie?

"I had hoped to use such a route to make a surprise foray. But the underworld knows of it now—knows that we know—that the radiation is down. So they will have it booby-trapped. We must make an overland attack."

Tyl looked relieved. "My tribe will take it for you."

The Master smiled. "I do not question the competence of your tribe. But your men are warriors of the circle.

What would they do against guns? Guns fired from cover, from a distance, without warning. And flamethrowers?"

"Flamethrowers?"

"Jets of fire that consume a man in moments."

Tyl nodded, but Var could see that he did not believe such a thing was possible, despite the other wonders they had learned about. Var didn't either. If fire were shot out in a jet, the wind would put it out.

"Do you remember when—someone—told you about white moths whose sting was deadly? About tiny creatures who could overrun armed warriors? Fire that would float on water?"

"I remember," Tyl said, and was sober.

Var did not see what relevance such rhetorical questions had to the problem, since everyone knew about the moths and the swarming shrews of the badlands. Floating fire was ridiculous. But now Tyl seemed to believe in flamethrowers.

"This will be ugly fighting," the Weaponless said. "Men will die outside the circle, never seeing the men who kill them. We are like the shrews—we must swamp a prepared camp, and we shall die in multitudes. But if we persevere, we shall take the mountain despite all the horrors there.

"Speak to your subchiefs. Tell them to seek volunteers—true volunteers, not coerced men—for a battle where half of them will die. They will not be using their natural weapons. Those that enlist will be issued guns and shown how to use them."

Tyl stood up, smiling. "I have longed for the old days. Now they return."

Three thousand men of Tyl's monster tribe put aside their given weapons and took instruction in guns. Day and night, Jim's small tribe spread out over the firing range, each man supervising one warrior at a time. When the gun had been mastered, the trainee was given the pistol or rifle and twenty rounds of ammunition and told to report back to the main camp. And *not to fire it* before the battle.

Var was kept busy relaying messages from the Master to Tyl and the subchiefs. The Weaponless pored over his map of the mountain and made notations for strategy and deployment. "We are shrews," he said mysteriously. "We

must utilize shrew tactics. They know we're here, but they don't know exactly when or how we'll attack. They won't kill their hostages until they're sure they can't be used for bargaining purposes. We shall try to overwhelm them before they realize it. Even so, I do not expect to leave this campaign a happy man."

The only hostage Var knew of was Sol, the prior Master of the empire. Why should his welfare loom so important now? The Master could hardly care for competition again.

They were ready. The men were trained and deployed in a ring entirely around the mountain. Special troops guarded the subway and its connected tunnels, and no strangers were permitted anywhere in the vicinity. Wives and children had no place in this effort; they were removed to a camp of their own a day's walk distant, and married non-volunteers guarded that region.

They were ready. But no attack was launched. Men chafed at the delay, eager to test their new weapons, eager to probe the dread defenses of the underworld. The mountain had a morbid fascination for them. They had guns and believed they could capture any fortress—but to take the mountain would be like conquering death itself!

Then, on the very worse day for such an effort, the Master put the troops in motion. He ignored Tyl's dismay and Var's perplexity. At the height of a blinding thunderstorm, they charged the mountain.

Var and Tyl stood beside the Nameless One, at his direction, each privately wondering what manner of man the leader had become. They watched the proceedings from an elevated and carefully protected blind. It was difficult to see anything in the rain, but they knew what to watch for.

"The lightning will knock out some of their television, temporarily," the Master explained. "It always does. The thunder will mask the noise of our firing. The rain will camouflage our physical advance—and maybe suppress the effect of their flamethrowers. That, plus the masses of men involved, should do it."

The old campaigner was not so confused after all, Var realized. The mountaineers would assume that no attack could occur in rain, and would not be ready.

The Master gave them field glasses—another salvaged device of the Ancients—and briefly demonstrated their use. With these, they were able to see distant sections of the mountain as though they were close. The rain blurred the image some, but the effect was still striking.

Var watched a troop of men, bedraggled in the rain, follow a line toward the first projecting metal beams at the base of the mountain. The mountain was actually a morbid mass of gray, with stunted trees approaching the base and a few weeds sprouting here and there on its surface. Buzzards perched on the ugly projections, looking well fed. Even in the rain they waited—and surely they would feast today!

But there were paths up through the twisted metal, and these had been charted from a distance. The troops were prepared with cleats and hooks, and would pass in minutes an obstruction that might take a naive man half a day to navigate. Already the column he watched was beginning to splay, rushing for cover adjacent to the mountain.

Then the earth rose up and smote them down. Men were hurled through the air, to land broken. Smoke erupted, obscuring the view.

"Mines," the Master said. "I was afraid of that."

"Mines," Tyl repeated, and Var was sure he was marking down one more thing to be well wary of in future.

"They are buried explosives. We have no way to anticipate their location. Probably the weight of a single man is insufficient to trigger them; but when a full column passes . . . " He paused meaningfully. "The area should be safe for other troops now, because the mines have been expended."

The sound of more distant explosions suggested that other regions around the mountain were being made similarly safe. How did he know so much, Var wondered. The Master seemed to spend most of his time reading old tomes, yet it was as though he had traveled the world and plumbed its secrets.

A second wave of men charged through the steaming basin where the mines had exploded. They reached the foot of the mountain, taking cover as they had been drilled to do. But there seemed to be no fire from the defenders. The warriors climbed through and under the twisted

beams, following the pathways they knew. From this distance the column resembled a lashing snake, appearing and disappearing in partial cover. Then men ran out on the first plateau above.

And fire spurted from pipes rising from the ground.

Now Var believed. He fancied he could smell the scorching flesh as men spun about, smoking, and died.

Many died, but already more were coming up. They charged the pipes from the sides, for the fire flicked out in only one direction at a time. They fired bullets into the apertures, and those who retained clubs and staffs battered at the projections and bent them down, and finally the fires died. The rain continued, drenching everything.

"Your men are courageous and skilled," the Master said to Tyl.

Tyl was immune to the compliment. "On a sunny day, none would have survived. I know that now."

Then the return fire began. The thinned troops moved up the mountainside—but they were exposed to the concealed emplacements of the underworld, and the weapons mounted there were more than pistols.

"Machine-guns," the Nameless One said, and flinched. "We cannot storm those. Sound the retreat."

But it was already too late. Few, very few, returned from the mountain.

When they totaled up the losses, known and presumed, they learned that almost a thousand men had perished in that lone engagement. Not one defender had been killed.

"Have we lost?" Var asked hesitantly in the privacy of the Master's command tent. He felt guilty for not finding and keeping properly secret a subterranean route into the mountain. All those brave men might have lived. . . .

"The first battle. Not the campaign. We will guard the territory we have cleared; they can't plant new mines or flamethrowers while we watch. Now we know where their machine-guns are, too. We will lay siege. We will build catapults to bombard those nests. We will drop grenades on them. In time, the victory will be ours."

A warrior approached the entrance. "A paper—with writing," he said. "It was in a metal box that flew into our camp. It's addressed to you."

The Master accepted it. "Your literacy may have turned the course of battle," he said. Flattered, the man left.

Var knew that many of the women practised reading, and some few of the men. Was it worthwhile after all?

The Master opened the paper and studied it. He smiled grimly. "We impressed them! They want to negotiate."

"They will yield without fighting?" Var didn't bother with all the awkward words, but that was his gist.

"Not exactly."

Var looked at him, again not comprehending. The Master read from the paper: "We propose, in the interests of avoiding senseless decimation of manpower and destruction of equipment, to settle the issue by contest of champions. Place: the mesa on top of Mt. Muse, twelve miles south of Helicon. Date: August 6, B118. Your choice of other terms of combat.

"Should our champion prevail, you will desist hostilities and depart this region for ever, and permit no other attack on Helicon. Should your champion prevail we will surrender Helicon to you intact.

"Speak to the television set in the near hostel."

After a pause, the Master asked him: "How would you call it, Var?"

Var didn't know how to respond, so he didn't.

"Sound sensible to you? You think our champion could defeat theirs in single combat?"

Var had no doubt of the Master's ability to defeat any man the underworld could send against him, particularly if he specified weaponless combat. He nodded.

The Master drew out his map. "Here is the mountain he names. See how the contours crowd together?"

Var nodded again. But he realized that this was only part of the story.

"That means it is very steep. When I surveyed it, I saw that I could not climb it. Not rapidly, anyway. I am too heavy, too clumsy in that fashion. And there are boulders perched on the top."

Var visualized rocks crashing down, pushed by a fast climber on to the head of a slow climber. The Nameless One was matchless in combat—but rolled boulders could prevent him from ever reaching it. Perhaps the site had

been selected to prevent him from participating, forcing the choice of a lesser man.

"Then—some other? We have many good warriors." Var said "we" though he knew he was not yet a part of the empire.

"It would be a test of climbing as well as fighting. And we have only two days to prepare, for today is August 4, by the underworld calendar."

"Tomorrow morning a climbing tournament!" Var said, knowing his speech had become incomprehensible in his excitement, but that the other would get the gist.

The Weaponless smiled tiredly. "You don't suspect betrayal?"

He hadn't, until then. But he realized the nomads could still take the mountain by force, just as originally planned, if the mountain master did not honor the decision of the champions. So it seemed worthwhile.

The Weaponless fathomed his thinking. "All right. Tell Tyl to select fifty top warriors for a climbing tournament. Tonight I talk to the mountain; tomorrow we practise on Mt. Muse."

But he still did not look optimistic.

At dawn on the day of the tournament, Var stood at the base of Mt. Muse, waiting for sufficient light to climb. Rather, for sufficient light for others to climb, for their eyes were less sensitive in the dark than his own. He had known he would be here the moment the Master agreed to hold the tournament. Var, with his horny hands and hooflike feet, and his years in the wilderness, was the most agile climber in the camp, and he had chosen to compete. Since he was not a member of the Master's empire, no one could tell him no.

Tyl had seen him, though, and smiled, and said nothing. And by noon Var was winner of the tournament.

"But he is yet a novice in the circle!" the Master protested, astonished by this development.

Tyl smiled. "Here are the next three winners of the climb. Test him against them."

The Weaponless, worried, agreed. So Var, tired from his morning effort but ready, faced the man who had

reached the top ten minutes after he had. Had it been the contest of champions, on the mesa of Muse, Var would have had ample time to cripple the man by dropping rocks on him. That was the point of the climbing exercise: the best warrior in the empire would lose if he were too much slower than the one the mountain master sent. But when it came to the actual battle, the champion had to be more skilled than the other, too.

The second finisher was a staffer, nimble and lanky, who had used his weapon cleverly to assist his climbing. Var entered the circle, running through in his mind the advice the Master and Tyl had given him in the past: stick against staff. The sticks were faster, the staff stronger. The sticks were aggressive, the staff more passive. The sticks could launch a dual offence . . . but it was hard to penetrate a good staff defense. And if the sticks did not break through early, eventually the staff would discover an opportunity and score.

The staffer was as well aware of the factors as was Var, and more experienced. His advantage was time, and he obviously meant to use it. He blocked conservatively, making no mistakes, challenging Var to come to him.

Var obliged. He rapped at the weapon, not the man, creating a diversion, while he searched for an opening. He feinted at the head, at the feet, at the knuckles holding the staff, until the man became a trifle slow in his responses, bored with the harassment.

Then Var directed fierce blows at head and body simultaneously. The staff spun to counter both—but not quite rapidly enough, because of the prior lulling byplay. The head shot missed, but the body attack was successful. One rib at least had been fractured.

As the man winced and brought his weapon over to catch Var's exposed arm, Tyle stepped up to the circle. "First blood!" he said. "Withdraw."

So Var had won. The advantage he had achieved would normally have been sufficient to bring him eventual victory, and that was all he had needed to demonstrate. There was no point in wearing himself out. His victory on that basis would only militate against him in the real contest tomorrow.

The next man was a dagger. Var quailed inwardly when

he saw that, for the knives were as swift as the sticks, and their contact more deadly. The sword and the club were impressive weapons; but the dagger, competently wielded, was more devastating in the confines of the circle.

But—the knives had to be properly oriented. A thrust with the flat of the blade was useless in many instances. And the daggers were not apt instruments for blocking. Though more effective offensively, they were less efficient overall than the dual-purpose sticks.

Var had no choice. He had to fence with the blades, paying first attention to his defense. If he could succeed in making an opening for himself without sacrificing personal protection, he could score. If not——

Now the dagger feinted at him, and Var had to react conservatively, just as the staffer had against him. And the result would be the same, with him the victim, unless he could break the pattern.

But the dagger was tired. He was an older man, as old as the Master. No doubt experience had made him a skilled climber, but his age had made him pay for the effort. Not much, not noticeably—except that Var did have a slight and increasing advantage in speed.

When he realized that, he knew he had won. With renewed confidence he beat back the blade thrusts, using his greater vigor to intercept every stroke and jar the hand that made it. Gradually he forced the man back, intercepting the thrust sooner, and finally the hard-pressed dagger made an error, was bruised on the wrist, and ruled the loser.

The third man was another sticker. "I am Hul," he said.

Var, fatigued from two circle encounters as well as the morning climb, knew then that he had lost his bid to be the empire's champion. For the sticker was one of the men Tyl had warned him about—one of the top fighters. Stick against stick, Var could have no advantage except superior skill—and against this man he didn't have that.

Hul stood just outside the circle. "Var the Stick," he said, his voice resonant. "I have studied you and assessed you, and I can take you in the circle. Perhaps not next year— but today, yes. But you would bruise me before you went down, for you are strong and determined. This would make me less able tomorrow on the mesa, and prejudice

the case of the empire. Will you yield your place to me without combat?"

The request was reasonable. Hul was fresh, for he was young and strong too, and he had rested while Var fought. And if he had been tired he still could have won, for he was a master sticker. Tyl did not make errors about such rankings, for it was Tyl's business to rank the leading weapons of all the empire. And—Var was not of the empire, so was answerable to no one but himself. Otherwise no subsidiary contest would have been necessary; the Master or Tyl could have selected the warrior with the best overall prospects and settled it. Var could step down with honor, having proven himself twice and now acting for the best interest of the empire.

But Var was not reasonable. The notion of losing the privilege of fighting for the Master, of being his champion —he thought he had won this in the climb and held it in the circle. Such a late sacrifice filled him with fury. "No!" he cried. It came out a growl. He would not give it up; it would have to be taken from him.

Unperturbed, Hul turned to Tyl. "Then, if the Weaponless permits, I shall yield to Var. One of us must conserve his strength; if we fight, neither will. He needs the respite; he *has* the spirit."

Tyl nodded, granting the Master's acquiescence. Var was to reflect on that act of Hul's many times in the years following, and to learn something more each time he did so.

CHAPTER NINE

Dawn again. This time he knew the best route—one that could cut as much as half an hour from his prior time. And he did not have to wait on any other man. But it was strenuous and dangerous, and he did not dare attempt it without suitable light. Natural light—if he used a flashlight, the other climber might spot him by it.

On the far side of Muse the mountain's champion would be ascending similarly. He would be naked, except perhaps for shoes, for the Master had stipulated that. Var was naked now. This was to ensure that no gun or other illicit weapon could be carried along secretly. The weapon the Master had specified was any of the recognized circle instruments: club, staff, stick, sword, dagger or star. Not rope or net or whip. Men of both groups would be watching from the fringes to see that neither climber was cheating on the terms in any other way.

Of course the fight on the mesa would not be very clear, because the watchers would be far below. But only the victor would descend alive, so there could be no doubt about that.

It was light enough. Var moved out, sticks anchored to his waist by a minimum harness. The chill of the morning pricked his skin. He was eager for the warming exercise—and, privately, to get away from the too-curious stares of the men at his exposed body. He knew he was not pretty.

He climbed. At first it was easy, for the slope was gentle and he avoided the crevices that might have trapped a foot in the dark. Then he struck the boulder-strewn wastes. This was where he gained time over his prior ascent, because of the superior route he had worked out. One man,

the day before, had led him at this point, and he had been careful to note the particular path that man had happened on. He knew the mountain's champion would have to be a remarkable athlete to better Var's own time, for the other man would not have had this practice.

Not recently, anyway. Of course he could have climbed Muse every day before the nomad siege began. That might be why such terms had been specified. Still, Var knew he was as fast as anyone, here.

And he was sure that the other side was no better than his own. He had checked that out from the summit. There was nothing in the agreement to stop him from circling to that side in order to ascend more rapidly or intercept the other man. And he had verified that there was no secret, Ancient-built tunnel there, either. So the terms were fair.

The last portion was the most difficult. Here the slope became so steep as to seem almost vertical. It wasn't; that was an illusion of perspective. But he did not peer down as he mounted it.

There were steplike terraces and crevices, ranging from mere lines in the wall to platforms several feet wide. Here Var's stubby, callused fingers and hard bare toes were important assets, for he could find lodging on a minimum basis. Up, across, and around he went, traversing the open face of the mountain, keeping a nervous eye for falling rocks. If the other champion *had* somehow reached the summit first——

But Var triumphed. No boulders were loosed on him, and when he poked his head over the brim, alert for attack, he found it bare.

Now it would be up to his ability with the sticks.

He trotted to the far side of the little mesa. The platform was only about ten paces in diameter—twice that of the battle circle, but hardly seeming so because of the frightening drop-off all around. He peered over.

The underworld's warrior was climbing. Var observed his bare back, his round head, his moving limbs, but was unable to make out much detail. He judged the man to be about five minutes from the summit. That was a kind of relief, for it meant that Var's selection as the empire champion had been valid. The slower warriors would have reached the top too late. Particularly Hul. What good

would Hul's skill and courage have done him, if his head was bashed in while he still climbed?

Var glanced at the available stones. Some were small, suitable for throwing. Some were good for accurate dropping. A few were large enough for rolling—and woe betide what lay in their crushing paths!

He picked up a throwing rock, nestling it in his palm. His grip was awkward, but he could throw well enough. He peered down at the warrior. The man was clinging to the rim of the shelf, inching from one narrow step to another. He was helpless; if he tried to dodge a falling object, he would fall himself. And he wasn't even looking up. It was as though the notion of such a premature attack had not occurred to him.

Var set the stone down, disgusted with himself for being tempted, and recrossed the mesa. The Master had invariably stressed the importance of honor outside the circle, until this present adventure. Within the circle there was no law at all except death and victory; outside there was no victory without honor. This plateau was the effective circle. The men of the underworld might not practise honor in the fashion of the nomads, but this one circumscribed case was plainly an exception. He had to let the warrior enter before making any hostile move.

Var was sitting crosslegged at his own side of the mesa as the other warrior clambered to the level section. The first thing Var saw was the sticks, slung from a neck loop. He was matched against his own weapon!

The second thing he saw was that the other warrior was small—in fact, diminutive to the point of dwarfism. His head would barely reach Var's shoulder—and Var, though large, was no giant.

The third thing he did not see. The naked warrior was either castrate——

Or female.

"I am ready," the mountain champion said, grasping the two sticks and dropping the harness over the edge.

It was a girl, definitely. Her voice was high, sweet. She had thick black hair cut short beneath the ears, delicate facial features, a lithe slender body, and tightly bound sandals on her feet. She could not be more than nine years old. Half his own age, by the Master's reckoning.

There could be no mistake. She was here, she was armed, she was not shy or surprised. The underworld had sent a child to represent its interests.

Why? Surely they were not depending on some chivalrous dispensation to give the little girl the technical victory? Not when the fate of mountain and empire was at stake. Not when a thousand men had died already in the larger combat. Yet if they *wanted* to lose, it had hardly been necessary to make such an elaborate arrangement, or to sacrifice a child.

Var got up and disposed of his own harness, mainly to have something to do while he tried to think. It occurred to him that he should be embarrassed to be naked in the presence of a girl—but his social conditioning dated only from his contact with civilization, and was not universally deep. The codes of honor were more immediate than personal modesty. And this was not a woman but a child. Except for her peeking cleft, she could be a young boy. Her hair was no longer, her chest no more developed.

He thought irrelevantly of Sola.

He came to meet the child cautiously, doubting that she could wield the full-sized sticks adequately.

Her slender arms moved rapidly. Her two sticks countered his own with expertise. She did know what she was doing.

So they fought. Var had size and strength, but the child had speed and skill. The match, astonishingly, was even.

Gradually Var realized that this outré situation was not at all a game. He had been prepared to battle a vicious man to the death, and had trouble coping with a female child. Yet if he did not defeat her (he could not, now, bring himself to think "kill"), he would be defeated himself—and the Master's cause would be lost.

Better to do it quickly. He attacked with fury, using his brute strength to beat the girl back toward the brink. She stepped back, and back again, but could not do so indefinitely. Stick met stick, no blow landing on flesh directly— but Var applied pressure as he had done with dagger the day before, and improved his position.

She was two steps from the edge, one. Then she spun about without seeming to look, knocked one of his sticks

up, ducked under it, scooted past him, and caught his wrist with a backhand swing that completely surprised him.

Var watched incredulously as one of his sticks flew from his numbed hand, to rattle down the mountainside. The maneuver had been so swiftly and neatly executed that he had not had the chance to defend against it. Now, half-disarmed, he was virtually lost. One stick could not prevail against two.

His inexperience in the circle had after all cost him the match. Hul would not have been caught so simply, and certainly not Tyl. Yet who would have expected such skill from a mere child?

Var waited for the attack that had to come. He was doomed, but he would not give up. Perhaps a lunge would catch her unaware in turn, or maybe he could throw them both off the mesa, making the battle a tie in mutual death.

She looked at him a moment. Then, casually, she tossed one of her own sticks after his—over the brink.

Dumbfounded, Var saw it clatter out of play. She could have tapped him on the skull in that moment without opposition, but she kept her distance. "You——"

"So you owe me one," she said. "Fair fight." And she came at him with the single stick.

Var had to fight, but he was shaken. She had disarmed herself to make the match even again. When she could have had easy victory. He had never imagined such a thing in the circle.

There was no doubt that she meant business, however. She pressed him hard with her half-weapon, and scored repeatedly on his unarmed side. It was a strange, off-balance contest, requiring unusual contortions and reflexes to compensate for the missing stick, and the finesse of the dual weapons was largely gone.

Thus, clumsily, they fought. And Var, because the reduction of finesse brought her skill closer to his own level without correspondingly upgrading her strength, gradually gained the initiative. But he pursued it with restraint, for he did not need a second such lesson as the one that had cost him one stick. The child was most dangerous when she seemed most beleaguered.

And—he still wasn't certain what her sacrifice of her

own stick meant. Surely she could not have been so confident of victory that she disarmed herself for the joy of enhanced competition! And surely she could not desire to *lose*. . . .

Var had not survived his childhood in the badlands without being alert to the dangers of the unknown. Not all unknowns were physical.

She was tiring, and he slacked off some more, supercautious. The height of the sun showed they had been at it for some three hours, and now the afternoon was passing.

But how would it end, with their life-and-death battle reduced to mere sparring. Only one of them could descend the mountainside. Only one team could prevail. Delay could not change that harsh reality.

If the contest did not end soon, the victor would not have enough time remaining before dusk to make a safe descent. Mt. Muse was challenging at any time, and seemed impossible in the dark.

It did not end soon. The battle had become a mockery, for neither person was really trying to win. Not immediately, anyway. Both were holding back, conserving strength, waiting for some more crucial move by the other—that did not come. Stick still beat against stick; but the force was perfunctory, the motions routine.

Dusk did come. The girl stepped back, dropping her weapon. "We shouldn't fight at night," she said.

Var lowered his own weapon, agreeing, but alert for betrayal.

She walked to the edge, leaving her stick behind. "Don't look," she said. She squatted.

Var realized that she had to urinate. But if he turned his back she could run up behind him, push——

Still, if he could not trust her during this period of truce, he had had no business agreeing to it. And there had been that matter of the extra stick. Her codes were different than his, but they seemed consistent.

He faced outward and relieved his own bladder into the gloom below.

Their toilets done, the two returned to the center of the plateau. Darkness filled the landscape like a great ocean, but their island remained clear. And lonely.

"I'm hungry," she said.

So was he. But there was nothing to eat. All concerned had assumed that the battle would be of short duration, so no provision for a prolonged stay had been made. Perhaps this had been intentional: if the champions did not fight with sufficient vigor, thirst and hunger would prompt them.

"You don't talk much, do you," she said.

"I don't talk well," Var explained. The mangled syllables conveyed the message more clearly than the language did.

Oddly, she smiled, a flash of white in shadow. "My father doesn't talk at all. He got hurt in the throat, years ago. Before I can remember. But I understand him well enough."

Var just nodded.

"Why don't you take that side, and I'll take this side, and we'll sleep," she said, gesturing. "Tomorrow we'll finish this."

He agreed. He took his stick and skuffed it across the center of the plateau, making a line that divided the area in halves. He lay down in his territory.

The girl sat up for a while, looking very small. "What's your name?"

"Var."

"Growr?"

"Var."

"I don't see any bad scar on your throat. Why can't you talk?"

Var tried to figure out a simple way to answer that, but failed.

"What's it like, outside?" she asked.

He realized that he did not need to reply sensibly to her questions. She was more interested in talking than in listening.

"It's cold," she said.

Var hadn't thought about it, but she was right. A hard chill was settling on the mesa, and they were both naked and without sleeping bags. He could endure it, of course; he had slept exposed many times in youth. But she was smaller than he, and thinner, and her skin was soft.

In fact, the cold would be more than an inconvenience to her. She could die from exposure. Already her hunched hairless torso was shaking so violently he felt the tremors in the ground.

Var sat up. "That favour I owe you, for the stick——" he called.

Her head turned toward him. He could see the motion, but nothing else in the fading light. "I don't understand."

"For the stick—my return favor." He tried to enunciate clearly.

"Stick," she said. "Favor." She was beginning to pick up his clumsy words, but not his meaning. Her teeth chattered as she spoke.

"The warmth of my body, tonight."

"Warm? Night?" She remained perplexed.

Var got up abruptly and crossed over to her. He lay down on his side, took hold of her, and pulled her to him. "Sleep—warm," he said as clearly as he could.

For a moment her body was tense, and her hands flew to his neck in a gesture he recognized from demonstrations the Nameless One had made. *She knew weaponless combat!* Then she relaxed.

"Oh—you mean to share warmth! Oh, thank you, Var!" And she turned about, curled up, and lay with her shivering back nestled against his front, his arms and legs falling about her. His chin, sprouting its sparse beard, came to nestle in her fluffy hair. His forearm settled on her folded thigh, his hand clasped her knee to gain the purchase necessary to keep them close together.

Var remembered the first time he had held a woman, not so many months before. But of course this was not the same. Sola had been buxom and hot, while this child was bony and cold. And the relationship was entirely different. Yet he found this chaste camaraderie against the cold to be as meaningful as that prior sexual connection. To stand even on the favors—that was part of the circle code, as he understood it, and there was no shame in it.

Yet in the morning they would do battle again.

"Who are you?" he asked now. For once the words came out succinctly.

"Soli. My father is Sol of All Weapons."

Sol of All Weapons! The former master of the empire, and the man who had built it up from nothing. No wonder she was so proficient!

Then a terrible thought struck him. "Your mother—who is your mother?"

"Oh, my mother knows even more about fighting than Sol does—but she does it without weapons. She's very small—hardly bigger than I am, and I'm not full grown—but any man who comes at her lands on his head!" She tittered. "It's funny."

Relief, until something else occurred to him. "She—your mother—brown curly hair, very good figure, smock—"

"Yes, that's her! But how could you know? She's never been out of the underworld—not since I've been there."

Once again Var found himself at a loss to explain. Certainly he did not want to tell her he had tried to kill her mother.

"Of course Sosa isn't my natural mother," Soli remarked. "I was born outside. My father brought me in, when I was small."

Var's earlier shock returned. "You're—you're Sola's dead daughter?"

"Well, we're not really dead in the underworld. We just let the nomads think that, because—I don't know exactly why. Sol was married to Sola outside, though, and I'm their child. They say Sola married the Nameless One, after that."

"Yes. But she kept her name."

"Sosa kept her name, too. That's funny."

But Var was remembering Sola's charge to him: *"Kill the man who harms my child."*

Var the Stick was that man, for he was pledged to save the empire by killing the mountain's champion.

CHAPTER TEN

Var woke several times in the night, beset by the chill of this height. A wind came up, wringing the precious warmth from his back. Only in front, where he touched Soli, was he warm. He could have survived alone—but it was better this way.

Every so often the girl stirred—but when her limbs stretched out and met the cold, they contracted again quickly. Even so, her hands were icy. Had she slept by herself she would hardly have been able to wield a stick in the morning. Var put his coarse hand over her fine one, shielding it.

Dawn finally came. They stood up shivering and jumped vigorously to restore circulation, and attended to natural calls again, but it was some time before they both felt better. Fog shrouded the plateau, making the drop-off unreal, the sky dismal.

"What's that?" Soli inquired, pointing.

Once more, Var was at a loss to answer. He knew what it was, but not what women called it.

"My father Sol doesn't have one," she said.

Var knew she was mistaken, for had that been the case, she herself would never have been born.

"I'm hungry," she said. "And thirsty too."

So was Var—but they were no closer to a solution to that problem than they had been the night before. They had to fight. The winner would descend and feast as royally as he or she wished. The other would not need food again, ever. He looked at the two singlesticks lying across the centerline. A pair—but one his, the other hers.

She saw his glance. "Do we have to fight?"

Var never seemed to be able to answer her questions. On the one hand he represented the empire; on the other, he had his oath to Sola to uphold. He shrugged.

"It's foggy," she said wistfully. "Nobody can see us."

Meaning that they should not fight without witnesses? Well, it would do for an excuse. The mist showed no sign of dissipating, and no sound rose from its depths. The world was a whiteness, as was their contest.

"Why don't we go down and get some food?" she asked. "And come back before they see us."

The simplicity and directness of her mind were astonishing! Yet—why not? He was glad to have a pretext to postpone hostilities, since he could not see his way clear either to winning or losing.

"Truce—until the fog lifts?" he asked.

"Truce—until the fog lifts. That time I understood you very well."

And Var was pleased.

They descended on Var's side of the mountain, after retrieving the stick harnesses. The third and fourth sticks themselves had bounced and rolled and been lost entirely, but the harnesses had stayed where they fell. Soli had feared that the underworld had ways to spot anyone who traversed her own slope of Mt. Muse. "Television pickups—can't tell where they're hidden."

"You mean sets are just sitting around outside?" Var knew what television was; he had seen the strange silent pictures on the boxes in hostels.

"Sets—outside," she repeated, interpreting. "No, silly. Pickups—little boxes like eyes, set into stones and things, operated by remote control."

Var let the subject drop. He had never seen a stone with an eye in it, but there had been stranger things in the badlands.

The fog was even thicker at the base. They held hands and sneaked up to the Master's camp. Then Var hesitated. "They'll know me," he whispered.

"Oh." She was taken aback. "Could I go in, then?"

"You don't know the layout."

"I'm *hungry*!" she wailed.

"Sh." He jerked her back out of auditory range. A warrior sentry could come on them at any time.

"Tell me the layout," she whispered desperately. "I'll go in and steal some food for us."

"Stealing isn't honest!"

"It's all right in war. From an enemy camp."

"But that's *my* camp!"

"Oh." She thought a moment. "I could still go. And ask for some. They don't know me."

"Without any clothes?"

"But I'm *hungry*!"

Var was getting disgusted, and didn't answer. His own hunger became intense.

She began to cry.

"Here," Var said, feeling painfully guilty. "The hostel has clothes."

They ran to the hostel, one mile. Before Var could protest, Soli handed him her harness and stick and walked inside. She emerged a few minutes later wearing a junior smock and a hair ribbon and new sandals, looking clean and fresh.

"You're lucky no one was there!" Var said, exasperated.

"Someone *was* there. Somebody's wife, waiting to meet her warrior. I guess they're keeping the women out of your main camp. She jumped a mile when I walked in. I told her I was lost, and she helped me."

So neatly accomplished! He would never have thought of that, or had the nerve to do it. Was she bold, or naive?

"Here," she said. She handed him a bundle of clothing.

Dressed, they reappraised the main camp. It occurred to Var that there should have been food at the hostel, but then he remembered that the nomads cleaned it out regularly. It took a lot of food to feed an armed camp, and the hostel food was superior to the empire mess. Otherwise they might have solved their problem readily. Their *food* problem.

"I'll have to go to the main tent," she said. Var agreed, hunger making him urgent, now that their nakedness had been abated. "I'll pretend I'm somebody's daughter, and that I'm bringing food out to my family."

Var was fearful of this audacity, but could offer nothing better. "Be careful," he said.

He lurked in the forest near the tent, not daring to

move for fear she would not be able to find him again. She disappeared into the mist.

Then he remembered what her motel-comment should have jogged into his head before: the entire camp was not only masculine, it was on a recognition-only basis. No stranger could pass the guards—particularly not a female child.

And it was too late to stop her.

Soli moved toward the huge tent, fascinated by its tenuous configuration though her heart beat nervously. She would have felt more confident with a pair of sticks, but had left them with Var because children—especially girl-children—did not carry weapons here.

A guard stood at the tent entrance. She tried to brush past him as if she belonged, but his staff came down to bar her immediately. "Who are you?" he demanded.

She knew better than to give her real name. Hastily she invented one: "I'm Sami. My father is tired. I have to fetch some food for——"

"No Sam in this camp, girl. I'd know a strange name like that, sure. What game are you playing?"

"Sam the Sword. He just arrived. He——"

"You're lying, child. No warrior brings his family into *this* camp. I'm taking you to the Master." He nudged her with the staff.

No one else was in sight at the moment. Soli vaulted the pole, shot spoked fingers at his eyeballs, and when his head jerked back in the warrior's reflex she sliced him across the throat with the rigid side of her hand. She clipped him again as he gasped for breath, and he collapsed silently.

He was too heavy for her to move, so she left him there and stepped inside, straightening her rumpled smock and retying her hair. She could still get the food if she acted quickly enough.

But the morning mess was over and she did not dare pester the cook directly.

"Kol has been attacked!" someone shouted, back at the entrance. "Search the grounds!"

Oh-oh. She hadn't gotten out in time. But her hunger

still drove her. She would have to make up for her vulnerability by sheer audacity, as Sosa put it. Sosa knew how to make the best of bad situations.

She retreated to just shy of the entrance, knowing what must happen there.

Warriors rushed up, hauled the unconscious Kol to his feet, exclaimed. "Didn't see it happen." "Clubbed in the throat." "Spread a net—he can't have gotten far."

Then a huge man came. Soli recognized him at once: the Nameless One, master of the enemy empire. He moved like a rolling machine, shaking the ground with the force of his tread, and he was ugly. His voice was almost as bad as Var's:

"That was a weaponless attack. The mountain has sent a spy."

Soli didn't wait for more. She ran out of the tent and threw herself at the monster, arms outstretched.

Surprised, he caught her by the shoulders and lifted her high, his strength appalling. "What have we here?"

"Sir!" she cried. "Help me! A man is chasing me!"

"A child!" he said. "A girl-child. What family?"

"No family. I'm an orphan. I came here for food———"

The Master set her down, but one hand gripped her thin shoulder with vicelike power. "The hand that struck Kol's neck would have been about the size of your hand, child. I saw the mark. You are a stranger, and I know the ways of the mountain. You———"

She reacted even before she fully comprehended his import. Her pointed knuckles rammed into his cloak, aiming for the solar plexus as she twisted away.

It was like hitting a wall. His belly was made of steel.

"Try again, little spy," he said, laughing.

She tried again. Her knee came up to ram hard into his crotch, and one hand struck at his neck.

The Nameless One just stood there chuckling. His grip on her shoulder never loosened. With his free hand he tore open his own cloak.

His torso was a grotesque mass of muscle that did not flex properly with his breathing. His neck was solid gristle.

"Child, I know your leader's tricks. What are you doing here? Our contest was supposed to be settled by combat of champions on the plateau."

"Sir, I—I thought he was attacking me. He moved his shaft——" She searched for a suitable story. "I'm from Tribe Pan." That was Sosa's tribe, before she came to the mountain, that trained its women in weaponless combat. "I ran away. All I wanted was food."

"Tribe Pan." He pondered. Something strangely soft crossed his brutal face. "Come with me." He let go of her and marched out of the crowd.

No other warrior spoke. She knew better than to attempt any break now. Docilely, she followed the Weaponless.

He entered a large private tent. There was food there; her empty stomach yearned to its aroma.

"You are hungry—eat," he said, setting the bowl of porridge before her, and a cup of milk.

Eagerly she reached for both—then fathomed the trap Nomad table manners differed from underworld practice. Her every mannerism would betray her origin. In fact, she wasn't sure the nomads used utensils at all.

She plunged one fist into the porridge and brought up a dripping gob. She smeared this into her mouth, wincing at its heat. She ignored the milk.

The Nameless One did not comment.

"I'm thirsty," she said after a bit.

Wordlessly he brought her a winebag.

She put the nozzle to her mouth and sucked. She gagged. It was some bitter, bubbling concoction. "That isn't water!" she cried, her anguish real.

"At Pan—they have neither hostels nor home-brew?" he inquired.

Then she realized that she had overdone it. Most nomads *would* know the civilized mode of eating, for the hostels had plates and forks and spoons and cups. And the truly uncivilized tribes must drink—brew.

Soli began to cry, sensing beneath this brute visage a gentle personality. It was her only recourse.

He brought her water.

"It doesn't make sense," he said as she drank. "Bob would not send an unversed child into the enemy heartland. That would be stupid—particularly at this time."

Soli wondered how he had learned her chief's name. Oh —they had communicated, to arrange the fight on Muse plateau.

"Yet no ordinary child would know weaponless combat," he continued.

She realized that somehow her very mistakes had helped put him off. "Can I take some back to my friend?" she asked, remembering Var.

The Nameless One looked as though he were about to ask a question, then exploded into laughter. "Take all you can carry, you gamin! May your friend feast for many days, and emerge from his orgy a happier man than I!"

"I really do have a friend," she said, nettled at his tone. She realized that he was mocking her, supposing that she wanted it all for herself.

He brought a bag and tossed assorted solids into it, as well as two wineskins. "Take this—and get out of my camp, child. Far out. Go back to Pan—they produce good women, even the barren ones. *Especially* those. We're at war here, and it isn't safe for you, even with your defensive skills."

She slung the heavy sack over her shoulder and went to the exit.

"Girl!" he called suddenly, and she jumped, afraid he had seen through her after all. Bob, the master of Helicon, was like that; he would toy with a person, seeming to agree, then take him down unexpectedly and savagely. "If you ever grow tired of wandering, seek me out again. I would take you for my daughter."

She understood with relief that this was a fundamental compliment. And she liked this enormous, terrible man. "Thank you," she said. "Maybe some day you'll meet my real father. I think you would like each other."

"You were not an orphan long, then," he murmured, chuckling again. He was horribly intelligent under that muscle. "Who is your father?"

Suddenly she remembered that the two men *had* met— for the Nameless One had taken the empire and her true mother from her father. She dared not give Sol's name now, for the men had to be mortal enemies.

"Thank you," she said quickly, pretending not to have heard him. "Good-bye, sir." And she ducked out of the tent.

He let her go. No hue and cry followed, and no secret tracker either.

CHAPTER ELEVEN

Var's body felt weak as he saw Soli come out of the thinning mist, alone. No one was following her; he let her pass him, and waited, just to be sure.

Yet he had heard the outcry and seen the men rushing to the main tent. Its entrance was hidden from him in the fog, but he had thought he heard her voice, and the Master's. Something had happened, and he had been powerless to act or even to know. He had had to wait, clasping and unclasping his rough fingers about the two sticks—his and hers—nervously. If she were prisoner, what would happen next?

She circled back silently, searching for him. Somehow she had talked her way out of it—if he had not imagined the whole thing, converting other voices to those he knew. "Here," he whispered. She ran at him and shoved a heavy bag into his hands. Together they hurried away from the camp. He knew no one would trace them in this fog, and the terrain was too rough for their traces to show later.

At the base of Muse they paused while he fished in the sack for the food he smelled. He found a wineskin and gulped greedily, squirting it into his mouth. It was good, sturdy nomad beer—the kind of beverage the crazies never provided. Then he got hold of a loaf of dark bread, and gnawed on it as they climbed.

The edge of his hunger assuaged, Var worried about the fog. If it let up before they reached the top, their secret would be out. Then what would they do?

But it held. With mutual relief they flopped on the mesa, panting. Then they emptied the bag on the ground and feasted.

There was bread, of course. There was roasted meat. There were baked potatoes. There were apples and nuts and even some crazy chocolate. One wineskin held milk, the other the beer.

"How," Var demanded around a mouthful, "did you get all this?"

Soli, not really hungry because of the porridge she had already had, experimented again with the beer. She had never had any before today, and it intrigued her by its very foulness. "I asked the Nameless One for it."

Var choked, spewing potato crumbs out wastefully. "How—why——?"

She gulped down another abrasive mouthful of beer, repressing its determined urge to come up again, and she told him the story. "And I wish they weren't enemies," she finished. "Sol and the Nameless One—they would like each other, otherwise. Your Master is sort of nice, even though he's terrible."

"Yes," Var murmured, thinking of his own intimate five-year experience with the man. "But they aren't really enemies. The Master told me once. They were friends, but they had to fight for some reason. Sol gave the Weaponless his wife, with his bracelet and all. Because she didn't want to die, and she didn't love Sol anyway."

She looked confused through most of that speech, having to puzzle out his inflections, but she reacted immediately to the last of it. "She did too love him!" she flared. "She was my mother!"

He backed away from that aspect, disturbed. "She's a good woman," he said after a moment. That seemed to mollify Soli, though he was thinking of the journey he had made with Sola. He could see the resemblance, now, between mother and daughter. But—could Sola have loved *anyone*, to have done what she did? Jumping from man to man, and putting her body to secret service for Var himself? Surely the Master knew—she had *said* he knew—yet he allowed it. How could such a thing be explained?

And once more he came up against the problem of his oath to Sola: to kill the man who harmed her child. What sort of a woman Sola was, or why she should be so concerned *now* for a child she deserted *then*—these things

had no mitigating relevance. He had sworn. How could he fight Soli now?

"Friends," Soli said forlornly. "I could have told him. . . ." She gulped more beer and let out a nomadlike belch. "Var, if we fight and I kill you—then the Weaponless will go away, and Sol will never see him. Again." She began to cry once more.

"We can't fight," Var said, relieved to make it official.

The fog lifted.

"They can see us!" Soli cried, jumping up. This was not true, for the ground remained shrouded, but the nether mists were thinning too. "They'll know. The sticks!" And she fell down again.

"What's the matter?" Var asked, scrambling to help her. She rolled her head. "I feel funny." Then she vomited.

"The beer!" Var said, angry with himself for not thinking what it would do to her. He had been sick himself, the first time he had been exposed to it. "You must have drunk a quart while we talked."

But the bag was not down nearly that much. Soli just hung on him and heaved.

Var grabbed a soft sugared roll and sponged off her face and front with it. "Soli, you can't be sick now. They're watching—your people and mine. If we don't fight——"

"Where's my stick?" she cried hysterically. "I'll bash your humpy head in. Leave me alone!" She tried another heave, but nothing came up.

Var held her erect, not knowing what else to do. He was afraid that if he let her go she would either collapse on the ground or stumble over the brink. Either way, it wouldn't be much of a show, and the watchers on either side would become suspicious.

A show! To the distant spectators, it must appear that the two were in a terminal struggle, staggering about the mesa after an all-night combat. This was the fight!

"Wanna sleep," Soli mumbled. "Lie down. Sick. Keep the cold off me, Var, there's a good nomad. . . ." Her knees folded.

Var hooked his arms under her shoulders and held her up. "We can't sleep. Not while they're watching."

"I don't care. Let me go." She lapsed into sobbing again.

Var had to set her down.

"It's that beer, isn't it?" she said, suddenly wide awake. "I'm drunk. They never let me have any. Sol and Sosa. Awful stuff. Hold me, Var. I feel all weak. I'm frightened."

Var decided that any further show of battle was hopeless. He lay down and put his arms about her, and she cried and cried.

After a time she regained self-control. "What'll we do, Var?"

He didn't know.

"Could we both go home and say it didn't work?" she asked plaintively. Then, before he could answer, she did: "No. Bob would kill me as a traitor. And the war would go on."

They sat side by side and looked out over the world.

"Why don't we tell them somebody *won*?" she asked suddenly. "Then it'll be settled."

Var was dubious, but as he considered it the proposal seemed sound. "Who wins?"

"We'll have to choose. If I win, you nomads will go away. If you win, they'll take over the underworld. Which is better?"

"There'll be a lot of killing if we go down there," he said. "Maybe your—maybe Sol and Sosa."

"No," she said. "Not if Helicon surrenders. And you said they were friends—Sol and the Nameless One. They could be together again. And I could meet Sola, my true mother." Then, after a moment: "She couldn't be better than Sosa, though."

He thought about that, and it seemed reasonable. "I win, then?"

"You win, Var." She gave him a wan smile and reached for the bread.

"But what about you?"

"I'll hide. You tell them I'm dead."

"But Sol!——"

"After it's over, I'll find Sol and tell him I'm not dead. By then it won't make any difference."

Var still felt uneasy, but Soli seemed so certain that he couldn't protest. "Go *now*," she urged. "Tell him it was a hard battle, and you fell down too, but you finally won."

"But I'm unmarked!"

She giggled. "Look at your arm."

He looked at both arms. His right was clean, but his left, the weaponless one, was laced with bruises. She had been scoring, that serious part of the fight. Soli herself was almost without blemish.

"I could bash you in the face a couple of times," she said mischievously. "To make it look better." She tried to suppress a titter and failed. "I think I said that wrong. The fight, I mean. It isn't that ugly. Your face, I mean."

Var left her there and began his descent. She would play dead until dusk, then make her way down the safest route as well as she could. He worried, but she told him that she knew the way and anyhow would have plenty of time to be careful. Certainly he couldn't wait for her. "I'll start down before it's all the way dark," she said. "So I'll be past the killer slope before I can't see any more."

He halted a few feet down and called up to her: "If anything happens—where can I find you?" He could not get rid of his morbid concern.

"Near the hostel, dummy," she called back. "Hurry up. I mean *down*."

He obliged, not avoiding abrasions since they would make his supposed fight to the death seem more authentic. He would be telling a lie—but at least he was doing the right thing, and he had also preserved his oath. He had learned the final lesson the Master had taught him.

"Var! Va-a-ar!" Soli was calling him, her dark head poked over the edge.

"What?"

"Your clothing!"

He had forgotten! He was wearing the stolen clothing. If he returned in that, everything would be exposed, ironically.

Embarrassed, he returned to the mesa and stripped to the skin. The material would help keep her warm, anyway.

There was jubilation that night at the Master's base camp, and Var was fêted in a manner he was wholly unaccustomed to. He had to eat prodigiously, not daring to admit he was not hungry. For the first time the women of the neighbouring camp, suspiciously quick to appear after word of the victory had spread, found him attractive. But

all he could think of was little Soli, struggling down the treacherous cliffs in the dark, carrying her bundle of food and clothing. If she fell, their ruse would become reality. . . .

The warriors assumed that he had fought a male sticker, and Var chose to avoid clarification of the matter. "I killed," he said, and stopped there. And fended off male congratulations and female attentions until finally Tyl saw the way of it and found him a private tent for the night.

In the morning the Master went to the hostel to talk to the television set, taking Var along. The Master had not questioned him, and seemed apprehensive. "If Bob pulls a doublecross, this is when it will happen," he muttered. "He is not the type to yield readily, ever."

Soli's own assessment of the underworld master seemed to concur. That must be a devil of a man, Var thought.

They entered the elegant cylindrical building, with its racks of clothing and sanitary facilities and its several machineries, and the Master turned on the set. As it warmed up, Var realized that once again they had blundered safely past disaster—for if that set had been on when Soli came, the underworld would have known what was happening.

The picture that came on was not the random, vapid collection of costumed posturings Var had observed from time to time before. Nor was it silent. It was a room—not like the hostel room, but certainly the work of crazy machines. It was square, with diagrams on the opposite wall, and airvents, and a ponderous metal desk in the center.

In fact, it was rather like a room in a building—such as he had prowled through in the badlands. But clean and new, not filthy and ancient.

A man sat in a padded, bendable chair behind the desk. He was old, older than the Master, at least thirty and possibly more. Var did not know how long a man could live if he suffered no mishap in the circle. Perhaps even as long as forty years. This one had sparse gray-brown hair (actually, the picture was colorless, but that was the way it looked) and stern lines in his face.

"Hello, Bob," the Master said grimly.

"Hello again, Sos. What's the word?" The man's tones were brisk, assured, and he moved his long thin arm as

though directing subordinates. A leader of men: yes. Var did not like him.

"Your champion did not return?"

The man merely stared coldly at him.

"This is Var the Stick our champion," the Master said. "He informs me that he killed your champion on the mesa of Muse yesterday."

"Impossible. Surely you realize no lesser man than yourself could have defeated Sol of All Weapons in honest combat."

The Master seemed stricken. "Sol! You sent Sol?"

"Ask your supposed champion," Bob said.

The Master turned slowly to Var. "Sol would not have gone. But if he had——"

"No," Var said. "It wasn't Sol." He didn't understand why the underworld leader should play such a game.

"Perhaps, then, his mate, if the term is not unkindly euphemistic," Bob said, his glance possessing a peculiar intensity. "She of the deadly hands and barren womb."

"No!" Var cried, knowing now that he was being baited, but reacting to it, anyway. The Master, astonishingly, was sweating. It was as though the real battle was taking place here, rather than on the mesa. A strange contest of deadly words and savage implications. And Bob was winning it.

Bob looked at his fingernails during the pause. "Who, then?"

"His—daughter. Soli. She had sticks."

The Master opened his mouth but did not speak. He stared at Var as though pierced by a bullet.

"I apologize," Bob said smoothly. "Var was there, after all. He did kill our designated champion. Her parents were too wary to cooperate, so are in our bad graces; but she was, shall we say, cooperatively naive. Of course she was only eight years old—eight and a half or better, technically —and I think we'll have to delay further action on this matter in favor of a rematch. . . ."

Var realized that the man's over-elaborate words signified his intent to renig. But the Master was not protesting. The Master continued to stare dumbly at Var.

There was another wait. "You—killed—Soli?" the Master said at last, so hoarsely as to be hardly comprehensible.

Var did not dare tell the full truth, here before the underworld leader. "Yes."

The Master's whole body shook as though he were cold. Var could not understand what was the matter. Soli was no relation to him; the Master had not even known her when she begged food from him. True, it was unkind to kill a girl—but he had had to meet the mountain's champion, in whatever guise. Had it been a mutant lizard, he still would have fought. Why was the Master so upset now, and why was Bob looking so smug? They were acting as though he had *lost* the battle.

"So I was correct about her," Bob said. "Sol never let on. But obviously——"

"Var the Stick," the Master said formally, his voice quivering with emotion. "The friendship between us is ended. Where we meet next, there is the circle. No terms but death. In deference to your ignorance and to what is past, I give you one day and one night to flee. Tomorrow I come for you."

Then he whirled and smote the television set with his massive fist. The glass on the face of it shattered and the box toppled over. "And after that, *you!*" he shouted at the dead machine. "Not one chamber will escape the flamethrower, and you shall roast on the pyre, alive!"

Var had never seen such fury in any man. He understood none of it, except that the Master intended to kill both him and the underworld leader. His friend had lost his sanity.

Var fled from the hostel, and kept on running, confused and ashamed and afraid.

CHAPTER TWELVE

"Var."

He whirled, grabbing for his new set of sticks. Then he relaxed. "Soli!"

"I saw you run from the hostel. So I came, too. Var, what happened?"

"The Master——" Var was stopped by an unmanly misery. "He——"

"Wasn't he happy that you won?"

"The——Bob reniged."

"Oh." She took his hand solicitously. "So it was for nothing. No wonder the Weaponless is mad. But that isn't your fault, is it?"

"He says he'll kill me."

"Kill you? The Nameless One? Why?"

"I don't know." It was as though she were the inquiring adult, he the child.

"But he's nice. Underneath. He wouldn't do that. Not just because it didn't work."

Var shrugged. He had seen the Master run amuck. He believed.

"What are you going to do, Var?"

"Leave. He's giving me a day and a night."

"But what will *I* do? I can't go back to the mountain now. Bob would kill me—and he'd kill Sol and Sosa too. For losing. He told me he'd kill them both if I didn't fight, and if he finds out——"

Var stood there having no answer.

"We weren't very smart, I guess," Soli said, beginning to cry.

He put his arm around her, feeling the same.

"I don't know enough about the nomads," she said. "I don't like being alone."

"Neither do I," Var said, realizing that it was exile he faced. Once he had been a loner and satisfied, but he had changed.

"Let's go together," Soli said.

Var though about that, and it seemed good.

"Come on!" she cried, suddenly jubilant. "We can raid some other hostel for traveling gear, and—and run right out of the country! Just you and me! And we can fight in the circle!"

"I don't want to fight you any more," he said.

"Silly! Not each other! *Other* people! And we can make a big tribe with all the ones we capture, and then come back and——"

"No! I won't fight the Master!"

"But if he's chasing you——"

"I'll keep running."

"But, Var——!"

"No!" He shook her off.

Soli began to cry, as she always did when thwarted, and he was immediately sorry. But as usual he didn't know what to say.

"I guess it's like fighting your father," she said after a bit. That seemed to be the end of it.

"But we can still do everything else?" she asked wistfully, after a bit more.

He smiled. "Everything!"

Reconciled, they began their flight.

By dusk they were ensconced in an unoccupied hostel twenty miles distant. "This is almost like home," Soli said. "Except that it's round. And everything's here—I guess the nomads haven't raided it this week."

Var shrugged. He was not at home in a hostel, but this had seemed better than foraging outside for supper. Alone, he would have stayed in deep forest; but with Soli——

"I can fix us a real underworld meal," she said. "Uh, you *do* known how to use knives and forks? I saw how the cooks did it. Sosa says I should always be able to do for myself, 'cause sometime I might have to. Let's see, this is a 'lectric range, and this button makes it hot——"

One word stuck in his mind as he watched her busily hauling out utensils and supplies. Sosa. That was the name of her stepmother, he knew. The little woman he had encountered underground, who had thrown him down so easily. The Master had spoken the name too. But there was something else——

Sos! Bob of the mountain had called the Master Sos! And so had Tyl, earlier; he remembered that now. As though the Nameless One *had* a name! And Sos would be the original husband of Sosa!

But Sol was married to Sosa, there in the mountain. And Sos was married to Sola. How had such a transposition come about?

And if Soli were the child of Sol and Sola—was there also a Sosi, born of Sos and Sosa? If so, where?

Var's head whirled with the complexity of such thinking. Somewhere in this confusion was the answer to the Master's strange wrath, he was sure. But how was he to untangle it?

Soli was having difficulties with the repast. "I need a can opener," she said, holding up a sealed can.

Var didn't know what a can opener was.

"To get these tomatoes open."

"How do you know what's in there?"

"It says on the label. TOMATO. The crazies label everything. That *is* what you call them, isn't it?"

"You mean you can read? The way the Master does?"

"Well, not very well," she admitted. "Jim the Librarian taught me. He says all the children of Helicon should learn to read, for the time when civilization comes back. How can I open this can?"

She called the mountain Helicon, too. So many little things were different! And she knew Jim the Gun's mountain brother, not the real Jim.

Var took the can and brought it to the weapons-rack. He selected a dagger and plunged it into the flat end of the cylinder. Red juice squirted out, as though from a wound.

He took the dripping object back to her. It *was* tomatoes.

"You're smart," Soli said admiringly. It was ridiculous, but he felt proud.

Eventually she served up the meal. Var, accustomed in childhood to scavenging for edibles in ancient buildings and

in the garbage dumps of human camps, was not particularly dismayed. He crunched on the burned meat and drank the tomatoes and gnawed on the fibrous rolls and sliced the rock-hard ice-cream with the dagger. "Very good," he said, for the Master had always stressed the importance of courtesy.

"You don't have to be sarcastic!"

Var didn't understand the word, so he said nothing. Why was it that people so often got angry for no reason?

After the meal Var went outside to urinate, not used to the hostel's crockery sanitary facilities. Soli took a shower and pulled down a bunk from the wall.

"Don't turn on the television," she called as he re-entered. "It's probably bugged."

Var hadn't intended to, but he wondered at her concern. "Bugged?"

"You know. The underworld has a tap so they know when someone's watching. Maybe the crazies do, too. To keep track of the nomads. We don't want anyone to know where we are."

He remembered the Master's conversation with the mountain leader Bob, and thought he understood. Television didn't *have* to be meaningless. He pulled down an adjacent bunk and flopped on it.

After a while he rolled over and looked at the television set. "Why is it so stupid?" he asked rhetorically.

"That's the way the Ancients were—before the Blast," she said. "They did stupid things, and they're all on tape, and we just run it through the 'mitter and that's what's on television. Jim says it all means something, but we don't have the sound system so we can't tell for sure."

"We?"

"The underworld. Helicon. Jim says we have to maintain 'nology. We don't know how to *make* television, but we can maintain it. Until all the replacement parts wear out, anyway. The crazies know more about 'lectricity than we do. They even have computers. But we do more work."

Var was becoming interested. "What *do* you do?"

"Man-facturing. We make the weapons and the pieces for the hostels. The crazies are Service—they put up the hostels and fill them with food and things. The nomads are 'sumers—they don't do anything."

This was too deep for Var, who had never heard of the underworld before this campaign and still had only the vaguest notion what the crazies were or did. "Why does the Master have to conquer the mountain, if it does so much?"

"Bob says he's demented. Bob says he's a doublecrosser. He was supposed to end the empire, but he attacked the mountain instead. Bob's real mad."

"The Master said the mountain was bad. He said he couldn't make the empire great until he conquered the mountain. And now he says he'll burn it all, after he kills me."

"Maybe he *is* demented," she whispered.

Var wondered, himself.

"I'm frightened," Soli said after a pause. "Bob says if the nomads make an empire there'll be another Blast, and no one will escape. He says they're the violent 'lement of our society, and they can't have 'nology or they'll make the Blast. Again. But now——"

Var couldn't follow that either. "Who made the mountain?" he asked her.

"Jim says he thinks it was made by post-Blast civilization," she said uncertainly. "There was radiation everywhere and they were dying, but they took their big machines and scooped a whole city into a pile and dug it out and put in 'lectricity and saved their finest scientists and fixed it so no one else could get inside. But they needed food and things, so they had to trade—and some of the smart men outside had some civilization too, from somewhere, and they were the crazies, and so they traded. And everyone else, the stupid ones, just drifted and fought each other, and they were the nomads. And after a while too many men in Helicon got old and died, and 'nology was being lost, so they had to take in some others, but they had to keep it secret and the crazies wouldn't come, so they only took in the ones that came to die."

"I don't think the Master would make another Blast," Var said. But he remembered the man's mysterious fury, his threat to destroy all the mountain, and he wasn't sure.

Soli was discreet enough not to comment. After a time they slept.

Twenty miles away, the Nameless One, known by some

as Sos, did not sleep. He paced his tent, sick with rage at the murder of his natural child, the girl called Soli—conceived in adultery but still flesh of his flesh. Since his time within the mountain he had been sterile, perhaps because of the operations the Helicon surgeon had performed on his body to make him the strongest man of the world. He carried metal under his skin and in his crotch, and hormones had made his body expand, but he could no longer sire a child. Thus Soli, legally the issue of the castrate Sol, was the only daughter he would ever beget, and though he had not seen her in six years she was more precious to him than ever. Any girl her age was precious, sympathetically. He had dreamed of reuniting with her, and with his true friend Sol, and with his own love, Sosa, the four together, somehow——

But now such hopes were ashes. It was not a girl but an entire foundation of ambition that had been abolished. Now the things of this world were without flavor.

Soli—perhaps she would have been like that gamin from Pan tribe, alert and bold yet tearful—artfully so—when balked. But he would never know, for Var had killed her.

Var would surely die. And Helicon would be leveled, for Bob had engineered that ironic murder. No party to the event would survive—not even Sos the Weaponless, the most guilty of all concerned.

So he paced, ruled by his despairing fury, awaiting only the dawn to begin his mission of revenge. Tyl would supervise the siege of Helicon until his own return. Tyl, at least, would enjoy being in charge.

CHAPTER THIRTEEN

In a month they were far beyond the Master's domains, but Var dared not rest. The Nameless One was slow but very determined, as Var had learned when they first met. He knew the local tribesmen would inform the Master of the route taken by the fugitive, so there was no escape except continued motion.

At first Soli had hidden whenever human beings were encountered, for she was officially dead. Then they realized that she could masquerade as a boy, and even carry the sticks, and no one would know. So they traveled openly together, an ugly man and a fair boy, and no one challenged them.

They went west, for the Master's empire was east and Soli had heard that ocean lay to the south. Extensive desert badlands forced them north. They avoided trouble, but when it came at them relentlessly, they fought. Once a foul-mouthed sworder challenged Var, calling him a pederast. Var didn't understand the word, but he got the gist and realized that it was supposed to be an insult. He met the sworder in the circle and flattened his nose and cracked his head with the sticks, and it was not pretty. Another time a small tribe sought to deny them access to a hostel; Var bloodied one, Soli a second, and the rest fled. The warriors beyond the empire were inept fighters.

In the second month they encountered so extensive a desert that they had to turn back. Fearing the Master, they took to the wilderness, avoiding the established trails.

But foraging while traveling these bleak hills was difficult. There was not time to set snares or to wait patiently for game. Soli had to turn girl-child again to enter occupied

hostels for supplies, while Var skulked alone. She returned with word that the Weaponless had passed this area two or three days behind them. He was outside his empire now, but no one could mistake the whitehaired brute of a man. He spoke only to describe Var and verify his transit, and did not enter the circle. He did not seem to be concerned about Var's boy companion.

So it was true. The Master was on his trail, leaving everything else behind. Var felt fear and regret. He had hoped that this murderous passion would fade, that the needs of the mountain campaign would summon the Nameless One back before very long. A minion might be dispatched to finish the chore, of course; but Var would have no compunction about destroying such a man in the circle. It was only the Master himself he could not bring himself to oppose—not from fear, though he knew the Master would kill him—but because this was, or had been, his only true friend.

Now he knew it was not to be. The Master would never give up the pursuit.

They veered north, moving rapidly and sleeping in the forest, the open plain, the tundra. Soli fetched supplies from the hostels, sometimes as girl, sometimes as boy.

Yet the word spread ahead of them. When they encountered strangers accidentally they drew stares of semi-recognition. "You with the mottled skin—aren't you the one the juggernaut is after?" But such acquaintances usually did not interfere, for Var was said to be devastating with the sticks. And, in this region of haphazardly trained warriors, this was a true description. The few who chose to challenge him in the circle soon became limping testimony to this.

And few suspected that his boy companion was even better at such fighting, possessing both sophisticated stick technique and weaponless ability. Only when they had to fight as a pair, against aggressive doubles, did this become evident. Soli, adept at avoiding blows, fenced around and behind Var, and the opposition was soon demolished.

In two more months of circuitous traveling they came to the end of the crazy demesnes. The hostels stopped, and the easy trails made by the crazy tractors terminated, and the wilderness became total. And it was winter.

Undaunted, they plunged into the snowbound unknown. It was an unkempt jungle of bareboned trees, fraught with gullies and stumbling stones hidden under the even blanket of white. At dusk the snow began to fall again, gently at first, then solidly. Soli became grim and silent, for she was unused to this. Never before had she dealt with snow; she had never emerged from the mountain above the snowline. To her it had been something white but not necessarily cold or uncomfortable. Var knew the reality exasperated her and frightened her, catching at her feet and flying in her face.

Var excavated a pit, baring the unfrozen turf and making a circular wall of packed snow. He spread a groundsheet and pegged a low sturdy tent, letting the snow accumulate on top. He sealed it in except for a breathing tunnel and brought her inside, where he took off her boots, poured out the accumulated water, and slapped at her feet until they began to warm. She no longer cried as freely as she had at their first meeting, and he rather wished she would, for now her misery just sat upon her and would not depart.

That night, after they had eaten, he held her closely and tried to comfort her, and gradually she relaxed and slept.

In the morning she would not awaken. Nervously he stripped her despite the cold, and dried her, and found the puncture mark: on the blue ankle just above the level of her unbooted foot. Something like a badlands moth had stung her, unobserved. They must have camped near a radiation fringe zone, far enough out so that his skin did not detect it, near enough for some of the typical fauna to appear. He might have recognized the area by sight, had it not been snowing. Probably there were hibernating grubs, and one had been warmed into activity by her body, and crawled and bit when disturbed . . . she was in coma.

There was no herb he knew, in this region, in this season, that would ease her condition. She was small; if she had taken in too much of the venom, she would sleep until she died. If she had a small dose, she would recover—if kept warm and dry.

The snowstorm had abated, but he knew it would return. At night it would be really cold again. This was no suitable place for illness, regardless. He had to get her to a heated hostel.

He struck tent, packed up everything hastily, and carried her dangling over his shoulder, swathed in bag and canvas. He stumbled through the knee-deep snow, the hip-deep drifts, never pausing for a rest, though his arms grew numb with the weight and his legs leaden.

After an hour he stepped into a snow-camouflaged burrow-hole, stumbled, caught himself, caught Soli as she slid off his shoulder—and almost collapsed as the pain shot up his thigh. Then he went on as before, ignoring it. Until the slower pain of his swelling ankle forced him to stop and remove his boot and rub snow on it. Then, barefooted, he continued.

After a time he had to stop again, to dispose of all superfluous weight. He hoisted Soli again and walked because he had to, no other reason. And before day was done he laid her limp body in the warm hostel, the last they had passed.

Soli's breathing was shallow, but she had neither the fever nor the chill of a serious illness. Var began to hope that he had acted in time, and that the siege was light.

He rested beside her, the sensation in his leg coming through with appalling intensity. The wrench would not have been serious, had he not continued to aggravate it, walking loaded. Now——

He heard something.

A man was coming up the walk to the hostel, treading the frozen path the crazies had cleared. Obviously intending to night inside.

Var had had perhaps half an hour—hardly enough for strength to creep back into his limbs, more than enough to make his ankle a torment. But he dragged himself up, hastily winding a section of crazy sheet around his leg so that he could stand on it more firmly. He and Soli had remained hidden until this time, but he knew their secrecy would be gone if anyone saw her now. They had lost a day of travel, and the Master would be very close; any exposure could bring him here within hours.

The approaching steps were not those of the Weaponless. They were too light, too quick. But Var could tolerate no man inside this hostel—not while Soli lay ill, not while they both were vulnerable.

He scrambled into his heavy winter coat, pulled its hood

tight around his face to conceal the discoloration above his beard, lifted his sticks, fought off the agony that threatened to collapse his leg, and pushed through the spinning door to meet the stranger outside.

It was bright, though the day was waning; the snow amplified the angled sunlight and bounced it back and forth and across his squinting eyes. It took a moment to make out the intruder.

The man was of medium height, fair-skinned under the parka, and well proportioned. He wore a long, large knapsack that projected behind his head. His facial features were refined, almost feminine, and his motions were oddly smooth. He seemed harmless—a tourist wandering the country, broadening his mind, a loner. Var knew it was wrong to deny him lodging at the warm hostel, especially this late in the day, but with Soli's welfare at stake there was no choice. The Master could get the word and come before she recovered, and they would be doomed. He barred the way.

The man did not speak. He merely looked questioningly at Var.

"My—my sister is ill," Var said, aware that his words, as always with strangers, were hardly comprehensible. When he knew a person, talking became easier, partly because he was relaxed and partly because the other picked up his verbal distortions and learned to compensate. "I must keep her isolated."

The traveler still was silent. He made a motion to pass Var.

Var blocked him again. "Sister—sick. Must-be-alone," he enunciated carefully.

Still mute, the man tried to pass again.

Var lifted one stick.

The stranger reached one hand over his shoulder and drew out a stick of his own.

So it was to be the circle.

Var did not want to fight this man at this time, for the other's position was reasonable. Var and Soli had fought together for their right to occupy any hostel at any time. Lacking an explanation, the other man had a right to be annoyed. And Var was in poor condition for the circle; only with difficulty did he conceal the liability of his leg,

and he was quite tired generally from his day's labor. But he could not tell the whole truth, and could not risk exposure. The man would have to lodge elsewhere.

If the stranger were typical of these outland warriors, Var would be able to defeat him despite his handicaps. Particularly stick against stick. Certainly he had to try.

The man preceded him down the path to the circle. This was a relief, for it meant Var could conceal his limp while walking. The man kicked the circle free of loose snow, drew out his second stick, removed his tall backpack and his parka, and took his stance. Suddenly he looked more capable; there was something highly professional about the way he handled himself.

Var, afraid to reveal his mottled skin, had to remain fully dressed, though it inhibited his mobility. He entered the circle.

They sparred, and immediately Var's worst fears were realized. He faced a master sticker. The man's motions were exceptionally smooth and efficient, his blows precise. Var had never seen such absolute control before. And speed—those hands were phenomenal, even in this cold.

Knowing that he had to win quickly if at all, Var laid on with fury. He was slightly larger than his opponent, and probably stronger, and desperation gave him unusual skill despite his injury and fatigue. In fact, he was fighting better than ever before in his life, though he knew he would lose that edge in a few minutes as his resources gave out. At this moment, Tyl himself would have had to back off, reassess his strategy, and look to his defenses.

Yet the stranger met every pass with seeming ease, anticipating Var's strategy and neutralizing his force. Surely this was the finest sticker ever to enter the circle!

Then, abruptly, the man took the offense and penetrated Var's own guard as though it were nonexistent and laid him out with a blow against the head. Half-conscious, Var fell backwards across the circle. He was finished.

His face sidewise in the snow, Var heard something. It was a noise, a shudder in the ground, as of ponderous feet coming down: crunch, crunch, crunch, crunch. An ear less attuned to the wilderness could not have picked it up, and Var himself would have missed it, had his ear not been jammed to the land.

It was the distant tread of the Master.

The victor stood above him, looking down curiously.

"Stranger!" Var cried, half delirious. "Never have I met your like. I beg a boon of you——" He was incoherent again, and had to slow down. "Let no man enter that hostel tonight! Guard her, give her time——"

The man squatted to peer at him. Had he understood any of it? It was unprecedented for the loser to beseech terms from the winner—but what else could he do now?

"A badlands grub—she will die if disturbed——" And Var himself would die if he didn't drag himself away immediately. Then who would take care of Soli? Would the Master linger to help her? Not while the vengeance trail was warm! No—it had to be this stranger, if only he would. Such exceeding skill in the circle had to be complemented by meticulous courtesy.

The man reached out to touch Var's injured leg. The sheet had come loose and a section of swollen skin showed. He nodded. This man would have won, anyway, but he could not be pleased to discover he had fought a lame opponent. He stood and stepped out of the circle, leaving Var where he lay. He donned his parka, then his pack, putting the sticks away. He walked down the trail in the direction the Master was coming from.

He was leaving the cabin to Var.

Var did not question the stranger's act of generosity. He climbed to his feet and limped back to the cabin, turning several times to watch the man's departure. At last he entered and shut the door.

The stranger would meet the Master. Var was at his mercy now. Who was this silent one, and how had he come by such fabulous fighting skill? Var knew that no sticker in all the empire could match this warrior.

But the Master was not a sticker. What would pass between them when they met? Would they fight? Talk? Come to this cabin together? Or pass each other, and the Master would come to find the fugitives here?

Soli stirred and he forgot all else. "Var . . . Var," she cried weakly, and he rushed to her side. She was recovering! If only they were granted the night——

They were. Though Var listened apprehensively for footsteps outside, no man came to the hostel.

In the morning Soli was well, though weak. "What happened?" she asked.

"You were stung by a badlands moth—its winter grub," Var said, though this was only conjecture. "It came alive when we warmed the ground, and got on you. I brought you here."

"What are those marks on you?"

"I fought a man who would intrude." And that was all he told her, lest she worry.

This time they picked up extra sheeting, so as to make possible a double layer on the ground and keep moisture and grubs out entirely. Var explained that they had lost time and had to move; he did not clarify how close he knew the Master to be, but she caught his urgency.

So they resumed their desperate trek. Soli was weak, but she could walk. In her residual disorientation she was not aware of Var's limp.

As they left the hostel, Var looked down the path once more, mystified. Who was the noble, dazzling, silent man who had made their escape possible? Would he ever know?

CHAPTER FOURTEEN

They marched northward through winter and emerged at last in spring, far beyond the crazy domains. Here they found complete strangers: men and women who carried some guns and bows but not true weapons, and who did not fight in the circle, and who lived in structures resembling primitive, dilapidated hostels. They burned wood to warm these "houses" because there was no electricity, and illuminated them with smoky oil lanterns. They spoke an unpleasantly modulated dialect, and were not especially friendly. It was as though every family were an island, cultivating its own fields, hunting its own preserve, neither attacking nor assisting strangers.

Still the Master followed, falling behind as much as a month, then catching up almost to within sight, forcing them to move out quickly. Now the silent man Var had fought accompanied the Nameless One. The scattered news reports and rumors described him well enough for Var to identify, though he said nothing to Soli about this. If she knew that a warrior of that quality had chosen to accompany the Master . . .

Had those two fought, and the Master had made the stranger part of the empire? Or had they joined forces for convenience, in the dangerous hinterlands?

Summer, and the country remained rugged and the pursuit continued. Soli was taller and stronger now, growing rapidly, and was quite capable. She learned from him how to make vine traps in the forest and capture small animals, and to skin them and gut them. How to strike fire and cook the meat. She learned to make a deadfall, and to

sleep comfortably in a tree. Her hair grew out, black and fine, so that she resembled her natural mother more than ever.

Soli taught him, in return, the rudiments of the weaponless combat she had learned from Sosa, and the strategies demonstrated by her father Sol. For they both knew that eventually the Master would catch up, and that Var, despite his reservations, would have to fight. The Nameless One would force the combat.

"But it's better to run as long as we can," she said, seeming to have changed her attitude over the months. "The Weaponless defeated Sol in the circle, long ago when I was small, and Sol was the finest warrior of the age."

Var wondered whether Sol could have been as good as the sticker now traveling with the Master, but he kept that thought to himself.

"It was the Weaponless who struck my father on the throat so hard he could not speak again," she said, as though just remembering. "Yet you say they were friends."

"Sol does not speak?" Var's whole body tingled with an appalling suspicion.

"He can't. The underworld surgeon offered to operate, but Sol wouldn't tolerate the knife. Not that way. It was as though he felt he *had* to carry that wound. That's what Sosa said, but she told me not to talk about it."

Var thought again of the fair stranger, the master sticker, now almost certain that he knew the man's identity. "What would your father do, if he thought you were dead?"

"I don't know," she said. "I don't like to think about it, so I don't. I miss him, and I'm really sorry——" But she cut off that thought. "Bob probably wouldn't tell him. I think Bob pretended I was being sent on an exploratory mission and didn't return. Bob almost never tells the truth."

"But if Sol found out——"

"I guess he would kill Bob, and——" Her mouth opened. "Var, I never thought of that! He would break out of the underworld and——"

"I met him," Var said abruptly. "When you were ill. We did not know each other. Now he travels with the Master."

"*Sol* is the Nameless One's companion? I should have realized! But that's wonderful, Var! They are together again. They must really be friends."

Var told her the rest of the story: how he had fought Sol, and tried to send him back to oppose the Master. About the strange generosity of the other man. "I did not know," he finished. "I kept him from you."

She kissed his cheek—a disconcertingly feminine gesture. "You did not know. And you fought for me!"

"You can go back to him."

"More than anything else," she said, "I would like that. But what of you, Var?"

"The Master has sworn to kill me. I must go on."

"If Sol travels with the Weaponless, he must agree with him. They must both want to kill you now."

Var nodded miserably.

"I love my father more than anything," she said slowly. "But I would not have him kill you, Var. You are my friend. You gave me warmth on the mesa, you saved me from illness and snow."

He had not realized that she attached such importance to such things. "You helped me, too," he said gruffly.

"Let me travel with you a while longer. Maybe I'll find a way to talk to my father, and maybe then he can make the Nameless One stop chasing you."

Var was immensely gratified by this decision of hers, but he could not analyse his feeling. Perhaps it was this glimmer of a promise of some mode of reconciliation with his mentor, the Master. Perhaps it was merely that he no longer felt inclined to travel alone. But mostly, it could be the loyalty she showed for him—that filled an obscure but powerful need that had made him miserable since the Master's turn-about. To have a friend—that was the most important thing there was.

The sea came north and fenced them in with its salty expanse. The pursuit closed in behind. The unfriendly natives informed them with cynical satisfaction that they were trapped: the ocean was west and south, the perpetual snows north, and two determined warriors east.

"Except," one surly storekeeper murmured smugly, "the tunnel."

"Tunnel?" Var remembered the subway tunnel near the mountain. He might hide in such a tube. "Radiation?"

"Who knows? No one ever leaves it."

"But where does it *go*?" Soli demanded.

"Across to China, maybe." And that was all he would tell them, and probably all he knew.

"There's another Helicon in China," Soli said later. "That's not its name, but that's what it is. Sometimes we exchanged messages with them. By radio."

"But we are fighting the mountain!"

"*The Nameless One* is fighting it. Or was. Sol isn't. We aren't. And this is a different one. It might help us—at least enough so I could talk to Sol. If we can find it. I don't know where it is in China."

Var remained uncertain, but had no better alternative. If there was any way to escape the Master, he had to try it.

The entrance to the tunnel was huge—big enough to accommodate the largest crazy tractor, or even several abreast. The ceiling was arched, the walls gently bowed— whether from design or incipient collapse. Var was uncertain at first. But closer inspection revealed its complete sturdiness. There was solid dirt on the floor, but no metal rails. It was a dark hole.

"Just like the underworld," Soli said, undismayed. "There's an old subway beyond the back storage room. With rats in it. I used to play there, but Sosa said there might be radiation."

"There was," Var said.

"How do you know?"

He summarized his foray to Helicon, before the first battle. "But the Master said she would tell them, so it would be booby-trapped. So we didn't use it."

"She never did. Bob knew it was there, but he said the geigers proved it was impassable, so he didn't worry about it. I guess the radiation was down when you came—but Sosa didn't say a word."

So they *could* have invaded that way! Why hadn't Sosa given the route away?

Then he remembered: Sos—Sosa. Sometime in the past she had been his wife, and she must still have loved him. So she hadn't told. But he had thought she had, and so the surface battle had begun. Just one more irony of many.

Soli lit one of their two lanterns and marched in. Var, perforce, followed.

Could this great tube actually cross under the entire ocean? What kept the water out, he wondered.

And why did no one emerge from it, if other men had entered? If the problem were radiation, he would discover it. But he feared that was not the case. There could be other dangers in fringe-radiation zones, as he knew so well. Mutant wildlife, from deadly moths to giant amphibians, as well as harmless forms like the mock-sparrow. And what else, here?

Deep in the tunnel the walls developed a tiled surface, clean and much more attractive than the bare metal and concrete. Var knew what had happened: the natives had pulled off the nearest tiles for their own use, but had not dared to penetrate too far. The mud on the bottom also slacked off, so that they walked on a fine gray surface, of a coarse texture in detail but marvelously even as a whole. It was ideal for running; their feet had excellent traction.

But how far could this continue? After an hour's brisk walk, he asked Soli: "How wide is the ocean?"

"Jim showed me a map once. He said this way was the Pacific, and it's about ten thousand miles wide."

"Ten thousand miles! It will take years to cross!"

"No," she said. "You know better than that, Var. You can figure. If we walk four miles an hour, twelve hours a day, that's almost fifty miles."

"Twenty days to cover a thousand miles," he said, after a moment's difficult computation. "To cover ten thousand— over six months to cross it all. We have supplies for hardly a week!"

She laughed. "It isn't so wide up here. Maybe less than a hundred miles. I'm not sure. I think the tunnel must come up for air every so often, on the little islands. So we won't have to walk it all at one stretch!"

Var hoped she was right. The tunnel was unnatural, and his nose picked up the dryness of it, the deadness. If danger fell upon them here, how could they escape?

They walked another hour, Soli swinging her lantern to make the grotesque shadows caper, and Var realized what it was that disturbed him most. The other tunnel, the subway passage, had teemed with life, though touched by radiation. This one had neither. Var knew that life intruded wherever it could, and should be found in a protected place like this. What kept it clean? There had to be a reason— and not any swarm of shrews, for there were no droppings.

They rested briefly to eat and drink and leave the substance of their natural processes on the floor, since there was nowhere to bury it. They went on.

Then down the tunnel came a monster. It rumbled and hissed as it moved, and shot water from its torso, and it was bathed in steam. A tremendous eye speared light ahead.

Var froze for a moment, terrified. Then his instincts took over. He backed and turned and started to run.

"No!" Soli cried, but he hardly paid attention.

As he plunged down the tunnel, she plunged too—and tackled him. Both fell and the rushing glare played over them.

"Machine!" she cried. "Man-made. It won't hurt men!"

Now the thing was bearing down on them, faster than they could run, and the clank of its sparkling treads was deafening. It filled the passage.

"Stand up!" Soli screamed. "Show you're a man!" She meant it literally.

Var obeyed, unable to think for himself. Men seldom daunted him, but he had never experienced anything like this before.

Soli took his hand and stood by him, facing the machine. "Stop!" she cried at it, and waved her other hand in the blinding light, but it did not stop.

"Its recognition receptor must be broken!" she shouted, barely audible above the din though her mouth was inches from his ear. "It doesn't know us!"

Var no longer had any doubts about what kept the passage clean. The water spouted out was probably a chemical spray such as the crazies used to clear pathways, that killed and dissolved anything organic. And men were organic.

They could not escape. The monster filled the tunnel, blasting its chemicals against the sides and ceiling, and he saw its front sweepers scooping dust into a hopper and wetting it down too. They could not get around it and could not outrun it. They had to fight.

Then it was upon them.

Var picked up Soli and heaved her into the air. As her weight left his arms, he leaped himself.

The machine struck.

Var clung to consciousness. He spread his arms, and

when one banged against something soft, he grasped it and fetched it in. He found a metal rod with the other hand and hung on to it.

He held Soli in his arms, and they were riding the machine—bodies spread against the warm headlight, feet braced against the upper rim of the hopper.

Once he was sure of his position, he checked Soli. She was limp. He hauled her about so that her head was against his and put his ear to her mouth, and felt the slight gout of air that proved she was breathing. He studied her head and body as well as he could, alternately blinded and shadowed by the cutting edge of light, and found no blood. She was alive and whole—and if the concussion were not severe, she would awaken in time. All he had to do was hold her securely until the machine stopped.

He shifted about, hunkering down against the hopper rim. The brushes whirled in front, highlighted in the spillage of light, and the water poured down from nozzles, but still the air was foul with dust. Something not quite visible whirred and ground inside the yard-deep hopper, reminding him of gnashing teeth. He kept his feet out of it, certain that he perched precariously over an ugly death. He wrestled Soli around again and draped her over his thighs, supporting her shoulders with his free arm and her feet with one leg. He did not want any part of her to dangle into that dark maw.

His muscles grew tired, then knotted, but he did not shift position again. He knew it could not be long, at this speed, before the machine reached the end of the tunnel—and he knew by the packed dirt where it had to stop. It only cleaned so far, for some reason. Once it did stop, they could jump free. They would be the first to escape from this ferocious tunnel.

In less than half an hour light showed, a dim oval beyond the focus of the machine's beam. The vehicle ground to a halt, steam rising thickly about the wedged passengers. Var made his effort—and discovered that his legs had gone to sleep.

Soli was still unconscious; there was no help there. If he dislodged himself now, he was likely to drop them both into the dread hopper.

The machine shuddered. The blasting water jets cut off.

The grinder beneath Var ceased its motion, and he saw that his fear had been well-founded. But at least now he could step down on those gears without losing his feet, and that would make it possible to recover his circulation and lever Soli out.

The light doused, leaving only the pale cast from the entrance. The machine jolted into motion again—the other way. Soli rolled off and Var had to grab for her. By the time he had her safe again, the motion was too swift. If he jumped with his prickling legs and her unconscious weight they would both be hurt.

But the grinder remained inert. Apparently it had been disconnected for the return trip, along with the spray and headlight. Var worked one foot down, then let Soli slide. Returning sensation made his legs painful, but now they were securely ensconced within the hopper, riding back along the tunnel at a good clip.

But why didn't she revive? Now, increasingly, he feared that she had struck her head too hard against the light, and suffered brain damage. He had seen warriors who had become disorganized and even idiotic after club blows to the head. If that were the case with Soli——

On and on the cleaner went, returning whence it had come. Var, helpless to do anything else, held Soli firm and slept.

He was jolted awake by bright light. The machine had come into the open. Soli still nestled unconscious in his arms.

The machine stopped again—and there were people. First men with strange weapons—no, they had to be tools— then tall, armed, armored women, peering in at him and Soli. Some carried round disks of stretched leather, so that one arm was fettered and useless for combat.

"Look at that!" one exclaimed wonderingly. "A beard-face and a child."

Var did not speak immediately, sensing trouble. These women were aggressive, militant, unfeminine and unlike those he had seen before. Their curiosity did not seem friendly. Their metal helmets made them look like birds.

Soli did not move.

"See if he has his finger," another woman said eagerly. There was something guilty and ugly about their atti-

tude—as though they were contemplating an intriguing perversion. Var drew out his sticks.

Immediately bows appeared and metal-tipped arrows were trained on him from several directions. He had no protection against these, and with Soli unconscious his position was hopeless. He dropped his weapons.

The quiet men were climbing on the machine, applying their tools to its surfaces. Evidently they cared for it the way the crazies cared for their tractors, checking it over after each trip. That was why it was still operating, so long after its makers were gone.

"Out!" cried the burly woman who seemed to be the leader. She held a spear in one hand, a shield in the other.

Var obeyed, lifting Soli carefully.

"The child is sick!" someone cried. "Kill her!"

Var held Soli with one arm about her chest. With his other arm he grabbed for the leader of the females, catching her by her braided hair. He yanked her against him, hauling back on her head so that her neck was exposed. Her shield got in the way, making her struggles ineffective. He bared his teeth. He growled.

"Shoot him! Shoot him!" the captive woman screamed.

But the archers were oddly hesitant. "He must be a real man," one said. "The Queen would be angry."

"If my friend dies, I rip this throat!" Var said, breathing on the neck he held bent. He was not bluffing; his teeth had always been his natural weapon, even though they were clumsy compared to those of most animals.

Another woman came forward. "Let go our mistress; we will medicate the child."

Var shoved the captive away. She caught herself, rubbing her neck. "Take him to the Queen," she said.

A woman made as if to take Soli, but Var balked. "She stays with me. If you kill anyone, kill me first, because I will kill anyone who harms her." He had made an oath to that effect long ago, to Soli's natural mother, but that was not the reason he spoke as he did now. Soli was too important to him to lose.

They walked down a pathway toward water. Var saw that they were on a small island—hardly larger than required to serve as a surfacing point for the tunnel. The cleaning machine stood athwart the road, grinders and

brushes and headlamps at each end, hissing and cooling as the mechanics labored over it. In this culture, it seemed, the men were crazies, the women nomad warriors. Well, it was their system.

Beyond the machine there was a level stretch; then the surface rose into a tremendous metal and stone bridge that traversed the extensive water and led out of sight.

At the waterside was a boat. Var and Soli had seen such floating craft in the course of their journey, and understood their purpose, but had never been really close to one. This boat was made of metal, and he did not understand why it did not sink, since he knew metal was heavier than water.

He balked at entering the craft, but realized that there was no reasonable alternative. Obviously the Queen was not on this atoll. And if he made too much trouble he and Soli both would die.

The boat rocked as they entered, but held out the water. Var could see that its bottom deck was actually below the surface of the sea. One of the women pulled a cord and a motor started banging and shaking. Then the entire thing nudged out from the dock.

It was astonishing that people other than the crazies or underworlders should possess and control motors. Yet obviously it was so.

The boat pushed along through the ocean. Var, unused to this rocking motion, soon felt queasy. But he refused to yield to it, knowing that any sign of weakness would further imperil himself and Soli.

How long would she sleep? He felt strangely unwhole without her.

The boat came to parallel the enormous bridge. Girders like those that rimmed the mountain Helicon projected from the sea and crossed and recrossed each other, forming an eye-dazzling network. But these were organized and functional, serving to support the elevated highway. Somewhere within this jumble that road was hidden; he could not see it now. He wondered why the amazons did not walk along it instead of splashing dangerously over the water.

At length they angled toward the bridge. There was an archway, here, where the water under the span was clear

for a space. And suspended in that cavity was something like a monstrous hornet's nest—all wood and rope and interleaved slices of metal and plastic and other substances Var could not guess at.

The boat drew up beneath this, where a blister hung scant feet from the surface of the water. A ladder of rope dropped down and the women climbed up with alacrity to disappear within.

Var had to ascend carrying Soli. He laid her over his shoulder and grasped the ladder with one hand. It swung out, seeming too frail to bear the double load.

Well, if it broke, he would swim. He was not really enthusiastic to enter the hive, and did not trust these armored women. He hauled himself and his burden up, rung by rung, carefully curling his clumsy fingers about each. The rope did not break.

The ladder passed through a circular hole, and was fastened above by a metal crosspiece. Var clung to this and got his feet to a board platform, and shifted Soli down. They were in a cramped chamber whose sides curved up and out. Metal cloth seemed to be the main element.

But there were other ladders to climb. Each level was larger, the curving walls more distant, until doors and intermediate chambers were all he could observe in passing.

At length they stood within a large room with adjacent compartments, rather like the Master's main tent.

On a throne fashioned of wickerwork sat the Queen: bloated, ugly, middle-aged, bejeweled. She wore a richly woven gown that sparkled iridescently. It fell from a high stiff collar behind her broad neck to the sides of her stout ankles, and was open down the front to reveal the inner curvatures of her monstrous breasts, her dimpled kettle stomach, and her hanging thighs.

Var, hardly prudish, averted his eyes. Sexuality as brazen as this repulsed him.

Weapons threatened. "Foreign beardface, *look* at the Queen!"

He had to look; it seemed this was protocol. She reminded him of a figurine the Master had shown him once: a fertility goddess, artifact of the Ancients. The Master had said that in some cultures such a figure was considered to be the ultimate in beauty. But for Var the female attributes

became negative when expanded to such grotesque proportion.

"Strip him," the Queen said.

Again Var had to make a decision. He could fight—but not effectively while supporting Soli, and both of them would be wounded or killed. Or he could submit to being stripped by these women. Nakedness was not a strong taboo with him, but he knew it was for others, and that the demand represented an insult. Still——

He yielded. "You promised to care for my friend," he said.

The Queen made an imperious gesture that sent gross quivers through her various anatomies. An unarmed woman came to take Soli. She brought her to a wicker divan and began checking the limp girl, while Var watched nervously. And the armed women removed his clothing.

"So he has his finger," the Queen said, staring as though studying an animal.

Now Var understood the term. It occurred to him that he had not had a close look at a man of this tribe.

The nurse attending Soli spoke: "Concussion. Doesn't look serious. Bruise on the neck, probably pinching a nerve, could let go anytime." She splashed water from a bowl on Soli's face.

The girl groaned. It was the first sound she had made since the leap to the tunnel sweeper, and Var felt suddenly weak with relief. If she could groan she could recover.

"He looks strong," said the Queen. "But mottled. Do we want any piebalds?"

No one answered. Evidently the question was rhetorical.

After a moment she decided. "Yes, we'll try one." She pointed to Var. "Your Queen will honor your finger. Bring it here."

Prodded by spearlike arrows, Var walked toward her. He had some idea what she meant, and was disgusted, but the weapons bristling about him discouraged overt protest. He saw Soli sitting up and wanted to go to her. If only he weren't restrained by the odds against him! Alone, he could have made a break, but he did not want to start trouble that would hurt the dazed girl.

He came to stand immediately before the gross Queen.

She was even more repulsive up close. Fat jiggled on her body as she breathed, and there was a steamy unnatural smell about her.

She reached out and caught what she termed his finger in her hand. "Yes, your Queen will use this once, now—and no woman after her." She spread her legs, hauling Var toward her.

It was no longer possible to pretend to mistake her meaning. Var acted. He whirled on his guards, grabbing at their weapons, shoving the women down. He caught the handle of a fighting hatchet and raised the blade toward the Queen.

The guards fell back, for they could not mistake his meaning either. He could split her head before they reached him.

"Bring her!" Var cried, gesturing toward Soli. He hoped they would not realize that they could nullify his threat by threatening Soli.

Bows came up, arrows nocked. Var put both hands on the hatchet and poised above the Queen. Even if a dozen arrows transfixed him, he would take her with him.

Soli came, listless but walking by herself. She still wore her two sticks; they had not been noticed by her captors.

Something flashed. Var jumped back as the Queen drove for his loin with a jewelled stiletto. "We shall remove it now, I think," she said.

In that moment of confusion Var saw the arrows coming. One grazed his thigh. The guards closed in.

In a fury, Var leaped at the Queen and clove her head with a two-handed stroke. A cry of horror went up. He did not need to look. He knew as he yanked free the blood-soiled blade that she was dead.

He caught Soli by the arm and sprinted for the nearest compartment behind the throne. For a moment no one followed. The women were too shocked by the fate of their breeder-Queen.

There was a ladder. "Climb!" he said at Soli, and she, unspeaking, climbed. Var stood with the hatchet, ready to fend off attack. He was sure that he himself would never have the chance to use the ladder.

Then, as the amazons advanced keening in fury, he struck at the wicker door supports. Rope and fiber sliced

easily, and the door began to collapse, and the floor beneath it sagged. He hacked some more until there was a tumble of material sealing him off, then dived for the ladder.

Soli waited for him at the next level. "Where are we, Var?" she asked plaintively.

"In a hive!" he gasped, drawing her through another door. "I killed the Queen-ant!"

They entered another large room. Men were working here, weaving baskets. Naked, flabby—Var saw at once that they were castrate. No wonder the women had been fascinated by the visiting male—they seldom saw a complete man!

But though these men were harmless, even pitiful, the amazon women were not. They burst through the door behind, screaming.

Var and Soli bolted again. But the next room was a blank cubbyhole, next to the gentle curvature of the exterior wall. They were trapped.

"Fire!" Soli cried.

Var cursed himself for not thinking of that sooner. He fumbled for his pack for a precious match and some kerosene. This dry hive would ignite rapidly.

His pack, of course, was not on him. It lay with the rest of his clothing in the Queen's hall.

But Soli was already making fire from the duplicate materials in her own pack. As the first female warrior charged into the compartment, she ignited a puddle of kerosene on the wooden floor.

The amazon stomped through the sudden blaze and screamed. Var clove her with the hatchet and she fell, her shield rolling away, the fire licking around her body.

"We're trapped, Var!" Soli cried. For the moment he was too glad to have her intelligible and functional to pay attention to her words. Perhaps the action had jolted her out of her concussion.

"We'll burn!" she screamed in his ear.

That registered. He went to the wall and began hacking. The fibers were tough, and several times the blade rang against metal, but he succeeded in ripping a hole to daylight.

"Hurry!" Soli cried, and he glanced at her while chip-

ping. He saw to his surprise that the fire was not consuming everything. Only the kerosene itself was burning. Soli stood just behind it, both sticks in her hands, fending off any amazons who tried to reach through. Fortunately the constriction of the surroundings prevented the effective use of arrows. But soon the flammable fluid would be gone, and the mass of outraged women would press through. Some were already trying to use their shields to block Soli's sticks.

"Out the hole!" Var shouted at her. Soli obeyed with alacrity while he covered her retreat.

He took a final swipe at a protruding spear and dived through the hole the moment her feet disappeared. As his head poked out he saw the water, far below. He had forgotten how high they were! How could they jump that dizzying distance?

Where was Soli? He did not spy her either on the wall or in the water. If she had fallen and drowned—

"Here!"

He looked up. She was clinging to the framework above the hole. Again, relief was almost painfully great.

And of course climbing was the answer. They could escape via the rope that supported the entire framework!

A helmeted head showed in the hole. Soli reached down negligently and tapped it ringingly with a stick. It vanished.

They climbed, Var carrying the hatchet between his teeth. It was easier than the ascent to the mesa had been, so long ago in experience. The woven ropes and struts provided plentiful handholds, and as the two rose the surface tilted toward the horizontal.

A trapdoor opened in the top and a head appeared. Var threatened it with the hatchet and the lid popped closed again instantly. They had command of the roof.

The rope by which the hive was suspended was much more sturdy than it had appeared from a distance. It was a good four feet in diameter at its narrowest, and the fibers were metal and nylon and rubber, interwoven tightly.

Var had had some notion of chopping through this cord and dropping the entire hive grandly into the sea. He gave it up; his battered little hatchet could not do the job.

They climbed the column, Soli still wearing her heavy pack because there was no time for adjustments. Fortu-

nately this stretch was short. Var didn't know how long she could last, after her prolonged unconsciousness. And if the amazons emerged and started firing arrows at them——

The women did emerge, but too late. Var and Soli were perched on the massive steel strut that supported the hive, and the arrows could not reach them directly. They were safe. All they had to do was mount the road surface of the bridge and be on their way.

Well, not *quite* all. A chill wind attacked Var's bare skin. He would have to find new clothing and traveling supplies. And new weapons——this hatchet, useful as it had been, was not to his liking.

He led the way up an inclined beam, going into the maze of supports. The angry cries of the amazons were left behind, and their arrows stopped rattling between the girders. He wondered why they did not follow; certainly they would know how to get around on the bridge, since they had built their hive within it.

His skin burned. First he thought it was windchap. Then he recognized the stigma of radiation.

"Back!" he cried, knowing Soli could not feel it, but would surely be affected. "Radiation!"

They retreated to a clean spot, where intersecting beams formed a gaunt basket. Now they knew why the amazons had not pursued them here. The women would have learned the hard way that the bridge was impassable. In fact, they would have constructed their vulnerable hive in the one place they knew to be safe from all marauders.

Var knew what he would find: the bridge ahead would be saturated with the deadly rays, making it a badlands. Probably some radiation touched it between the hive and the island where the tunnel emerged, too——but even if not, the amazons would be waiting at the island with drawn bows.

Soli, so brave until this point, suddenly gave out. She laid her head against Var's shoulder and cried. She had not done that for many months.

The wind was colder now and night was coming.

CHAPTER FIFTEEN

It was an uncomfortable night. Soli's pack contained food and some clothing, so Var was able to fortify himself somewhat internally and externally. But the hardness and narrowness of the beams, the cutting edge of the intermittent wind, their several flesh wounds, and the general hopelessness of their situation made sleep a misery.

They clung together as they had done on the mesa of Muse, and they talked. "Does your head hurt?" Var asked, trying to make the inquiry seem more casual than it was.

"Yes. I think I banged it. How did we get out of the tunnel?"

Var told her.

"I think I started to wake when you made me stand," she said. "I heard voices, and something shook me, but it was all very far away, maybe a dream. Then I woke again and saw water, but I didn't know what was happening so I didn't move. I was pretty much alert when you carried me into the hive—but then I *knew* I had to stay out of trouble. I kept my eyes closed, so I didn't really know what it was."

That explained how she had been able to function almost normally once she woke up officially. She had been smart enough to play dead until she knew more. It had been hard on Var, but he knew that it would have been worse any other way. The amazons had treated him more carefully because they knew he was not much of a threat while he held the unconscious girl.

"Those men," she said. "They were almost like my father Sol, except that he's no weakling."

Var was aware of that. "They're castrates."

293

"No. They had—part. Like you. But——"

He realized she was right. He had seen testes but no members. They were only partial castrates—as he would have been, had the breed-queen's thrust at him scored.

"I've seen animals since we've been outside," she said. "I know what happens, I think. They breed by putting it—there." She touched her rear. This was, as it happened in their present circumstance, nestled firmly against his groin. Var visualized the way the four-footed animals performed and understood her inference. She did not really comprehend sex, yet. "But those hive-men—how could they——?"

He didn't know, and did not want to conjecture. It was an awkward subject to discuss with any female, particularly a nine-, almost ten-year-old child.

"What are we going to do, Var?" she asked after a while.

"When it gets light, we can climb down to the water and swim. Maybe we can get around the radiation."

"I don't know how to swim."

She had been brought up in the mountain. She would never have had the chance to sport in open water, he realized. And in the summer and winter and summer they had traveled together, they had never had occasion to swim. What were they to do now?

"Will you teach me, Var?" she asked shyly.

Again she had provided the answer herself. "I will teach you," he agreed.

Finally they did sleep. The wind died down and that was better.

The amazons, as though confident of their quarry, were not on watch in the morning. Var and Soli descended to the water with some difficulty, as the girders merged into isolated smooth pylons and plunged into the sea. He showed her the motions of swimming in the cold water and told her to keep her head up. She mastered the art quickly, though she splashed a good deal and stayed very close to him. "It's so deep!" she explained. They set out west along the bridge.

The radiation came, and they veered out into the ocean. This frightened Soli, but they both knew there was no other way. After a time he treaded water while she clung to him, exhausted. He could not tell whether the droplets

on her face were from the sea or her eyes. Certainly she was tired, tense and miserable.

Var wondered whether it would be feasible to steal a boat, but decided negatively. They wanted to hide, not advertise their presence by such activity. They would be safest on the bridge—once they got past the radiation.

Progress was slow. Several times they came all the way in to a pylon safely, and hung on while Soli coughed out mouthfuls of salt water. Her lips were blue and her face forlorn. Finally Var mounted a pylon and climbed stiffly until he encountered the radiation. They had to continue swimming.

But on the second try, half an hour later, he found no radiation. He helped her up. The sun came out and they soaked up its warmth as they ate sodden bread from the pack.

Then on down the highway, marching along its level thread toward China. Their supplies had been halved by the loss of Var's pack, but he thought they might catch some fish. And if there were other islands, there might be fruit or berries or at least rats.

Later in the day the road descended to land, and it was a larger island, many miles across, with trees and seals and birds and houses.

But they were wary, for there could also be men here, and the hive experience had taught them not to trust their own kind. Var had not before appreciated the true strength of the crazy/nomad system, and still did not comprehend its mechanisms. But somehow men were civilized there, as they were not at the hive. A man did not have to worry about castration, or fight outside the circle, in America.

There were no people. The island was vacant. They found old cans of food, but did not touch these. A few berries grew in patches, and these provided a supplement to their pack supplies. One of the houses seemed reasonably tight, and so they set up there after driving out the rats. (Soli said she'd rather not eat any rats just yet.)

At dawn the sound of a motor approached. They hid, watching through a dirt-crusted window that still had glass, and saw a boat with amazons pull up to the shore. This island was their foraging ground.

The women stepped out and surveyed the area effi-

ciently. Evidently they did not come here often, or they would not have needed to check it out so carefully. Fortunately they did not approach the house where Var and Soli lurked. Then several of the half-castrate men emerged. They were herded to one of the berry areas and put to work picking into wicker baskets, while the armored women took turns practising with their weaponry.

After a couple of hours the baskets were full and the men returned to the boat. Var and Soli relaxed.

Then they tensed again, for two people came ashore and headed for the houses. A man and a woman. They walked slowly, the man leading and listless, the woman prodding him along every so often.

"This one," she said, stopping at a house, She jerked open the door. Wood and plaster crashed down, and she coughed in the dust. She said a word Var had not heard before from distaff lips.

She tried the next house, but the door was jammed. She was a hefty woman, quite stout under her armor, but the house was sealed. Var had had the same experience the night before.

Then the amazon came to the one Var and Soli occupied.

The fugitives scrambled for the back room as the door pushed open. Var scooped up the pack, Soli their scattered belongings.

"Good," the amazon said as the door opened. "This one's tight and even fairly clean. You'd hardly know it's been deserted for years."

Var controlled his breathing and peered out of the gloom of the back room, Soli doing the same. There was a back exit—they had made sure of that before settling in—but that door creaked, and if they used it now they would be discovered. Then they would have to kill the two visitors, and the hunt would be on again, with no radiation to hide behind. And other couples were entering neighboring houses; he could hear them. Any noise would bring them running. Better to wait it out.

"Strip," the woman said, as imperiously as her erstwhile Queen.

The man obeyed with resignation. Once more Var saw his mutilation—a scrotum without an instrument. What purpose, this cruel cut?

Now the woman stripped, helmet to greaves. Gross of breast and belly, she stood and smiled.

And Var realized: they had come here to make sex! And the other couples would be doing the same.

Fascinated and disgusted, he watched. The woman was shaven below so that she resembled a ponderous child. The Queen had been barbered similarly, he remembered. The man, too, was hairless in that region, adding to his indignity. But that was superficial. Var's main question was how any effective connection between these two could be possible.

He looked across at Soli, wondering what her thoughts were. Her face was concealed in the shadow.

"There will have to be a new Queen," the Amazon murmured, leading the man to the worn mattress Var had slept on. "I have borne four healthy girls. One more and I will be in contention as a breed-leader, and can claim the Queenship—after I kill the other claimants. You, my pretty, have given me two of those girls, and you shall be well rewarded if you give me another."

"Yes," said the man unenthusiastically.

"Of course, if you disappoint me with a boy, it will go hard with you."

The man nodded.

Var, to his dismay, felt a surge of sexual excitement as he craned his head to see what transpired. This was perverted, it was awful—but compelling.

The amazon lay down and raised her knees. The man squatted between them. Her hands reached down——

Var, overbalanced at last, fell into the room.

Then it was rapid. Committed, Var and Soli had to strike. Almost before Var realized what had happened, the amazon pair lay sprawled unconscious, and there were shouts from the boat and other cabins in response to the noise of the brief battle. Var took up the amazon's bow and arrows, and Soli her spear; they grabbed their own possessions as well and ran out the back.

Despite the strait his guilty curiosity had brought them to, Var regretted that he had not learned how the amazons mated. Would he ever know?

Armed women were charging from the boat and emerging—in dishabille—from houses. Five of them were

headed toward Var and Soli, while the men milled uncertainly on the shore. Three were closing in on the house just vacated. Two split off to cover the path to the bridge. Var saw that that route was hopeless. In fact, now that the hornets had been aroused, the entire island was hopeless. The women were tough, and odds of five to two in daylight were prohibitive. And the men would naturally assist their females.

"The boat!" Soli whispered piercingly. "This way!"

Var knew that direction to be the very height of folly. But she was already running at right angles to the path of the approaching trio, and he had either to follow or to let her go alone. He could not call to her, for that would pinpoint their location immediately. So he followed.

She circled toward the boat. The amazons, not suspecting this maneuver, remained in the village. He could hear them exclaiming over the fallen couple and banging through the houses in that section. Soli stopped just before they came in sight of the men.

"They're weaklings," she gasped. "The men don't fight. If we run at them and yell, they'll flee." And she set off again, running and yelling and waving her arms.

Var had to follow once more.

The men did scatter, though there were four of them here, all full grown. Var marveled.

"Now the boat!" Soli said, clambering in.

As Var settled beside her, the amazons realized what had happened and gave hue and cry.

"Start the motor!" Soli yelled at him.

He looked at her blankly.

"The pull cord!" she cried. She grabbed a handle on the engine and jerked. It came out on a string, and there was a bang. Var remembered that he had seen an amazon do this on the other boat that took them to the hive.

He took hold and gave it a tremendous yank. The cord came out a yard—and the motor roared.

"I'll steer!" Soli screamed over the noise. She grabbed the wheel in the middle of the boat and began doing things with handles. To Var's amazement, the craft began to move. She knew what she was doing!

Under Soli's guidance, it nudged out from the bank and swashed into deeper water. The amazons ran up,

brandishing their spears, but there was twenty feet of water separating them from the boat. Then the women kneeled and lifted their bows.

Soli jerked another handle and the motor multiplied its sound. The boat jerked forward.

The arrows came. They were not random shots. They passed well wide of the engine section, that the archers did not want to damage, and centered on the personnel. They did not miss by much. Only Soli's sudden burst of speed spoiled their aim.

The second volley was already nocked, and Var knew this one would score, though the boat was now fifty feet away and moving swiftly. He grabbed one of the round amazon leather shields and held it behind Soli's back, for she could not see the arrows coming while she was driving.

Three arrows plonked into the shield—surely fatal to her, had they not been intercepted. Two struck Var. One was in his right arm, rending flesh and bone; the other was in his gut.

He clung to consciousness, for they were not out of danger yet. He left the arrows where they were, but shifted the shield to his left hand and kneeled behind Soli, protecting her by both his shield and his body.

Two more arrows plunged into the leather, their points coming through but without much force. Another skewered his unprotected thigh. One more passed just beside his head and struck the wood near Soli.

"Var, can't you——" she said, turning.

Then she saw his situation and screamed.

Var passed out.

CHAPTER SIXTEEN

He woke and fainted many times, conscious of pain and the passage of time and the rocking of waves and Soli's attentions, and of very little else. The arrows were out from his arm and leg and gut, but this brought him no relief. His body was burning, his throat dry, his bowels pressing.

She took care of him. She propped him up inside the boat's cabin and held water to his mouth, and it made him sick and the heaves wrenched his abdomen cruelly, but his lips and tongue and throat felt better. He soiled himself many times and she cleaned him up, and when she washed his genitals they reacted and that made him ashamed but there was nothing he could do. He kept bleeding from his wounds, and she would wash them and bandage them, and then he would move and the blood would flow hotly again.

He thought deliriously of the Master, in the badlands seven years before, his illness from radiation. Now Var knew what the man had gone through, and why he had sworn friendship to the wild boy who had aided him then. But the thought brought another torment, for he still could not fathom why the Master had reversed that oath and become a mortal enemy.

But most of all, he thought of Soli—she who cared for him now in his helplessness. A child yet—but a master sticker and faithful companion who had never remarked on the colors of his skin or the crudity of his hands and feet and hunch. She could have returned to her father, whom she loved, but had not. She could even have gone to the Master, who had offered to adopt her as his daugh-

ter. Such offers were never casually made. She had stayed with Var because she thought he needed help.

And he did.

It was night and he slept. It was day and he moved fitfully and half-slept, hearing the roaring of the motor, smelling the gasoline she poured from stacked cans into the funnel. It was night again, and cold, and Soli hugged him close and wrapped rough blankets about them both and warmed him with her small body while his teeth knocked together.

But he did recover.

In one of his lucid moments—and he was aware they were not frequent—she talked with him about the mountain Helicon and the nomads.

"You know, I thought you people were savages," she said. "Then I met you, and the Nameless One, and I knew you were merely ignorant. I thought it would be good to have you joined with underworld 'nology."

"Yes——" He wanted to agree, to converse on her level, sure he was able to do so now. But the sentence played itself out in silence.

"But now I've seen what it's like beyond the crazy demesnes, where the common man does have some 'nology—technology—and I'm not so sure. I wonder whether the nomads would lose their primitive values, if——"

Yes, yes! He had wondered the same. And been unable to express it succinctly. The amazons and their motors and their barbarism. . . . But he could remember no more of that fragment. The boat went on and on beside the bridge. Once he felt radiation, and cried out, and she veered away from it.

Then time had passed or stopped and the boat was docked and there were people. Not amazons, not nomads. Soli was gone and then she was back, crying, and she kissed him and was gone again.

A man came and stabbed him in the arm with a spike. When Var woke once more, his abdomen hurt with a different kind of hurt—a mending hurt—and he knew he was at last recovering. But Soli was not there.

Women came and fed him and cleaned him, and he slept some more. And days passed.

"I believe you are well now," a stranger said one day. He was old enough to be losing his hair, and somewhat stout and flabby. No warrior of the circle, he!

Var *was* well, though weak. His arm and leg and gut had healed, and he was now able to eat without vomiting and to eliminate without bleeding. But he did not trust this man, and he missed Soli, who had not come again since the time she kissed him and cried.

"The girl—what is your relationship to her?" the man asked.

"We are friends."

"You speak with a heavy accent. And you appear to have suffered serious radiation burns at one time, and childhood deformities. Where do you come from?"

"Crazy demesnes," he answered, remembering Soli's term.

The man frowned, "Are you being clever?"

"Some call it America. The crazies share it with the nomads."

"Oh." The man brought him strange, elegant clothing. "Well, you should be advised that this is New Crete, in the Aleutians. We are civilized, but we have our own conventions. The girl understands this, but feels that you may not."

"Soli—where is she?"

"She is at the temple, awaiting the pleasure of our God. You may see her now, if you wish."

"Yes." Var still did not like the man's attitude. It was not exactly cynicism of the Helicon vintage, but it wasn't friendly either.

He dressed, feeling awkward in the long loose trousers and long-sleeved white shirt, and particularly in the stiff leather shoes that hurt his clubbed feet. This was not what Var considered to be civilized attire. But the man insisted that he wear these things before going out.

They were in a city—not a dead badlands city, but a living metropolis with lighted buildings and moving vehicles. People thronged the clean streets. Var felt less uncomfortable when he saw that most men were garbed as he was.

The temple was a tremendous building buttressed by

columns and a high wall. Guards armed with guns stood at the front gate. Var, so weak that even the short walk fatigued him, and weaponless, felt nervous.

Within the temple were robed priests and elaborate furnishings. After several challenges and explanations, Var's guide brought him to a chamber whose center was crossed by a row of vertical metal bars, each set about four inches from its neighbor.

Soli entered the other half of the room. She saw Var and ran up to the bars, reaching through to grasp his hand. "You're all right!" she cried, her voice breaking.

"Yes." He was not so certain about her. She looked well, but there was something wrong about her manner. "Why are you here, behind these bars?"

"I'm in the temple." She was silent a moment, just looking at him. "I agreed to do something, so I have to stay here. I can't see you again after this, Var."

He was not facile with words. He did not know how to protest eloquently, to make her tell the truth. Particularly not with the stranger listening. But he knew from her tight, controlled, desperate manner that something terrible had happened while he lay sick, and that Soli expected never to see him again.

And she did not want him to know why.

She had been alienated from him as surely as had the Master—and also by the agency of some third party.

"Good-bye, Var."

He refused to say it to her. He squeezed her hand and turned to go, knowing that this was not the occasion for effective rebuttal. He knew too little.

And during the walk back he worked out what he had to do.

"You will have to go to the employment agency and make application for training," the man said. "Even the menial jobs will be complicated for you at first."

"What if I want to leave here?" *Not without Soli, though!*

"Why of course you may—if you purchase a boat and supplies. This is a free island. But to do that you will need money."

"Money?"

"If you don't know what that is, you don't have any."

Var let that pass. In time he would find out what money was, and whether he needed it. It sounded like some variation of barter, however.

They entered the hospital and returned to Var's room. "You'll be moving out of here in a day or so," the man said.

Var looked around. None of his or Soli's prior possessions were in evidence, except the bracelet he wore, and that was dull and scratched. He thought he knew why they hadn't taken that: they didn't know it was gold.

The bed was similar to some he had seen during his childhood in the badlands. It had high rods of metal projecting at either end, rather like the grates to certain ancient windows—or the bars in that temple room. Generally, these could be screwed loose. . . .

"And a final word," the man said. "Don't go bothering them at the temple. They won't let you see your friend again."

Var placed a hand on one of the rods and twisted. It was tight. "Why not?"

"Because she is now a temple maiden, dedicated to our God Minos. These girls are kept in seclusion for the duration."

Var tried another bar. This one turned. "Why?"

"Regulations. When they approach nubility, there is too much danger of their losing their value to the God."

The rod came free. Var held it aloft and advanced on the man, suppressing a tremor of weakness. *What will happen to her?*

The man looked at him and at the improvised club as though ignorant of the threat. "Really, there is no need for that——"

"Tell me—or you die." Var, driven by fear for Soli, was not bluffing. He was weak, but this man was obviously untrained for combat. One or two blows would suffice.

"Very well. She is to be sacrificed to Minos."

Var wavered, suddenly feeling his weakness redoubled. His worst fear had been brutally confirmed. "Why——"

"You were dying. Medical attention is expensive. She agreed to enter the temple—it has to be voluntary, for we are civilized—if we made you well again. Because she will

be lovely, and the God likes that, we acceded to the unusual commitment. Today we demonstrated that we kept our bargain, and now she will keep hers."

"She will—die?"

"Yes."

Var dropped the bedpost and sat down, befuddled and horrified. "How——"

"She will be chained to the rock at the entrance to the labyrinth. Minos will come and devour her in his fashion. Then fortune will smile on New Crete for one more month, for our God will be satisfied."

One last thing Var had to know. "When——"

"Oh, not for a couple of years yet. Your friend is still a child." He glanced obscurely at Var. "Otherwise I dare say she would not have proved eligible."

Var did not follow the man's nuances and did not care to. The relief was as debilitating as the threat. Two years! There were a thousand things he could do to save her in that time.

"Remember, nomad—she made a bargain. Young as she is, she strikes us as a person of integrity. She will not break her vow, that saved your life, no matter what you may do."

And that, Var realized with dismay, was the truth. Soli had always been keen to keep a bargain, any bargain. She didn't object to little ploys, such as passing for a boy or stealing the food they needed to live on, but she liked the formal things to be right.

The man stood up. "I know it is hard for you to accept the ways of an unfamiliar culture, just as I would have trouble adapting to your crazy-circle system of America." Var noted that the man, despite his prior attitude, did after all know something of nomad existence. Maybe Soli had told him, and he had been verifying it with Var. "But you will find us fair and even generous, if you cooperate with the system. Tomorrow you will be released, and I'll direct you to the employment agency. They will test you for aptitude and provide the individual indicated training. From then on, it is up to you. If you work well, you will eat well."

He left.

Var lay on the bed. He appreciated the efficiency of the system—it had points of similarity to the empire—but he had no intention of letting Soli die.

Still, he did have time to plan carefully. Until he came upon a suitable course of action, he could afford to cooperate.

Var became a trash collector. Because he was ugly and the proffered training perfunctory, he could not aspire to any prestige position. Because he was illiterate and had poor hands, he could not handle most of the more sophisticated jobs of New Crete, a literate, technological society. And hauling refuse on a daily basis kept him in excellent physical condition. People left him alone because of the dirt and the smell, and that was the way he wanted it too. He had a room with running water and heat in the winter and even an electric light that snapped on when he yanked at a string, and he earned enough of the metal tokens that were "money" to purchase clothing and regular meals and occasional entertainment.

It was a year before he discovered just how valuable his golden bracelet of manhood was here. He had thought it would bring a few of their silver tokens, but the truth was that had it been appraised and sold it would have paid for all his initial hospitalization. Gold, so common in the crazy demesnes, was at a premium here, for they used it in their machinery in ways he did not understand. Soli must have suspected this—yet sold herself into the temple rather than take advantage of it.

Her generosity had been foolish. A man wore the bracelet only to give it to the woman of his choice. What could she care whether he wore it? He had no woman to give it to.

By day Var cooperated and had no trouble. By night he stripped his conventional clothing, dressed in warm rags, and ranged barefoot in the wilderness regions of New Crete. The island was large—at least twenty miles across—and he was able to explore it without disturbing the inhabitants, and to practice his weaponry. He made himself a fine set of sticks from seasoned wood, and became as proficient with them as he had ever been in the circle with the metal ones. It was not the implement but the skill of the hand that counted. He learned the lay of the land, and

even ventured some distance into the dark tunnel that left the island on the west. It was clogged with refuse; no mechanical sweepers cleaned it, and it had been used as a dump.

And he scouted the temple preserve. This was a walled enclosure between one and two miles in diameter, patrolled but not heavily. Var had no problem sneaking in. Every day the maidens were exercised, Soli among them, and Var observed that she was well cared for. Every month at full moon one of the older ones was taken to a canyon and chained there. Next evening she would be gone. Var never actually saw the God Minos, because the God struck not by the light of that full moon, oddly, but by day. The maidens were put out before dawn and remained as it grew light. Var could not do so; he had to work by day, every day, and had he remained in the compound he would have run the double risk of absence at his assigned location and discovery at his forbidden location.

In the second year he built a boat. Not a good one, not nearly as good as the amazon one they had arrived in (what had happened to it? Why hadn't *that* value been charged against his medical bill?) and certainly not one he would trust to the open seas. Even if he were sailor enough to manage it. But the craft would do to spirit Soli away and hide her until better arrangements could be made. First he had to save her from Minos.

For if she were chained in the canyon for the God, then rescued, her bargain would be complete. She would have offered herself in sacrifice and found unexpected reprieve. All he had to do was stop Minos from eating her, then take her away, and the temple would never know the difference.

The morning came. Var was watching, for he knew the monthly date of the ceremony (he could look at the moon as well as a priest could) and had been aware that her turn was incipient. Most of the girls were now younger than she, and the temple did not provide board and keep longer than necessary. This was the day he would not go on his rounds—indeed, not ever again.

Soli, grown barely nubile in two years, was taken by hooded priests to the canyon and anchored there. The

men—Var could not be certain of their sex, but assumed this was man's business—hammered spiked shackles into the stone. Soli's slender wrists were pinned within them at shoulder height. She was naked, her lustrous black hair falling down around her shoulders, her small breasts standing erect, her rather well-fleshed thighs flexing nervously as she fidgeted about.

Var felt an acute pang. Soli now looked very much indeed like her natural mother Sola. Once her hips and breasts filled out completely——

But what would never happen unless he saved her from the sacrifice.

Var lurked in the trees as the priests departed. He waited half an hour, making sure they would not return and that no other parties were watching. The canyon face was shielded from the direct view of the temple, probably intentionally and mercifully for the remaining maidens. Var now knew how most of them came here: they volunteered in order to spare their families hunger, for there were many poor people on the island. The he-who-won't-work-won't-eat philosophy was a thin cover for subjugation of the unfortunate. The wage that had been adequate for Var was not enough for a family, so there was continual and large-scale distress. The way of the crazies and the nomads was better, for no one hungered in America.

Assured that he was unobserved, Var let fly his random philosophies, emerged from hiding, and entered the canyon. Soli heard him and looked up with a poignant little cry of dismay, thinking the god had come already. Then she gasped. "Var!"

He approached and put his hand to one manacle. "I never forgot you," he said. "Did you think I would let you be eaten?"

But the bond was tight, and he had no leverage to pry it loose.

"I——" she started, her eyes suddenly streaming. "I—thank you, Var. But I can't go with you. I made a vow."

"You fulfilled it!" He cast about for some way to get the metal out of the stone. Why hadn't he anticipated this detail?

"No. Not until—the sacrifice," she said.

Var yanked at the other manacle. There seemed to be some give in it.

"I can't let you do this," she said through her tears.

Var ignored her and continued to work on the metal. His sticks would not pry it, being too thick to squeeze in beside her wrist, and the outside offered no purchase. He might hammer the metal with a stone—but the sound would bring the priests—or Minos himself.

Then he was thrown back.

Soli had raised her bare foot and shoved him hard in the chest. Now he understood: she meant it. She would resist him physically not permitting him to labor on the bonds.

That meant he could not free her unless he knocked her out. And what kind of cooperation would she give him thereafter, if he violated her oath by such force?

In any event, he could not bring himself to strike her. Anyone else, yes; Soli, no.

He stood up and faced her. "Then I'll go slay Minos," he said.

"No!" she screamed in horror. "He's a beast! No one can hurt him!"

"I have sworn to kill the man who harms Sola's child," Var said. "I swore it long before you made *your* oath. Would you have me wait until after the—after the creature comes?"

"But Minos is a god, not a man! You can't kill him!"

"He devours maidens—but he's not a beast?" Then he was ashamed of his irony with her. "Whatever he is, I must meet him—unless you come with me now."

"I can't."

Var saw that further argument was useless. He marched down the canyon into the labyrinth, heedless of her low cries.

There was a large, open cave where the walls merged. From its rear several smaller passages opened. Var held his sticks up and went cautiously into one.

It led to a medium chamber lined with bones. Var did not investigate them closely; he knew their source. If he did not succeed in his mission, Soli's bones would be added to the collection. He went on.

The next chamber had several dry skulls. The third was mixed. There was no present sign of Minos.

It occurred to Var that the beast-god could go out and attack Soli while he searched the empty caverns. Hastily he retreated toward the entrance, passing through the skull chamber and an empty one.

And realized that he was lost in the labyrinth. He had missed a passage and now did not know where he was or in what direction lay the entrance. His wilderness exploring sense, normally an automatic guide to such things, had let him down in this moment of preoccupation.

He could find his way out. He could sniff out his own spoor, or, failing that, make lines of bones to show his route, eliminating one false exit after another. But this would take time, and Soli might be in danger this moment. So he acted more directly.

"Minos!" he bawled. "Come fight me!"

"Must I?" a gentle voice replied behind him.

Var whirled. A man stood in one of the passages.

No—not a man. The body was that of a giant warrior, but the head was woolly and horned. No mere beard accounted for the effect. The front of the face pushed out in a solid snout, and the horns sprouted from just above the ears. It was as though the head of a bull had been grafted on to the body of a man. And the feet were hoofs—not blunted toes, like Var's own, but solid round bovine hoofs. The teeth, however, were not herbivorous; they were pointed like those of a hound.

This was Minos.

Var had seen oddities before and had been expecting something of the sort. He made a motion with one stick, the excitement of battle growing within him. He supposed this was what some called fear.

"What brings you here by day, Var the Stick?" the god inquired quietly. "Always before you have come in darkness, and never to my domicile."

"I came to fight," Var repeated. No one had told him the god could speak, or that he knew so much. How had Minos learned Var's name?

"Of course. But why at this moment? I have a busy day ahead. Yesterday I could have entertained you at greater leisure."

"It is Soli out there. My friend. For the sacrifice. I have sworn to kill the man—or beast, or god—who harms her. But I would not wait to have her harmed."

Minos nodded, his woolly locks shaking. "You have fidelity and courage. But do you really believe you can kill me?"

"No. But I must try, for I have no life without Soli."

"Come. We can settle this without unpleasantness." Minos turned his broad back and trod down the passage, his horny feet clicking on the stone.

Var, nonplussed, followed.

They came to a larger chamber, in whose center was a boulder. "I lift this for exercise," Minos said. "Like this." He bent to grapple the stone, seemingly not concerned that an armed enemy stood behind him. Muscles bulged hugely all along his arms and sides and back. Var had not seen might like that since training with the Master.

The stone came up. Minos lifted it to chest height, held it there a few seconds, then eased it down. "Have to watch how you let go these monsters," he panted. "Most hernias come after the load, not during it."

He stood back. "Now your turn. If you can hoist it, you may be a match for me."

Var hung his sticks at his belt and approached the rock. The god had trusted him and he was obligated to extend trust in return.

He strained and hauled at no avail. He could not budge it. The thing would not even roll.

He gave up. "You're right. I am not as strong as you. But I might beat you in combat."

"Certainly," Minos said genially. His face was strong when he spoke, because he had to stretch his mouth closed around the muzzle and form the words with part of it. Even so, his enunciation was odd. "And we shall fight if you insist. But let us converse a time first. I seldom have opportunity to chat with an honest man."

Var was amenable. As long as the god was with him, Soli was safe. He wondered what would have happened had he attacked Minos while the god lifted the rock. That boulder might have come flying at him. . . .

They sat on crude chairs fashioned of bone tied with tendon, in another chamber. "Have a bite to eat," Minos

said. "I have nuts, berries, bread—and meat, of course. But you know where that comes from."

Var knew. But the notion was not as shocking to him as he knew it was to others, for he had eaten many things in his wild childhood state. "I will share your food."

Minos reached into a pit and drew out a meaty rib. "I roasted these yesterday, so they remain wholesome," he explained, handing it to Var. He lifted a second for himself.

Var gnawed the rib, finding it far more tasty than raw rat meat. He wondered to which maiden it had belonged. Probably the last one; she had cried endlessly as they staked her out, and hadn't been very pretty. A bit fat—as this morsel verified. Momentarily queasy, Var washed his first mouthful down with the tepid water Minos provided.

"Where do you originate?" the god inquired.

Var explained about the circle culture.

"I have heard of it," Minos said. "But I must confess I thought it a myth, a fabrication, no offense intended. Now I see that it is a marvelous land indeed. But why did you and the girl depart?"

Var explained that, too. It was remarkably easy to talk to this enemy giant, and not entirely because of the stay it granted Soli.

"And you say her father is a castrate? When did that happen?"

"I don't know. No one spoke of it. I don't see how it could have been while he was Master of Empire, and Soli says it wasn't in the underworld."

"Then it must have been before. Perhaps in childhood. Some tribes, I have heard, practice such things. But in that case——"

Var shrugged. "I don't know."

"Is it possible—I am postulating from ignorance, understand—that the Nameless One is in fact her father?"

Var sat and chewed the maiden-meat, and diverse things began to fall into place in his mind, as though bees were settling into a hive. *The Master thought Var had slain his natural daughter!*

"Ironic," Minos said. "If that is the case. But the solution is simple. You have merely to show her to him when next you meet."

"Except——"

"Unfortunately, yes."

"Do you have to take her?" It was hard to believe that so affable, reasonable a creature could balk on this point.

Minos sighed. "I am a god. Gods do not follow the conventions of man, by definition. I wish it were otherwise."

"But surely you have enough meat here to last another month?"

"I do not, for it spoils and I am not a ghoul. Some day I must require them to install refrigeration equipment. But that is not the problem. It is not primarily for the meat that I take the sacrifices."

Var chewed, not understanding.

"The flesh is only an incidental product," Minos said. "I use it because it is handy and I dislike waste. I make the best of the situation foisted on me by the temple."

"The temple makes you do this?"

"All temples, all religions make their gods perform similarly. So it has always been, even before the Blast. The New Crete priests pretend that they serve Minos, but Minos serves them. It is a method of population control, in part, for the birthrate is governed by the percentage of nubile girls in the population. But mostly it is a way to retain power that would otherwise drift with the winds of politics and time. The common people have an abiding fear of me. I lurk near the bedstead of every disobedient child, I breathe misfortune on every tax-evader. I impregnate the wanton wives. Yet I am single and mortal. The temple produced me by mutation and operation———"

"Like the Master!" Var exclaimed.

"So it seems. I should like to meet that man some day. And in the course of that adaptation to godhood, they provided me with—this." Minos opened his garment. Var was impressed. "The opposite of castration, you see. My appetite differs correspondingly from that of the normal male. But it waxes only with the moon."

"Then Soli—and the others———"

"You will note that I have stayed well within my domicile. Should I go near enough to the entrance to pick up the nuptial odor I should immediately lose control of myself. That is the way I have been designed; it is in my blood, my brain, my gonad. My onslaught is such that my partner does not survive."

Var pictured the member he had just seen, and the force with which it would be wielded, and shuddered to remember that Soli awaited this. Better a full underhand smash by a club! "Why don't they provide—old women?"

"Who would die soon anyway? Because they are not virgins. Minos must have chastity. This is part of it. My glands simply do not tolerate any other condition."

This seemed remarkable to Var, but no more so than other things he had seen and learned in his travels. "What happens if a mistake is made—if the sacrifice is not chaste?"

Minos smiled hideously, all his teeth exposed on one side. "Why then I betake myself to the temple and I raise a fuss. And it is said that bad luck follows for a month."

Var attacked the last of his repast. He remembered something. "Do you know about the amazons—the hive-women?"

"Oh, yes. Fascinating subculture there. I had them in mind when I mentioned ritual mutilation."

"The men—how do they do it?"

"No problem at all. The women do it. Simple manipulation of the prostate and seminal vesicles so as to force out the ejaculate at the critical moment. Not the most comfortable mode for the man, particularly if he has hemorrhoids or if she has a broken fingernail, but effective enough."

Var nodded, not caring to admit that this explained nothing to him. He had never heard of a prostate, and obviously babies were not conceived by fingernails, whole or broken.

The meal was done. "I must fight you," Var said.

"Surely you know I would kill you. I should think you would find a more romantic solution, pun intended. I would not like to have the blood of both of you on my horns—not when you have traveled so far, and worked so hard, and suffered such ironies already. Particularly when it is so easily avoided."

Var looked at him, not understanding. "She won't go with me. Not until the sacrifice."

Minos stood up. "There are things a god does not tell a man. Go now, or assuredly we *shall* fight, for the need is rising in me."

Var drew his sticks.

Minos knocked them numbingly from his hands with one lightning swipe. "Go! I will not reason with a fool."

Var, seeing that it was hopeless, picked up his sticks and went. This time he found the proper passage.

CHAPTER SEVENTEEN

Soli remained at the rock. Var ran to her. "You must go with me. Minos is coming!"

She hardly seemed surprised to see him alive. "I know. It is nearly noon." Her fair face was reddening in the slanting sun, and her lips were cracked.

"He doesn't want to kill you! But he has to, if he finds you here."

"Yes." She was crying again, but he could tell from her expression that she had not changed her mind.

"I can't stop him. I'll try, but he will kill us both."

"Then go!" she screamed at him explosively. "I did this to save your stupid life. Why throw it away?"

"*Why?*" he screamed back. "I would rather die than have you die! You gave me nothing!"

She glared at him, abruptly calm. "Sosa told me all men were fools."

Var didn't see the relevance. But before he could speak again, there was a bellow from the labyrinth.

"Minos!" she whispered, terrified. "Oh, Var—please, please, *please* go! It's too late for me now."

The shape of the giant loomed at the cave entrance. Vapor snorted from the god's nostrils.

Var threw himself on Soli as though to shield her from the onslaught of the god, knowing this to be futile but determined not to desert her. He held her close and tight though she fought him, tearing his clothing with her feet and teeth. Finally he got her body pinned firmly against the wall so that her legs split and kicked behind him ineffectively while she hung by the manacles. "I will not leave you," he panted in her tangled hair.

Then her resistance collapsed. "Oh, Var, I'm sorry!" she sobbed. "I love you, you idiot."

There was no time to be amazed. He kissed her savagely, hearing the tramp of Minos' hoofs, the blast of Minos' breath.

Desperately they embraced, experiencing what had been building for three years; compressing it all into these last moments. Sharing their love absolutely, exquisitely, painfully.

And Minos came, and stopped, and paused, and made a noise half fury and half laughter, and passed on.

Only then did Var realize what had happened. What Minos had tried, subtly, to suggest to him.

He had, indeed, been a fool. Almost.

There were screams from the temple as Var yanked and pried and banged at the manacles still pinning Soli's bruised wrists against the stone. If he could get even one prong out, her hand would be free—but the stone and metal were too strong.

He found a corroded spike in the dirt just beyond the canyon and wedged it under one bond and pounded it with a stone—and finally, reluctantly, one prong pulled out. But his spike snapped as he pried up, and was useless for the other manacle.

The furor at the temple subsided. After an interval Minos came back, carrying two bodies. Var and Soli waited apprehensively.

The god halted. "This one's the high priestess," he remarked with satisfaction. "She deserved this, if anyone does. Poetic justice." He looked at Soli, who averted her face.

"Hold this," Minos said, handing Var a dead girl. Var took her, not knowing how to decline. She was about Soli's age, still warm, and blood dripped from her. There was something incredible about her posture, even in death; it was as though her guts had been pulped, leaving a human-shaped shell. He knew how close this corpse had come to being Soli herself.

Minos reached forth with the hand thus freed and grasped the stubborn manacle. The muscles of that great

arm twitched. The metal popped out of the wall with a spray of stone and fell to the ground. Soli was free.

Then the god fished a small package from his torn clothing and gave it to Soli, forcing it into her reluctant hand. "A gift," he said. "There never was anything personal about this——but I'm glad you became ineligible."

Soli did not answer, but she held on to the package. Minos took back the second corpse and marched into his labyrinth, humming a merry tune. He had reason to be happy: he would eat well this month.

"We'd better get out of here before the temple recovers," Var said. "Come on." He took Soli's hand and led her away.

Once they were in the forest he took off his tattered shirt and put it about her. It formed into a short, baggy, but rather attractive dress, for her exposed legs were firm, her torso slender, and her face, despite the sunburn, lovely.

Soli, mutely curious, opened the package Minos had given her. It contained two keys and a paper with writing on it. She stared.

"What good are keys?" Var demanded. "We have no house."

"They belong to a powerboat," she said, reading the paper.

There were sea-charts aboard the craft, and voluminous tanks of gasoline and fresh water and canned goods. How Minos had arranged this they could not guess, but the boat had obviously been ready long before the two of them had entered the picture. Perhaps he had intended to escape himself, but had given up the notion because of his biological urgencies. Or maybe he was less a slave to the temple than he had admitted. He could have many luxurious boats tucked away. . . .

From the maps they learned that they were far south of where they had supposed. The tunnel to China—actually, to Siberia—left from farther along. They had taken the Aleutian series, that led nowhere. However, with this stout craft it should be possible to make the crossing, following the island chain to the Kamchatka peninsula. From there they could either trek overland north and west and

south around the Sea of Okhotsk, or continue island-hopping directly southwest toward Japan.

Var's head spun with the unfamiliar names Soli pieced out. This weird map was like the Master's books: it predated the Blast, and so contained much nonsense. Some of the islands might not be there any more.

Somehow neither person suggested that they go back—back past the amazon hive, on to Alaska, north to the true crossing. Or even back to America. China had become a fixed objective, for no good reason now. Obviously they were not going to be satisfied with anyone's culture but their own. And if the Master were still on their trail, he should have caught up by this time.

They could go home and Soli could rejoin whichever father she chose, and Var could be a warrior again, and their relationship would be over. They would never need to see each other again. Yet they continued west, non-sensically.

A storm blew up and they hastily docked the boat on the shore of a deserted islet. Then fair weather, and they moved through deep water at top speed, letting the fine engine do the work.

They did not discuss the implications of what they had done to escape Minos, and after a time it became as though it had not happened. Indeed, the entire New Crete residence of two years tended to encyst itself as a thing apart, an unreal memory. Soli was the child again, Var the ugly warrior.

But with a difference. Hide it as they might, Soli was nubile and Var male. They could no longer embrace with complete innocence and candor, for now an embrace implied an adult relationship and inspired adult reactions that neither cared to admit. Nor could they talk quite so frankly, for the frankest subject of all was sex.

They were not ready for love. For a moment it had been forced upon them, emotionally and physically . . . but that moment had faded like the storm tide, and they were left to their unbridged isolation. Two people united by a common purpose and an unspoken affection.

This was, at any rate, the way Var saw it, though he did not work it out neatly or consciously. More than once

he observed Soli staring at his bracelet. Perhaps she was remembering the way she had preserved it for him, at the near sacrifice of her own life. He was sorry that he had told her this was foolish, for that must have hurt her feelings—but it was true. Had the bracelet been sold, they need never have suffered those two years on New Crete.

That reminded him circularly of another point, the one Minos had made. *Could* the Master be Soli's natural father? Now this seemed less reasonable than it had in the cave, and Var could not bring himself to present the notion openly. How would Soli react, having the paternity of Sol questioned? She loved Sol dearly, and hardly knew the Master. And if it *were* true, how would the Master react, knowing that Var had lied to him, making him believe his daughter had been slain? And when he learned what had happened on New Crete, what Soli had been set up for, how she had been reprieved. . . .

The wide expanse of the sea went on and on, hypnotic, beautiful, boring. The sparse islands were barren, and did not conform exactly to the indications of the map. They took turns steering, following a marking on the compass— a dial that always pointed north. The sun and the stars also served, and whenever they encountered a feature recognizable on the map, they corrected course accordingly.

And a few days after they thought the ocean would never end, they sighted the mainland of Asia.

And the people spoke incomprehensibly.

"Yes, of course," Soli said in response to his bewilderment. "They speak Chinese. Or they will, when we reach China. The map says it's—well, see, we have a long way to go yet."

Two thousand miles or more, it seemed to Var. Months of travel.

They were sick of the ocean, but the overland route looked worse. They searched out a place to buy gasoline, paying for it with artifacts from the boat, and hopped southwest along what the map called the Kuril islands, then north inside of Sakhalin, and finally back to the mainland of Manchuria. The preposterous pre-Blast names were fascinating.

Now the land route promised to be more direct and safe. They had either to use the boat or dispose of it, and

they remained more at home afoot. So, regretfully, they decided to sell it. They went to a place that had similar craft and inquired until an old man was brought who spoke a little American.

"America?" he asked, amazed. "Destroyed—Blast."

By and by they conducted a party to the boat, and the sale was completed. Soli was cynical about the value, expecting to be cheated, but there seemed to be little choice. At any rate, they obtained enough currency to buy local outfits and equipment, and some written primers in the language—including an ancient, pre-Blast text with American equivalents.

They hiked again and drilled each other on the written symbols. Soli said they were not like the writing she knew, but that they made sense once she got used to them. And though there were many spoken dialects, so that travelers like them would be constantly confused, the written language covered the entire region. With these symbols they could always communicate—provided they met someone literate.

Overall, the landscape resembled what they had known on the other continent—mountainous, wild, and riddled by patches of badlands radiation. The natives near the coast were civilized in the fashion of New Crete—without human sacrifice, but with other cultural problems. Those inland were more primitive—like the American nomads, but without the substantial benefits of crazy technology or supplied hostels. Most left the strangers alone, but some were belligerent, and no circle circumscribed the combat. Had Var and Soli not been apt at self-defense, they would not have lived very long.

They followed the river Amur inland, not from any love of the water but because it showed the best route through the formidable mountain ranges. When it veered northwest, they shifted to a large tributary. Months passed and they came at last to the fringe of the actual Chinese territories. The Chinese influence, like that of the crazies in America, extended through the entire region, perhaps all the continent; but their written language unified the divers peoples in a subtle but comprehensive way. Var, having learned the very real constraints upon the seemingly free nomad society, was sure that similar factors operated here.

Similar in principle, if not in detail. There must, indeed, be a Chinese Helicon.

Yet as they neared their supposed destination, their camaraderie became more strained. Soli was filling out, and Var was too well aware of this. Sometimes he touched his bracelet, thinking of offering it to her—but this always reminded him of what had happened when he first took his manhood. Girls of band-borrowing age did not appreciate ugly men, and Var knew himself to be grotesque.

And—she was beautiful. Perhaps in the flower of her maidenhood her mother Sola had been like this, so lovely that the mightiest warriors of the age contested for her favor and lived lies without complaint. Soli tended to hide her charms under rough, loose clothing; but when she bathed—as she did even now without embarrassment— her naked body was wonderous.

Soli had never remarked on it, but she could hardly favor his mottled skin, battered countenance and clubbed extremities. Children did not care so much about such things, but Soli would never be a child again.

Var saw, occasionally, the literate ladies of this core-Chinese culture. They were like crafted dolls, delicate and delightful, their motions constrained, their demeanors diffident. In contrast, the peasant women were brutes—stout, plain, hunched of body, coarse of expression.

Var knew that the wandering life he was making for Soli would shape her into the peasant mold. He could not bear the thought. Increasingly it preyed upon him, and when he saw some crone he fancied Soli's face on her.

The background level of civilization rose as they entered the Chinese heartland. The people here were yellowish of skin and their eyes were different, and their manners tended to be almost ritualistically polite. The women were eloquent—the highborn ones. Var learned that they attended institutions somewhat like the crazy schools, that brought them to the mature state. Then, as sophisticated ladies, they married, and did not do hand labor again. Household servants performed the chores.

Var decided that this would be a better life for Soli. But he didn't know how to explain this philosophy, and feared she would not understand his intent, so he didn't try.

One night when she slept beside him in the forest, he rose stealthily. She woke, however. "Var?"

"Have to—you know," he said, feeling a pang of guilt for his lie. To reassure her, he urinated noisily against a tree, then squatted. In a moment her breathing became even and he moved quietly away.

Just as he passed beyond the normal hearing range, he heard something—either an animal moving, or Soli rolling over and striking dry leaves. His pang came again, quite forcefully, and he wavered and almost went back. But he heard nothing else, and forced himself to go on.

He ran five miles back to one of the schools they had passed that day. He pounded on the gate for admittance and finally roused an old caretaker—a near-sighted, gray-bearded, bony man who was not pleased to be disturbed at this hour. Var tried to talk to him, but his words were evidently of the wrong dialect and inadequate to the concept. He did make the oldster understand that he had to see the authority figure for the school. With grumbling, the man retired into the bowels of the building to search that person out, while Var waited nervously outside the gate.

Ten minutes later he was admitted to the presence of the head matron. She had obviously just gotten up, and wore a nightrobe, but he could tell from her aspect that she was sharp of mind. Her face was lined though she was heavyset, and her hair was glossy black.

She could not understand him either, though she appeared to speak a number of dialects. Then she made a symbol on a sheet of paper, and Var knew they could communicate after all. For these symbols were universal, here, and had the same meaning regardless of the dialect spoken, or even the language. Var was borderline-literate, now, so far as these symbols were concerned; he had picked up several hundred in the past few months, as had Soli, and could use them for making purchases and clarifying posted directives such as 'Radiation Ahead."

For two hours they passed messages back and forth. At the end of that silent dialogue Var had purchased admittance for Soli to the school. He was to pay the tuition by doing brutework for the maintenance department.

He described her location, and a party went out, armed. Var reported to the cellar, where the gray-bearded man showed him to a wooden bunk near the giant furnace. He was now the assistant to this man, for good or ill.

He had sold them both into a kind of servitude. But Soli would emerge with her future secure.

It was a month before he saw her again, for the hired help had no legitimate contact with the élite girls. But as he hauled wood and peat for the furnace, and pounded stakes for new fencing, and carried supplies for the daily wagon to the kitchen, and did the thousand things the older man had somehow managed before, he picked up hints. He mastered the common local words and received the local gossip.

They had brought in a spitfire, that night. A wild country urchin who struck out with sticks as devastatingly as a seasoned fighting man. They had threatened her with guns, but she had not yielded, and they had not dared to use them because she was supposed to be captured and trained as a lady. They had finally subdued her with a net, after suffering several casualties.

Soli! Soli! Var ached with her misery, ashamed to have brought this on her. How could she know that it was for the best, that she might spend the rest of her life at leisure?

The old man shook his head. He could not understand why they should want to train a wild peasant—and an outlander at that, for she was fair of skin and round of eye. But rather attractive, he confessed, once subdued and cleaned up.

Var realized that the man made no connection between him and Soli. This once, his discoloration had worked to his advantage. He wanted to watch, to be sure the terms of the bargain were fulfilled—but not to associate with her, for that would hurt her manufactured image. She was to be a lady; he could never be a gentleman.

Then he was cutting back shrubbery beside the wall and she was taken for a walk inside the grounds. He saw her with a matron and three other girls, dressed in chaste gowns. He was reminded horribly of her stay in New Crete, waiting for the sacrifice. Then, as now, he had been

the instrument that confined her. The whole thing suddenly seemed so similar that he longed to grab her and run for the forest and undo what he had done.

He averted his face, afraid of the consequence if she should see him now.

The little party walked along the flowered pathway, treading in step to the murmured cadence of the matron. Each girl took tiny steps. Var heard the petite patter, aware of their motions peripherally. They were learning to walk like ladies, daintily, intriguingly.

Var continued clipping, his back to the walk. The girls passed so close he could smell their fragrance. They did not stop. After a while they were guided inside, and Var was both relieved and saddened. It would have been folly to speak to Soli—but the urge had been almost unbearably strong.

Regret it as he might, he knew that the school was honoring the agreement they had made. He could not be the first to break it.

That night, as the oldster lay in the heat ready to sleep, a hooded visitor came to the cellar. The old man went to investigate, was given something, and stood aside. The figure came to stand over Var's bunk.

Jarred out of his reverie, Var looked up.

It was Soli. Her eyes were luminous under the hood.

"You did it," she said softly.

Var just looked at her, struck by the beauty of her features. Already the training had had its impact on her bearing, and the cosmetics had enhanced her splendor.

"I saw you in the garden," she murmured, continuing to look down on him with an expression he did not understand.

Then her hand came from under the cloak, holding a slipper. Down it came against his stomach, stingingly.

"I thought you were dead!" she cried, and now he recognized her emotion: fury. Then she turned and left.

She had thought him dead. He had never suspected that, but in retrospect it was obvious. Attacked in the night, captured, hauled away to a strange institution without sight of him—what would her natural interpretation have been, except that he had been killed in the same fracas?

So she had resigned herself . . . and discovered suddenly that it was a lie.

Why had he meddled? He had never intended to have it come out that way.

The old man returned, chuckling. Obviously he had now made the connection between the spitfire and the handyman. Would he keep the confidence? It didn't matter, since the arrangement was legitimate and Soli knew the truth.

Var lay awake a long time, not certain whether to be pleased or saddened by Soli's attitude. The sudden sight of her had been a shocking stimulus. So lovely, so angry! Did she hate him for deceiving her? Or would she recognize the advantage he had arranged for her? Surely she could see that they could not have wandered endlessly across the continents of the world. A beautiful girl and an ugly man. Such a life would not hurt him, of course, for he had no higher potential; indeed, it would be easy for him to revert to the wild state and range the badlands. But Soli— Soli could be the Lady, graceful and cultured. He owed it to her to make that life possible.

He still felt guilty. He still longed for her free companionship, as it had been in the early days, before New Crete. It was impossible, for she would never be young again, but still he wished, and suffered.

Two weeks later, as he gathered fallen wood in the forest and loaded it on a hand wagon for hauling, she came to him again. This time she was dressed in boy's clothes, with her hair concealed and artful smudges on her face. She looked like a marauding urchin—a guise she had long been versed in, as he knew.

"I'm running away," she said. "Come with me, as you used to."

Var grabbed her and carried her back toward the school enclosure. She could have disabled him in a number of ways, but she offered only token resistance.

"I know you're paying for me," she said. "I hate you."

He knew she didn't mean it, but the words stung just the same.

"Why do you want me here?" she asked pitifully. "Why can't we tour the countryside together? That's all I want."

Var shifted his grip and continued carrying. She was lithe in his arms, all curve and tension.

She drew her head up and kissed him on the lips, as a woman might. As Sola, her mother, had. "Just to be with you, Var."

Temptation smote him savagely. It was the child he remembered, but the woman had hold on his longing too. Yet he walked, unanswering.

"Do you want me to cry?" But she didn't cry, though it would have broken him. And when he didn't answer, she murmured: "I'm sorry I hit you with my slipper." And then, when they came in sight of the buildings: "It should have been a *star!*"

And had she *had* a morningstar mace, he reflected, she might very well have bashed him with it, such was her momentary fury.

He turned her over to a matron. As he tromped dejectedly back to the forest he heard her beginning screams, part agony, part rage. They were beating her for the infraction. The instrument was padded, so as not to leave any disfiguring mark, but he knew it hurt. And they both had known the penalty. The matron had made that clear at the outset: discipline was her watchword.

But Soli, veteran of stick combat, could not be made to scream through pain. She was merely letting Var know, and satisfying the matron, who of course was not fooled. The ritual had to be complete, lest the other girls grow similarly wilful.

Var was given one day off in every ten, though he was willing to work. The head matron, fair-minded, insisted on this too. There was a town near by, and his second holiday he went there to look about. But he was not comfortable and a number of the natives treated him with subtle disrespect, not desiring his company. It was so hard to know when to smile and when to react, when no circle marked the boundary between courtesy and combat. Once a young rowdy laid a hand on him and Var struck him to the ground, but it changed nothing.

No—for him the badlands were best. He understood neither this culture nor the American nomad culture, and was better off alone. Once he had seen Soli through the

training, he would doff civilization of any type and become completely, happily wild.

But he remembered Soli, and knew that he was deceiving himself. He would never be happy without her, child or woman.

CHAPTER EIGHTEEN

"I have found out whose men have been assembling here the past month," the oldster said.

In the course of nearly a year Var had learned to converse with him, though he had never had occasion to learn his name. The man was always full of gossip, and Var was not interested. He had observed the troops and known them to be the advance guard for some royal personage. Most of the girls of the school were high born, and it was a mark of distinction to graduate and depart in style with an armed retinue, even if one had to be hired for the purpose. Often the men assembled in advance, waiting for their masters to appear, so that as the end of term approached the school grounds resembled a battle camp. Var had jousted familiarly with some, showing off his ability with the sticks. But most were armed with handguns.

"The ones in gold livery," the oldster said, perceiving the waning attention of his limited audience. "Who speak to no one and drill on a private field."

Those were intriguing. No one seemed to know which lord they served or what girl would be honored by them—but over a score were present, in beautifully matched uniforms. And they were crack troops; Var had covertly observed their practice maneuvers and firing.

Seeing that he had Var's interest at last, the oldster continued: "They serve the emperor of Ch'in. He must have chosen another bride."

Var was impressed. Ch'in controlled the largest of the rival kingdoms of the south, and through political intrigue and judicious force of arms had expanded his sphere of

influence considerably in the last generation. Just as the Master had controlled an empire in America, this man had built one here in China—though it was not as large as the Master's and did not extend into the region this school was located in. He had at least thirty wives already, but was always on the lookout for attractive girls or politically expedient unions. Evidently his eye had fallen on one of these here, and he intended to see that nothing happened to her before he arrived.

But none of that concerned Var. He hoped to see Soli graduated and placed in some prosperous household, after which he could retreat to the badlands. He would regret never seeing her again—regret it intensely—but this was the hard choice he had made when he brought her to the school. She would, in time, be happy, and that was what was most important. Her childhood was behind her, and he was part of that childhood.

The head matron summoned him. "I have excellent news for you," she said, studying him in a way that hinted at a dark side to that news. "We have found a placement for your ward."

The information crushed him. Suddenly he realized what the matron had probably known all along: that he didn't want Soli placed. He couldn't voluntarily give her up, when that moment came, despite all his plans and pretensions.

"That *is* what you required," she reminded him gently.

"Yes." He felt numb.

"And as is customary in such cases, her tuition will be refunded. We shall return it to you in lieu of your wages this past year. You will find it to be a comfortable amount."

Var followed this with difficulty. "You—aren't charging for her training?"

"Certainly we're charging! We are not a charitable institution. But another party has undertaken to cover it. So it is no longer necessary for you to do so, though we have been well satisfied with your contribution. We shall be owing you money, as I said, at graduation."

"Who—why——?"

"The lord who is to marry her, of course." Again that intent look. "We're rather pleased with this placement; it is an auspicious one."

"Ch'in!" he cried, making the connection.

"He prefers anonymity, prior to the ceremony," she said. "That is why I did not mention it to you before. But you *do* deserve to know, and with his livery so evident. . . . He desired a foreign bride, being momentarily sated with domestic affairs."

Her nicety of expression was wasted on him. "But Ch'in!"

"Isn't this what you said you wanted? The highest possible placement for your ward, that she should never again be in want, never again run with a savage?" Once more that obscure glance.

Yes, it was what he had wanted. What he had *thought* he had wanted, once. The matron had more than fulfilled the bargain. He could not back out of it now.

"It is not necessary for you to be separated from her," she continued with a certain wise compassion. "The Emperor Ch'in is always in the market for strong men-at-arms . . . and he seldom pays close attention to a wife for more than a year. His earlier wives have considerable freedom . . . provided they are circumspect."

Var had once been naive about such things, but he had learned from experience. In this land, the appearance was often more important than the reality—as it was in America, too. She was suggesting to him that he take service with the emperor now . . . and make his overtures to Soli after a year or so, when she might have borne a child to Ch'in and when some newer bride would command Ch'in's attention. Such arrangements were common, and the emperor, though cognizant, did not object—so long as no public issue was made. Soli could have a royal life, and Var could have Soli—if he were patient and discreet.

The matron had showed him the expedient course. He thanked her and left. But he was *not* satisfied, and expedience had seldom appealed to him before. Suddenly the thought of Soli rolling in the arms of a stout Chinese emperor repelled him. He had never thought it through to this point—to realize that she would buy her luxury with her body, as surely as he had bought her training with his own body. He was furiously jealous—of the suitor he had never seen, and whom Soli had never seen.

He remembered Soli's insistence that she did not favor

the schooling and only wanted to travel with him. Now, suddenly, this loomed far more importantly. Now that she could marry richly—would she feel the same?

It became imperative that he ask her.

But of course he could not simply walk into the school dormitory and put the question to her there. There were strict regulations. She would be beaten if she were caught speaking to him, just as any girl was beaten who disobeyed any school rule, however minor. But this late in the term they were supposed to discipline themselves, and increasing social stigmata attached to infractions. Soli, a foreigner, had become quite as sensitive to this as any native. So—Var approached cautiously. She would speak to him if he were circumspect: that is, if they were not caught.

And he discovered that the emperor's men were on the job. Every approach to Soli's dormitory was subtly guarded.

Var, not to be put off by merely physical barriers, picked the weakest section of the defense and moved through. This was the garden behind her second-floor window. He intended only to knock the lone sentry out with one blow from one stick—but the man was alert, and escaped the blow, and fired his pistol. Var brought him down, but roughly, and there was no chance to scale the wall before reinforcements came.

They were well organized, and they had rifles. A semicircle of uniformed men closed in, pinning him in a shrinking area beside the wall. A vehicle crashed through the bushes, making him wince because he had carefully tended those plants. A light speared from it, catching him.

Var stood still, knowing he was trapped. He had not suspected that they would act so competently. He could not make a break against lights and guns.

"Who is it?" a voice called from the truck.

"A maintenance worker," another replied. "I've seen him around."

"What is he doing here?"

"He cuts the hedges."

"At *night*?"

"What are you doing here, laborer?" This was directed at Var.

"I have to talk to—a girl," he said, realizing that he was hurting himself by his directness.

"*Which* girl?"

"Soli."

There was a huddle behind the light. Var remembered that they had renamed Soli for school purposes, in the interest of minimizing her vulgar origin. The name he had used was not familiar to them, and he could avoid the truth even now. "The one you guard—betrothed to Ch'in."

"Bring him to the barracks," the officer snapped.

They brought him. "What do you want of this girl?" the officer demanded, in the privacy of the temporary building the soldiers used.

"To take her away, if she wants to come." The truth comforted him in the telling, despite the effect it had on these men. He *did* want Soli, even though it might cost her luxury. He knew that now.

"Do you understand that we shall kill anyone who tries such a thing?"

"Yes."

The officer paused, thinking him a fool or a simpleton. "You struck down the sentry?"

"Yes."

"Why do you want to take this particular girl?"

"I love her."

"Why do you think she might go with you, an ugly hunchback, when the pinnacle is within her reach by staying?"

"I brought her."

"You knew her before?"

"For four years we traveled together."

"Fetch the matron," the officer said to one of the men. "Heat the knife," he said to another. And to Var: "If she denies your story, you shall die as an example to those who would thwart Ch'in. If she confirms it, you will merely lose your interest in this girl. In any girl."

Var watched the knife being turned over and over in the flame of a great candle and pondered how many he could kill before that blade touched him.

The matron came. "It is true," she said. "He brought her, and has paid for her keep by his labors, and kept her here when she wanted to escape. It is his right to take her away again—if she wishes to accompany him."

"It *was* his right," the officer said grimly, "until the

Emperor Ch'in selected her for his retinue. No other rights exist."

She faced him without alarm. "We are not in Ch'in's demesne."

"You may readily be added to it, madam."

She shrugged. "A strike into this region at this time would unite the enemies of Ch'in in the north, at a time when his main force is occupied to the south. Is one bride worth it?"

The officer pondered, taken aback by the political acumen of the matron. "The Emperor does not wish bloodshed to mar his wedding day. We shall pay this man a fair price for his prior claim, and deport him unharmed from the vicinity. Should he return before the nuptial, he will be held until that day is passed—then suffer the death of a thousand cuts." He fetched a bag of coins. "This will cover it."

The matron looked at Var soberly. "His compromise is reasonable. Accept it, nomad. And take this too." She handed him a packet.

Var was reminded of the manner of Minos, god of New Crete, as he gave Soli the keys to the power boat. He realized that in some subtle manner she was helping him. He could either start fighting now—sure death, however many he took with him—or trust her guidance and acquiesce to the officer's terms.

He accepted the money and the package and accompanied the guards to their truck. He had not given up, but this did seem to be the best present course.

Six hours later he was set down, alone, a hundred miles to the north. Dawn was breaking over the badlands.

The packet contained a map and a human thumb.

The map was routine, covering all this region. Except for a single location marked in red. The thumb——

Var was familiar with digits, since his own were misshapen. He could recognize certain men as readily by their hands as by their faces. This was not a Chinese digit; it was American. Massive, with fine mesh under the skin, scarred.

This was the Master's thumb.

Obviously the matron knew where the Master was,

alive or dead, and had known for some time. She must then also know the connection between Var and Soli and the Nameless One. Now she had chosen to reveal her information to Var. Why?

He shook his head, not comprehending that part of it. She was an honest woman, but, like so many of these people, mysterious in her ways.

He had less than a fortnight to recover Soli—if he intended to do so before Ch'in took her to his couch. If he wanted to present her with a fair choice between the ugly nomad and the rich powerful emperor.

He could return to the school in time, for they had underestimated his capacity for walking. But he knew the officer had not been bluffing about the fate that awaited him there. And suddenly he was unsure what Soli's reaction would be. She *had* been angry with him, and she *could* have a luxurious life. . . .

He could get to the indicated spot on the map in a week's strenuous marching. Surely the Master's thumb had come from there. It was time for him to settle his difference with his longtime friend and mentor—or to know for certain that it could never be settled. If the great man were dead. . . .

It was an arena. Gladiators met each other and wild animals in mortal combat, for the delight of paying spectators. The star attraction was a pair of foreign savages— prisoners captured half a year before by troops of a lesser kingdom in a border skirmish. Sol and the Master, of course.

Brief inquiry enabled Var to come at some semblance of the truth. The two had followed Var into the Aleutian tunnel but, more canny than he, had avoided the menace of the automatic sweeper. They had fought off the amazons, but had been balked by the radiation at the bridge. So they had taken the long way round, knowing that Var would not stop until he reached the mainland across the ocean. Back through the tunnel, overland north to the true transpacific tunnel, and down the Asiatic coast. They had traversed a lot of territory, fighting off enemies of animate and inanimate types, and had taken years in the process. Then they had run afoul of one border patrol too

many—actually a quasi-official bandit band—and had been taken under the threat of massed rifles.

After their wounds had healed, the two had been sold to the arena. Their left thumbs had been cut off, to mark their status. Now they were earning out their contracts—at fees that would necessitate a decade to meet the price.

"I will pay off the contract," Var said. He put the bag of coins into the hand of the agent at the gate.

The man counted the money and nodded. "Ch'in currency. Very strong. For which one?"

Var described the Master.

"Very well." Var had expected haggling, for his little bag could hardly be worth a ten-year contract. The man gave him a receipt, written in the Chinese symbols. Var took it eagerly and entered the grounds, finding his way toward the gladiators' accommodations. It had been surprisingly easy.

But he had a second thought, and paused to puzzle out the symbols. The note was phony; it granted admission to the grounds and nothing else. He had been cheated.

Angry, he started back—but soon realized that the man would have hidden the money and perhaps disappeared himself, after this illicit haul. No one else would choose to believe Var's complaint. Arenas were known to be dens of vice and corruption; he should have been alert.

Still, they had set the pattern, meeting his honest if naive approach with dishonesty. Var's ethics of civilization were not fundamentally ingrained, for he had come by them only through his contact with the Master, and had not had them reinforced by his adventures beyond America. He treated other men as they treated him—and he knew how to look out for himself, thus warned.

He threw away the paper and continued to the gladiatorial pen. This was a high wire stockade at whose corners wooden towers rose. A man with a rifle stood watch within each edifice, facing toward the center.

Nearby were the animal cages. Tigers, bison, snakes, vicious dogs—and some mutants from the badlands. These were set up as a sideshow when not in use. From the healing wounds some had, Var inferred that they were used repeatedly. Probably the gladiators were given a bonus for defeating an animal impressively without killing it.

He scouted the rest of the compound. This was an off day. The shows only took place every three of four afternoons. Relatively few sightseers like himself were about. In one side lot there were several trucks, used for transporting animals and equipment from time to time. The show traveled every few months, seeking new pasture and new audience—and perhaps as a hedge against too great an accumulation of vengeance-minded suckers.

Satisfied, Var retreated to a comfortable wilderness patch and slept. He would be busy tonight.

At night, refreshed, Var re-entered the compound, using his well-versed stealth. He prised down a window in a locked truck, got the door open, used pliers on the wiring in the manner he had learned as a handyman dealing with balky equipment, and unblocked the wheels. Then he moved to the nearest guard tower, climbed it noiselessly and tapped the rifleman on the head with a makeshift singlestick. He did the same for the second tower, having learned from his brief experience with Ch'in's men not to give a man with a gun any chance to react. The section of fence between these two points was partially out of sight of the far towers, so a passage was clear. Var took metal clippers and made a hole. He entered, carrying a handgun and flashlight taken from the second guard.

The gladiators were in a locked shed that reeked of excrement. Var used screwdriver and crowbar to unlock it with minimum noise, working on the side away from the manned towers. He knew the occupants would overhear, but would not give him away. They might, however, attempt to overpower him and make their own escape. He had to be ready.

He kicked open the door, shone the light inside, and stood back. "I have a gun," he said softly in the local dialect. Then, in American: "Come out singly and make no sound—if you want your freedom."

"Var the Stick!" the Master said at once, but low, for he was well aware that they had to stay below the hearing level of the tower guards. His bulk showed in the doorway. "Do you bring a gun to meet me?"

That familiar voice sent a shiver through him, but Var answered firmly. "No. This is not the circle. You swore

to kill me because you thought I had killed your daughter. I did not kill her. I will take you to her now."

There was a long pause. "Not my daughter—*his*," the Master said at last. And Sol appeared beside him, a somber shape. "We suspected as much, when we had the description of the boy you traveled with. But we didn't *know*—and you kept running. So we had to follow."

So the entire chase had been for nothing! Var could have taken Soli to the Master, or even let Sol see her, that time they met in the circle, and the oath would have been voided. It would not even have affected the contest for the mountain, because Bob had already reneged on that agreement. Such irony!

Var looked up to discover the Master before him, well within striking range. But of course the Weaponless would not have struck, outside the circle—not against one who shared that convention. And had he wanted to violate the code, he could have thrown something. Except that his thumb was missing; that would have made it harder.

"I should have questioned you," the Nameless One said. "A day after you were gone, I knew I had acted wrongly, for you had done only what I sent you to do. It was the mountain Helicon that betrayed us both. Betrayed Sol too, for he did not know that his child had been sent—until he learned that she was dead."

Var remembered that Soli had said her parents hadn't known, that Bob almost never told the truth, and that she had cooperated because of Bob's threat against their lives. Ugly business—the underworld master's revenge for the nomad attack. "That's why he came—to avenge her?"

"To bury her. He had already avenged her when he slew Bob and fired Helicon. Sosa—disappeared in that carnage. All that was left was to bury Soli—but he could not find her body. So he came—and by the time we met and worked it out, you were gone again, with your . . . sister."

They were wasting time. "Come with me," Var said. "She is in—in a school. There will be trouble."

It was as though there had never been strife between them. They came: the Master, Sol, and four other gladiators of diverse and grotesque aspect. Var led them through

the fence and past the animal cages, ready to loose the beasts upon the compound if any alarm were cried. But, almost disappointingly, there was no disturbance. They piled into the truck and Var started it, using the shorted wiring. They were off.

Emperor Ch'in had arrived, together with more of his retinue, by the time the truckful of gladiators nudged into the vicinity and parked surreptitiously near the school grounds. Uniformed troops were everywhere. A frontal attack would have been sheer folly. And—they still were not sure how Soli would feel about it.

"She did not ask to attend the school?" the Master inquired. "She was satisfied to travel with you?"

"So she said," Var admitted. "A year ago. But she was growing up. . . ."

"Now she is grown—why should the situation be otherwise? Would you have her roam again?"

Terrible uncertainty smote him. "I don't know."

"This Ch'in—I have heard of him. Isn't that a good marriage?"

"Yes."

"But you don't want her to have it?"

Var became even more confused. "I want to talk to her. If she *wants* to marry Ch'in——"

The Master grunted. "We shall put her to the test."

They spent the night in the truck in the woods. The Chinese gladiators went after food and gasoline zestfully, enjoying this lark. The Master questioned him on every aspect of his association with Soli, while Sol, eerily silent, listened. It occurred to Var that he did not know what was in the minds of these men. So far as Soli was concerned, their reactions were suspect. They might have no sympathy whatever with his blunted desires.

But he discovered that he had lost his independence of action since releasing these men. The Master dominated the entire group, and his intelligence radiated out almost tangibly. Var thought he recognized in this man some of the qualities that made Soli what she was—that had, in fact, attracted him to her—yet the Master denied siring her. So things had been thrown into confusion again.

Var peered from the concealed truck while the others marched off to attend the graduation ceremony, his heart pounding. Eager to act, he was helpless, dependent on the motives of others, uncertain of his own.

CHAPTER NINETEEN

Soli slept fitfully. The events of her life passed through her mind, now that she faced a drastic change. She did not remember her early residence among the nomads—only snow and terrible cold, her father Sol protecting her though they both meant to die. Then, somehow, they were alive again, painfully so, and Sosa was her new mother. And after the shock of change, it had been good, for Sosa was a remarkable woman—at once devastating in combat and loving in person. And the underworld was fascinating. Until Bob had acquainted her with the brutality of politics and sent her out with her sticks to defend her way of life from the savages.

She had supposed all nomads to be mutilated, for Sol had been one and he had no genitals, and Sosa had been one and she was barren. Var had had splotched skin and funny hands and a hunch in his back. Yet Sosa had taught her that appearance meant little in a man; that his endurance and skill in combat were more important, and his personality more important still. "If a man is strong and honest and kind—like your father—trust in him and make him your friend," had been her advice.

The men of the underworld had not met this simple set of standards. Jim the Librarian was honest and kind and intelligent, but not strong; a single blow to the gut would have put him in the infirmary. Bob the Leader was strong but neither honest nor kind. In fact, only her father Sol met Sosa's standards. So she learned the art of the sticks from him, and learned it well, and waited.

And Ugly Var had been strong, if not as skilled with the sticks as she. And he had been honest, for he had not

341

dropped rocks on her, though she would have dodged any that might have come. And he had been kind, for he had protected her against the awful cold, even as her father had done before. That was the one enemy she could not face boldly: she hated and feared the cold.

So she had known him for a good man, though he was an enemy savage—and she had never been disappointed subsequently. Oh, he was not exactly smart—but neither was Sol. Men like Bob and the Nameless One were awesome, because their minds were more deadly than their bodies. She preferred an associate whose motives she could fathom.

At what point this appreciation had phased into love she was not certain. It had been a gradual thing, deepening with further association and ripening with her womanhood. But she tended to place the transition at the time she had been stung in the cold by the poisonous bug, and he had carried her all the way back to the cabin and cared for her there. She had been conscious much of the time, but unable to move or respond. Thus she had observed him when he supposed himself effectively alone, and knew that he had fought for her long before he confessed as much.

She had decided then to take his golden bracelet—when she was old enough to do so and to honor the full commitment the act implied. When she had learned that Sol was following them, too, she had stayed with Var despite her ache to rejoin her father, knowing she would lose Var if she let him go on alone. Then he had saved her from the tunnel sweeper, and from the vicious amazons, and yet again from the radiation she could not detect for herself. And once more, in the boat: he had intercepted with his own body the arrows marked for her.

Five times he had preserved her life at peril to his own, asking nothing in return, not even her company unless freely given. He was quite a man, and not merely for his courage and sacrifice. If she had not loved him already, she would surely have done so then. But when she brought them to New Crete he had been dying. Then she had seen the manner she had to repay her debt to him. For a moment she had been tempted to cash in his golden bracelet, realizing its disproportionate value there; but that

would have made it unavailable for her own subsequent possession and what went with it. And they might just have taken it as they took the boat, with no return favor. Though they both might die, she could not bring herself to give up that dream.

So it had had to be the temple—the one offering they could not simply claim offhand, the one bargain she could hold them to. She had cried, not so much for herself as for her loss of him. She had known, via the temple grapevine, that he had settled into a mundane task, and she suffered to imagine how that demeaned him while she thrilled to believe that he missed her as she missed him. Sweet girlish dreams, nonsensical but essential. She even fancied that he watched her from time to time, romantically; that he might even challenge the god Minos for her.

And then he *had* come, just when she was resigned to her violent demise. And she had told him no, crying yes! inside, and pushed him away while yearning for his embrace. For it was her commitment that had saved him, and it would have been a denial of it all had she reneged at the end. And she had watched him go into the labyrinth, and condemned herself for her idealistic folly.

"If ever I see him again alive," she had sworn to herself as she stood chained and helpless, "I shall clasp him to me and tell him I love him." But it had been the abandoned conviction of desperation.

Yet it had happened.

And somehow, from that moment, she had ceased to understand him. She was woman now, ready and able to accept him as man, and the proof had been made. Still he treated her as child. Why—when they had already made spectacular love? Why did he withdraw when she approached? *Why had he stayed two years, retaining his bracelet, and come for her and taken her—only to ignore her offerings now?*

She had gone along, powerless to change the situation. And gradually she discovered that she had changed, not he—and that he did not realize this. Not quite. Var was naive. He had begun his journey with a child, and in his mind he still traveled with a child. Apparently he did not comprehend what had happened on New Crete. In his eye, she would always be a child.

Then, just as she was adjusting to that situation, a raiding party had caught her unaware and brought her here. At first she thought Var was dead; then she learned that he had arranged it. Her fury had lasted for weeks.

Until it occurred to her that she could emerge from this inane purgatory a woman—in his estimation. He wanted her here so that he could officially accept the transition that had already taken place. So that he could present her his bracelet honorably.

That changed her attitude. She discovered that there was a good education to be had here. The matrons were rigorous but sincere, and they knew a great deal of value. Soli perfected her reading ability in the symbols of this continent and mastered other disciplines she had hardly been aware existed. Most important, she became adept at female artistries that would twist and remold the impetus of almost any male. This, indeed, was as intricate a combat as any with weapons, and as potentially rewarding.

Var had some surprises coming.

Now she had been betrothed—against her will—to the emperor Ch'in. It was an advantageous liaison, no question of that. His very name emulated the founding dynasty of this realm, thousands of years before the Blast—or so the local mythologies had it. No doubt Ch'in's public relations department had had a hand in that. But her studies had also pin-pointed Ch'in for what he was: a pompous, arrogant, middle-aged prince with the supreme good fortune to have a loyal tactical genius for an adviser. Thus Ch'in could sate himself in ever-younger distaff flesh while his masterfully managed empire expanded. Many women were flattered to attract his roving eye and to join his luxurious harem; Soli was not. She had long since chosen her man, and she was not readily diverted.

But there remained the problem of foiling Ch'in while snaring Var. She had confidence in her ability to do either —but not to do them simultaneously.

Var had come to her at last, barely before graduation— but, manlike, he had bungled it. He had tried to scale the wall, and had been intercepted by Ch'in's minions and questioned and deported. They might have castrated him had they been certain of his purpose. She had asked the head matron to intercede, and that stern, kindly, coura-

geous woman had obliged. So Var had been reprieved of his folly and set down in another territory, unharmed, with money. He would be safe for the time being, so long as he did nothing else foolish.

Still she slept fitfully. For the situation was by no means tied up neatly, and many things could go wrong. She had not yet decided how to deal with Ch'in. If she simply refused to oblige him, she might find herself kidnapped and ravished and murdered. The emperor had an infamous temper, especially when his pride was bruised. And the school would suffer too, perhaps harshly. No—an outright balk would not be expedient.

She could give Ch'in a gala wedding night, then spin a tearful tale of frustrated love. A proper appeal to his protective vanity might work wonders, particularly if the suggestion of political advantage were not too subtle. A romantically enhanced image would mitigate the effect of certain crude military policies, such as dethumbing valiant prisoners and selling them to gladiatorial arenas. Not that Ch'in was the only offender; the practice was general. But still it rankled. Image was very important here.

Yes, the wedding ploy seemed best. She could always run away, after a reasonable interval, if her plan didn't work. That way the school would not be blamed. Then she could locate Var and bring him to terms.

Except—she was not sure of Var. Oh, she could bring out the male in him, no question of that. But she distrusted his common sense. She could not assume that he would *not* do anything foolhardy. He might get tardily jealous and make some blundering move against Ch'in, or even come back to the school before graduation. Var just was not bright about such things, and he could be preposterously stubborn. His defiance of Minos had been incredible folly. . . .

And of course that was why she loved him.

Maybe she had been wrong to encourage him to seek the Chinese Helicon. There was one, somewhere, but they were obviously not at all close to it. Probably its underworlders were fully as secretive as those of the American unit, so that such a search would be quite difficult. But her purpose had not been to *find* it, only to give Var a suitable mission. A mission she could participate in, while she grew.

She wondered what had happened to her father and the Nameless One. Had they finally given up the chase? She doubted it. Once she had Var in hand, she would have to arrange a reconciliation. It had hurt her to run from Sol, but she knew she could not return to Helicon with him, and it was essential to keep track of Var. Sol had been the man of her childhood; Var was to be the man of her womanhood.

But the thought of Helicon reminded her of Sosa, the only mother she remembered. In certain ways the loss of Sosa was worse than that of Sol. What was that proud small woman doing now? Had she resigned herself to the absence of both husband and daughter? Soli doubted it, and this hurt.

Finally her memories and alarms and conjectures subsided, and she slept.

Ch'in was more portly than she had heard. In fact he was fat. His face retained the suggestion of lines that in youth would have been handsome, but he was long past youth. Not even the grandeur of his robes could render him esthetic.

Soli glimpsed him momentarily, as she peered from a front window graduation morning. He was reviewing his troops, not even bothering to rise from the plush seat of his chauffeured open car. Suddenly she was unsure of her ability to play on his emotions; he looked too set, too jaded to be affected by a mere girl.

She ate a swift breakfast and performed her toilette: first a warm shower, then a tediously meticulous dressing, layer by layer. Then the combing of her hair to make it lustrous; nail-filing, makeup—a complete conversion process, to convert girl into Lady. She inspected herself thoroughly in the mirror.

She was a colorful creature of skirts and frills and beads and sparkles. Her feet appeared tiny in the artful slippers, her face elfin under the spreading hat. No woman in America wore clothing like this—yet it was not unattractive.

The graduation ceremony occurred precisely on schedule. Thirty-five girls received their diplomas and minced, single file, to the courtyard where proud relatives awaited them. Soli was last—a place of honor, for it was acknowl-

edgement that small attention would accrue to any girl following her. This was partly because she was the lone representative of her race. But she was also aware that though she was younger than some—thirteen—she was beautiful in her own right. She knew this because it was to her advantage to know it, and she possessed the poise to show herself off properly. Had she not mastered the essential techniques, she would not have graduated.

Ch'in was waiting for her, buttressed by a phalanx of soldiers. He was resplendent in a semi-military uniform girt with medals and sashes; indeed, had he been smaller around the middle there might not have been room for all the decorations. But of course he wore no golden bracelet—and that made all the difference.

She smiled at him, turning her face to catch the sunlight momentarily so that her eyes and teeth flashed. Then she walked to him, moving her body with just that flair to heighten breast and hip and slender waist, and took his hands.

Oh, she was giving the audience the show Ch'in had bought. She *had* to sparkle, to validate the training she had had. Appearance was everything.

The emperor turned, and she turned with him as though connected and accompanied him toward the royal car.

People thronged behind the line of guards, eager for an envious glimpse of the Emperor and his lovely bride. Most were locals, owing no present allegiance to Ch'in but fascinated by the trappings of power—and well aware that tomorrow or next year they might very well come to owe him that allegiance. But a number had evidently traveled far for this occasion. Conspicuously absent were the patrols of the monarch of this territory; he wanted no trouble at all with Ch'in.

Near the polished car stood a somber, cloaked man. Momentarily she met his gaze, glanced on——

"Sol!" she breathed.

The sight of her father, so unexpected after five years and thousands of miles, overwhelmed her. She had seen him last in Helicon, but his dear face was still as familiar to her as any she knew.

Ch'in heard her exclamation and followed her gaze. "Who is that man?" he demanded.

The soldiers whirled immediately and grasped Sol. His hands came into sight—and she saw that his left thumb was gone.

First she felt shock, then fury. *They had sold her father as a gladiator!* And, unreasonably, she fixed the blame on Ch'in.

She struck, using the technique Sosa had versed her in so well. Ch'in gasped and tottered, completely surprised. The soldiers drew their pistols.

Then Sol was moving, striking left and right, throwing the guards aside. A sword appeared in his hand. He leaped and came to stand beside Soli, the blade at Ch'in's throat.

The cordon of soldiers broke, letting the amazed spectators throng close. Soli saw guns level, and knew that Sol would be killed where he stood, whatever he did. There were too many troops, too many guns. Someone would shoot in the confusion, even though it cost the life of the emperor.

Then grotesque figures rose up within the crowd and began throwing people about. Gladiators—rampaging outside their arena! Hungry tigers could not have wreaked more havoc! In moments, every man with a gun had been incapacitated. Some weapons fired, but not with accuracy. The mêlée became inchoate and purely muscular.

Sol pushed Ch'in roughly away, put his arm about her, and lifted her into the car. A giant hurled the chauffeur out and vaulted into the driver's seat. The motor roared. Two more tremendous men piled in, shaking the vehicle as it moved out. They held curved bright swords aloft and swung them warningly at other trespassers. When the car became mired in the press of surrounding bodies these two jumped down to shove people out of the way of the wheels, working so quickly that no organized resistance could develop.

Soli hung on and watched. Suddenly she recognized the driver. He was the Nameless One—the man who had sworn to kill Var!

Now there were shots and screams, as the departure of the gladiators allowed the soldiers to recover their guns. But the crowd was such that the bullets scored only on innocent targets, not the fugitives. Then the car was finally free of the press, and speeding over the roadway. Soli had

supposed the vehicle was just for show, but it was a fully functioning machine.

"Hope Var makes it," the Nameless One said, glancing back.

"Var?" she asked breathlessly. "You found Var?"

"He found us. Freed us. Brought us here. We were——" He held up the stub of his thumb.

"You didn't—fight? You and Var?" But obviously they hadn't.

"Do you want to travel with the wild boy?" he asked instead.

She wondered why the Nameless One should care how she felt about Var. But she answered. "Yes."

The car sped on, northward.

CHAPTER TWENTY

Var, galvanized into action when he heard the shots, started the truck and nudged forward toward the crowd. If Soli had been hurt, he would run down the emperor!

Then he saw the car pull out, the Master driving, Soli beside him, two gladiators aboard. They had done it!

But the troops, only temporarily nonplussed, were massing, leveling their rifles. Var goosed the motor and careered across their path, spoiling their aim while the car fled. Men jumped at him. He veered, then recognized the naked thews of the remaining two gladiators. He eased up, allowing them to clamber aboard. Then he took off.

No one else got hold of the truck—not with those two free-swinging bodyguards on it. But there were no other vehicles to cross his own path and interfere with the aim of those rifles. There were shots; his tires popped. Var drove doggedly on, knowing that if he stopped for anything, they all were doomed.

The wheel wrenched at his hand. The motor slowed and knocked. He used the clutch, raced the engine, and eased it back into harness. The truck bobbled and throbbed with the irregularity of skewed rubber, but it moved.

It was not fast enough. The troops had been left behind, and now a hillock in the road cut off the direct fire, but other cars would catch up in minutes. "We'll have to run for it!" Var cried, as the motor finally overheated and stalled.

They piled out and charged into the forest as the first pursuing car appeared. There were cries and shots as the troops spied the truck, not realizing that it was empty.

Var and the two gladiators kept running, knowing the emperor's men would pick up their trail soon enough. Alone, he could have lost himself easily, for the forest was his natural habitat and he could hide in the badlands. But the other men, skilled as they might be in combat, were behemoths here. The end was inevitable—unless they separated soon.

He could elude the gladiators. No problem about that. But was it fair? They had helped him free Soli, at the risk of their lives, and one of them was wounded in that action. Though he had freed *them* initially, at the risk of his own welfare. Where did the onus lie?

"We have repaid you," one of them panted. "Now we must hide among our own people, as you cannot. Otherwise we all will die, for Ch'in is ruthless."

"Yes," Var agreed. "You owe me nothing. It is fair."

The gladiator nodded. "It is fair. We regret—but it must be."

They thought they were protecting *him*! And that he would die if they deserted him. The three had almost brought destruction on their own heads, through misplaced loyalty.

"It is fair. Go your way," Var repeated. He saluted them both and faded into the wilderness.

Secure at last from pursuit, he had opportunity to worry about the others. Soli and her father and the Master had driven north. Would they be able to outdistance the emperor's men and make a lasting escape? And if they did— could he locate them?

In fact—would they let him locate them? Sol had been reunited with his daughter, after Var inadvertently kept them apart these long years. They could go home to America. They did not need the wild boy. And might not *want* him. For what would he do, except try to take Soli away again?

If Soli had any such inclination. Now he doubted it. She had been furious when he put her in the school, and cool to him since, the few times he had seen her at all privately. She had been set up for an excellent marriage— until he had arranged to break it up. Now she was with her father, a better man than Var. Surely she would either stay with Sol—or go back to Emperor Ch'in.

So he would be best advised to hide in the badlands and let her go her way.

He circled back to the road, knowing no one would expect to find him there, and trotted in the direction the car had gone, north. He never *had* taken the best advice.

Every so often a vehicle passed, and Var leaped into the ditch and hid, emerging immediately afterwards to continue his solitary trek. Sooner or later he would catch up to the car—or discover the trail where the party left it. Then——

Another truck was bouncing south and he jumped for cover. He smelled the dust of it, underlaid by gas fumes, manure odor . . . and Soli's perfume.

He charged into the road, shouting. Either Ch'in's men had captured her already, or——

The truck stopped. Soli stepped down prettily and waved her bonnet, looking incredibly genteel. "Get in, you mangy idiot!" she cried. "I knew you'd get lost."

So the four were together for the first time: Var, Soli, Sol and the Master. The two remaining gladiators had gone their own ways, having fulfilled their obligation.

"Now we'll have to plan our escape," the Master said as he drove. "There'll be road blocks. We foiled them by doubling back in another vehicle, but that won't work a second time. So we'll have to take to the hills soon, and they'll be tracking us with dogs. This Ch'in is not one to give up readily, and that general of his is an expert at this sort of chase. We'll probably take losses—better count on fifty per cent."

Var didn't recognize the term. "How many?"

"Two of us may die."

Var looked at Soli. She perched on Sol's lap, between Var and the Master, and her elegant coiffure was undisturbed. She was as lovely and distant a lady as he had ever seen, and a striking contrast to the brutish, stinking men about her. How well she had responded to the training!

And how aloof from him now! His tentative fancies were ludicrous. She had no need of him. She was with her father again, and the chase was over, and Var was superfluous. They had returned to pick him up out of common courtesy, no more.

"You've been here a year, Var," the Master said. "You know the region. What's our best escape route and where can we make a stand if caught?"

Var pondered it. "The land is fairly open to the south, but that's Ch'in's territory. There are mountain ranges east and west, so that no truck-roads go through, though we could scale one of the passes on foot. Except for the dogs," he added, realizing that they *had* to stay with the vehicle. "To the north is really best, except for the———"

He stopped, appreciating as he suspected the Master had already, the predicament they were in. Far north the land was wild and open, so that pursuit would be awkward even with many men and dogs. Wild tribes fought anything resembling an organized, civilized force, but tended to ignore refugees. Ideal for this group. But the near north was a bottleneck. Hardly fifty miles beyond the area where he had found the gladiators potent badlands began. These intense bands of radiation extended east and west for hundreds of miles, acting as an invulnerable natural barrier between the civilized southerners and the primitive tribes.

Only one road went through, for only one pass was clear of the deadly emanations, and that barely. This was fortified and always garrisoned; he and Soli had had to pass through it and pay token toll even as foot travelers, on their original journey south. This was not in Ch'in's domain, but the personnel were friendly to him. Ch'in's public relations with such key outposts were uniformly good—one of the reasons his power was on the ascent.

"I think we shall have to take the badlands pass," the Master said.

No one answered. The feat was of course impossible.

"In my time as a gladiator," the Master said, "I pondered this as a theoretical problem. How half a dozen bold men might overcome the garrison and hold the pass indefinitely."

"But we are four!" Var protested, knowing that with even a hundred it could not be done. That fortress had balked entire armies in the past.

The Nameless One shrugged and drove on. When they passed other vehicles the passengers hunched down so as not to attract unwelcomed attention. In due course he

turned off the main road, heading toward the badlands section adjacent to the pass. "Give warning," he said to Var.

Var gave warning. The Master stopped immediately and backed away from the radiation thus advertised. "Now find a hot rock that we can put aboard with some shielding. Several, in fact. Don't touch them, of course—just point them out. We'll rig a derrick and hook them in at the end of a pole. A ten foot pole," he said, smiling momentarily for some reason.

It was done. Var located several small stones with intense radioactivity, and they levered them into the back of the truck by rope and stick. The men were dosed, inevitably, but not seriously. Soli looked on, concerned and not quite approving. Var privately agreed with her. This was dangerous work, to no apparent purpose—and it consumed time far better spent in fleeing the searching Ch'in forces.

Then they dumped larger rocks and dirt into the main body of the truck, to serve as a shield between the cab and the radiation. When Var pronounced the cab clean, they poured their remaining fuel—the last of several big cans the truck carried as a standard precaution, since fuel stations were far between—into the tank and set off for the pass.

"Now comes the rough part," the Master said, as they ground up the winding approach. "The garrison has geiger counters, and we can be sure they're thoroughly leary of radiation. In fact, this is known as a hardship post, because of that danger. There's a rapid turnover in personnel, to prevent low-grade illness from peripheral radiation, too."

The Master had obviously done more than just think about that pass. He had studied it, probably reading books on the subject. Var wondered how a gladiator would get hold of books. But no amount of study could get them past.

"Those men will shy away from radiation automatically, and go into blind terror if trapped in it," the Master said.

"Who wouldn't?" Soli inquired. "It's a horrible death. I bit my tongue three times just watching you play with those stones."

Var remembered the Master's own experience with radiation, in the American badlands, and marveled that

he was not more leary of it himself. But he was beginning to see some method in this cargo. They carried a truck-load of terror. . . .

"We can use this to drive them off," the Master said. "They won't even shoot, because that could blast radio-active fragments all over the station. They'll retreat with alacrity. They'll have to."

"But why should they fear it—in a shielded truck?" Var asked.

"It won't stay in the truck. We'll bring it inside."

Var felt a shock of horror he knew the others shared. "Carry it? Without the poles?"

"Two people can do the job. And hold the pass for hours afterward. So two can escape, and reach the wilds and later the coast, and——"

"No!" Var and Soli cried together.

"I did mention fifty per cent casualties," the Nameless One replied. "Perhaps you youngsters have become soft-ened by civilized life. Have you any illusions what it would mean to fall into the hands of Ch'in's men now? We shall surely do so if we do not escape this region promptly. Already the dogs must have been unleashed—and those hounds are not gentle either. Sol and I have met a few in our business."

Var knew he was right. The gladiators were better equipped to face reality and to take the prospect of torture and death in stride. They had to get through the pass, and they could not do so by bluff. They were known now, and their crime was known, and these soldiers were tough and disciplined. No appeal would move them, no ruse con-found them, no empty threat cow them. Nothing short of artillery would dislodge them . . . except radiation.

"Who escapes?" Soli asked in a small voice.

"You do," the Master said brusquely. "And one to guard you."

"Who?" Soli asked again.

"One close to you. One you trust. One you love." A pause, then: "Not me."

That left two to choose from, Var saw. Himself and Sol. He understood what was necessary. "Her father."

"Sol," the Master said quickly.

Sol, being voiceless, did not say anything.

So it was decided. Var felt cold all through, knowing he was going to die, and not swiftly. His skin would warn him of radiation, but could not protect him otherwise. He survived it by avoiding it, where others received fatal dosages unawares. If he touched one of those stones——

Yet there was a morbid satisfaction in it too. He had never asked for more than the right to live and die beside the Master. Now he would do so. And Soli would be saved, and her father would guard her, as he had before. They would return to America, to the land of true solace, land of the circle code. He felt a tremendous nostalgia for it, for its courtesies and combats, even for the crazy crazies.

That was what meant most to Var: that Soli be safe and happy and home. That was what he had really tried, so unsuccessfully, to arrange for her before. A safe, happy home.

He would die thinking of her, loving her.

The challenge point came into sight. Metal bars closed off the road. As the truck stopped before them, other bars dropped behind, powered by a massive winch. "Dismount!" the guard bellowed from his interior tower.

The four got down and lined up before the truck.

"That's the girl!" the guard cried. "Ch'in's bride, the foreign piece!"

The Master turned—and suddenly a bow was in his hands, an arrow nocked, loosed, swishing up—and the tower guard collapsed silently, the missile through his windpipe.

Now was the time to pick up the rocks. Var stepped toward the back, girding himself for the flashing pain of contact—and the Master's huge hand fell on his arm. Var stumbled back, bewildered. Then he was shoved brusquely forward.

At the same time Sol whirled on his daughter, grasping her by the upper arms and lifting her bodily before him. She and Var met face to face, involuntarily, each held from behind. The Master's hand clapped down on Var's wrist, twisting off the bracelet. Sol reached out to take it and shove it on to Soli's wrist and squeeze it tight. Then Var and Soli were dropped, clutching at each other to keep from falling.

As they disengaged and righted themselves, they saw that Sol and the Nameless One had already grabbed hot stones. The two men leaped for either side of the grating, climbing rapidly with the deadly stones tucked into their waistbands. That was a talent the Master had not had before! They were at the top by the time the other guards discovered what had happened.

The Master hurled a stone toward a panel. "Listen!" he bellowed. Var heard the fevered chatter of crazy-type click boxes, the screams of amazement and fear.

The Master began to crank up the forward grill. Var saw the counterweights descending, the road opening ahead.

"Drive!" the Master shouted down. Var obeyed unthinkingly. He scrambled into the driver's seat, Soli into the other. The motor was running; it had never been turned off, he realized only now. The Master had planned every detail.

As the gate cleared, he nudged out. The top of the cab scraped the bars; then they were free.

As he started down the north slope, Var heard the portcullis crash behind. The Master had let it drop suddenly. Probably he had cut the counterweight-rope, so that the barrier could not be lifted again without tedious repairs. There would be no vehicle pursuit.

Safely away from the fortress, Var braked the truck. "This isn't right," he said, recovering equilibrium. "*I* should be back there———"

"No," she said. "This is the way they meant it to be."

"But Soli———"

"Vara," she said.

Var stared at the gold band on her wrist, realizing what it meant. "But I didn't———"

"Yes, you did," she said, pretending to misunderstand. "Back on New Crete, by Minos' cave. And you will again, tonight. With more art, I trust. And then we shall go back to America and tell them what we know: that we have the best social system in the world, and dare not destroy it through empire. Helicon must be rebuilt, the nomads must disband, the guns must be abolished. We shall go to the crazy demesnes and tell them, my husband."

"Yes," he said, seeing it clearly at last.

Then, remembering the valiant sacrifice of her two fathers, Vara fell against him and sobbed, the little girl again.

"They die together—friends," Var said. And that was true, but it was scant comfort.

Neq
the
Sword

CHAPTER ONE

"But you are too young for the circle?" Nemi cried.

"If I am, then you are too young for that bracelet you've been eying! You're fourteen—the same as me." His name was the same as hers, too, for she was his twin sister. He refused to use that name now, for he no longer considered himself to be a child.

In fact he had already chosen his manhood name: Neq. Neq the Sword—as soon as he proved himself in the battle circle.

Nemi bit her lip, making it artfully red. She was full-bodied but small, like him, and could not term herself adult until she had borrowed the bracelet of a warrior for at least a night. After that she would shed her childhood name and assume the feminine form of the warrior she indulged. Between bracelets she would be nameless—but a woman. And twice a woman when she bore a baby.

"Bet I make it before you do!" she said. But then she smiled.

He tugged one of her brown braids until she made a musical trill of protest. He let go and walked to the circle where two warriors were practicing: a sticker and a staffer. It was a friendly match for a trivial point. But the metal weapons flashed in the sunlight and the beat of the weapons' contacts sounded across the welkin.

This was what he lived for. Honor in the circle! He had taken a sword from the rack in a crazy hostel four years ago, though it was so heavy he could hardly swing it, and had practiced diligently since. His father, Nem the Sword, had been pleased to train him, and it was excellent training, but he had never been allowed in a real circle.

Today he was fourteen! He and his sister were no longer bound by parental conventions, according to the code of the nomads. He could fight; she could borrow a bracelet. Whenever either was ready.

The sticker scored on the staffer, momentarily stunning him, and the two stepped out of the circle. "I'm hot today!" the sticker cried. "Gonna put my band on someone. That girlchild, maybe—Nem's kid."

They hadn't noticed Neq. His sister's challenge, "Bet I make it before you do," meant nothing. But though they were close as only twins could be, their rivalry was also strong. Neq had a pretext to act.

"Before you put your band on Nem's girlchild," he said loudly, startling both men, "suppose you put your stick on Nem's boychild. If you can."

The sticker smiled to cover his embarrassment. "Don't tempt me, junior. I wouldn't want to hurt a nameless child."

Neq drew his sword and stepped into the circle. The weapon looked large on him, because of his small stature. "Go ahead. Hurt a child."

"And have to answer to Nem? Kid, your dad's a good man in the circle. I don't want to owe him for roughing up his baby. Wait till you're of age."

"I'm of age today. I stand on my own recognisance."

That silenced the sticker, because he wasn't familiar with the word. "You *aren't* of age," the staffer said, looking down at him. "Anybody can see that."

At this point Nem approached, trailed by his daughter. "Your boy is asking for trouble," the staffer told him. "Hig don't want to hurt him, but—"

"He's of age," Nem said regretfully. He was not a large man himself, but the assurance with which he wore his sword suggested his size in the circle. "He wants his manhood. I can't deny him longer."

"See?" Neq demanded, smirking. "You prove your stick on me, before you prove anything on my sister."

All three men stiffened. That had been a nasty jibe. Now Hig the Stick would have to fight, for otherwise Nem himself might challenge him to keep Nemi chaste. It was no secret that the sworder was protective toward

both his children, but particularly toward his pretty daughter.

Hig approached the circle, drawing his stocks. "I gotta do it," he said apologetically.

Nemi sidled near. "You idiot!" she whispered fiercely at Neq. "I was only fooling."

"Well, *I* wasn't!" Neq replied, though now he felt shaky and uncertain. "Here is my weapon, Hig."

Hig looked at Nem, shrugged, and came to the white ring. He towered over Neq, handsome and muscular. But he was not an expert warrior; Neq had watched him fight before.

Hig stepped inside. Neq came at him immediately, covering his nervousness with action. He feinted with his blade in the manner he had practiced endlessly, emulating the technique of his father. The sticker jumped away, and Neq grinned to show greater confidence than he felt. It had actually worked!

He drove at Hig's middle while the man was catching his balance. He knew that thrust would be blocked, and the next, but it was best to maintain the offensive as vigorously as possible. Otherwise he'd be forced to the defensive, which did not favor the sword. Especially against the quick sticks.

But he scored.

Adrenaline had made him swift. The sword thrust inches deep into Hig's abdomen. The man cried out horribly and twisted away—the worst thing he could have done. Blood welled out as the sword wrenched loose. Hig fell to the ground, dropping his sticks, clutching the gaping mouth in his belly.

Neq stood dazed. He had never expected it to be this easy—or this gruesome. He had intended the thrust as another ploy, braced to get clipped a few times while he searched for a genuine opening. To have it end this way—

"Hig yields," the staffer said. That meant Neq could leave the circle without further mayhem. Ordinarily the man who remained in the circle longest was the victor, regardless what happened inside, since some were clever at feigning injury as a tactical ruse, or at striking back despite wounds.

He was abruptly sick. He stumbled away from the circle, heedless of the spectacle he made. He retched, getting vomit in his nose. Now, calamitously, he understood why his father had been so cautious about the circle.

The sword was no toy, and combat was no game.

He looked up to find Nemi. "It was awful!" she said. But she was not condemning him. She never did that when the matter was important. "But I guess you won. You're a man now. So I fetched this from the hostel for you."

She held out a gold bracelet, the emblem of adulthood.

Neq leaned against her sisterly bosom, crying. "It wasn't worth it," he said.

After a while she took a cloth and cleaned him up, and then he donned the bracelet.

But it *was* worth it. Hig did not die. He was packed off to the crazy hospital and the prognosis was favorable. Neq wore the invaluable bracelet clamped around his left wrist, proud of its weight, and his friends congratulated him on his expertise and assumption of manhood. Even Nemi confessed that she was relieved to have had her liaison with the sticker broken up; she hadn't liked Hig that well anyway. She could wait for womanhood—*weeks,* if need be!

There was a manhood party for Neq, where he announced his name, which was duly posted on a hostel bulletin board for the crazies to record. There was no eligible girl in this group, so he was unable to consummate his new status in the traditional fashion. But the truth was that he was as leary as was his sister of the actual plunge. Man-man in the circle was straight-forward. Man-woman in the bed . . . that could wait.

So he sang for them, his fine tenor impressing everyone. Nemi joined him, her alto harmonizing neatly. They were no longer technically brother and sister, but such ties did not sever cleanly at the stroke of a sword.

A few days later he commenced his manhood trek: a long hike anywhere, leaving his family behind. He was expected to fight, perfecting his craft, and to move his bracelet about, becoming a man of experience. He might return in a month or a year or never; the hiatus would

establish the change of circumstance, so that all nomads would respect him as an individual. Never again would he be "Nem's kid." He was a warrior.

It was a glorious moment, this ceremony of departure, but he had to hide the choke in his throat as he bid farewell to Nem and Nema and Nemi, the family he had set aside. He saw tears forming in his sister's eyes, and she could not speak, and she was beautiful, and he had to turn away before he was overcome similarly, but it was good.

He marched. The hostels in this region were about twenty miles apart—easy walking distance, but not if a man tarried overlong. And Neq tended to tarry, for many things were new to him: the curves and passes of the trail, unfamiliar because he had never seen them alone before, and the alternating pastures and forests and the occasionally encountered warriors. It was dark by the time he found his first lodging.

And lonely, for the hostel was empty. He made do for himself, using the facilities the crazies had provided. The crazies: so-called because their actions made no sense. They had fine weapons that they did not use, and excellent food they did not eat, and these comfortable hostels they never slept in. Instead they set these things out unguarded for any man to take. If everything were removed from a hostel, the crazies soon brought more, with no word of protest. Yet if a man fought with his sword outside the circle reserved for combat, or slew others with the bow, or barred another from a hostel, and if no one stopped him, the crazies cut off their supplies. It was as though they did not care whether men died, but how and where. As though death by arrow were more morbid than death by sword. Thus there was only one word for them: crazy. But the wise warrior humored their foibles.

The hostel itself was a thirty-foot cylinder standing as high as a man could reach, with a cone for a roof. Somehow the cone caught the sunlight and turned it into power for the lights and machines within. Inside there was a fat column, into which toilet facilities and food-storage and cooking equipment were set, and vents to blow cool air or hot, depending on the need.

Neq took meat from the freezer and cooked it in the

oven. He drew a cup of milk from the spout. As he ate he contemplated the racks of bracelets, clothing, and weapons. All this for the taking without combat! Crazy!

At last he pulled down a bunk from the outer wall and slept, covering his head from the stillness.

In the morning he prepared a pack with replacement socks and shirt, but did not bother with extra pantaloons or jackets or sneakers. Dirt did not matter, but the items that became sweatsoaked did need changing every so often or discomfort resulted. He also packed bread and the rest of the meat: waste was another thing the crazies were sensitive about, despite their own colossal waste in putting this all out for plunder. Finally he took a bow and a tent-package, for he intended to do some hunting and camping on this trek. The hostels were fine for occasional use, but the typical nomad preferred to be independent.

The second night he camped, but it was still lonely and he had forgotten to take mosquito repellent. The third night he used a hostel, but he had to share with two other warriors, a sworder and a clubber. It was friendly, and they did not talk down to him though they had to be aware of his youth. The three practiced in the circle a bit, and both men complimented Neq on his skill: meaning he still was a novice. In serious combat no compliments were needed; the skill spoke for itself.

The fourth night he found a woman. She prepared a meal for him that was immeasurably superior to his own makings, but did not make any other overtures, and he found himself too shy to proffer his bracelet. She was as tall as he, and older, and not really pretty. He took a shower in her presence so she could see he had hair on his genitals, and they slept in adjacent bunks, and in the morning she wished him good fortune in a motherly fashion and he went on. And cursed himself for not initiating his bracelet, at the same time knowing he was even more afraid of somehow mishandling it and being ridiculed. How could a man feign experience in such a matter?

The fifth day he arrived early at a hostel set near a beautiful small lake, and a man was there. By his fair, unblemished features he was not much older than Neq,

and he was not substantially larger, but he had the bearing of a seasoned warrior.

"I am Sol of All Weapons," he announced. "I contest for mastery."

This set Neq back. Mastery meant the loser would join the tribe of the winner. Because it was a voluntary convention, it did not violate the crazies' stricture against deprivation of personal freedom, but a man honor-bound was still bound. Neq had only fought once and practiced some, and didn't trust his luck in serious combat. Not so soon, anyway. He didn't want to join a tribe so soon, and had no use for a tribe of his own.

"You use all weapons?" he asked, putting off the implied challenge. "Sword, staff, sticks—all?"

Sol nodded gravely.

"Even the star?" He glanced at the morning star maces on the weapons rack.

Sol nodded again. It seemed he wasn't much for conversation.

"I don't want to fight," Neq said. "Not for mastery. I—I just achieved my manhood last week."

Sol shrugged, amenable.

About dusk a woman showed up. She wore the sarong of availability, but she was if anything less young and less pretty than the one Neq had met before. She must have borrowed many bracelets in her time, yet no man had retained her. Sol paid her no attention; he was without his own bracelet, showing he was married. So it was up to Neq again—and again he did nothing.

The woman prepared supper for them both, at this was the function of the available distaff. She had the same assurance about her cooking that Sol did about his weapons. This must be her territory, so that she was used to catering to any men who came here, hoping that some would prefer capability to beauty and would leave the bracelet on her. No woman ever took her bracelet directly from the rack; it had to come from a man.

Before the meal was served, a third man arrived. He was a large warrior, paunchy, gruff, with many scars. "I am Mok the Star," he said.

"Sol of All Weapons."

"Neq the Sword."

The girl said nothing; it was not her place. She made another setting at the table.

"I contest for mastery," Sol said.

"You have a tribe? This boy and who else?"

"Not Neq. My tribe is training in the badlands."

"The badlands!" Mok's surprise matched Neq's own. "No one goes there!"

"Nevertheless," Sol said.

"The kill-spirits—"

"Do you question my word?" Sol demanded.

Mok bridled at the tone. "Everyone knows—"

"I have to agree," Neq said—and was immediately aware that he had spoken out of turn. This was not his quarrel.

"In the *circle* you challenge my word!" Sol said. He glanced at the rotating transparent door, noting that it was dark outside. "Tomorrow."

Mok and Neq exchanged glances. Both were stuck.

"Tomorrow," Mok agreed. "For mastery." Then as an afterthought: "But you will see my weapon is not for games."

The girl smiled at Mok. He smiled back, stroking his bracelet. And that night Sol and Neq pulled down bunks from the wall on the east side, while Mok took the woman to the west side, putting his bracelet on her wrist.

Neq lay in the dark, listening, feeling guilty for it. But he couldn't really tell anything from the sounds.

Sol had a barrow filled with weapons. "What would you face in the circle?" he asked Mok.

"You really use them all? Let's have the star, then."

Sol brought out his ball and chain. Neq was fascinated. He had never seen a star in action, and had never heard of a star-star encounter in the circle. The weapon was unreliable but terrifying, as it could not be used defensively. Either the heavy spiked ball connected or it didn't, and the outcome of the battle depended on that. Serious injury was a probability, in this match.

The two men entered the circle on opposite sides, each whirling his deadly steel ball over his head so rapidly that the short chains were blurs. Now the stars were beautiful, flashing the sunlight in rings of fire as the men's torsos flexed rhythmically. The fight had to be short, for the out-

ward pulling weight of the ball would rapidly tire the arm.

It was short. The two bright arcs intersected, the chains crossed, the balls spun about each other fiercely, striking sparks. Both Mok and Sol jumped as their chains yanked—but it was Sol who hung on to his star. Mok's handle slipped from his grasp, and he was disarmed.

Neq realized that this was exactly what Sol had intended. He had deliberately engaged the other weapon, not trying for the man at all, and had jerked sharply the moment contact was made. Mok had expected the entanglement to interfere with both warriors, so that he could use his weight to advantage in the clinch. Sol's strategy and timing had been superior.

Or could it have been sheer luck?

"What would you face?" Sol asked Neq.

Already! Not the star, certainly! Was it courtesy or confidence the man showed? What to answer!

A sword or dagger in a skilled hand could hurt him severely, like Hig. The sticks were blunt, but the pair of them could rattle his brain. The club was blunt and slow, but a real mauler when it connected. The staff—

"The staff!" One piece, slow, no edges, safe.

Sol calmly brought out his staff.

They entered the circle and sparred. Neq felt guilty for his cowardice. A real warrior would have chosen to oppose his own weapon, so the threats were equal. The quarterstaff was safe, but hard to circumvent. Neq feinted—

When he came to, his head was throbbing. He was on a bunk in the hostel. The woman wearing Mok's bracelet—Moka—was sponging his face.

Neq refrained from asking what had happened. Obviously he had been felled by a blow he had never seen. Could Mok have struck him from behind? No—that would have been a gross violation of the circle code, and there had been no evidence that either Sol or Mok were the type to practice or tolerate such dishonor. The staff must have passed his guard—

He touched his head. The welt reminded him. An astonishingly deft maneuver, the staff avoiding his sword as if it were fog, whipping in—ouch!

Well, he was a member of Sol's tribe now. The badlands tribe. If there were kill-spirits there, they hadn't hurt Sol

much! On balance, it wasn't such a bad outcome. Nem had always said there were advantages to serving a strong leader. What a man lost in independence he gained in security. Provided he joined a good tribe.

Neq wasn't quite confident he had joined a good one, for there remained some doubt whether Sol was an excellent warrior or merely lucky. But Neq put the best face on it: would he have let himself be taken by a fluke?

He traveled with Mok, following instructions, while Sol continued in the opposite direction. Mok had reclaimed his bracelet after the second night, and Neq didn't question him. Maybe the man just didn't care to take a wife to the badlands, though Sol said the kill-spirits—he called them roents—had gone back beyond the camp. They were on the trail several days.

Sol's tribe, or at least the portion of it they joined, seemed to consist of about thirty men encamped in and about another hostel under the general eye of his wife Sola. She was a sultry beauty of about sixteen, inclined to sharpness when addressed and brooding silence at other times. But she wore her gold bracelet proudly.

For two weeks they tarried there, their numbers augmented by other converts Sol sent back. A number of men had families, so that the drain on the supplies of the hostel was considerable. They hunted with bow and arrow in the forest to supplement those waning rations, though twice the crazy van came to restock them.

The crazies were as funny in person as their name indicated: strangely garbed, unarmed, almost devoid of muscle, and ludicrously clean. Yet their truck was a monster, capable of crushing many warriors if misdirected. Why should they act like servants to the nomads, when they could so easily assume power? Some thought it was because the crazies were weak and foolish, but Neq doubted that it could be that simple.

Eventually Sol returned with another fifteen men, swelling the tribe to over fifty. Then the whole group marched —to the badlands. Neq viewed the red crazy warners with alarm, knowing they marked the boundaries of the kill-spirits as surveyed by the crazy click boxes. But nothing happened.

A camp had been established in the wilderness beside

a river, with a flooded trench around it. The leader of this camp was Tyl of Two Weapons; but the man who really ran it was Sos the Weaponless. Sos drilled the men mercilessly, setting up subtribes for each weapon and ranking each man according to his skill. Neq began as the bottom sworder of twenty, chagrined, but he prospered under the training and rose eventually to fourth of fifty. The camp was growing all the time, as Sol traveled and sent more warriors. There was no doubt of the tribe's power now; he had never seen such discipline.

Strange that it was all the doing of a man who would not fight in the circle himself. Sos obviously had an enormous store of information about combat, and he was no weakling physically. Yet he kept a stupid little bird on his shoulder, the ridicule of all the tribe, and obviously loved Sola without admitting it. Neq once saw her go to his tent in winter and stay there until dawn. The whole situation was incredible.

When spring came, the tribe was ready to move out as a unit, and Neq was a ranking member. He was eager for the promised conquest.

Only one thing marred his success: he had not yet had the courage to offer his bracelet to a girl. He wanted to, but he was not yet fifteen, and looked thirteen, and a live naked woman was just too much for him to contemplate. The mistakes he might make!

Sometimes he dreamed of Sola. It wasn't that he loved her, or even liked her; it was that she was a lusciously constructed female who stayed in another man's tent though her husband was master of the tribe. Dishonor . . . but excruciatingly tantalizing! She was the kind to keep a secret. . . .

That was one reason he had improved so much as a sworder: he spent almost all of his free time practicing, while others allowed themselves to be diverted by romantic concerns. They thought him dedicated, but he was tormented.

Some day—some day he would really be a man!

CHAPTER TWO

Neq prospered in battle, too, winning his matches easily. His first match was against the first sword of a smaller tribe. The other master had not wanted to fight, and Neq had been one of the carefully picked hecklers who taunted him into a commitment. His opponent in the circle was good, and Neq was so nervous he feared his weapon would quiver—but incredibly his intensive winter's training had made him better. Sos had drilled him until he was furious, not only against swords but against all other weapons, and had matched him in pairs with others to fight other pairs. It had been tedious, hard work, and since the practice sessions were never for blood he had only Sos's opinion to certify his actual skill. But that opinion was justified; as Neq saw the little crudities of the other man's technique he knew it was all true. Clumsy victories and confused losses were no longer Neq's lot. He really *was* a master sworder, not far behind Tyl himself, who was first.

Then, suddenly, Sos the Trainer left. It was an ironic question who mourned his departure more: Sol or Sola. Had Sol found out? But the tribe continued operating as Sos had organized it. Sola birthed a baby girl, though nine months before her husband had been away a great deal. . . .

The tribe became so large through conquests that it had to be broken up into ten subtribes formed into an empire. One was under Sol and the others under his major lieutenants: Tyl of Two weapons, who had the finest warriors; Sav the Staff, who took over the badlands camp as a training area and was the other songsinger of the

empire; Tor the Sword, with his great black beard . . . and, gratifying, Neq himself. Each subtribe went its own way, acquiring more warriors, but all were subject to Sol ultimately.

At first it was wonderful, for Neq's fondest dreams of glory had been exceeded. He was chief of a hundred and fifty warriors, which was more than most independent tribes boasted. He visited his family and showed off his status. His sister had married and moved away, but hometown doubters he gladly convinced. He packed half a dozen of them off to the badlands camp, and even demonstrated his skill against his father Nem, though not for blood or mastery. Neq was the finest sworder this area had ever seen, and it was good to have it known.

But in a year such things palled, for administrative duties kept him from practicing in the circle as much as he liked, and there seemed to be rivalries and enemies on every side. He decided that he was not, at heart, a leader. He was a fighter.

By the end of the second year he was heartily sick of it, but there seemed to be no way down the ladder. He longed just to run away by himself, meeting people honestly, without the barrier his present responsibility erected.

And—he still wanted a woman. He was sixteen now, more than man enough—but the very notion of offering his bracelet to a girl, any girl, filled him with dread. If one would ask *him*, make it clear she was amenable . . . but none did.

Neq suspected that he was the shyest man in all the empire—and for no reason. He could command men without qualm, he could meet any weapon with confidence, he could run a tribe of hundreds. But to put his bracelet on a woman . . . he *wanted* to, but he *couldn't*.

Then disaster came to the empire. A nameless, weaponless warrior appeared—one who entered the circle and defeated the empire's finest *with his bare hands*. It seemed impossible—but the Nameless first took Sav's tribe, breaking Sav's arm; then Tyl's tribe, shattering Tyl's knees; then Tor's—by killing Bog the Club, the one warrior even Sol had not beaten. And finally he brought Sol himself to the circle, and took all the empire and Sola too for his own, sending Sol to die with his girlchild at the mountain.

Neq's tribe had been ranging far from the scene of that action, and by the time he got there the issue had been settled and Sol was gone. There was nothing for him to do but go along with the new Master. Tyle remained second in command, acting in the name of the grotesque Weaponless conqueror, who seemed to have little interest in the routine affairs of empire. "Go where you will," Tyl advised Neq privately. "Battle where you will. But no more for mastery. Query your warriors and release any who wish to leave, asking no questions. The Nameless has so decreed."

"Why did he conquer, then?" Neq demanded, amazed.

Tyl only shrugged, disgusted. Neq knew Tyl much preferred Sol's way—but he was a man of honor to match his station, and would not act against the new Master.

So it came to pass. For six years the empire stagnated. Neq turned over his administrative duties to other men and took to wandering alone, incognito. Sometimes he fought in the circle—but his blinding skill with the sword made such encounters meaningless, and destroyed his alias. And still his bracelet had never left his wrist, though he dreamed of women, all women.

At the age of twenty-four, with a decade of nomadic brilliance behind him, Neq the Sword was over the hill. He had no present and no future, like the empire.

Then the Master invaded the mountain, using his own and Tyl's subtribes—and disappeared. Tyl returned with news that the mountain fortress had been gutted; that the men who went there in the future really *would* die, whatever had been the case in the past. But Tyl could not claim the leadership of the empire. No one had defeated the Weaponless. He might or might not return.

The chiefs met—Tyl, Neq, Sav, Tor and the others— and formally suspended the empire, pending that return. Each subtribe would become a full tribe, but they would not fight each other.

Neq wanted only freedom, so he dissolved his own tribe completely. The top warriors immediately began forming their own tribelets and moving out. Neq, truly independent for the first time in his life, wandered alone again.

* * *

The third time he came to a lodge in a hostel and found it gutted and broken, Neq grew perplexed and angry. Who was doing this, and why? The hostels had always been sacrosanct, open for all travelers all the time. When one was destroyed, every person suffered. Too much of this would hurt the entire nomad society—that had supposedly been saved by the razing of the mountain underworld.

There was no hope of catching the perpetrators; the deed was weeks past. Easier to inquire of the crazies themselves, who were often knowledgeable about nomad affairs but who never acted positively.

Neq, missionless until this moment, had found a mission of a sort.

The local crazy outpost was under siege. Its foolish glass windows had been broken in, and now fragments of wood and metal furniture barred them ineffectively. The flower beds around the building had been trampled. Two unkempt warriors patrolled in semicircles at a distance, one on either side, and three more chatted around a nearby campfire.

Neq accosted the nearest of the marchers, a large sworder. "Who are you and what are you doing?"

"Beat it, punk," the man said. "This is private soil."

Neq was not young or impulsive any more. He replied calmly: "It looks to me as though you are molesting a crazy outpost. Have you any reason?"

The man drew his blade. "This is my reason. Got it clear now, shorty?"

Neq saw that the others had been alerted, and were coming at a run. They were all sworders. But he held his ground. "Are you challenging me in the circle?"

"Hey, this guy's a troublemaker!" the man cried, amused.

"Cut off his balls—if he has any!" one of the others said, approaching with weapon drawn.

Neq was assured by this time that these were noncircle outlaws: clumsy fighters who banded together informally to prey on whoever was helpless. Such wretches had never been tolerated within the crazy demesnes before, and the empire had systematically run them down and executed them. That is, they were forced to meet a capable warrior in the circle, contesting for life. There was no sense in having the crazies halt maintenance because of the actions of outlaws.

But the empire was gone now, and the weeds were encroaching. He would have no compunction about cutting down such cowards. Still, he made sure: "Give me your names."

They ringed him now. "We'll give you a bleeding gut!" the first man said, and the rest chuckled.

"Then I give you mine. I am Neq the Sword." He drew his weapon. "The first to move against me defines the circle."

"Hey—I've heard of him!" one man cried "He's dangerous! Got a tribe—"

But already the others, no students of the empire heirarchy, were closing in, thinking to overwhelm him by their dishonorable mass attack.

Neq swung into action the moment they moved. He thrust ferociously at the one directly in front, driving his point into the man's unguarded chest and yanking it out again immediately. Then he whirled the bloody blade to the left, catching the next man at the neck before he could raise his sword in defense. Such tactics would never have worked against competent warriors—but these were combat oafs. He swung right, and this man had his guard up, so that sword clanged on sword.

Neq leaped away, passing between the two bleeding men. Two remained, for the fifth had fled after recognizing him. Neq spun to face them as they looked at their fallen comrades, appalled. Novices frightened of blood!

"Take your wounded and get out of here," he snapped at them. "If I see you again, I kill you both."

They hesitated, but they were inept cowards and he knew it. He turned his back on them contemptuously and went to the outpost building. He knocked on the door.

There was no answer.

"The siege is lifted," he called. "I am Neq the Sword— Warrior of the circle. You have me in your records."

Still silence. Neq knew that the crazies kept track of all the nomad leaders, and had duplicate dossiers.

"Stand before the window," a voice called at last.

Neq walked to the shattered window. He saw that the rough sworders were stumbling away with their comrades.

"There *is* a Neq-sword listed," another voice said. "Ask him who his father is."

"Nem the Sword," Neq answered without waiting for the question. These crazies! "And my sister is Boma; she took Bom the Dagger's band and bore two boys by him."

"We have no record of that here," the second voice said after a pause. "But it sounds authentic. Did he serve in the nomad empire of Sol of All Weapons?"

"Bom? No. But if you saw my action of a moment ago, you know *I* served."

"We have to trust him," the first voice said.

Neq returned to the door. There was the sound of laboriously shifting furniture. Keys. It opened.

Two old men stood within. They were typical crazies: cleanshaven, hair shorn, parted and combed, spectacles, white shirts with sleeves, long trousers with creases, stiff polished leather shoes. Ludicrous apparel for any type of combat. Both were shaking visibly, obviously unused to personal duress and afraid of Neq himself.

"How did you hold them off?" Neq asked, genuinely curious. A nomad in such decrepit condition would begin excavating his cairn.

One crazy picked up a vaguely swordlike instrument. "This is a power drill, operating off house current. I turned it on and put it against any part of the body that entered the building. It was sickening but effective."

"And we do have weapons," the other said. "But we aren't adept at their use."

Obviously. "How long has this been going on?"

"For two days. We've had similar attacks recently, but our supply trucks were able to disperse them. This time the truck did not come."

"Probably ambushed, boarded and wrecked," Neq said. "I found three gutted hostels too. But those jackals never had the nerve to attack you before. What's the reason?"

"We don't know. Supplies have been short, and we have not been able to stock our hostels sufficiently. The nomads seem to have been making war against us."

"Not the nomads! Those were outlaws!"

They peered at him dubiously. "We don't question your values, but—"

"My values aren't hurting," Neq said. "You have evidence that regular warriors are rampaging against you?"

"It seems so."

"But that's suicidal! We are not completely dependent on the hostels, but they do make possible a special way of life. Their sanctity has always been honored."

"So we thought. But as you have seen—"

Neq sighed. "I have seen. Well, I want you to know that I do not condone this destruction, and I'm sure most nomads agree with me. How may I help you?"

The two exchanged timid glances. "Would you be willing to bear a message to our main depot?"

"Gladly. But the way things are going, you need protection here. If I go, you won't survive long."

"We can not desert our post," one man said sadly.

"Better that than death," Neq pointed out.

"It is a matter of principle."

He shrugged. "That's why you are called the crazies. You *are* crazy."

"If you will carry the message—"

"I'll take the message. But first I think I'd better see to your defenses. I can round up a few men—"

"No. We have never worked that way."

"Crazies, look," Neq exclaimed, exasperated. "If you *don't* work that way now, your post will surely and shortly be a smoking hole, and you buried under it. You have to take some note of reality."

"A compelling case," the man admitted. "You have obviously had tactical experience. But if we do not function according to our philosophy, we have no point in functioning at all."

Neq shook his head. "Crazy," he repeated, admiring their perverse courage. "Give me your message."

The main post was a school. The message was for one Doctor Jones, and he meant to deliver it personally to the man.

A blonde crazy girl sat at a desk as though guarding her master from intrusions. "And who is calling?" she asked, her professional eye analyzing him comprehensively. She was quite clean, and that was mildly annoying too.

"Neq the Sword."

"N E K or N E G?"

He merely stared at her.

"Oh, illiterate," she said after a moment. "Dr. Jones will see you now."

He entered the interior office and handed over the written message. The aged, balding crazy within broke the seal immediately and studied the scribbled sheet of paper. He looked grave. "I wish we had been able to install telephonic cables. So our trucks have not been getting through?" he obviously knew the answer.

"Those two men are probably dead by now," Neq said. "Crazies just won't listen to reason. I offered to protect them, but—"

"Our ways differ from yours. Otherwise we would be nomads ourselves—as many of us have been, in youth."

"You were a warrior?" Neq asked incredulously. "What weapon?"

"Sword, like you. But that was forty years ago."

"Why did you give it up?"

"I discovered a superior philosophy."

Oh. "Well, those crazies at the outposts are *dying* by their philosophies. You'd better call them in."

"I shall."

At least the crazy master had some sense! "Why is this happening? Attacks on your posts, hostels—it was never this way before."

"Never in your memory, perhaps. I could give you an answer, but not a completely satisfactory one." Dr. Jones sat behind his desk and made figures with his hands. He had long spindly wrinkled fingers. "We have been unable to supply the hostels properly in recent months. Normal attrition thus reduces some of these to virtual uselessness for travelers. When that happens, some men react adversely—and lacking the stability of civilization, they strike out senselessly. They are hungry, they want clothing and weapons—and none are available. They feel they have been unfairly denied."

"But why can't you supply them anymore?"

"Because our own supplies have been cut off. We are chiefly distributors; we do not manufacture the implements. We do have a number of mechanized farms—but food is only part of our service."

"You get the weapons and things from somebody else?" Neq had not realized this.

"Until recently, yes. But we have had no shipments for several months, and our own resources are practically exhausted. So we are frankly unable to provide for the nomads, with the unfortunate results you have noted."

"Didn't they tell you what happened? Your suppliers, I mean?"

"We have had no contact. Television broadcasts ceased abruptly, so there seems to have been a severe power loss. Our suppy trucks have not returned. I fear that now the very restlessness our lapse promotes is rebounding against us: a feedback effect. The situation is serious."

"Your whole hostel system will break down?"

"And, I am very much afraid, our schools and hospitals and farms. Yes. We cannot withstand the concerted attacks of so many armed men. Unless we are able to resolve this matter expeditiously, I have grave reservations about the stability of our society in its present form."

"You're saying we're all in trouble?"

Dr. Jones nodded. "You are succinct."

"What you need is someone to go find out what's wrong at the other end. Someone who can fight. If your truck drivers are like the men I met at the outpost—"

Jones nodded again.

"*I'll* go, if you like."

"You are most generous. But you would not be conversant with the details. We would require a written report—"

"I can't write. But I could guard a literate."

Jones sighed. "I will not claim your offer is unenticing. But it would be unethical for us to use you in this fashion. And you might have difficulty protecting a 'crazy'."

"You're right. I can't help a man who won't listen."

"So I thank you for your service in bearing this message." Jones stood up. "You are welcome to remain with us for as long as you desire. But I doubt that you are inclined toward the quiet life."

"I doubt it's quiet anymore," Neq said. "But it does differ from my—my philosophy." He put his hand on the hilt of his sword. "By this I live."

"Doctor."

Both men glanced over to see the blonde girl in the

doorway. "Yes, Miss Smith?" Dr. Jones said in his question-statement tone.

"I listened over the intercom," she said, looking rebelliously guilty. "I overheard Mr. Neg's offer——"

"Neq," Neq said, pronouncing it carefully. "Neq the Sword."

"With a Q, I'm sure," Jones said, smiling. "One of the most skilled of the nomad swordsmen today."

Neq was startled, for Dr. Jones had given no hint of his information before. But of course an ex-sworder would keep track of such things, and Neq was in the crazy records.

"I could go with him," Miss Smith said, and a flush came to her rather pretty features. "I haven't entirely forgotten the wild life—and I could make the report."

Jones looked pained. He had an excellent face for it. "My dear, this is not the type of enterprise——"

"Doctor, you know our whole structure will collapse if we don't do *something!*" she cried. "We can't go on much longer."

Neq stayed out of this debate, watching the girl. She was young but quite attractive in her animation. Her two breasts were conical under her light crazy sweater and her skirted legs were well proportioned. She was worth a man's contemplation despite her outlandish attire. He had heard that "Miss" applied to a crazy woman signified her eligibility for marriage; they used words instead of bracelets.

Jones faced Neq. "This is somewhat awkward—but she is technically correct. Our need is imperative, and she would seem to be equipped to do the job. Of course it is not incumbent on you to——"

"I can guard a woman as easily as a crazy man," Neq said. "If she'll do what I say. I can't have her standing on 'principle' when a warrior's charging us."

"I'll do what you say," she said quickly.

"My mind is not easy," Jones said. "But we *do* require the information. Even a negative report—which I very much fear is to be anticipated—would enable us to make positive plans to salvage a very limited sphere. If both of you are amenable——"

Neq considered more carefully. How far would he travel in a day, fettered to this doll-pretty crazy woman? She would faint at the sight of blood, surely, and collapse before they had walked sixty miles. And the ridicule he would evoke, marching with a crazy companion, *any* crazy, but particularly a *female* crazy—

"It wouldn't work," he said. And felt a certain familiar frustration, knowing that his shyness with women had as much to do with it as logic.

"It *has* to work," she said. "Dr. Jones can do amazing things, but only if he has exact information. If you're worried about my keeping up—we'll take a truck. And I don't have to look this way. I'm aware of your contempt. I can dress like a nomad. I'll even put on some dirt—"

Jones almost smiled, but Neq shrugged as though it wasn't that important to him. If they didn't get there, they didn't get there. The notion of traveling with a handsome woman, even a crazy, had its subtle but developing appeal. This was business, after all; his private problem could not be permitted to interfere. "All right."

"All right?" She looked surprised.

"Put on some dirt and get your truck and we'll go."

She looked dazedly at Jones. "All right?"

Dr. Jones sighed. "This is against my better judgment. But if both of you are willing—"

CHAPTER THREE

The change in blonde Miss Smith was amazing. She had unbound her hair to wear it loose and long in nomad fashion, and she had the one-piece wraparound of the available. Gone was the crisp office manner: she spoke only when addressed, knowing her place in the presence of a warrior. Had Neq not known her origin, he would have been fooled. Of course his close experience with women was meager.

She, however, had to drive the truck. Neq had seen the crazy vehicles on occasion, but had never actually been inside one before. The handling of such machinery was not his forte, obviously. So he rode beside her in the cab, sword clasped between his knees, and clung to the seat as the wheels bumped over the ruts. The velocity of the thing was appalling. He kept expecting it to start panting and slow to a walk, for no one could run indefinitely! He had been told a truck could cover in one hour a distance equivalent to a full day's march, if it had a good track, and now he believed it.

The road was no pleasure. What suited for foot traveling became hazardous for wheels, particularly at this speed, and he was privately terrified. Now he understood why the crazies had always been so fussy about the maintenance of their trails, cutting back the brush and removing boulders. Such natural obstacles were like swinging clubs to the zooming vehicle. Neq refused to show it, of course, but his hands were clammy on the sword and his muscles stiff from tension.

But in time he became acclimatized, and watched Miss Smith's motions. She controlled the truck by turning a

wheel around: when she pushed the top of it north, the truck swung north. When she wanted to stop she pushed a metal pedal into the floor. Driving was not so difficult after all!

All day they drove, stopping only to let Neq be sick from the unaccustomed motion, and to refuel. The first was mortifying, but Miss Smith pretended not to notice and in time his gut became resigned. The second was just a matter of pouring funny smelling liquid she called gasoline into the motortank from one of the large metal drums carried in the back. "Why don't you just pipe it in from the drums?" he asked, and she admitted she didn't know.

"These trucks were designed and probably built by the Ancients," she said. "They did a number of inexplicable things—like making a gas tank far too small for a day's driving. Maybe they *liked* pouring gas from cans."

Neq laughed. "That's something! To the crazies, the Ancients are crazy!"

She smiled, not taking offense. "Sanity seems to be inversely proportional to civilization."

Inverse proportion: he knew what that meant, for he had been drilled like the others in the empire training camp. They had used numbers to assess combat ranking: the smaller the number, the higher the warrior stood.

They drove on, until they had to stop to do patchwork on the road. A gully had formed, the result of some cloudburst, and made a tumble of boulders of the roadbed. Here Neq felt useful, for Miss Smith could not have budged all those rocks or shoveled enough sand into place to make the passage.

Despite these delays, Neq estimated that they had come a good five days march by dusk.

"How much do you normally march?" she inquired in response to his remark.

"Thirty miles, alone. More if I'm in a hurry. Twenty, with a tribe."

"So you make it a hundred and fifty miles today."

He worked it out, counting off fingers. He knew how to count and calculate, but this was a different problem than the type he normally encountered. "Yes."

"Speedometer says ninety-four," she said. "It must have

seemed faster than it was. On a paved road it would have been double that."

"The truck keeps track of its own travels?" he asked, amazed. "Maybe it forgot to count the section between the tank-filling and the roadwork."

She laughed again. "Maybe! Machines aren't bright."

He had neither worked with nor talked with a woman this way before, and was surprised to realize that it wasn't difficult. "How far is this supplier?"

"About a thousand miles from the school, direct. Somewhat farther by these backwoods trails."

He figured again. "So we have about ten days of travel."

"Less than that. Some areas are better than others. Let me show you our route on the map. I think we've been through the worst already."

"No."

"No?" She paused with the map in her hand.

"The worst is what stopped your other trucks from returning."

"Oh." She was prettily pensive. "Well, we'll find out. The others didn't have an armed guard along."

She opened the map and pointed out lines and patches of color to him, but it was largely meaningless to Neq, who could not relate to the continental scope of it. "I can find the way back, once I've been there," he said.

"That's good enough." She studied the map a bit more, then put it away with a small sigh.

There were canned and even frozen goods. Miss Smith lit a little gas stove and heated beans and turnip greens and bacon, and she opened the little refrigerator and poured out milk. Neq had never had a woman do for him on a regular basis, and this was an intriguing experience. But of course she only looked like a woman; she was a crazy.

They slept in the truck—he in the back beside the gas drums, she curled in the cab. She seemed to feel there would be something wrong if they both slept in the back, though there was far more room there and she had to know that no honorable nomad would disturb her slumber without prior transfer of the bracelet. She could not know, of course, that Neq had never had relations with

any woman. The only girl he had been close to was his sister. In fact, had Miss Smith not been a crazy, he would have been extremely nervous. As it was, he was only moderately nervous, and relieved to sleep alone.

But in his dreams women were ubiquitous, and he was not bashful. In his dreams.

The second day of travel was uneventful, and they made almost two hundred miles. The novelty of riding in the truck palled, and he stared moodily into the rushing brush and covertly at Miss Smith's right breast, shaped under the cloth as she steered. She seemed less like a crazy, now.

He began to hum to his sword, and when she did not object he sang to it: the folk songs he had picked up from happy warriors like Sav the Staff, in the glad days of the empire's nascence.

Oh, the sons of the Prophet were hardy and bold
And quite unaccustomed to fear.
But the bravest of all was a man so I'm told
Named Abdullah Bulbul Ameer.

The references were meaningless, as were the names, but the melody always brought pleasure to him and he responded to the warrior mood of such songs. From time to time he was tempted to change the words a bit, adapting to the things he knew, but that forfeited authenticity. "Oh, the warriors of empire were hardy and bold . . ." No—songs were inviolate, lest they lose their magic.

After a time he realized with a shock that she was singing with him, in feminine harmony, the way Nemi used to do. That jolted him back into silence. Miss Smith made no comment.

The third day they encountered a barricade. A tree had fallen across the road.

"That isn't natural." Neq said, alert for trouble. "See— it has been felled, not blown. No nomad cuts a tree and leaves it."

She stopped the truck. In a moment men appeared— unkempt outlaws of the type he had encountered before. "All right, you crazies—out!" the leader bawled.

"You stay here," Neq said. "This will be unpleasant for you. Maybe you'd better duck down so you can't see." He got out in one bound and lifted his weapon. "I am Neq the Sword," he announced.

This time no one recognized the name. "You think you're pretty smart, dressing like a man," a big clubber said. "But we know you're crazies. What's in your truck?"

Miss Smith had not followed his suggestion. Her pale face showed in the cab window. "Hey!" the leader cried. "This one's a lady-crazy!"

Neq advanced on his man. "You will not touch this truck. It is under my protection."

The man laughed harshly and swung his club.

He died laughing.

Neq let him drop and moved to the next, a scarred dagger. At the same time he watched for bows, for outlaws were capable of anything. He would have to perform some deft maneuvers if arrows came at him. "Run," he suggested softly.

The dagger looked at the bleeding clubber corpse and ran. That was the thing about outlaws: they were easily frightened.

Neq charged the leader, another dagger. This man, at least, had some courage. He brought up his knives and sliced clumsily.

It was axiomatic that a good dagger would lose to a good sworder when the combat was serious. This man was not good, and Neq cut him down immediately.

No one else remained. "Scream if you see anything," he told Miss Smith. "I'm scouting the area." He had to be sure that all the teeth of the ambush had been drawn before he tackled the fallen tree.

She just sat there, her features stiff. He had known she would not like it. Crazies and women were similar in that respect, and she was both.

He located the outlaw camp. It was empty. The cowardly dagger had lost no time spreading the word. From the traces there had been at least two women and four men. Well, now it was two women and *two* men—and he doubted they'd attack any more trucks.

He went back. "It's clear," he told Miss Smith. "Let's haul this trunk out of our way."

She seemed to wake, then. He surveyed the tree and decided it was too much for him to move without cutting in half. He made ready to hack at it with his sword, but Miss Smith called to him. "There is an easier way."

She brought out a rope and hitched it to the base of the tree trunk. Then she looped the other end into the front bumper of the truck. Then she started the motor and backed the vehicle away slowly until the tree was dragged out lengthwise along the road. Neq gaped with a certain confused respect.

She brought a peavy from the back. He limbed the tree and used the tool to roll the main mass clear of their path. This was still heavy work, but far more efficient than his original notion.

He wound the rope and put the peavy away. They got back into the cab. "Let's move," he said gruffly.

She drove mechanically, not looking at him.

"You surprised me," he said after a while. "I never thought of using the truck like that."

She didn't answer. He glanced at her, and saw her lips thin and almost white, her eyes squinting though the light was not strong.

"I know you crazies don't like violence," he said defensively. "But I warned you not to look. They would have killed us if I hadn't wiped them out first. They didn't set that ambush just to say hello."

"It isn't that."

"If we hit any more bands like that, it'll be the same. That's why your trucks aren't coming back. You crazies don't fight. You think if you're nice to everyone, no one will hurt you. Maybe once that was true. But these outlaws just laugh."

"I know."

"Well, that's the way it is. I'm just doing the job I promised. Getting the truck through." Still he felt awkward. "I was sick myself, the first time I fought a man and wounded him. But you get used to it. Better than getting hit yourself."

She drove for a while in silence. Then she braked the truck. "I want to show you something," she said, her face softening.

They got out under the shade of spreading oak trees. She stood before him, breathing rapidly, her yellow hair highlighted momentarily by a stray beam of sunshine. She was as pretty a girl as he had seen, in that pose. "Come at me."

Neq was abruptly nervous. "I meant no offense to you. I only tried to explain. I have never attacked a woman."

"Pretend you're an outlaw about to ravish me. What would you do?"

"I would *never*—"

"You're shy, aren't you," she said.

It was like a blade sliding wickedly through his defense. Neq stood stricken.

Miss Smith shook her hand—and there was a knife in it. No lady's vegetable parer—this was a full-length warrior's dagger, and her grip on it was neither diffident nor clumsily tight. There was a way of holding that was a sure signal of circle readiness, and this was her way.

Instantly Neq's sword was in his hand, his eye on the other weapon, his weight balanced. One never ignored a blade held like that!

But Miss Smith did not attack. She unwrapped her wraparound, revealing one firm fresh breast, and tucked the knife into a flat holster under her arm. "I just wanted you to understand," she said.

"I would never have struck you," he said, numbed by both her weapon-readiness and the glimpse of her torso. But it sounded ridiculous, for there he stood with sword ready. He sheathed it quickly.

"Of course not. I checked your file, once I got your name straight. You were a tribal chieftain, but you never took a woman. What I meant was: understand about *me*. That I was wild once. I'm not really a crazy. Not when it counts."

"You—used the dagger?"

"When I saw you fighting those brutes—the blood—it was as though a dozen years had peeled away, and I was the gamin again. I found the knife in my hand, there in the cab."

"Twelve years! You fought as a small child?"

Her mouth quirked. "How old do you think I am?"

"Nineteen." It was an unfortunate fact that most married women lost their beauty early. At fifteen they were highly desirable; ten years later they were faded. The unmarried lacked even that initial freshness. Miss Smith was obviously not in the first bloom, but still pretty enough.

"I am twenty-eight, according to Dr. Jones' best estimate. No one knows for sure, since I had no family."

Three years older than Neq himself? That was incredible. "Your breast says nineteen."

"When I was nineteen——" she said, mulling it over. "When I was nineteen, I met a warrior. A strong, dark man. Maybe you know of him. Sos—Sos the Rope?"

Neq shook his head. "I knew a Sos once, but he had no weapon. I don't know what happened to him."

"I would have gone nomad with him—if he had asked me." She thought for a moment, still breathing quickly. "I would have gone nomad with anyone."

This was all awkward, and Neq's hands were clammy, and he didn't know what to say.

"I'm sorry," she said. "It was the blood, the action—it made me react in an uncivilized way. I shouldn't have shown you."

"I thought you were sick. In the cab."

"I was. Emotionally. Let's forget it."

They climbed back into the truck, but he didn't forget it. He kept trying to coincide that ripe breast with her advanced age. What secret did the crazies have, to preserve a woman so?

And her knife. That motion had been swift and sure. She *had* run wild once; such talents were not readily come by, and a woman did not carry a weapon unless she knew how to use it.

Dr. Jones had said that many crazies including himself had once been nomads. This was one such.

They stopped and had a supper heated on the engine —that saved time and fuel—before he brought himself to the point. "Why did you come with me?"

"The real reason? As opposed to the one I claimed?"

He nodded.

"I suppose I still crave what I can't have. A way of life, a—a freedom from responsibility. A—a man."

A half-pleasant chill went through him. "There are crazy men."

"A *man*," she said with emphasis. "Like you."

"Are—are you asking for my bracelet?"

Even in the dusk he could see the flush rise to her face, and he hoped his own cheeks were not betraying him as mercilessly. "A woman doesn't ask."

His heart was beating, and suddenly he desired her intensely despite her age and her crazy ways. She *had* asked, in her fashion, and she was more approachable than the women he had encountered before. Perhaps because of the very things that had seemed to put her beyond any such connection. A literate, knife-bearing, twenty-eight year old crazy!

He had come to know her as a person before seriously considering her as a potential sex object, and that made a considerable difference. Three days . . . and that was longer than he had known any other woman this intimately . . . except Nemi.

"I never gave my bracelet—even for a night."

"I know. But I don't know why."

"I—was afraid of being refused." He had never spoken this truth before. "Or that it wouldn't work."

"Would that be so bad? To—fail?" Now he could see her pulse actually making the clothing quiver rhythmically. She was as wrought up about this conversation as he was. That helped, in a way . . . and hurt, in another way.

"I don't know." It made no sense, intellectually, for he could face defeat in the circle without such shame. But with a woman, his fear seemed insurmountable.

"You are handsome enough, strong enough," she said. "I don't think I've seen a more comely nomad. And you sing beautifully. I don't think you would be refused."

He studied her yet again, comprehending her meaning. It was darker now, but his night vision illuminated her more clearly than ever. He was shivering with tension and incredulous passion. Slowly he reached his right hand over to his left wrist, touching the gold band there.

She did not move. Her eyes were on his hands.

He grasped the bracelet, twisting. It slid about his

wrist but did not come away. He would have to spring it out a little, for that. But his hand would not cooperate.

Miss Smith watched him, the flush remaining on her face. It enhanced her beauty.

Neq forced his fingers apart as though he were straining at hand-wrestling and hooked them into the open section of the band. Slowly he applied pressure. Sweat trickled down his neck. His arm jerked nervously.

At last he got the metal off. His wrist felt naked, cold. He lifted the bracelet, seeing the sweat marks on it. He wiped it ineffectively on his shirt, trying to make it clean. Then, inch by inch, he carried it toward her.

Miss Smith raised her left hand. Unsteadily their two arms came together. The gold touched her wrist.

And she snatched her arm away. "No—no—I can't!" she cried.

Neq was left with his bracelet extended, refused. It was the very thing he had feared, all these years.

"Oh Neq, I'm sorry!" she said. "I didn't mean it like that. I didn't know this would happen."

Neq remained with the bracelet extended, his eyes fixed on it. He didn't know how he felt.

"It isn't what you think," she said. "I—I'll take it. The first shock . . ." She raised her wrist again . . . and dropped it. "I *can't!*"

Slowly Neq brought the band back to his own arm, and clasped it there.

"I'm ashamed," she said. "I never thought—please, don't be angry."

"I'm not angry," he said around a thick tongue.

"I mean—don't feel rejected. It's me, not you. I never —I—I'm worse than you. Oh, that sounds awful!"

"You never had a man?" Neq discovered that analyzing her problem was much easier than doing something about his own.

"Never." She forced a laugh. "If I had been a normal nomad, I'd be a grandmother by now."

Not far from the truth. "Not even this Sos?"

"I don't think he was ever really aware of me. He had some nomad woman on his mind; that's why he came to the school."

"I guess it's all right," he said after a pause.

"I don't understand." She spoke more freely now that the crisis had passed.

"I didn't really want to give you my bracelet. I just wanted to see if I could do it. So that I wouldn't have to see myself as a coward."

"Oh."

He saw that he had been cruel. And it had been a lie. "I don't mean that I don't want *you*. It's the—the principle." Now he sounded like a crazy himself, and it was still a lie. "It's that you're old—older than I am. And a crazy."

"Yes." Yet she was *not* a crazy, not exactly. And had she been a full nomad, he would not have been able even to proffer his bracelet, ironically.

And her simple agreement to his lies and his half-lies made it worse. "You don't *look* old. If you hadn't told me—"

"Can't we let it drop?"

He should have been silent from the start. It would have spared her needless shame and improved his own image. He had failed—not in proffering the bracelet, but in trying to talk about it.

So the matter dropped—but not very far.

CHAPTER FOUR

Next day it rained steadily. They tried to keep driving, but the trail became so mushy that the wheels were in obvious peril. If they became mired here today, they might not get out tomorrow. Miss Smith pulled up on the crest of a low hill and parked.

"We have a long wait," she said. "It will take at least a day for those ruts to firm up again."

Neq stared out at the steady rain and shrugged. It was not that rain bothered him, but it was an inconvenience generally and a hindrance to this mission. He might have gone foraging in the forest and checked out the local lay of the land, but he couldn't leave Miss Smith here alone. Her knife would not help much if outlaws attacked the truck again.

"Well," she said with a certain artificial brightness. "Shall we try it again?"

Neq looked at her, uncertain of her meaning.

"We're stuck here together for some time," she explained. "We both need the experience. Yesterday was bad, but I think I'm stronger now. If we keep trying, maybe—"

Oh, the bracelet! "Right now? Here?"

"Maybe day is better than night. Fewer spooks. Have you anything better to do? Or did you mean it, about not—"

"No!" To both questions.

"Maybe if we do it quickly, we won't balk."

Suddenly the idea appealed to him. He was sorry for the way he had insulted her before, and she was giving

him a chance to make it right. She carried no grudge. His sweat was only beginning; if he treated the matter like circle combat, acting automatically, he might do his part before she could work up too much fear to do hers.

He clapped his hand on his bracelet, jerked it off, thrust it at her. She met him halfway.

Their wrists banged. The bracelet fell to the floor.

"Oh, *damn*!" she cried, using the crazy expletive. "I'll get it. She reached down just as Neq did. Their heads bumped.

Embarrassed, he began to laugh.

"It's not funny," she said. "I'm trying to find the—"

Impulsively he caught her by slim shoulders and hauled her upright. He brought her face to his and kissed her.

There was no magic in it. Her lips, taken by surprise, were mushy. The bracelet dangled from her fingers.

"Put it on," he said. "I think we'll make it."

She looked at the gold, then back at him.

Something struck the cab on her side.

"Down!" Neq barked. He was already in motion, ducking, flinging open the door, tumbling to the muck near the wheel. Sword in hand, he crouched by the truck, watching for the enemy.

He had recognized the striking arrow by the sound. That meant outlaw attack. Probably not well organized, because they had parked randomly, but no matter to be taken lightly.

He was right. Through the rain he heard two men talking. They were debating whether to approach the vehicle now, or try more arrows first. They had not seen the door open.

They decided to charge. "Those crazies can't fight," one said. "Just yank it open and haul them out."

They came up, touched the driver's door—and Neq charged them from the side. The battle was brief. In a moment two bodies lay in the mud.

"Let's go," he called to her.

"Go?" She pushed open her door. "We can't move the—"

"Not the truck. Us. Where there are two, more may be on the way. We can't stay in the obvious target."

She jumped down, one foot striking one of the corpses. She moved away quickly.

They were not dressed for the rain, but did not tarry. He led her into the forest, away from the truck. Neither spoke.

Neq found a gnarly yellow birch and climbed it, searching out a suitable perch that would be hidden from the ground. Miss Smith followed, and he put her astride one fat round limb. He took another. Water poured down their backs, but this was a good defensive situation just in sight of the truck.

They waited that way for three hours.

A man came—an ugly clubber. He passed about thirty feet from their tree, evidently searching for someone.

He discovered the truck, and what lay beside it. He ran back. He was alone. Neq jumped down. "Hey, outlaw!"

The man swung to face him, club lifted.

"I killed them," Neq said. "As I shall kill you, if you don't—"

The clubber was no coward. He charged Neq, swinging viciously. That was all Neq needed to know. A true nomad would have protested the designation of "outlaw" and demanded satisfaction in the circle. He would not have attacked like this.

Neq ducked the blow and slashed in return. He wanted this one alive. There was information he needed.

The clubber swung again. This time Neq parried, sliding his blade down along the shaft of the club until it nipped the man's hand. Not a serious wound, but enough to convince the man he was overmatched. As, indeed, he was.

"Tell me what I want to know, and I let you go."

The clubber nodded. Neq backed off, and the man relaxed. Miss Smith remained hidden in the tree, wisely; it was best that the outlaw not know of her presence.

"If you lie to me, I will take up your trail and kill you," Neq said. "But I would not take the trouble—except for vengeance."

The clubber nodded again. Vengeance was something even outlaws understood well. The man might betray Neq if he had the chance, but he would be exceedingly

careful about it. He would certainly answer questions honestly.

"How many in your tribe?"

"Twelve. Ten, now. And their women."

"All outlaw?"

"No. We're a regular tribe. But we take what offers."

"And if a crazy truck comes, you take it too?"

"Not before this. That must've been Sog's idea. If he saw it stopped, mired——"

"And your chief doesn't care?"

"He has to eat too. The hostels don't stock any——"

"Because the trucks are being raided!" Neq said. "The crazies can't stock the hostels when their trucks are hijacked."

"I can't help that," the clubber said sullenly.

Neq turned away in disgust, hoping the man would strike at him from behind and justify a killing return thrust. But the clubber stayed honest, perhaps aware of the trap.

"Go tell your chief to stay away from this truck," Neq said finally. "I'll kill anyone who comes near."

The man left.

Neq made sure he was gone before returning to the tree. "Do you think that will work?" Miss Smith asked him. She was shivering, but that would be from the wet chill.

"Depends on the chief. If he's a full outlaw, he'll try to swamp us. If he's halfway nomad, he'll let us be."

"Then why did you let that man go? Now the tribe will know where we are."

"I want to know what's really stopping those trucks. This is one way to find out."

She climbed down stiffly. Her garment was clinging to her torso and she was blue with the cold. "I wish there were an easier way."

"There isn't. If I hadn't stopped him, he would have brought the tribe to the truck anyway. If I had killed him, the others would have come looking. No tribe can let its members just disappear. It was better to give them warning."

"This could happen any time any truck stops," she said.

"Are *all* the nomads outlaws now?"

"No. I'm not. But if only one man in five is, no truck will get through."

"They're so quick to turn against their benefactors!"

Neq shrugged. "As the club said: they have to eat."

"I didn't think it would be like this."

"We'll go back to the truck."

"But that's where they'll attack, if—"

"That's why we have to be there, now. I'll set some traps and keep watch; you can sleep."

"I can't sleep, waiting for them to come!"

"Then I'll sleep while you keep watch," he said, heading back to the vehicle.

He hauled the men away from the side and left them near the yellow birch as a reminder to approaching tribesmen. Then he checked the cab. "Where's my bracelet?"

She flushed. "I—" She poked her arm out of the sodden cloth. The bracelet was on it, far back because of the much smaller girth of her forearm, but there.

"You put it on!" he said, amazed.

"There wasn't anything else to do with it, when you jumped out," she said defensively.

"All right, Neqa. Sing out if you see anything."

"I'll give it back!" she said. "I didn't mean—"

"You meant. Let it stay. It's never been on a woman before."

"But I still can't—"

"Do you think *I* can? But I'd like to. Maybe after a few days." Oddly, he wasn't sweating, though of course he was completely wet. *She* was on the defensive now, not he.

"Yes," she said. "That would be nice."

"I'll squeeze it tight for you." He took her limp arm, slid the band down to her wrist, and applied his thumbs to the heavy metal ends. The gold gave way, and slowly the bracelet constricted to match her size.

"Euphemism makes it so much easier," she murmured. "Thank you." She was still shivering, though it was warm in the cab. She was afraid, all right—of outlaw attack, of the meaning of a man's band on her arm, of indecision. She needed protecting.

"I never was kissed before . . ." she said, as though nothing had happened in the interim.

Had he done that? Suddenly he felt as though a sword had grazed his scalp, and he was weak with reaction.

Neq lay in the back of the truck and slept, ignoring the continuing drizzle. He was a warrior; he could sleep anywhere, regardless of the weather. Miss Smith—Neqa pro tem—needed the shelter of the cab.

He dreamed. He had treated the transfer of his bracelet lightly, but it was fundamental. For the first time a woman had accepted it, and they were married, however tenuously. The rest would surely follow. That was his dream, and all of it: a lovely woman bearing his bracelet, loving him.

"Neq!"

He woke immediately, sword ready. She was right: there were men approaching the truck. In the face of his warning there could only be one reason, and no mercy.

Silently he dropped from the back and flattened himself against the side. He identified the marauders by their sounds: they were clumsy stalkers. Six, seven, eight or more.

It was dusk—bright in the sky yet, but dark under the trees. An advantage for him, for he could strike anywhere, while they had to watch for each other.

Neq wasted no time. He ran noiselessly at the nearest, a sworder. The man was dead before he realized the fight had started. Neq took his place and stalked the truck with the others. Nothing showed in the cab. Good—Neqa was staying down.

"See anything?" a clubber whispered as they converged. "That guy is dangerous."

It was the man Neq had warned before. He walked up as though to whisper a reply—and ran his point into the man's neck so that he died without a cry.

But the group had converged too much for further secrecy. "That's him!" someone cried.

Then Neq was lashing out, dancing here and there, cutting down whatever he could reach and jumping away in a fury of swordsmanship. Six men hemmed him in—

two sworders, two clubbers, a staffer and a dagger. It was the staffer he was most cautious about, for that weapon could interfere with his action while the others closed in. He retreated toward the truck.

Two more men ran out of the forest and climbed on the truck. "Neqa—defend yourself!" Neq cried. Beset as he was, he could not go to her himself.

One man yanked open the door. "A woman!"

He reached in, then fell back, grunting. Neq knew she had used the knife. In the cramped space of the cab, it would be more effective than a sword.

The cab door swung closed, and the second man backed away from it, joining the main force. Seven warriors remained to the tribe, and now they knew the limits of their opposition. The element of surprise was gone. Neq had hoped to do more damage before it came to this. Had it been down to three or four functional enemies, in the near-dark, he could have brought them down. But seven threw the balance against him unless they were extraordinarily clumsy or unlucky. He could dodge and run, but he couldn't fight them long without getting hurt himself, and ultimately killed.

Then the motor of the truck started. It roared, and the blinding headlights came on. She was going to try to drive it away!

But the truck backed and turned, its rear wheels spewing up gouts of wet earth. The lights speared toward him. The motor roared again, like some carnivorous animal at bay, and the vehicle bounced toward the group of men.

She wasn't going to stop! Neq threw himself to the side, out of the path of the great rubber tires. Mud and sand sprayed at him.

Not all the outlaws were as quick to realize the danger. They hadn't ridden this machine for three days, and didn't respect its potential. They stared, confused.

The front bumper caught two, not striking them hard enough to kill at this slow speed, but knocking them down. One screamed horribly as the wheel went over him. The other scrambled to safety, only getting clipped on the foot.

In the confusion Neq clove a sworder across the face,

and one more was down. *Two* more, counting the one under the wheel. He retreated again, but did not go far from the truck.

The huge machine crashed into a tree, shattering a headlight. The wheels spun, digging holes. The gears growled. Then it backed, lifting out of its own trench in one mighty contortion.

Neq ran to it and jumped on the back. A clubber, catching on, tried to follow him. A backhand slash dispatched that one.

Back across the road they went, slowing in the deepening mud, and the remaining outlaws scattered. The single headlight caught one; the gears howled again, and the truck jumped forward toward that man. He fled to the side, waving his two sticks. The bright beam followed him.

Neq had not until that moment appreciated the fact that *the truck was a weapon*. A terrible one, for no man could stand against it, even though its footing was treacherous in this rain. Miss Smith—*Neqa!*—was making it a living, ravening monster, spreading terror and carnage within its limited domain.

Back and forth the one-eyed creature went, hurling mud behind, lurching at any moving thing its light caught, bumping over the bodies in the road. One man was buried face-down in that dark pudding of mud, only his legs clear. To and fro endlessly, as though hungry for more.

And the enemy was gone. Five of the tribe's number were dead, and Neq knew that others were wounded, the rest intimidated. The battle was won.

The truck stopped. The motor died, the headlight went off. Neq climbed down and went around to the cab.

"Is that you, Neq?" she called. He saw the small glint of her blade in the lingering light of the dashboard.

"Me." He climbed in.

"Oh God!" And she was sobbing like any jilted nomad girl. Neq put his arms about her and pulled her across the seat to his chest, and she clung to him in her sudden misery of relief.

"I was so afraid they'd attack the tires!" she said.

"No, they only attacked me."

"Oh!" she cried, beginning to laugh. It was stupidly funny, somehow.

She had his bracelet, she was in his arms, she was overflowing with reaction and need . . . but that was as far as it went. This was not the time.

CHAPTER FIVE

The following day he sang again, as the sun same down
and steamed the forest floor into solidity. He pretended
to sing to his weapon, but it was really to her, and she
knew it.

> I know my love by her way of walking
> And I know my love by her way of talking
> And I know my love by her suit of blue—
> But if my love leaves me, what will I do?

"You sing very well," she said, reddening a bit.

"I know it. But it isn't all real. When I sing of battle, I
know what it means. But love—those are words I don't
understand."

"How do you know?" It was as though she were afraid
to ask, but was fascinated anyway.

He looked at his bare wrist. "I never gave my—"

She held up her own wrist with the heavy gold bracelet
clasped about it. "You gave. I accepted. Is that love?"

"I don't know." But he was breathing jerkily.

"Neq, I don't know either," she admitted. "I don't feel
different—I mean I'm still *me*—but the gold seems to
burn, to lead me along, I don't know where. But I want
to know. I want to give—everything. I'm trying to. But
I'm old, and crazy, and afraid. Afraid I have nothing *to*
give."

"You're beautiful, and warm, and brave. That business
with the truck—"

"I hate that! Being a killer, I mean. But I had to do it. I
was afraid for you."

403

"That must be love."

"I like the sound of that. But I know better, Neq. I could hate you and still need you. If anything happens to you, I have no way home."

That was the wonder of it: she was as afraid of him as he was of her. She fought rather than see him hurt—yet she could not come to him in peace. She had to impose practical reasons to justify what needed no justification. As he did, too. "Show me your breast," he said.

"What?" She was not shocked, only uncomprehending.

"Your knife. Your—when you put away your knife, you—"

"I don't understand." But she did.

"Show me your breast."

Slowly, flushing furiously, she unwrapped her shoulder, exposing her right breast.

"It is nineteen," he said. "It excites me. A breast like that—it *can't* be old, or crazy, or afraid, or have nothing to give. It has to be loved."

She looked at herself. "You make me feel wanton."

"I will sing to your breast," he said.

She blushed again, and her breast blushed too, but she did not cover herself. "Where do you learn these songs?"

"They go around. Some say they come from before the Blast, but I don't believe that." Yet he did believe it as much as he disbelieved it, for so many of the words made no sense in the nomad context.

"The books are that old. The songs might be." Her flush was fading at last.

He sang, contemplating her breast:

> Black, black, black is the color
>   of my true love's hair.
> Her lips are something rosy fair.
> The prettiest face and the neatest hands
> I love the ground on where she stands.

She blushed yet again. "It's so real when you sing like that. I'm glad my hair's not black."

"Are you?" He was vaguely disappointed.

"No. I wish the song *did* fit."

"Enough fits. All except the hair."

"Does it?" She looked hopeful.

"No. I'd like it to fit." After a pause he added: "Neqa."

She couldn't seem to stop blushing. "You make me all confused when you say that. Neqa."

"Because of the bracelet."

"I know. I'm your wife as long as I wear it. But it isn't real."

"Maybe it will be." If only it were that simple!

"You nomads—you just pass the bracelet and that's it. Instant love, for an hour or a lifetime. I don't understand it."

"But you were a nomad once."

"No. I was a wild girl. No family. The crazies took me in, trained me, made me like them, outside. They do that with anyone who needs it. I never was part of the nomad society."

"Maybe that's why you don't understand the bracelet."

"Yes. What about you?"

"I *understand* it. I just can't *do* it."

"Maybe that's the trouble with us. You're too gentle and I'm too timid." She laughed nervously. "That's funny, after we killed all those men. Gentle and timid!"

"We could hold each other tonight. It might help."

"What if the outlaws come back?"

He sighed. "I'll stand watch."

"You watched last night. I should do it this time."

"All right."

She laughed again, more easily, so that her breast moved pleasantly. "So matter of fact! What if I said 'take me in your arms, crush me, make love to me!'?"

He considered the prospect. "I could try. If you said it before I got too nervous."

"I can't say it. Even though I want to."

"You want to do it—but you can't ask me?"

"I can't answer that." This time she forgot to blush.

"I want to do it," she said seriously. "But I can't just start. Not unless you say. And even then—"

"It is funny, you know. We know what we want, we know how each feels, but we can't act. We can even speak about speaking, but we can't speak."

"Maybe tomorrow," he said.

"Maybe tomorrow." And the look of longing she gave

him as she put away her breast made his heart pause and jump.

Tomorrow was another clear day, and the ruts were hardened, and there seemed to be the first whiff of something from the corpses around the truck, and so they moved out. Nature compensated for the day's delay by providing an excellent route.

That night Neqa joined him in a double sleeping bag in the back of the truck and pressed her breast against him, but she did not ask and he did not do. They both were frustrated, and they talked about it, and they agreed the whole thing was ridiculous, but that was all.

They had to keep alert against possible marauders, so they took turns sleeping even though together, and while she slept he tried to touch her breast with his hand but didn't . . . but it was against his hand when he woke after her turn awake.

The next night they slept together naked, and he ran his hands over both her fine breasts and her firm buttocks, and she cried when she could not respond, and that was all.

The night after that he sang to her and kissed her, and she ran her hands over his torso and did not avoid what she had avoided before, huge as it was, and she pressed against him and he tried . . . but she cried out with a pain that might have been physical and might have been emotional, and he stopped, chastened, and she cried quietly for some time.

Meanwhile, they were making much faster progress toward the supplier. Their union unconsummated, they pulled up to a hostel near what Neq recognized with shock as the mountain: the place of nomad suicide. Gaunt rusty girders projected from it, hiding the summit; he knew that no man who had passed that barrier had ever returned . . . until recently.

Yet Tyl of Two Weapons and the Master had laid siege to this bastion, for there had been living men within it. They had gutted it, and now it was truly dead.

Neqa consulted her map. "Yes, this is it."

"This—your supplier?" he demanded.

"Helicon. But something is wrong."

"We destroyed it," he said. "The Weaponless did, I mean; I was not there. I could have told Dr. Jones, if I'd known he was talking about the mountain!"

"Oh, no!" she cried. "Helicon manufactured all the technical equipment! We cannot do without it!"

"Maybe some are alive, inside." Knowing Tyl's efficiency, he doubted it, but he had to offer her some hope.

She moved around the center column of the hostel, looking for something. This hostel had not been ravaged, but there was no food in it. She opened the shower stall and stepped in.

"You're still dressed," Neq reminded her.

"I know it's here," she said, as though he hadn't spoken. "I memorized the instructions." She counted tiles along the wall, then pressed on one. She counted from another direction and pressed again. And once more. Nothing happened.

"You have to turn the knobs," he said. "One for hot, the other for cold. But you don't need to take a shower right now, just when you're beginning to smell like a true nomad—"

"I must have done it too slowly," she said. "Now I know the tiles, I'll try it faster."

She went through her mysterious ritual again, while Neq watched tolerantly. The crazies were crazy!

Something snapped inside the inner wall. Neqa pushed on yet another tile and it tilted out, revealing a handle. Neq gaped; he had never known there were handles behind the shower wall! If not for hot or cold water, what?

She twisted and gave a sharp jerk—and the entire wall swung toward her.

There was a compartment behind the shower—in the heart of the hostel's supposedly solid supporting column!

"Come on," she said, stepping inside.

Neq joined her, clasping his sword nervously. There was barely room for them both. She pulled the wall shut and touched a button inside. There was a hum; then the floor dropped.

Neq jumped, alarmed, but she laughed. "This is civilization, nomad! It's called an elevator. We have them in our buildings, and the underworld uses them too. This is

a secret entrance, that we use for transfer of supplies. When nomads see a crazy truck outside, they assume it's a routine servicing—but the truth is we're taking supplies *out*. Most of the heavy stuff comes through other depots in the area, of course, that the nomads never see."

The floor stabilized. She pushed open the side again, and now there was a tunnel, curving into darkness.

"Bad," she said. "The lift is on hostel power, that charges whenever the sun shines. But the tunnel is on Helicon power. That means the underworld is dead, as you said." She turned on a flashlight Neq hadn't known she possessed. "But we'll have to look."

The passage opened into a room where empty boxes were stacked. "Someone's been here," she remarked. "They took the merchandise. But the crates were never restored."

"Probably the last truck—that didn't return."

"Our men never went beyond this point," she said. "But obviously there is a pasage to Helicon. We'll have to find it."

"It may not be pretty." He had heard the tales of labyrinthine underground tunnels choked with bodies. Such claims were probably exaggerated; still. . . .

"I know it." She kissed him—she was able to do that now, and was proud of herself—and began pushing again at places in the wall, randomly.

"If they didn't want you inside, it wouldn't open that way," he pointed out. "Might even be booby-trapped."

"I don't think so. They might guard it, but they wouldn't do anything to antagonize us. The crazies, I mean. Helicon needed us as much as we needed it, because they'd largely shelved their hydroponics and couldn't grow really decent vegetables, and of course no wood. It was more efficient to trade with us, so they concentrated on the heavy industry we couldn't touch. Dr. Jones can talk endlessly about such things—what he calls the essential interactions of civilization."

"So it's safe to break in, you think," he said.

She continued to tap at panels without effect. Neq studied the wear-marks on the floor, analyzing their pattern as though he were verifying the situation of a vacated campsite. "There," he said, touching one section of the wall. "It opens there."

She joined him at once. "Are you sure? This seems solid."

He pointed to the floor marks her flash illumined, and she understood. With this hint, they were able to locate a significant crevice. "But it doesn't open inward," he said. "No hinge on this side, no scrape-marks."

"I don't find any other crease," she said. "But it has to open somehow." She banged at the corner with the butt of the light. "Unless it slides—"

Neq forced the point of his sword into the crevice and leaned on it. The wall gave a little, sidewise. "It slides— but it's locked or blocked."

"Naturally it would lock from the other side," she said. "Can you free it?"

"Not with my sword. But we can get a crowbar from the truck. Enough leverage, it'll give."

They returned to the vehicle and collected an armful of tools. And in due course they had it open.

Behind the wall was a set of tracks. "They used a railroad!" she said. "To haul the supplies along, maybe by remote control. How clever."

But there was no wheeled cart, so they had to walk between the tracks. Neq was nervous about this, not liking the confinement, but she didn't seem to mind. She took his hand in the dark and squeezed it.

He counted paces. It was over a mile before the tracks stopped. There were platforms, with boxes stacked, and sidings with several carts. Neq opened one crate and discovered singlesticks—perhaps fifty of the metal weapons.

So it was true: the underworld had made the nomad arms. Hadn't the Weaponless known that when he destroyed it?

They walked along to the end of the platform and passed through a dark doorway. Then up a gradual ramp, through a charred aperture, and into a larger hall. The air was close and not sweet. Neqa passed the beam of the flashlight over the floor.

Ashes lay across it, with occasional charred mounds. The ambient odor was much stronger here.

"What happened?" she inquired, perplexed.

Neq saw that she didn't comprehend. "Fire. They couldn't get out in time."

"They?" Then she recognized the shape of the nearest mound and screamed. It was the remains of a human being.

Neq led her back down the ramp. "See—after they were dead, the wooden door finally burned through. It must have locked or jammed, like the panel back there. Someone must have poured gasoline all over everything and—"

She turned to him in the darkness, the flashlight off. "The nomads did this?"

"Tyl said it happened before they broke in, actually. The fires were still hot, and the smoke was everywhere, so they didn't stay long. I don't know."

She made a choking sound. He felt something warm on his arm, and knew that she was vomiting against him.

"Helicon was the last hope of man!" she exclaimed, and heaved again.

"I don't think we need to look any more," he said. He took the flashlight from her flaccid hand and guided her away.

CHAPTER SIX

Neqa insisted on writing her report. "In case anything happens, this will tell the story," she explained. "Also, I'm sure of the details now. I hope I forget them by the time we get back."

They slept in the truck that night, though the hostel bunks were handy. The tunnel connection to the Helicon carnage was too direct; it felt as though the fumes of death were filtering along, enclosing the hostel in their horror. Neq had been objective about the scene at the time, but at night his imagination enhanced the under-world's gruesomeness. Fresh death in the circle, or fighting outlaws—that was one thing. But this helpless doom of confined fire. . . .

There was no question of trying to make love. They clung tightly together, holding the morbid blackness off.

Next day Neqa completed her report and locked it in the dash compartment of the truck. They moved out. Neq still didn't see any reason for a written description; the place was dead, and that was it. Such a message would hardly be any comfort to the crazies. They would be finished anyway, and the nomad culture would degenerate into complete savagery.

What colossal folly had led the Weaponless to lay siege to Helicon? He had brought it down, somehow—but had destroyed both the crazies and the nomads with it. The dark age of man was beginning.

Neqa didn't say much either. He was sure that similar thoughts were obsessing her. If information was all they had come for, the mission had been successful. But what a miserable mission it was!

The second day of the return trip they encountered a barricade that had not been there before. Neq was instantly on guard; this surely meant trouble.

"Coincidence?" Neqa inquired.

"Can't be. They saw us go by before, knew we would have to come back this way. So they set it up."

They had to stop. There was no way around, no room to turn.

"If we're lucky, they won't have more than a guard or two here right now. They wouldn't know exactly when we might come along," he said.

They were not lucky. Men converged from both sides. Sworders, clubbers, staffers—at least a score of warriors. A number stood back with drawn bows.

"Do you think this is where the other trucks were lost?" she inquired as though it were an interesting footnote for her report.

"Most of them. This is well organized." He studied the situation. "Too many to fight. And if we try to back out now, those arrows will get us. See, they're aiming at the tires. We'll have to go along—as far as we can."

A sworder strode up to Neq's side. "You're a warrior. What are you doing in a crazy truck?"

Before Neq could reply, a man called from the other side: "Hey, this one's a woman!"

"What luck!" another exclaimed. "Is she young?"

" 'Bout nineteen."

"OK. Out, both of you!" the sworder said.

Neq was furious, but glanced again at the bows covering them and dismounted. No honest nomad would use the hunting bow against a man, but that didn't diminish its effectiveness as a long-distance weapon. Neqa slid over to step down on his side. She stood close to him, but clear of his sword, so as not to obstruct his draw. He knew she was ready to snap her dagger into her hand: she was tense.

"Know what I think?" the sworder said. "I think they're crazies, both of them, pretending to be nomads. They want us to think they hijacked the truck themselves, so we'll leave 'em be. See, her hands are smooth, and he's too small to really handle a sword. And unmarked—no scars on him."

"Pretty smart," a staffer said.

"The crazies are awful smart—and awful stupid."

"All right, crazy," the sworder said. "We'll play this game. We got the time. Who do you claim to be?"

"Neq the Sword."

"Anybody hear of any Neq the Sword?" the man shouted.

There was a reaction. "Yeah," a dagger said.

"Me too," a clubber agreed. "In Sol's tribe. A top sworder—third or fourth of a hundred swords, I heard. And better against other weapons."

The sworder smiled. "Crazy, you picked the wrong name. Now you'll have to prove it—in the circle. With your doll watching. And if you can't—"

Neq didn't answer. The circle was exactly where he wanted to be—with Neqa in sight. These were certainly outlaws, but the tribe seemed to be large enough to require the discipline of the circle code. It was a matter of logistics: one tough man could control five or ten warriors by force of personality on an informal basis, and a few more by judicious intimidation; but when the number was thirty or forty, it had to be more formal. The circle code was not purely a matter of honor; it was a practical system for controlling large numbers of fighting men in an orderly fashion.

And where the circle code existed, even imperfectly, Neq could prevail. He had indeed been third or fourth sword of a hundred. But first sword had been Tyl, who had retired largely to managerial duties of empire. Second had been killed in a noncircle accident. Third had been Tor, now retired. And Neq had kept practicing. The result was that at the time of the breakup of the empire he had been unofficially conceded second sword—of three thousand. And he had had private doubts about Tyl's continuing proficiency in the circle.

It was true, too, that the empire training had brought particular competence in inter-weapon combat. There had been half a dozen staffers who could balk Neq in the circle, one or two stickers, Bog the Club who was now dead, and no daggers or stars. Against these men he would take his chances, sometimes prevailing in friendly matches, sometimes not.

Neq feared no man in the circle.

They were conducted to a camp similar to those of the empire. A large canvas tent was surrounded by a number of small tents, and there were separate latrine, mess, and practice sections. A good layout.

The chief of this tribe was a huge sworder, grizzled and scarred. Chiefs were generally sworders, for the weapon had a special quality that awed others into submission that an equally competent staff could not. When the man stood, he towered over Neq.

"Neq the Sword, eh? I am Yod the Sword. And she wears your band?"

"Yes."

"Now I know of Neq," Yod said. "Maybe the top sworder of the empire, a few years back. He never gave his bracelet to a woman. Isn't that strange?"

Neq shrugged. The chief thought he was toying with the captive.

"Well, all shall be known," Yod said. "I shall give you the tour."

And a tour it was. "I have fifty excellent warriors," Yod said, gesturing to the tent. "But for some reason we're short of young women, and that makes the young men restive. So the girl will have a place with us, regardless."

Neqa walked closer to Neq and let her bracelet show, defensively.

"I have supplies enough for many months," Yod boasted. "See."

Four crazy trucks were parked behind the main tent. There was no longer any doubt who was the main hijacker. But it made little difference, since Helicon was dead.

"And entertainment." Yod gestured to a hanging cage.

Neq looked at this curiously. There was a man inside, huddled within a filthy blanket. Metal cups lay on the wire floor, evidently for his eating, and ordure had cumulated underneath. Apparently they did not release him even for natural functions. He had room to move about some, making the cage rock and swing, which no doubt provided much of the tribe's "amusement." By the look and smell of it, he had been there some weeks.

"We caught this crazy using our hostel," Yod said. "He

claimed to be a surgeon, so we're giving him a chance to carve his way out. We don't like fakes." He glanced at Neq.

"A surgeon?" Neqa asked. "We haven't—" She stopped, remembering her guise as a nomad woman. But it told Neq that this man was not a crazy, for she would have known of it. Perhaps he deserved his punishment.

The prisoner looked dully at them. He was a small man with graying hair, very old by nomad definition.

"He says he's literate!" Yod said, laughing. "Show our guests your writing, Dick." In an aside to Neq: "All crazies have funny names."

The man reached around and found a tattered piece of cardboard, probably salvaged from one of the rifled crates the trucks had carried. He held this up. There were lines on it that did resemble the crazy writing of Neqa's recent report.

"Mean anything to you?" Yod asked Neq.

"No."

"Because you can't read—or he can't write?"

"I can't read. I don't know about him. Maybe he can't write either."

"Maybe. We could use a literate man. Some crazy books we found, don't know what's in 'em. Maybe something good."

"Why not test them on the crazy in the cage?" Neq asked.

"He lied about being a surgeon. We brought him a wounded man and gave him a dagger and he wouldn't operate. Said it wasn't clean, or something. Lot of excuses. So he'd lie about the books, too. He could tell us anything—and how could we know the difference?"

Neq shrugged. "I can't help you." He knew Neqa could, but he had no intention of giving her away.

"You're still Neq the Sword?"

"I always was."

"Prove it and you can join my tribe. We'll have to take your girl away, of course, but you'll get your turn at her."

"The man who touches her is dead," Neq said, putting his hand to his sword.

Yod laughed. "Well spoken. You have your part down well—and you shall have your chance to enforce it. Here

is the circle." He glanced around and made a sweeping signal with his hand. Ready for this summons, the men of the tribe gathered.

In the temporary confusion, Neqa touched his hand. "That man in the cage—he *is* literate," she murmured. "He's from Helicon—a survivor. He may not be their surgeon—they had the best surgeon in all the crazy demesnes—but he's worth questioning."

Neq considered. If there were Helicon survivors. . . . "When I fight, you cut him down. I'll put on a show to distract them. You take him to the truck and get out. Use your knife; this bunch is rough. I'll find you later."

"But how will you——"

"I can handle myself. I want you out of here before it starts." He brought her to him suddenly and kissed her. Stolen this fleetingly, the kiss was very sweet. "I love you."

"I love you," she repeated. "Neq! I can say it now! I mean it! *I love you!*"

"Touching," Yod said, breaking it up. "Here is your first match, crazy."

Neq let her go and faced the circle. A large clubber was there flexing his muscles. Most clubbers were large, because of the weight of the weapon; by the same token, most were clumsy. Still, no one could ignore the smashing metal, that could bash sword and torso right out of the circle in one sweep. Bog the Club had been astonishing. . . .

Suddenly, incongruously, Neq remembered how Bog had been balked. Once by Sol of All Weapons, the greatest warrior of all time; once by the Weaponless, who had broken his neck and killed him by a leaping kick. But once between those two honest contests, by the man Neq had not been able to remember before. The Rope! Sos the Rope—the man Miss Smith had remembered. He had looped the cord about the club, surprising Bog (who was not bright) and disarming him. Then the man had talked Bog into joining forces for doubles combat. The story of that audacity was still going the rounds. The Rope had not been nearly the man Bog was, but he had known how to use his luck. With Bog on his side, he had torn up several regular doubles teams. Bog plus a two-year child would have been a winning team! The Rope had finally

overrated himself so far as to challenge Sol himself, and Sol had sent him to the mountain.

He would have to tell Neqa that, when they were out of this. And ask her whether by any chance her Sos had carried a little bird on his shoulder. Not that any of it was important today.

"That's Nam the Club," Yod said. "He says he's going to diddle your crazy blonde right after he diddles *you*. Should be no threat at all to—the fourth sword of a hundred?"

Neq gave Neqa a parting squeeze on the arm and urged her toward the caged man. The cage was beyond the immediate circle of spectators, partially concealed by the tree it hung from. If all of them faced toward the circle, and if there were enough noise, she would be able to cut open the cage and free the surgeon. Neq would have to arrange his fights—he knew they would keep sending men against him until they tired of this sport—to attract the complete attention of the outlaws. All of them.

She moved away, and he walked slowly toward the painted circle, drawing his sword. He stepped inside without hesitation.

Nam roared and charged. Neq ducked sidewise, staying within the ring. The clubber, meeting no resistance, stumbled on out.

"One down," Neq said. "Not much of a diddler, I'd say—either kind." He wanted to insult both clubber and tribe, to make them angry and eager to see the stranger get beaten. He wanted nobody's attention to wander.

Nam roared again, and charged back into the circle. This was another direct proof of his outlaw status, for no true warrior would re-enter the circle after being thus ushered out of it. To leave the circle during combat was to lose the battle—by definition. That was one of the ways the circle code avoided unnecessary bloodshed.

Neq did not wish to appear too apt with his blade too soon. If they recognized his true skill immediately, the game would be over, for they would know that he was the man he claimed to be, and that none of them could hope to match him. Yod would play fair only so long as he was certain of winning.

So Neq sparred with the clubber, ducking his clumsy blows, pinking him harmlessly, dancing him about in the circle. Meanwhile Neqa was edging toward the cage, not facing it but making covert progress.

When it seemed to him that interest was beginning to flag, Neq skewered Nam with a seemingly inept thrust, very like the one he had made against Hig the Stick at the outset of his career as a warrior. It looked like a lucky stab by a novice sworder—as intended.

"So you *can* fight," Yod remarked. "But not, I think, quite up to the measure of your name. Tif!"

A sworder stepped toward the circle as men dragged the bleeding, moaning clubber way. Neq could tell at a glance that Tif was a superior sworder. The ante had been raised. The outlaws watched with greater anticipation.

Neqa was now close to the cage.

It required less art to fence with Tif, for the man was quick and sure with his blade, making defensive measures mandatory, not optional. But he was no threat to Neq. They jockeyed around, blade meeting blade clangingly, keeping the tribe absorbed. Every nomad liked a good show, even an outlaw.

Then Tif drew back. "He's playing with me," Tif called to Yod. "He's a master. I can't touch—"

Neq put a red mouth across Tif's throat and the man spouted his life's blood and fell. But it was too late. The "secret" had been exposed.

Neqa was working at the cage.

"So you *are* Neq the Sword!" Yod exclaimed. "We can't trust you, then. You'd want the tribe for yourself."

"I disbanded a tribe ten times this size!" Neq said scornfully. "This is nothing to me, and you are nothing. But you called me a crazy—so fight me for your tribe!" That might be an easy way out: take over the tribe, reconstitute it along honest nomad lines, bring all the trucks back to Dr. Jones.

Yod made an obscene gesture. "I'm not that kind of a fool. We'll have to shoot you."

If they brought out the bows again, Neq would have little chance. "I'll take on any two of you pitiful cowards in the circle!" he cried.

Yod was quick to accept the opportunity to save some

face. It was always better for a leader to dispose of his competition honorably, if at all feasible. Otherwise other leaders would arise quickly to challenge him, suspecting his weakness.

"Jut! Mip!" Yod shouted.

A dagger and a staffer came up, but not with the same eagerness the first two warriors had shown. Neq knew why: they were aware that one of them would likely die, even if the other finished off the challenger. Two men could generally defeat one—but the one could generally pick his man and take him out, if life were not the supreme object. Also, the tribe was beginning to mull the possibility of new leadership. If Neq were a better sworder than Yod, he might improve the lot of the tribe. So a certain discretion in loyalties was developing. As Yod was surely aware.

This was a smart combination. The staff would block Neq's sword and defend the pair of them, while the dagger would slice out from under that cover with either hand.

But Neq, like all warriors of the former empire, had been well trained in doubles combat. His reflexes sifted through automatically and aligned on "partner incapacitated; staff and dagger opposed." Except that he had no wounded partner to protect. That made it easier.

Yes, he owed a debt now to that Sos he had known! The interminable practice against all doubles combinations had seemed a waste of effort, for singles combat was the normal rule. But Sos had said that a top warrior had to be prepared for every eventuality. How right he had been!

As he engaged the pair, he saw that Neqa was still working at the cage. She could not devote her full attention to it, because she had to appear innocent. But she would shortly have the prisoner free.

Neq made the battle look good. He concealed none of his skill now. He kept the dagger at bay with a steadily flashing blade, and beat the staffer back by nipping at his hands and slamming against the staff itself. The pair had not fought like this often; they got in each other's way at crucial moments. A duo could be less effective than either warrior singly, if they were not properly coordinated. He could take them; it was only a matter of time. And they knew it; they were desperate, but had no way out.

Meanwhile, the tribe was watching, pondering loyalties, gravitating toward the strongest candidate for leadership.

"The crazy's escaping!" Yod cried.

Heads whipped about, Neqa and Dick the Surgeon were running away from the open cage.

Neq's ploy had almost worked. But that one small hitch—the random glance back of one spectator, perhaps only because a fly was bothering him—or because he was desperate himself to break up a pattern that did not favor him—had undone it all.

Now there would be hell to pay.

CHAPTER SEVEN

"After them!" Yod screamed. "Don't kill the girl!"

Men lurched to their feet, drawing their assorted weapons. Now they had to follow the leader they knew, for there was an immediate crisis. Had Neqa and the cage-man escaped cleanly while Neq fought, so that it was obvious that there was no chance to recapture them, then the leadership of Yod the Sword would have been open to serious question. Then Neq might have killed him quickly, and assumed command of the tribe. All that had been nullified by this one bad break.

Neq leaped from the circle and charged the chief. He still had a chance: he could take Yod hostage and buy time, and perhaps bargain for his own release and that of the other two. Or kill Yod outright, leaving the tribe no choice.

But Yod was too canny for that maneuver. Yod met him with drawn sword, yelling constantly to his men, stiffening their wavering loyalty.

Suddenly Neq was surrounded again. The warriors did not approach the battling sworders too closely, for he could still catch Yod in a desperation lunge; but that circle of weapons did prevent his escape. There were drawn bows—but again, he and Yod were moving so swiftly and the pack of other men was so great that the archers dared not fire until forced.

"The gun!" Yod yelled.

Then Neq despaired. He knew what a gun was. Tyl's tribe had returned from the mountain with guns and grenades and demonstrated them on targets. Guns had been employed against the underworld, and without them the

assault would have been impossible. They were metal tubes that expelled metal fragments with great speed and force. The effect was similar to that of an arrow—but the gun could shoot farther and quicker, and it required far less skill to use. A cripple could kill a master sworder, with a gun.

Tyl had later decided that guns were inimical to the nomad mode of existence, and had called all such weapons in and hidden them. But he lacked authority over the complete empire, and some few had been lost. . . .

If Yod's tribe had a gun, Neqa and the surgeon would not escape. A gun could penetrate the metal of a truck.

Neq made his desperation lunge, breaking through Yod's guard and wounding him in the thigh. But as Neq recovered his stroke there was a blast of noise. Something struck his own thigh, and not an arrow.

The gun had been fired at him.

First he was relieved: they were not using it on Neqa!

Then he realized that it meant his own doom. The gun could kill him, and he would never get back to Neqa, and she would have to make the return journey alone. Unless the surgeon could protect her. But that man had not even been able to protect himself from being caged!

"Yield!" Yod panted. "Yield—or we shoot you down now!"

There seemed to be no choice. This was not a bluff. They might kill him anyway if he yielded—but they certainly had the means to do so if he did not. If Neqa was going to get away at all, she had had time enough; he could not help her by fighting longer.

Neq threw down his sword and stood waiting.

"You're smart," Yod said, as men grabbed Neq by the arms. "You saved your life." He touched his leg gingerly. "And you proved who you are. No lesser man could have wounded me in fair combat."

That was an exaggeration. Yod was good, but a score of empire sworders could have taken him handily. But Neq didn't feel obliged to enrage the man by pointing that out. He was now dependent on Yod's mercy, and the more Yod felt like an honorable victor, the more honorably he would act.

"But you did make a lot of unnecessary trouble by not

yielding sooner," Yod continued. "And we can't trust you. I have promised you life—but I will consider your punishment. Tie him, men."

This time the tribesmen sprang to obey. They tied him: arms behind his back, tight, and a hobble-rope on his ankles. They propped him up against a post with his arms hooked behind it while they attended to other things.

Neq's wound smarted increasingly. The puncture was small, but through the large muscle. The fragment had to be lodged inside somewhere. There was not much bleeding; a sword would have been far worse. Except that the blade would have exited cleanly, permitting better healing.

There was a clamor as the pursuit party returned. "We got her!" A man exclaimed.

Neq saw to his grief that it was true. Neqa was being hauled along between two men, her wraparound torn, portions of her torso exposed. She did not seem to be injured, however.

"She had a knife. Stabbed Baf," another man said. "Real wild girl. But we didn't hurt her."

"The crazy got away," another said. "But who cares?"

Yod's wound, not serious, had been bound. He was probably in as much pain as Neq, but did not show it. He had to maintain his facade before his tribe. "So she freed the crazy and stabbed one of our men," he mused. "And her man messed us all up, pretending to be a crazy, and killed Tif." He looked calculatingly at Neq. "OK—we'll teach them both a real lesson."

Yod walked up to Neqa. While the men held her arms, he ripped away the remainder of her clothing, flinging pieces of cloth aside to the delight of the others. "Man, she's a beauty!"

Neq struggled with his bonds, but they were firm. Some of the outlaws, watching him, chuckled; they *wanted* him to struggle. As they would have wanted Yod to struggle, had things worked out otherwise.

"Han!" Yod cried.

A youthful dagger approached nervously. Neq judged him to be a novice, perhaps fourteen.

"You never had it with a woman, did you?" Yod demanded.

"No—no." Han said, not looking at Neqa's nakedness.

"Now's your time. Go to."

Han backed away. "I don't understand."

"This crazy doll with the smooth skin and the sweet breast—you got her first. Right now."

Han glanced at Neqa, then guiltily away again. "But she's—she has his bracelet!"

"Yeah. That's funny. Leave it on."

"But—"

"He's going to watch this. On his own band. That's his punishment. And some of hers."

Han's body was shaking. "That's not right. I can't do that."

Neq strained furiously, but only skinned his wrists on the rope. "I'll kill any man who touches her!" he screamed.

Neqa stood with her eyes closed, still held by two men. She seemed to have withdrawn from the proceedings. Her body was fair and slender and wholly out of place amid this rough crowd. Neq saw the outlaws looking at her, licking their lips.

Yod laughed. "You'll kill us all then, crazy-lover. 'Cause every man here's going to touch her—right now, where you can see."

"No!" Han cried. He ran at Yod.

Yod smashed him down backhanded. "You missed your chance, you sniveling kid. Now it's my turn."

Han stumbled back, bleeding from the lip, and fell near Neq. One of his daggers skidded on the ground.

Yod opened his pantaloons. The outlaws laughed. Neqa opened her eyes, struggled silently, and kicked her feet.

"Hold her legs too," Yod said. Two more men jumped forward to grasp her thighs.

Neq jabbed Han with his bound legs. When the youth turned dazedly toward him, Neq nodded toward the knife just out of his reach.

Han looked at the struggle going on as four men held Neqa by the hands and feet, spread-eagling her on the ground. Then he swept the blade toward Neq. It was still out of reach, for Neq could not pick it up.

Now Neqa screamed. Neq did not look. He had to get that knife immediately. He arched his body against the post, sliding his shoulder up, until his arms unhooked

over the top of it. He fell over to the side, rolled, grabbed. The blade of the dagger sliced his hand, but he had it.

No one noticed. They were all intent on the show Yod was putting on.

Neqa screamed again, piercingly, as Yod's body covered her. She writhed on the ground and one of her hands slipped loose, but Yod stayed with her, grunting. The men grinned as they held her legs apart.

Neq twisted the knife, but he could not get it angled properly at the cord. His hands became slippery with his own blood. Then the strands began parting, reluctantly, as the flat of the blade wedged against them.

It seemed to take forever for the rope to give.

The outlaw chief stood up, short of breath. Neqa was sobbing brokenly.

"Hey—she was a virgin!" Yod exclaimed. "Look at that!"

The men crowded close to look. Neq, numbed to physical pain, sawed at the infernal rope.

"Why'd she have his bracelet, then?" someone demanded.

"I *heard* he wasn't much of a man outside the circle!"

Still the bands held. Han the dagger got up and fled, looking sick.

"All right—line up and take your turn," Yod said. "Every man of you. She's a good one."

The men lined up. Neqa had stopped crying. Three men still held her supine and spread on the ground.

Three more completed their business before Neq's hands finally were free. He severed the hobble-cord and lurched to his feet. He plunged the blade into the back of the fourth man as he lay astride Neqa. One down—four to go.

"Hey! He's loose!"

They piled on him. Neq fought savagely, but the dagger was not his weapon and he was grossly outnumbered. In moments they had him prisoner again.

Helpless, he had to watch while forty-four more men ravished his wife.

But it was not over.

"That's another he killed—and several more wounded," Yod said angrily.

"Kill him!" several cried.

"No. I granted him life. I want this bastard to suffer."
Yod considered. "Cut off his hands." He lifted his sword.

Neqa, momentarily forgotten, climbed slowly to her
feet. Her eyes were staring. The dagger Neq had used lay
near her on the ground. She stooped to pick it up.

Then, silently, she launched herself at Yod. Her blade
sliced down the side of his face, catching part of one eye
and eyeball.

Yod whirled, swinging his sword in an automatic reaction. It caught her across the neck, sinking in.

"Damn!" Yod cried, not seeming to realize the extent of
his own wound. "I didn't mean to kill her! We *need*
women!"

Neqa dropped to the ground, her blood spouting. Neq
heaved his captors forward and they all fell.

It was too late for Neqa. Her teeth were bared in the
rictus of the terminal agony; her red blood pooled in the
dry dirt.

"Damn!" Yod repeated. "It's *his* fault. Hold him!"

They held Neq. Under Yod's grim direction they tied
his hands again by the wrists, this time stretched forward.
Four men hauled against his body while two pulled each
rope, putting a terrible strain on his arms.

Yod positioned himself and swung his sword as though
he were splitting wood.

Neq felt horrendous pain, and blanked out.

He came to immediately, or so it seemed. The pain had
intensified unbearably, and sweet smoke stung his nostrils.
They were holding torches to his wrists, burning them so
the flesh bubbled and popped.

Then nothing more.

CHAPTER EIGHT

He woke at dusk. His arms terminated in great crude bandages, hurting ferociously. Neqa lay beside him, pale and cold. His bracelet was still on her wrist.

He woke again, shivering, in the dark. Nothing had changed but the hour.

Toward morning he became delirious.

Light again, and someone was tending him. It was the cage-man, the surgeon. "You'll live. I'll bury her. You two saved me; I owe you that much."

"*I'll* bury her!" Neq cried weakly. But he had no hands.

He cursed meaninglessly as he watched Dick do it, as the dirt fell over her dead lovely face, over his bracelet, over his dreams. He had loved a crazy.

Miss Smith was gone forever. Neqa was dead.

Time passed. Dick the surgeon turned out to be no phony; he knew his medicine. The fevers and the chills subsided, strength of a sort came back; the thigh wound, excavated and cleaned, healed. But the hands were gone, and so was love.

Dick did everything, though he was no nomad. "I owe it to you," he said. "Her life, your hands—all because of me."

"They would have done it anyway," Neq said, not caring how the blame was parceled out. "They ambushed us before we ever saw you. We were already prisoners."

"She took several minutes to get me out of that cage, and she waited while I got some circulation back into my legs so I could walk. She would have gotten away, otherwise."

"You can't bring her back. If you owe me a favor, kill me too. Then I won't hurt any more—any way."

"I deal in life, not death. After Helicon, this is just an incident. I do owe you, but not that." He looked about. "We should get away from here. They dumped you both and left—but they could come back at any time. I was lucky they didn't see me following them."

Neq was not in a position to argue further. He talked with only a part of his consciousness, the least important part. The rest was obsesssed with what had happened, and his impotence in the face of such calamity.

Only one thing kept him going. At first it was intangible, nebulous, a background emotion that gave him strength without comprehension. But gradually, as the days passed, it became solid, better defined, until it occupied the clear forefront of his mind, and he knew the need for what it was.

Vengeance.

"You are a surgeon," Neq said. "From what was mooted, the best in the world."

"Not necessarily. I was trained by a master, and he trained others. I've heard of remarkable surgery in the Aleutians—"

"You *do* talk like a crazy. Can you operate on me?"

"Without my equipment, my laboratory, drugs, competent assistants—"

"Was that what you told Yod?"

"Essentially. Surgery without sterilization procedures, anesthetics—"

"They sterilized my wrists, all right. With living torches!"

"I know. Yod is an outlaw, but he keeps his word. He wanted you to live."

"I keep my word too," Neq said. "But if there *are* ways to sterilize, why couldn't you—"

"Try a flaming torch on abdominal surgery!"

Neq nodded. "So Yod figured you were lying."

"I wasn't going to help him anyway. Any life I might save for him would mean death for others. His tribe deserves extermination."

"That may come," Neq said, but decided against clarifying the matter. "We'll get equipment, somewhere."

"Yes, with the necessary facilities I could operate. But

in what manner? I can't give you back your hands. No one can do that."

"Tyl said—he said that the Nameless One, our Master of Empire, the Weaponless—by whatever name you know him—he said that man had been made strong by an underworld surgeon. You?"

"I had considerable assistance. And there was a strong possibility of failure. As it was, I understand I rendered him sterile."

"If you could do that for him, you can do this for me."

"What do you want?"

Neq held up his truncated right arm. "My sword."

Without a hand?

"My sword will be my hand."

Dick studied him appraisingly. "Yes, I could do that. Insert a metal brace, attach the blade—it wouldn't be flexible, but there'd be plenty of power."

Neq nodded.

"It would be awkward," Dick continued, considering it further. "For sleeping, for eating. You would not be able to use that hand for any constructive purpose, except chopping firewood. But once you learned to control it you might re-enter the circle. Much of your fighting skill is in your brain, I'm sure; you could overcome a substantial flexibility handicap. You would not be the warrior you were, but you could still be more than most."

Neq nodded again.

"I could give you a hook on the other arm, maybe even pincers. So you could dress, feed yourself."

"Start now."

"But I told you: I'll need anesthetics, instruments, sterilization—"

"Knock me out. Pass your knife through the fire."

Dick laughed without humor. "Impossible!" Then: "You're serious."

"Every day she lies cold while her murderers live is a torture to me. I must have my sword."

"But only Yod killed her, actually."

"They're all guilty. Every man who touched her—every one shall die."

Dick shook his head. "I'm afraid of you. I thought I had learned complete hatred during my time in the cage,

choking on the miasma of my own refuse, but I fear what you will do."

"You won't have to watch."

"I'll be responsible, though."

"If you will not do it, tell me you will. Then kill me in my sleep."

Dick shuddered. "No, I'll fix you up. In my own way. We'll have to go back to what remains of Helicon for my supplies. They aren't all gone. I went back once to make sure. Gruesome experience."

"I know. But such a trip would take time!"

Dick looked at him. "You may dismiss pain when you're fighting in the circle or elsewhere. But this, when you're calm—let me make a small demonstration. Hold out your arm."

Neq held out one bandaged stump.

Dick took hold of it and applied pressure.

The pain started slowly, but built up appallingly. Neq took it, not flinching, knowing he was being tested but not knowing how long he could withstand it.

"That's just hand pressure," Dick said. "How will you like it when I start cutting? Scraping off the new scar tissue, cauterizing living flesh, laying open the muscle and tendons and tying wires to them? Hamering a metal spike into the radius—the long bone of the forearm? And another into the ulna, so that you will be able to twist your weapon as you once twisted your wrist, and perhaps to flex it a little. You're fortunate that your hands were severed below the wrists, leaving the main bones connected; that gives us much more leeway for reconstruction. But the pain—" As he talked, he twisted.

"Knock me out!" Neq cried again.

"I can't knock you out for the duration. I'd be substituting brain damage for hand damage. And I'll need your cooperation, because I'll be working without assistants. You have to be conscious. That means a local anesthetic—and even so, it will hurt a fair amount. Like this."

Neq, sweating acceded. He had not known there could be so much pain remaining in his mutilated limbs. "We'll go to Helicon."

"One other thing," Dick said. "I don't want to exploit your weakness by bartering with you now, not on a

matter like this, but I have my own welfare to look out for. Once you have your sword, you won't need me or want me along."

"That's true."

"I'm not strong. I spent weeks, months in that cage. I lost track. I was able to exercise some, and I knew which muscles to concentrate on, but I never was strong for the wilderness life. I'm in no condition to survive by myself. I'd only get captured again, or killed by savages."

"Yes."

"Deliver me to the crazies before you start your mission."

"But that would take months!"

"Steal one of Yod's trucks. You can kill some outlaws in the process. I can drive; I can teach you—even with metal instead of hands. That's worth knowing."

"Yes . . ." Neq said, realizing that the man had a point. Dick had repaid anything he owed for his freedom by tending to Neq after the amputation and finding food—probably stolen from Yod's tribe at great risk—for otherwise Neq would have died. The operation was a new obligation. So it was a fair bargain.

And Neq *could* do some damage while taking the truck. Then the tribe would be on guard—pointlessly—while the two made their journey to the crazies.

It was, on balance, worthwhile.

Dick had a different entrance to Helicon. It was a stair-way under a nomad burial marker, leading into a dank tunnel that in turn led to the main vault. Neq speculated privately that there must be numerous such ports—perhaps one for every underworld inmate of rank. That meant that many more could have escaped the flames and slaughter. No wonder the defense of the mountain had collapsed so quickly!

They fetched the drugs and instruments. Under the film of ash much of Helicon was untouched. Had the under-worlders had any spunk they could have restored it to a considerable extent. Nomads would have.

Neq could not do much, but he could carry. Dick fixed a pack for him and he hauled everything they needed to the nearby hostel and set up for the operation.

Time passed.

When Neq emerged from the intermittent haze of drugs and pain, his right arm terminated in a fixed full-length sword. His left had dull pincers that he could open and close with some discomfort by flexing wrong-seeming muscles.

The first time he tried to practice with the sword, the pain was prohibitive. But as his flesh healed around the metal and callus and scar-tissue formed, that problem eased. Eventually he was able to strike quite hefty blows without wincing.

His swordsmanship was hardly clever. Deprived of a real wrist, he had to maneuver mainly from shoulder and elbow. But he had power, for there was nothing to break or loosen. Skill would come with practice, for his mind had all the talent it had ever possessed.

He had to work with the pincers, too, flexing them each day, gaining proficiency. They were actually quite mobile when under proper control, and would lock onto an object or a knob like pliers, enabling him to pick up and squeeze without destroying. They, too, had great power.

Neq and Dick returned to Yod's territory to stalk a truck. There was a guard: Neq cut him down with an axe-motion swing of his sword, almost severing the man's head from his body. One more down. . . .

"Find a good one," he told the surgeon. "Load plenty of fuel. I'll watch for intruders."

"OK," Dick said, relieved. Neq knew the man did not like the killing, much as he hated the men who had tortured him. With Dick, hate was general, not subject to specific implementation; with Neq it was otherwise.

When he was alone, Neq hauled the body about with his clumsy pincers. He wanted to sever the penis that had violated Neqa, but he realized this would be meaningless. What he needed was a true token of his vengeance. That every man of the tribe would comprehend.

He struck down with his sword-arm, chopping at the gory neck. He struck again, and the head came loose.

He left it on the ground for a moment and walked to a sapling. He cut it down with one sweep, then caught the shaft in his pincers and held it for stripping. Finally he carved crude points on each end of the pole.

He returned to the loose head. He braced one foot on it and jammed with the pole. After several attempts he got the point wedged firmly inside the neck. He lifted the head, bracing the pole with both pincers and sword, and tried to set it upright in the ground.

It wouldn't go. Angry, and aware that he was wasting time dangerously, he jammed his sword down, making a cavity in the soil. He dropped the end of the pole in this and twisted it firm. It stood crookedly, but well enough.

Neq's monument was complete: the staring, dirt-smirched head of one of the men who had raped his wife. Mounted on a pole.

He had killed one of the men in the act, with the dagger, so this was the second. Of the forty-nine he had counted . . . Forty-seven to go.

If the tribe heard the truck take off, it was too late. No pursuit developed. If only they had been this lax before, Neq thought bitterly, he and Neqa would never have been caught. . . .

Dick had done well. Not only was there spare gasoline, there were blankets and tools and food. Apparently Yod used the trucks for supply storage, and had kept them in running condition. That was good management, for few nomads had knowledge of trucks.

The journey back was routine. There were roadblocks, but none by a major tribe, and Neq had little trouble discouraging them. In fact it was excellent practice for his stiff arm and sword.

He learned to drive, passing his sword through the wheel and using it to steer. His left extremity and his feet did the rest of the handling.

He delivered Dick to Dr. Jones, and trusted the under-worlder to make the report Neqa had intended. Had his luck reversed all the way, this would have been the original truck, with her notes in the dash—but it was not. At least Dick himself had been there at Helicon for virtually all of it, so the report would be complete.

Then he turned back, driving the truck alone. His mission awaited him. Forty-seven lives. . . .

Vengeance.

CHAPTER NINE

Yod's camp was on guard day and night. It had been alert the whole time Neq had been absent. Ever since that first spiked head.

Good. He wanted them to suffer, just as they had wanted *him* to suffer. They had succeeded in torturing him . . . and now he would repay them in equal measure. He wanted every man to remember what the tribe had done, that day Neqa died, and to know that the time of reckoning was at hand. To know that every man of Yod's tribe would be staring on a pike.

First he took the guards—one each night, until they began to march double, and after that two each night. When they marched in fours he desisted; that was too chancy. He didn't care about himself, but he didn't want to die or become further incapacitated before he had completed his vengeance.

He avoided the foursomes and moved instead into the camp, killing a warrior in his sleep and taking the head. After that there were men on guard everywhere—one sleeping, one busy with chores, the third watching. The tribe was down to forty, and it was terrified.

Neq made no killings for a week, letting them wear themselves out with the harsh vigil. Then, when they relaxed, he struck again, twice. That brought them alert again.

They had to take the offensive. They swept the forest for him, trying to rid themselves of this stalking horror. He killed two more and left their heads for their fellow-searchers to find.

They went back to the perpetual alert, the men haggard.

But they had to leave their immediate campside to fetch water, to hunt, to forage. Three men, resting in the forest, gave way to fatigue and slept. They never woke.

Thirty-three remained.

There were fifteen women in the camp and twenty children. Now these noncombatants began standing guard over their men. Neq disliked this; he did not know what would happen to them once their men were gone. The women might be culpable for not encouraging some restraint in their men—no woman had shown herself during the whole of that nefarious day—but the children at least were innocent.

But he remembered Neqa, her piercing screams, her struggle as Yod raped her, and her failure to cry thereafter. His heart hardened. How often had this sort of thing happened before, with the women and children knowing and doing nothing? A person of any age who would not speak against such obvious wrong deserved no sympathy when the consequence of that wrong came back to strike him personally.

Three men came after him, guided by a dog. A clubber and two daggers. They must have borrowed the canine from some other tribe, for there had been no animals at the camp before. Neq had known it would come to this: small cruising parties tracking him down relentlessly. He was ready.

He looped about, confusing the scent-trail, then attacked from behind. He killed one dagger before they could react, and swung on the other.

"Wait!" the man cried. "We—"

Neq's sword-arm transfixed his throat, silencing him forever. But as the blade penetrated, Neq realized he had made a mistake. He recognized this youth.

Han the Dagger.

The boy who had balked at raping Neqa. Who had helped free Neq, however temporarily. Who had fled while the sexual orgy continued, after trying to stop it.

"Wait!" the third man, the clubber, cried, and this time Neq withheld his stroke. "We did not do it. See, I am scarred. Where you struck me when we fought in the circle, and I—"

Now Neq recognized him too. "Nam the Club—the first

of Yod's men I engaged," he said. "I tagged you in the gut." Nam might be better now, but he could not have participated then; not when that wound was fresh.

"The other dagger," Nam said, pointing to the first dead of this trio. "Jut—you fought him and Mip the Staff together. You did not wound them, but Jut hid. He knew what was coming. He never—"

Neq reflected, and realized that Jut's face was not among those he had seen at the raping. He had just killed two innocent men.

Not quite. Jut had not raped, but he had not protested either. He had fled, letting it go on. Even Han had had more courage than that.

"There were fifty-two men in Yod's tribe—plus Yod himself," Neq said. "Fifty-three altogether. Forty-nine did it, after hearing my oath. If you three did not, that accounts for fifty-two. What other man is innocent?"

"Tif," Nam said. "Tif the Sword. You killed him in the circle before—"

"So I did." Neq hesitated, feeling sick as he looked down at Han. "Tif I do not regret, for it was a fair combat. Jut I might have spared, had I realized. But Han helped me, and—" Here regret choked off his words.

"That's why we came to you," Nam said. "We knew you did not have cause against us. We thought—"

"You turned traitor to your tribe?"

"No! We came to plead *for* our tribe!"

Neq studied him. "You, Nam the Club. You bragged of diddling. Had you been fit, would you have raped my wife?"

The man began to shake. "I—"

Neq lifted the tip of his sword. Blood dripped from it.

"I am a clumsy warrior," Nam said with difficulty. "But never a liar. And I am loyal to my leader."

Answer enough. "Were you friend to Han the Dagger?"

"No more than any other man. He was a stripling, softhearted."

Yes, the clubber was no liar. "I spare you," Neq said. "For the sake of this lad who was innocent and whom I wrongly slew. With choice, I would have cut you down instead, but now I spare you. But take this message to Yod: I spare no other."

"Then kill me now," Nam said simply. "Yod is a good leader. He is a rough man to resist, and he has bad ways about him, so that when he tells us to do something—even something like that—we must do it or suffer harshly. But he takes care of his tribe. He had to make an example."

"Not with my wife!"

"Discipline. He had to show—"

Neq's sword sliced off his nose and part of his talking mouth.

Then, sorry, Neq killed him cleanly.

And vomited, just as though he were a lad of fourteen again, at his first blooding.

At last he buried the bodies in honorable nomad fashion, digging the grave and forming the cairn with his sword. He did not mount their heads.

Twenty-five remained, and they were dying more readily now. But Neq performed his ritual with a sense of futility. He knew that vengeance would not bring Neqa back or right the wrong he had done the nonraping tribesmen. Han the Dagger—there was no justifying that murder. Already Neq was guilty of acts as bad as those perpetrated against him—but he could not stop.

The second party to find him was female. Neq had learned caution, and did not attack them: five young women. He stood his ground and parlayed.

They were hauling a wagon covered by a tarpaulin. Neq watched it, judging that it was large enough to hold a man. A man with a gun. Neq stood in such a way as to keep one of the girls between himself and the wagon.

"Neq the Sword," their leader said. "Our tribe wronged you. But we offer atonement. Take one of us to replace your wife."

Surprised, he studied them more closely. All five were pretty—evidently the pick of the tribe.

"I have no quarrel with the women," he said. "Except that you did not protest the dishonoring of one of your kind. But I can not trust you and do not want you. Your men must die."

"It was our leader who was responsible," the woman replied. "Our men were bound to do Yod's bidding, or to die cruelly. Kill Yod and you have vengeance."

"I will kill him last," Neq said in fury. "He must suffer as he has made me suffer, and even then it will not be enough. Neqa was worth more than your entire tribe."

She seemed nonplussed for a moment, but made a decision. "We have brought him to you," she said. She gestured, and the other four approached the wagon.

Neq grabbed the leader with his left arm, his pincers threatened near her face, and held her before him as a shield against Yod's gun. She did not resist. Her sleek buttocks touched him.

The cover came up. The man inside was exposed.

It was Yod. But the man had no gun. He was dead, his hands servered, the hilt and blade of a dagger protruding from his mouth, and soaking in his own blood.

"Our men were bonded to him, and afraid," the captive woman said. "But *we* were not. We have brought your vengeance to you. Only spare the rest, for our children will perish if we are left without men."

"This is not vengeance," Neq said, troubled. "You have denied me my vengeance."

"Then kill us too, for we five killed Yod. Only leave this place."

Neq considered killing them, as she suggested, for they were trying to buy the reprieve of the guilty. But he found himself sick of it all. Now both Neqa and vengeance had been taken from him. What else was left?

He turned loose the woman. She merely stood, awaiting his response, and the others stood too, like waking dead. They were all young and fair, but there were pockets under their eyes and tension lines about their mouths, and they were less buxom than they might have been. Their vigil and their act of murder had scarred them already.

Neq lifted his sword and touched it to the leader's bosom. She blanched but managed not to flinch. He slid the blade along her front so that it cut open her dress of availability and the handmade halter beneath it, exposing her breasts and letting them droop. Yet they were full and handsome.

He had only intended to check her for weapons. If she had a knife on her person he would know for whom it had been intended, and that would justify what he might

do. But there was no knife. Those breasts reminded him forcefully of Neqa's breasts . . . and suddenly he just wanted to forget.

Vengeance was too complicated.

He pushed her away and fled.

CHAPTER TEN

When Neq next took stock of himself, three years had passed. He was a scarred veteran of 28, still deadly in combat at an age when injury or death had retired many warriors. He had killed more men than any nomad he knew of—most of them outside the circle, for the circle code was virtually dead.

Abruptly he realized three things—or perhaps it was these things that had brought him to this sudden awareness. First, he was now the age Neqa had been when he knew her. Second, he was no closer to true vengeance than ever. Third, the true culprit had not been Yod and Yod's tribe, but the situation that had brought about the dissolution of the circle code. In the old days no woman had been molested, and no man had been required to fight unless he chose.

It came to him that his only true vengeance had to be constructive. Killing gained him nothing. What he had to abolish was not the *men* who had injured him, but the *system*.

That meant that Helicon had to be rebuilt.

Perhaps he had been working it out subconsciously the whole time. A concept of this complexity could not have struck him full-blown. But suddenly he had a mission, and the hurt that was the memory of Neqa abated, and the blood on his sword-arm assumed a certain vindication. He had no further desire to kill, for he had plumbed the depths of that and found it futile. He had no need to impress women, for there had been only one for him. He required no tribe, no empire, for he had long since experi-

enced the heights of power and tired of them. He had his mission, and that was enough.

Rebuild Helicon, and the circle code could be restored. There would be supplies for the crazies, who would restock the hostels and subtly enforce their usual requirements, and the nomads would find themselves conforming, and the world he had known would come back. Slowly, perhaps; it might take decades. But it would surely come. And when the circle code lived again, outlaws like Yod would have no chance. Women would pass freely from hostel to hostel and from bracelet to bracelet, never forced, never hurt. The circle code was civilization, and Helicon was the ultimate enforcement of that code.

First he marched to the ruins of the mountain. He entered by Dick the Surgeon's passage and cleaned out the bones and the ashes. He reconstructed the damaged exits as well as he could and resealed the premises against intrusion and made the entire labyrinth bare but theoretically habitable. He worked slowly and carefully, pausing to feed himself when the need came and to search out supplies. A surprising amount had *not* burned. Perhaps the fire had suffocated soon after the people. Under layers of ashes the majority of Helicon's furnishings remained salvageable.

Neq sought no help, though his metal extremities were inefficient for this type of work and greatly extended the time that would normally have been required. It was tedious shoving a mass of cloth across interminable floors with his sword, mopping up the grisly grime, and his pincers were poor for setting hinges in new doors. But this was the place he had shared with Neqa, however briefly and horribly, and Helicon was somehow suffused by her presence, and blessed by it.

When he was done, a year had passed.

Then he went to see the crazies.

The minor crazy outposts had all long since been devastated, but the fortress-like administration building of Dr. Jones remained intact. And the old crazy chief was there, much the same as ever. He seemed never to have been young, and he did not age.

But there was now no girl at the front desk.

"How have you survived, with no defense?" Neq de-

manded. "It has been four years since I was here, and they have not been kind years. By the sword men live. But no man challenged me as I entered here. Anyone could ravage this place."

Jones smiled. "Would a guard have prevented you from entering?" When Neq merely glanced at his weapon, he continued: "I am tempted to inform you that our philosophy of pacifism prevailed . . . but that would not be entirely accurate. We hoped that the diminished services we offered would dissuade the tribesmen from violence, but there always seemed to be another more savage tribe on the horizon whose members were immune to reason. Our organization has been devastated many times."

"But you live unchanged!"

"Only superficially, Neq. My position remains tenuous." Dr. Jones began unbuttoning his funny vest.

The old crazy must have hidden when the outlaws invaded, Neq thought, and emerged to rebuild after the region was clear again. Tribes would not stay here long, for there would be little food, and the building itself was alien to the nomad way. Still, Dr. Jones must have courage and capability that did not show on the surface.

The crazy had finally finished with his buttons. He opened his vest and began on the clean white shirt beneath.

"How did you know me?" Neq inquired, hoping the man wasn't senile.

"We have met before, you remember. You took Miss Smith and released Dr. Abraham——"

"Who?"

"The Helicon Surgeon. He has been of immense assistance to us. Do you recognize his handiwork?" He opened his shirt to reveal his bony old chest.

Scars were there. It looked as though a dagger had cut him open, chopped up the ancient ribs, and made a careless foray into the meager gut. But somehow everything had been put together again, and what should have been a fatal wound had healed.

"Dick the Surgeon," Neq said. "Yes, he worked on me too." But did not raise his sword to demonstrate the surgery, afraid the gesture would be mistaken.

"I think it safe to assume I would have perished after that particular episode," Dr. Jones said, beginning the

slow task of buttoning his shirt and vest. "But Dr. Abraham restored me. Since he would not have been present except for your timely assistance, I belief it is not farfetched to infer that I owe my preservation to you."

"For every life I may have saved," Neq said, "I have taken fifty."

Dr. Jones seemed not to have heard. "And of course his report enabled us to dispense with any further effort in the region of Helicon."

"Neqa died."

"Miss Smith . . . your bracelet . . ." Dr. Jones murmured, sifting through his information. "Yes, so Dr. Abraham informed us. He said the two of you were very close, and I am gratified to know that. She was a remarkable person, but alone." He did not say more, and Neq was sure the old crazy knew everything.

"I come to avenge her."

"Your reputation precedes you. But do you feel that more killing will satisfy your loss?"

"No!" And, with difficulty, Neq explained his conclusion about the real cause of Neqa's death, and his determination to rebuild Helicon.

Dr. Jones did not respond this time. He sat as if suffering from his venerable wound, eyes almost closed, breathing shallow.

Neq waited for several minutes, then raised his pincerarm to touch the man and determine whether he was all right. Death by old age was something he had never encountered and was almost too horrible to contemplate. What were its symptoms?

Dr. Jones was alive, however. His eyes reopened.

"Do you require proof that I was there, in the mountain?" Neq asked. "I brought papers for you. I do not know what they say." He had saved out these singed writings because of Neqa's literacy; any writing reminded him of her.

Now the crazy reacted beautifully. "Papers from Helicon? I would be extremely interested! But I do not question your veracity. My thoughts were momentarily elsewhere."

Momentarily? Crazies were crazy, naturally!

Then Dr. Jones got up and left the room.

Neq remained, baffled.

A few minutes later Dr. Jones returned with another man, a rotund crazy in spectacles. "Please tell Dr. Abraham and you told me," Jones said. "About your plans."

It was Dick the Surgeon—the man Neqa had rescued from the cage! Now he only remotely resembled the thin fugitive of four years ago.

Neq repeated his philosophy and his plan.

"Why do you come to us?" Dick asked, as though he had never had experience with the wilderness.

"Because I am a sworder, not a builder. I can't read, I can't operate the machinery of Helicon. You crazies can."

"He knows his limitations," Dr. Jones observed.

"But he is a killer."

"Yes," Neq agreed. "But I have had enough of killing." He lifted his arm. "I would make this sword into—"

"A plowshare?" Dr. Jones asked.

Neq did not answer, not being familiar with the term.

"Your former leader, Robert of Helicon," Dr. Jones said to Dick. "Was he not a ruthless man?"

"Robert? Oh, you mean Bob. Yes, ruthless but efficient. Maybe you're right." Dick looked at Neq. "It is ugly, but—"

Neq did not follow much of this. "I have cleaned and restored the mountain, but I cannot do more without your help. I can't fill it with people who can make it function. That is why I'm here."

"It would take a year for a man in your condition to tidy up that carnage!" Dick exclaimed.

"Yes."

There was a silence. The crazies hardly seemed enthusiastic!

Finally Dr. Jones brought out a sheet of paper. "Bring me these people," he said, handing it to Neq. "Those who have survived."

"I can not read. Is this the service you require of me in exchange for your help?"

"In a manner of speaking, yes. I must ask you to tell no one of your project. And I must advise you that your weapon will be valueless in this endeavor—perhaps even a liability."

That seemed to be the extent of his answer. Neq glanced at his sword, wondering whether he should remind the old

crazy that it was impossible for him to set aside his weapon, useful or not. "Tell me the names."

"You can remember them accurately?"

"Yes."

Dr. Jones picked the paper out of Neq's pincer-grasp and read. "Sos the Rope. Tyl of Two Weapons. Jim the Gun."

Neq halted him, astonished. "Sos the Rope went to the mountain . . . oh, I see. He may be alive after all. Tyl is master of the largest remaining tribe. Jim the Gun—"

"You may know Sos better by his later designation: the Weaponless."

"The Weaponless! Master of Empire?" And yet of course it fit. Sos had gone to the mountain; the Weaponless had come out of it. To take the wife he had always wanted—Sola. Neq should have made the connection long ago.

"Have you changed your mind?"

Angry, Neq kept silence while he considered. The crazies were trying to set him an impossible task! Was it to be certain he would fail? Was this really their way of refusing assistance? Or was Dr. Jones serious, having decided that it was necessary, before Helicon could be rebuilt, to eliminate its destroyers? The Weaponless, Tyl, Jim the Gun—these had been the architects of Helicon's demise. The Weaponless had provided the motive; Tyl the manpower; Jim the weapons. . . .

Perhaps it made sense. But how to locate the Weaponless now! If the man lived, so did the empire, and Neq himself still owed him fealty!

"I think the Weaponless is dead," Neq said at last.

"Then bring his wife."

"Or his child," Dick said.

"And if I bring these people to you, then you will give me the help I need for Helicon?"

"There are more names." Dr. Jones read them: all unfamiliar.

"I'll bring every one that lives!" Neq cried recklessly. *Will you help me then?*"

Dr. Jones sighed. "I should be obliged to."

"I do not know where to find them all."

"I will travel with you," Dick the Surgeon said. "I know

many of the Helicon refugees by sight, and have some notion where they might hide. But it would be your job to persuade them to come—without killing them."

Neq mused on this. The company of the surgeon did not appeal to him, but it did promise to facilitate an onerous task. "I can't tell them and I can't kill them. Yet I must make them come. The leading warriors of the old empire, including the very man who—" He shook his head. "All because I want to rebuild Helicon, and restore your source of supply, so that you can bring back the circle code."

Dr. Jones didn't seem to comprehend Neq's irony. "You have the essence, warrior."

Angry and disappointed, Neq walked out. But Dick the Surgeon followed.

CHAPTER ELEVEN

Tyl's tribe was not as large as it had been in the heyday of empire, for he had taken losses in the Helicon reduction and in the anarchy following. But its demesnes were larger because of the general decimation of nomads in recent years. Now it represented a kind of civilization itself, for shelters had been built, fields cultivated, weapons forged, and the circle code was enforced. There was now a preponderance of staffs, clubs and sticks, mostly wooden weapons, because metal was much cruder than Helicon's product. The fine old weapons were increasingly precious now. Neq knew that those who carried swords of the old type were veterans, for today a man was challenged as frequently for possession of a superior weapon as for woman or service or life.

"You come to challenge *me*?" Tyl demanded incredulously. "Have you forgotten the code of empire: the subchiefs of the Weaponless may not war against each other?"

"They may not war for mastery," Neq answered. "No, I have not forgotten. But the empire is dead, and so are its conventions."

"It is not dead until we know the Weaponless is dead—and he is a difficult man to kill, as you would know had you ever met him in the circle. And the circle code is not dead where my tribe travels."

"It is dead wherever your tribe departs, however." But Neq approved the fine order Tyl maintained. "I did not say I came to challenge you with weapon, for I may not use my sword on this mission. Were any man to question my competence in the circle, I should be glad to show him my blade—but not for mastery, not for death, only

447

for demonstration, no blood shed. I challenge you only to do a service for me, and perhaps for the nomad society."

Tyl smiled. "I would do you a service without inducement in the circle, however circumspectly hinted, for we were comrades in better days. And I would aid the nomad society if I only knew how. What is it you wish?"

"Go to the crazies."

Tyl laughed.

"Nevertheless," Neq said, remembering how Sol had reacted to disbelief, so many years ago. More than half Neq's life had passed since his conquest by Sol of All Weapons.

Tyl looked at him more closely, responsive to the tone. "I have heard—this is merely rumor—that you were injured in a conflict with outlaws."

"Many times."

"The first time. That they overcame you by means of the advantage of fifty men and a gun, and cut off your hands."

Neq glanced down at his cloth-wrapped extremities, nodding.

"And that you achieved some semblance of vengeance . . . nevertheless."

"They slew my wife."

"And she was a crazy?"

"She was."

"Yet now you espouse another crazy cause?"

Neq's sword-arm twitched under the cloth. "Do you slight my wife?"

"By no means," Tyl said quickly. "I merely remark that you have had adventures I have not, and must have strong motive for your mission."

Neq shrugged.

"I will go to the crazies," Tyl said. "If I do not find reason to stay, I will return to my tribe."

"That suffices."

"Any other favor I can do you?" Tyl inquired dryly.

"If you can tell me where the Weaponless might be."

Tyl controlled his surprise. "He has been absent five years. I doubt he resides within the crazy demesnes."

"His wife, then."

"She remains my guest. I will take you to her."

"I thank you."

Tyl stood, a fair, rather handsome man, a leader. "Now that our business is done, come with me to the circle. I would show my men swordsmanship of the old style. No blood, no terms."

It was Neq's turn to smile. On such basis he could enter the circle. It had been long since he had sworded for fun, following the rules of empire.

And it was a pleasure. Whether Tyl remained his superior no one could say, for Neq's technique had necessarily changed, and they were not fighting in earnest. But Tyl's art was beautiful, rivaling that of Sol of All Weapons in the old days, and the display the two of them put on left the more recent members of the tribe gaping. Feint and counterfeint; thrust and parry; offense and defense, with the sunlight flashing, flashing, flashing from living blades and the melody of combat resounding to the welkin.

When they finished, panting, the tribesmen remained seated around the circle, rows and rings of armed men, silent. "I have told you of Sol," Tyl said to them. "And of Tor, of Neq. Now you have seen Neq, though his hands are gone. Such was our empire."

And Neq felt a glow he had not experienced in years, for Tyl was giving him public compliment. Suddenly he longed for the empire again, for the good things it had brought. And his determination to complete his mission despite the barriers the crazies were erecting was doubled.

Sola had aged. Neq remembered her as a rare beauty, truculent but gifted with phenomenal sex appeal, fit for a single man to dream about. Now her face was lined, her body bent. Her long dark hair no longer flowed, it straggled. It was hard to believe that she was only two or three years older than he.

"This is Neq the Sword," Tyl said to her, and departed.

"I would not have recognized you," Sola said. "You look old. Yet you are younger than I. Where is the shy young warrior with the magic sword and the golden voice?"

To each his own perspective! "Does the Weaponless live?"

"I fear he does not. But he would not return to me, regardless."

Neq was surprised. "To whom, then?"

"His other wife. She of the underworld."

His interest intensified. "You know of Helicon?"

"I know my husband laid siege to the mountain, because she was there. She has his bracelet and his name."

"She lives?"

"I do not know. Do *any* live—who were there when the fire came?"

"Yes," he said. Then, quickly: "Or so it is rumored."

She was on the slip immediately. Sola had never been stupid; she had taught the warriors counting and figuring. "If any live, *she* lives. I know it. Seek her out, tell her I would meet her. Ask her—ask her if my child—"

Neq waited, but she only cried silently.

"You must go to the crazies," he said finally.

"Why not? I have nothing to live for."

"This woman of the Weaponless—what name does she bear?"

"His old name. Sos. The one I would have had, had I not been a foolish girl blinded by power. By the time he was mine, he was *not* mine, and he was nameless."

"So she would be Sosa. She would know if the Weaponless lives?"

"She is *with* him if he lives. But my child—ask her—"

Neq made a connection. "Your child by Sol? Who went with him to the mountain?"

"More or less," she answered.

He thought of the skeletons he had swept from the underground halls. A number had been small—children and babies. Yet there had been several exit passages such as the one Dick the Surgeon had used. There had been some unburned caverns as well as the little wagon-tunnels to scattered depots. Some adults had escaped, perhaps many; no one knew how large Helicon's population had been. Some children could have. . . .

"I have one more name for you," Sola said. "Var—Var the Stick."

Neq had some vague recollection of such a warrior, a helper to the Weaponless who had disappeared at the same time. "He will know where to find the Weaponless?"

"He must know," she said fervently. "He was the protégé of my husband, and sterile like him."

Neq wondered how she could know such a thing. But he remembered the rumors about this woman, and how she had gone to Sos's tent in the badlands camp, and wondered again. "I will seek Sosa," he said. "And Var the Stick."

"*And* my child—Soli. She would be thirteen now, almost fourteen. Dark-haired. And—" She hesitated. "You remember the way I used to be?"

"Yes." Her figure had stimulated him many times, fifteen years ago.

"She favors me, I think."

Soli would be a beauty, then. Neq nodded. "I will send them all to the crazies—if they live."

"I will wait there." And for some reason she was crying. Perhaps it was the weakness of an old woman who knew she would never see her husband or her daughter again; who knew that their bones lay charred and buried near the mountain of death.

Dick the Surgeon located several of the strangely-named fugitives in the next few months. Men like John and Charles and Robert, men old and feeble and obviously unused to the way of the nomads despite their recent years among them. Some were refugees from Helicon; others seemed to be crazies, cut off by the breakdown of civilization. Dick talked to them, and glimmers of hope brightened their forlorn faces and they agreed to come with Neq—to Neq's suppressed disgust. Now he had to forage for them, and guard them against outlaws, for they were almost unable to do for themselves and could not make the trek to Dr. Jones alone. A man with no hands taking care of men with no gumption!

But these creatures had survived because they had talents certain tribes wanted—literary, hand skills, knowledge of guns. Most of the names on his list seemed not to have survived; no doubt they belonged to bones he had swept in Helicon.

When he could, he inquired about his other names: Var, Sosa, Soli. But there was no memory of these among the nomads—not since the destruction of Helicon.

Finally he brought his small group back to the crazy building. Almost a year had passed.

"You are still determined to rebuild Helicon?" Dr. Jones inquired.

"Yes." He did not add *in spite of you*.

"You did not locate all the persons listed."

"I have not finished. I merely deliver these to you, who could not deliver themselves. Many of the rest are dead. You saw Tyl and Sola?"

"They are here."

So Tyl had remained! What had the crazy said to him?

"I have not found the Weaponless—but now I search for his underground wife, Sosa, and for Sola's child, and for Var the Stick. These may help me to locate him—or his cairn."

"Interesting you should mention those names," Dr. Jones murmured. "You are illiterate, as I recall."

"I am a warrior."

"The two abilities—reading and fighting—are not necessarily mutually exclusive. Some warriors are literate. But you have no notion of the content of the papers you delivered to us?"

"None."

"Let me read some excerpts to you, then." And the old crazy brought a similar sheaf up from the bowels of his desk.

AUGUST 4, B118—The siege has abated, but the mood is ominous. Bob has arranged some kind of contest of champions, but has as yet selected no man to represent Helicon. We are not geared for this nomad circle-combat; it is folly. We have in Sol the Nomad one of the most formidable primitive fighters of the age, but I know he will not take up weapon against his own kind. He hates it here; he really did come to die, and he resents what we did to him: making him live because we made his daughter live. Sosa has kept him pacified somehow; I don't know how that marvelous woman does it. Sol's daughter *is* his life.

But I ramble too much about other people's business, as an old bookworm will. Surely I have concerns of my own: this premonition that this is the terminus, the extinction of the life we have known, and perhaps of civilization itself. . . .

"The mountain!" Neq exclaimed. "The siege of Helicon!"

"These notes are by Jim the Librarian—a literate and sensitive man."

"He is on my list! A man of the underworld!"

"Yes, of course. But it will not be necessary to look for him further."

"To rebuild!" Neq cried, comprehending what should have been obvious all along. "The men who *know*!"

"Certainly. Obviously nomads could not rebuild the foreign technology of Helicon unassisted, however noble their motives. But a nucleus of such survivors, together with the most capable nomads and, er, crazies, under a strong, sincere leader—it can be done, we suspect."

Dr. Jones looked at him with compassion. "I hope you will not be disappointed that we do not deem you fit to lead the actual restoration. What you are attempting is noble, and you shall certainly receive due credit for your dedication and effort; but the complexities of technology and discipline—"

"No, you are right," Neq said with mixed emotions. He *was* disappointed, but also relieved. "I never thought to stay in Helicon myself. I saw the carnage—only crazies could *like* it there, away from the sun, the trees—" As he spoke he realized why Tyl had been on the list. They needed strong and competent leadership, and Tyl was that. He had been second in command to the Weaponless, and before that to Sol of All Weapons. He had as much experience in managing men as any nomad, and he was a top warrior who never let discipline slide. The underworld would be a kind of empire.

"I'm glad you understand. Training and temperament are paramount. In a pressure situation where swords and clubs are not the answer—"

"But the Weaponless—he *destroyed* Helicon! Why should he help it now?" Yet obviously Dr. Jones wasn't depending entirely on the Weaponless. He was grooming Tyl as an alternate.

"Sos the Weaponless was *of* Helicon. Dr. Abraham made him what he was, on the unfortunate directive of their leader." Dr. Jones cogitated for a moment. "Dr. Abraham was not aware of the politics leading to the

disaster. He was sleeping when the fire started, and dazed when he escaped. He supposed the nomads had done it."

"Hadn't they?" Leading question!

"Not directly. Here is Jim's final entry."

AUGUST 8, B118—How can I express the horror I feel? Soli was my child too, in the sense that I taught her to read and I loved her as my own. Almost daily she came to the library, an absolutely charming little girl—indeed, I believe she divided her time almost evenly between my books and her father's weapons. Yet now—

I blame myself. She came to me in tears just three days ago with a story I refused to credit: that Bob intended to murder both Sol and Sosa, her Helicon parents, if she did not go on a dangerous mission *outside*. She had been sworn to secrecy, she claimed, lest they be slain regardless—but she had to tell someone, and I agreed to keep her confidence, thinking it a fantasy of a juvenile mind. I advised her that she had misunderstood, that Bob had the best interest of Helicon at heart, and had only meant that her parents' lives might be endangered, as we are all endangered, by this continuing nomad siege. I recommended that she agree to the secret mission, for surely (if it were not a product of her own lively imagination) it was merely a device to get her safely from the scene of action before another crisis occurred. 'We value our children most of all,' I informed her fatuously.

Now she is dead, and I deplore my hopeless naivete. Bob sent her to Mt. Muse, to engage in physical combat with the nomad champion, and of course the brute killed her. The nomads are celebrating; we can overhear their foul carousing. 'Var the Stick!' they cry—but I don't believe they realize that their precious barbarian champion, shielded from their view on the flattop mesa a dozen miles south of here—was pitted against *an eight year old girl*.

Confound the promise of secrecy I made! I have told Sosa what Soli told me. I had to, for Sosa is more the mother of that dear girl than her nomad dam could ever have been. Sosa would have learned of it

soon enough, less sympathetically. I am sure she will relay it to Sol, and I do not speculate what will develop now. Were I a warrior-type in such a situation I am sure I would not be gentle. But I am only a futile old man.

I am taking poison.

There was a pause.

"Var the Stick—he was the nomad champion? He killed Sol's child?"

"So it would appear. If you were Sol—"

"I *am* a warrior-type! I would have put Var's head on a spike in the forest for all to see. And Bob's. And all others responsible. And—"

Dr. Jones steepled his hands in a way he had. "And . . . ?"

"And accomplished nothing," Neq said slowly. "Vengeance is not the answer. It is only vengeance. Only more sorrow."

Dr. Jones nodded. "I believe you are in a position to comprehend Sol's motives, then and later. He was a thorough nomad, despite his residence in Helicon for those years. Would he have ignited the incendiary stores there?"

"I don't know about that," Neq said, not understanding one of the words. "But I think there was gasoline down there. And other stuff that would burn. I think he fired it all. In the name of vengeance. Those bodies were scorched!" And more than scorched.

"And later—would he have returned?"

"To view the destruction, after he knew it had accomplished nothing? No, he would not return. . . ."

"Yes. Yet if we were to rebuild Helicon, how could we be certain that such a thing would not happen again?"

"I do not know," Neq said honestly.

"Go and find out," Dr. Jones said.

"But you agreed to help if I brought you these people!"

"And we shall. But of what use is it to rebuild Helicon if it remains liable to destruction by the forces that brought it down before? The human forces."

Neq had no answer for that.

"Forget the remaining names on the list," Dr. Jones

said kindly. "The nucleus is almost sufficient now. Look instead for Sol and Sosa and Var, should he somehow have survived Sol's quest for vengeance. Learn whether Sos the Weaponless was more directly involved; perhaps his disappearance is relevant. Ascertain the truth—and suggest how we may prevent any conceivable recurrence. Only then will we be assured that our endeavor is secure."

CHAPTER TWELVE

The six year old spoor of both Var the Stick and Sosa had to begin at Helicon. The one had been with the nomads, the other with the underworld. Both had vanished in that final, devastating encounter. Probably both were dead— but then his quest for information was dead, too. Sol and the Weaponless had much better chances of survival— but neither would have been party to the heart of Helicon's failure: the inner workings of Bob's mind. For had Bob not sent an innocent child to her death, both he and Helicon might have weathered the siege. The underworld defenses were certainly formidable enough. Why had Bob, by all accounts a capable leader, erred so brutally and calamitously? Would the next leader err the same way? There was the key.

Helicon was as he had left it: tight and clean. He re-explored its several exits, pondering whether a woman might have used one to escape. Certainly she might! To this extent Sola's intuition must be correct: Sosa, with forewarning of Sol's intent, was the most likely of all the underworlders to have escaped cleanly. Sol could have been trapped in his own conflagration—and the Weaponless, outside, could well have entered Helicon in a desperate attempt to find Sosa . . . and failed, and died.

He scouted the exterior again, and made a trek to Mt. Muse, to see where a warrior might have gone after slaying a child. But he could not climb to the mesa—and anyway, Var had returned to the nomad camp to be feted for his barbarism. There was no answer there. Tyl himself had seen Var after the "combat of champions" but had only known that Var disappeared shortly thereafter, and

then the Weaponless. Neither had given any advance hint of what was to happen. There had been no evidence of foul play.

There were outlaw tribesmen in this region. Some Neq and Dick had encountered before; no one had known of Var or Sosa. Of course there was considerable turnover here, for the outlaws warred constantly with one another in this land of no honor, and few lived long.

The locals were not eager to answer more questions. Neq's uncovered sword convinced them. Still he learned nothing.

He moved out, making great circles around Helicon, searching out men and tribes he had not met before. Many balked—but as the blood dripped from his sword, his questions were answered. Negatively. Only six years had passed, but many of these men did not know what he meant by "Helicon."

Months passed, his circles widened, and he accomplished nothing. But he would not stop. Instead he became more devious in his questioning. "Six years ago, perhaps seven—did a stranger pass through your territory? A lone sticker? A small woman? Someone masked or hidden or mysteriously wounded?"

And finally he got a meaningful response, from an old warrior of the defunct empire, who had drifted to this region before the siege and remained, retired. "I saw a stranger then—a pale, slender man who spoke no word."

This did not sound like Var the Stick, who was a large, grotesquely mottled youth. "What was his weapon?"

"I did not see it. But he hauled a barrow with a staff protruding, and he reminded me of—"

"Of whom?" Neq prodded, remembering a man who had hauled a barrow.

"Of Sol of All Weapons. But that could not be, for Sol went to the mountain half a dozen years before."

So he had looked for Sosa, but found Sol! But that was almost as good, for surely they had escaped Helicon together. His long search had been rewarded . . . perhaps.

Suddenly the trail was hot. There were passes where a man would normally travel, places where he might camp. Neq traced Sol's course, finding many who had seen the barrow-man pass. Some had challenged him to the circle,

for that was before the effect of Helicon's fall had been felt in the nomad society and honor was strong, but the man had avoided all such contacts. No one Neq met claimed to have fought the barrow-man in the circle.

That proved they were speaking honestly. Sol had been the greatest circle warrior of all time, except for the artificially forged juggernaut of the Weaponless—and the battle between the two had been so even as to be merely chance in the decision. Sol might have lost his edge during six years in Helicon—but not much, if he were training his daughter regularly. Any man who brought Sol to combat against his preference must have paid the obvious penalty. Only those who had *failed* to fight him could have survived.

And why had Sol avoided encounters? Obvious, now: because he had more important business. He was going somewhere.

But not, it seemed, with Sosa. No one had seen her. Sol was traveling alone. Why should that be?

Neq knew. Sol was following the man who had killed his daughter. Var the Stick.

Vengeance.

A lone warrior would not have been remarkable. That's why Var himself hadn't been remembered. But the barrow —that stuck in many minds, because it was unusual. Because it brought to mind the one warrior everyone knew about. Now that Neq inquired about that specifically, the long faded memories returned.

Sol had departed Helicon and traveled northwest, detouring around badlands and avoiding established tribes. Why northwest? Because Var the Stick must have fled that way.

And he had! Neq picked up the memories now—the skin-mottled man, also no talker, deadly with the sticks . . . and his boy companion.

Boy companion?

And abruptly—the Weaponless. He was on this route too, incredibly. Was he following Var—or Sol? To protect the first from the second? What a battle of titans, if Sol and the Weaponless should meet again!

Yet none of them had returned. All the key figures had vanished, and not in the Helicon conflagration. Where had they gone?

And where had the boy come from—the boy with **Var** the Stick? Had he had a little brother? After months of finding too little, Neq had found too much!

He continued the chase doggedly. His hopes for the restoration of Helicon were somehow bound in with this mystery, and he would not stop without the answer. His cast of characters remained set: three men and a boy, not together, traveling northwest. The riddle of Helicon's demise . . . perhaps.

But the trail faded near the northern limit of the former crazy demesnes. Neq cast about for a month in the increasingly bitter winter, but the natives knew nothing. He had either to give up, or to leave the territory of the nomad society, as his quarry seemed to have done.

He hesitated to go farther north. His metal extremities were excellent for combat and simple hunting, for he had a bow he could brace on his sword and fire lefthanded with the pincers with fair accuracy. But against true wilderness and snow he was weak, and he knew that guns were more common in the northern realm. He could not use a gun himself, and had to be extremely wary in the presence of such a weapon.

And so he continued his futile search in the land of the nomads long after his real hope of success was gone.

One day Tyl of Two Weapons appeared, alone. "Are you ready for help?" Tyl inquired as if this were routine.

Neq's pride had suffered with the winter. "I welcome it," he said.

Tyl did not clarify the obvious: the word had reached him of Neq's futility. "I do not wish to bargain with a comrade of empire, but the crazy has laid his stricture on me as on you. My help is for a price."

Dr. Jones' peculiar yet subtly forceful hand again! "What price?"

"I will name it when the occasion arises."

Neq knew Tyl for an honest man. "Accepted."

"We travel north?"

"Yes." With Tyl along, they could manage. The search could resume. "Sol of All Weapons. The Weaponless. Var the Stick. A boy. All went north, none returned. Find one of these, and we may learn why Helicon failed. Var might

have learned the truth from Soli, before he killed her; Sol might have gotten it from Bob of Helicon, before he killed him. The Weaponless . . . may have his notions, for he negotiated with Bob about the combat of champions. The boy—I don't know."

Tyl considered. "Yes. The secret lies between Bob and Soli. Too bad neither survived. . . ." He trailed off, pondering something; but he did not amplify his thought.

Tyl had a gun, and was competent with it. Tyl had hands. Tyl had a way with strangers that Neq lacked. The trail reappeared.

And disappeared. They followed it to the northern ocean, where a forbidding tunnel went under, and there it stopped. "If they went in there," the natives opined, "they are gone forever. The machine-demon consumes intruders."

Tyl distrusted it for a more practical reason. "I saw strange things come from the tunnels as the mountain burned. Animals with tremendous eyes and mouths, that a sword would not stop. Rats with no eyes. Some of my men died after merely touching such creatures. Jim the Gun said they carried radiation kill-spirits; he heard them on his click-box. I would not enter such a place without an army, and then I would need good reason."

Neq agreed. He had seen strange corpses in the fringe passages beyond the burn-zone of Helicon, and many radiation markers, and at night he had heard the scamperings of things that could have been similar to those Tyl described. Had he not had strong motivation, he would never have completed the long chore of cleaning the underworld rooms and passages. It would be folly to brave this unfamiliar tunnel as anything but a last resort. Rumors of horror were often well-founded, these days.

So they quested north, along the coast—and the trail resumed! Two men, one grizzled and huge, the other pale and silent. No blotch-skinned sticker; no boy.

Then Tyl spied a nomad campsite. "See—they built a fire, here, and pitched some kind of tent here, with guides around it to lead off the water from rain. The locals don't do that; they stay in square houses."

"But this is recent. Five, six days, no more. It can not be our quarry."

"True. But what would nomads be doing here? We should question them."

"Question the locals. Some would have seen the nomads pass."

Tyl nodded thoughtfully. "Strange we have heard nothing of these before."

They questioned the locals, and learned that two nomads, a man and a woman, had passed through, traveling south.

"South?" Neq demanded. "Where did they come from?"

The people only shrugged, not knowing or caring what the barbarians did or which direction they went.

Sol and the Weaponless had gone north; these others were *from* the north. Their trails might have crossed.

They made a rapid excursion south again, tracing the strangers, following a course that skirted dangerously close to posted radiation zones. A large, gruff man and a rather pretty woman who kept to themselves and made swift progress. Tyl would question native villagers—a village was a kind of stationary tribe, unique to this locale—while Neq scouted the countryside for further traces.

Neq looked up one such afternoon to discover a grotesque man watching him. Huge and shaggy, hunched-backed, with grossly gnarled hands curled about home-made singlesticks, and mottled skin showing under his heavy winter coverings—the man was more like a badlands beast that a nomad. But nomad he was, and he had already assumed a stance of combat. His long arms and heavy chest suggested enormous power; he would be savage with those sticks!

Mottled skin. . . .

"Var the Stick!" Neq cried, amazed.

The other spoke, but it sounded more like a growl. By concentrating, Neq made out the gist. "You followed me for days. Now give cause why I should not drive you off."

Neq unveiled his sword. "Cause enough here. But first you must answer my questions, for I have sought you long."

"A changeling!" Var rasped, seeing Neq's arms. "Do you know the circle?"

Neq was surprised. "You speak of the circle? *You*, slayer of children?"

"Never!" Var roared, coming at him. There was something wrong about his legs; though he wore boots, he did not walk like a man. A true beast in nomad outfit . . . it was no longer a mystery why he had killed the young girl Soli. He had probably eaten her.

Var struck at him and Neq parried, smiling grimly. He had no fear of hand-hewn weapons, and a clumsy charge was the simplest to terminate. But first he needed information.

Var was more artful than his appearance suggested. As Neq dodged aside, so did he, so that they met squarely. One stick shot toward Neq's face while the other blocked his sword. Var had met many a blade before!

So much the better. Neq's pincers also blocked defensively while his sword whistled. He struck first at the other's weapon, seeking to cut a stick in half. He preferred to disarm this monster gradually, lingeringly, not hurting him much . . . until after the truth was known.

"Before I down you," Var grunted, "tell me your name."

"Neq the Sword." This courtesy of identification was due even for a beast.

Var fought for a while, quite skillfully, pondering behind his overhanging brows. "I know of you," he grunted. But he showed no fear, only caution.

It was increasingly apparent that this was no warrior of the decadent post-empire ilk. Var's technique was unconventional, but he was years younger than Neq, and much larger, so that even with his considerable stoop he stood taller. He had quick brute power, and the crude-seeming sticks were more solid than they looked, blocking sword-thrusts with considerable authority. The wood tended to catch the blade, holding it instead of bouncing it back, and that was dangerous indeed. The two sticks beat a tattoo on both his metal arms, their violent force bearing him back. Had his sword not been part of him, Neq could have been disarmed early, and certainly he was giving way before the onslaught.

Yet there was a certain eloquence about Var's attack,

ferocious as it was. His balance was excellent. Without pausing, the man kicked off his boots and exposed horny bare feet—and then his footing was not clumsy at all. He was astonishingly agile for his bulk, yet his motions were economical.

A master sticker, in fact. Neq had encountered only two empire stickers with power and finesse like this. One was Tyl—greater on the finesse, less on the power—and the other was Sol . . . whose whereabouts Var must know.

But the sticks were not like the sword, and Neq's sword was not like others. His wrist was invulnerable. Though he was not young himself, he knew of no man who could match him in fair circle combat today, other than Tyl. Var might hold him off for some time, but Var had to tire, to make mistakes, to overreach himself. The real strength of a sticker lay in his endurance under stress and his continuing judgment. There was where Neq had him: experience.

Neq fended off the blows and maneuvered for a clean opening himself. This was difficult, for Var danced about on his hooves and ducked his shaggy head sometimes almost to the ground—without ever exposing it.

"You are skilled, man of metal hands," Var muttered. "As befits a chief under the Master."

Neq eased his fencing, spying an opportunity to learn something. If Var were attempting to lull him by conversation, he would fail. "You are skilled too. I heard the Weaponless trained you himself."

"The Master is dead," Var said, relaxing his attack.

Neq let the pace slow, but remained vigilant. Var's companion might be near, ready to pounce treacherously during the double distraction of battle and dialogue. What kind of woman would mate with this kind of man, if not a beast-woman? "You could not have slain the Weaponless."

"Not in the circle," Var said grimly.

Neq stiffened. In that moment the sticker could have scored, had he been alert. Then the sparring resumed. "Sol of All Weapons followed you. You could not have slain him either."

"Not with the sticks."

This time Neq stiffened deliberately, proffering a seem-

ing opening. Still Var did not strike. He was either too clever or too stupid. "You admit you killed them treacherously?"

"The radiation."

That blotched skin of his! Neq remembered now—there had been a story that the beast-boy could feel radiation, avoiding lethal concentrations himself while leading others into some badlands trap. So it was true, and Var had doomed both his friend and his enemy by luring them through an unmarked radiation pocket! Now he dared to return with his bitch, thinking his crime unknown or forgotten.

So Neq's sources of information were gone. But there was one more thing to know. "Soli—the child of Helicon—"

Var actually smiled. "Soli exists no more."

Neq could hardly speak. "The radiation?" he whispered with biting irony.

But this question Var avoided, as though some lode of buried guilt had finally been tapped. "We have no quarrel. I will show you Vara."

Then the opening came, and Neq's sword struck true.

CHAPTER THIRTEEN

Tyl returned at dusk, with a companion. "Neq! Neq! Look what I found in the village!"

Neq looked up from the cairn he had been fashioning. As the two approached he saw that the stranger was a woman. "I'm so glad to find you!" she exclaimed.

Neq stared. It was a crazy woman! She wore the typical skirt and blouse despite the cold, and her long dark hair was bound the crazy way. And she was lovely.

"Miss Smith," he murmured, reminded achingly of his love though there was little actual, physical similarity between the two women. This one was neat to the point of precision, as Miss Smith had been; she was beautiful in that fragile manner; and she was incongruous in the wilderness. That was the connection. Intelligent, literate, innocent. His heart felt as though a dagger had nudged it.

"This is one of the two we traced," Tyl said. "She was reconnoitering in the village, the same as I, and when we met—"

"She traveled with a nomad?" Neq asked, still bemused by the parallel to his own experience of six years before. "A crazy?"

"I am Vara," she said. "I travel with my husband. He should be around here somewhere—"

Neq still had not come out of his fog. "*Var*? The Stick?"

"Yes! Did you meet him? From what Tyl says, we have a common mission—"

Then Neq came to total and ugly awareness. He touched the fresh burial mound with one foot. "I—met him."

Tyl looked at him and at the cairn, comprehending. He went for his sword, but stopped. He turned away.

Vara went to the cairn and carefully removed a section of the stone lining. She excavated the fresh earth and sand with her slender fingers while Neq watched. Finally she uncovered a foot, with its blunted, hooflike toes. She touched it, feeling its coldness.

By this time it was dark, and night closed in completely as she contemplated that deformed, dead foot. Then she covered it gently, filled in the hole, and replaced the stones.

"My two fathers are dead," she said wistfully. "Now my husband. What am I to do?"

"We met. We fought."

"I served Sol," Tyl said from his section of the night, still facing away. There was an anguished quality to his voice that Neq had not heard before. "I served the Weaponless. Var the Stick was my friend. I would have barred you from the circle with him, had I been certain of what I suspected. When I saw Vara, I was certain. But you met Var too soon."

"I did not know he was your friend," Neq said, hating this. "I knew him only as a slayer of men by treachery, and of a child at Helicon."

"You misjudged him," Tyl said in the same quiet tone Vara had used. "He was bold in combat but gentle in person. And he had an invaluable talent."

"Var slew only of necessity," Vara said. "And not always *then*."

Neq was feeling worse, though it had been an honest combat. He had struck too hastily, as he had so often before. His sword outreached his intellect. He could have disengaged, waited for Tyl's return. Now he had to defend his action. "What need had he to slay the child of Sol?"

Vara turned to him in the dark. "I am the child of Sol."

Neq's stomach heaved with the pang of unwarranted killing, knowing what was coming. "He killed Soli at Mt. Muse, when she was eight years old. All accounts agree on that."

"All but one," she said. "The true one. He claimed to have killed me, so that the nomads would win, and my

two fathers could be together again. But then I couldn't get back to tell Sol the truth, and the Weaponless was seeking Var for vengeance—"

"Vengeance!" Abominable concept!

"So we had to flee. We went to China, and I took his bracelet when I came of age. Soli exists no more."

Now Neq recognized her face, though it was no longer visible in the night. The classic beauty of Sola! The crazy dress and his own dawning guilt had blinded him to her identity.

"The boy Var traveled with, going north—" Neq murmured. "A girl with her hair hidden."

"Yes. So no one would know I wasn't dead. I can't do that now."

She certainly couldn't! The child of eight had become a woman of fifteen. "And Sol pursued you too, not knowing . . . he must have met the Weaponless on the way!"

"They learned in China. And gave their lives carrying radioactive stones into the enemy stronghold, so that we could escape. Var always felt that it was his fault they died, but it was mine. I knew they would do it."

Var had blamed himself . . . and so had let Neq's accusation stand. Now Var's assumed guilt was Neq's.

"It was a mistake," Tyl said after a long pause. "Var told everyone he had killed the mountain champion. Helicon itself was fired and gutted to avenge that murder—it does not matter by whom. Neq did not know. Only *I* knew Var would not have slain a child. And I know the kind of terms Sola makes. She was kind to Var, but her price was surely the life of her daughter."

"Var did say something," Vara admitted. "He had sworn to kill the man who harmed me. And for a long time he was reticent, though he loved me. . . ."

Neq remembered Sola's comment about Var's sterility. Strange, driven woman!

"Yet I knew it could have happened," Tyl continued. "Mt. Muse is high and steep, and there are rocks to drop. Had you attacked him with stones while he was climbing, he might have had to fight before he knew, and he was deadly in rough terrain. So he *might* have killed you, and I could not bar Neq from combat until I was sure. It was my mistake; I am to blame for your husband's death—"

"No!" Neq and Vara cried together.

There was silence again, as each person sifted his tangled motives. The conversation was unreal, and not because it emanated from darkness. Neq's emotions were partly in suspension. "Why do you not curse me? Why do you not weep? I killed——"

"You killed because you did not understand," Vara said. "I have some share of guilt for that, for I agreed to play dead. Tonight I make you understand. Tomorrow I kill you. Then will I weep for you both."

She meant it. She was like Miss Smith, who died Neqa. Changed of name, precious beyond all imagination, but loyal to her man. Neqa had tried to kill Yod when Yod made ready to cut off Neq's hands. Would Vara do less?

Yod had killed Neqa by accident. Now Neq had killed Var. The guilt was the same. Vengeance would be the same.

She would not have it, any more than he had. Neq bent his elbow, bringing his sword-arm to his own throat. It was past time for him to die.

"I claim my price," Tyl said, startling Neq as his muscles tensed for the fatal slice.

Of all times! Yet Neq had a debt of honor, and he would have to acquit it. "Name your price."

"Give back what you have taken this day."

Neq delayed answering, trying to discover Tyl's meaning. Obviously he could not restore Var to life.

"What you have to do," Vara said evenly, "do before dawn. When daylight comes I will destroy you in the circle."

"In the circle!" Now Neq could not fathom her meaning either. Women did not do battle. "What is your weapon?"

"The stick."

The morbid situation could not suppress Tyl's interest. "So Sol *did* train you in combat!"

"My father. Yes. Every day we practiced, inside the mountain. He hoped to take me away from Helicon some day, but Sosa wouldn't let him. And I have practiced since."

Now Tyl's voice was more concerned. "Mere practice can not make a woman into a man. My daughter is older than you, and she has a child of her own now—but this

would never have come to pass if she had ever entered man's province. The circle is not for you."

"Nevertheless." Sol's child, all right!

"This man," Tyl continued persuasively, "this man, Neq the Sword, was second only to me in the empire, when the Weaponless departed. Now he has no hands, but he retains his weapon. He is less clever in technique, but more deadly than before because he cannot be disarmed. His sword is swifter than his mind. I think no man can stand against that sword today."

"Nevertheless."

"I can not permit this encounter," Tyl said.

Her voice was cold. "Your permission is irrelevant."

"Var was my friend. He taught me to use the gun. I hurt with his loss, as you do. Yet I say this: do not lift stick against Neq the Sword. We must not make this terrible mistake again."

"Var was more than friend to me," she pointed out caustically.

"Nevertheless."

"You have no right," she said.

Tyl did not answer, and the strange, tense conversation ended.

Neq did not know whether he slept that night, or whether the others did, but slowly the morning came.

Vara had changed. She no longer resembled an ineffective crazy woman. That guise must have been for the benefit of the local villagers, who were rather like crazies themselves in their dress, so that she could pass among them freely. Now she wore a nomad smock, and her hair was loose and long, falling down over her shoulders on either side and curling about the soft mounds of her breasts. She remained stunning by any definition.

She carried sticks—the twin thin clubs that Var had used.

Neq felt another chill. He had buried Var's weapon beside him, according to the normal courtesy of warriors. Neq's sword had cut open the ground and scooped it out, and his pincers had levered the stones into place: the work of several hours. Yet these were Var's sticks, for they

carried the recent marks of the sword. Neq could recognize the scars of a weapon as readily as he could a face.

"As you fought my husband," Vara said, "so shall I fight you. As you slew him, so shall I slay you. As you buried him, I'll bury you. With honor. Then will my mourning begin."

"Neq will not fight a woman," Tyl said. "I know him, even as I knew Var."

Vara lifted her sticks and stood beside the burial mound. "He may fight or flee as he chooses. Here is the circle—beside my husband's cairn. The world is the circle. I will be avenged."

The words struck Neq like blows of the sticks. Her sentiments were so similar to his own when Neqa died! He could not have forgiven Yod and his rapist tribe; he had not forgiven them now. The thrust of his vengeance had changed, now applying to the entire outlaw society and its roots in the ashes of Helicon, but vengeance it remained. How could he say to her that a life for a life was not enough?

"Var was my friend," Tyl repeated. "He shamed me before my tribe when he was but a child, a wild boy of the badlands, and I meant to take him to the circle when he became a man. But Sola interceded on his behalf, and when I came to know him—"

Vara gripped her sticks and moved purposely toward Neq. He saw the savage grief in her eyes, the kind he had had, the kind that cast aside all thought of honor and permitted murder by stealth, the kind that was futile. But he had done it; he had killed without cause. He would not lift his sword to perpetrate further evil.

Tyl stepped between them. "Var was my friend," he said once more. "In any other case I would avenge him myself. Yet I forbid this conflict."

Vara did not speak. She whipped one stick at Tyl, a lightning stroke, her eyes not leaving Neq. It was no feeble womanish blow; lovely as she was, she did know the use of her weapon.

Tyl caught it on his forearm. "Now you have struck me," he murmured softly, though a massive welt was forming. Had there been a man's weight behind the blow, or

had Tyl been unprepared for it, his arm could have been broken. "Now give me leave to fetch my weapon, for this conflict is mine."

Vara waited stonily. It was obvious she had not wanted to battle Tyl, and did not wish to engage him now. But she *had* struck him, and he had been unarmed—deliberately, for Tyl always knew where his weapons were. She was committed by the code of the circle.

Tyl fetched his sticks. Neq was relieved; had Tyl taken the sword to her, that death would have been charged to Neq's own conscience. Tyl intended only to interfere.

Yet why was he bothering? First he had balked Neq's own attempt at suicide; now he balked Vara. He was preserving Neq's life—when he should have been satisfied to see it end.

Now Vara threw off her smock and stood naked but for sturdy hiking moccasins, despite the chill of the air: as fine a figure of a woman as Neq had ever seen. She was full-breasted and narrow-waisted, well-muscled for a girl yet quite feminine. Her black hair flowed proudly behind her, almost to her hips.

Full bosomed . . . Neq was fascinated. Each breast stood round and true, a work of private beauty, an aspect of passionate symmetry. He had serenaded a breast like that, so long ago. . . .

It was fitting that such a breast now declared vengeance against him.

But Tyl stood between, and if Vara thought to dazzle him with her bodily attributes and so diminish his guard, she had forgotten that he had a daughter older than she.

She fenced with him, impatient at the delay Tyl represented. She wanted only to get at Neq, who had not moved.

The sticks spun and struck, wood meeting metal. Tyl had the advantage of superior Helicon weapons, and his experience was more than Vara's whole life. He parried her blows without effort.

Neq could not bring himself to care particularly about the fight or its outcome. The twin shocks of this final unjustified slaying of Var, and the identity and appearance of Vara, had almost completely unmanned him. Discover what had gone wrong with Helicon? He could not discover what had gone wrong with himself!

Meanwhile, man and woman fought. Vara ducked and whirled about, her hair spinning about her breasts and hips like a light cloak. From that floating coiffure her sticks came up to rap sharply at Tyl's wrist, one side and another. A deft maneuver! Vara was, if anything, a better sticker than her husband had been.

But Tyl flicked his wrist out of the way and engaged in a counter maneuver that sent her stumbling back far less gracefully. "Very nice, little girl! Your father Sol disarmed me with a similar motion and made me part of his empire, before you existed. He taught you well!"

But there was more to the circle than good instruction, obviously. Tyl had never since been defeated by the sticks.

Had Neq been fighting, even with no guilt-related inhibitions, he would have been bemused by those dancing breasts playing peek-a-boo behind that black hair, and completely unable to strike at Vara's lovely lithe body. In fact he was bemused now. Her femininity was as potent in combat as her sticks.

Suddenly she turned away and kicked back, her heel striking for Tyl's knee. But again he moved aside in time.

"The Weaponless—your other father?—crippled me with that blow when he was driving for the empire himself. But after my knees healed they became leary, and have not been injured since."

If Vara had not realized she was sparring with the top warrior of the old empire, she surely knew it now. Tyl was no longer young, but nothing short of Neq's sword had hope of moving him out of the circle. Vara was fifteen and female; those were insurmountable obstacles.

Tyl was merely blocking, of course. He had no interest in hurting this beautiful girl; he only meant to convince her that she could not have her way.

Vara required considerable convincing. She whirled, she feinted, she sent a barrage of blows against the man. She knew an astonishing variety of tricks—but there was no trick that could overmatch Tyl's reach and strength and experience.

Finally, panting, she yielded far enough to speak. "Warrior, what is it you want?"

"Neq slew Var in fair combat. Even as I could disarm

you now, so could Neq defeat Var. I would not face Neq with the stick myself. Forswear your vengeance."

"No!" she cried, and launched another flurry of blows at him.

"No!" Neq also cried. "It was not fair combat. Var withheld his attack, he opened his guard, saying we had no quarrel. Then I slew him."

Tyl retreated, dismayed by the words rather than by the girl's offense. "This is not like you, Neq."

"It is too much like me! I have slain innocent men before. I did not understand in time. I thought it was a combat mistake, or a ruse. My sword was there—"

"Desist, girl," Tyl said, just as though she were his daughter playing a game. And Vara desisted. "Neq, you place me awkwardly."

"Let her have her vengeance. It is fair."

"That I cannot."

"You admit you slew him unguarded!" Vara blazed at Neq.

"Yes. As I have others."

"In the name of vengeance!" Tyl cried, as if proving a point.

"In the name of vengeance." Neq was sick of it.

"In the name of vengeance," Vara repeated, and now the tears showed on her cheeks.

"Yet you could have slain him fairly," Tyl said. "And you thought you were avenging—her."

"I misunderstood. I did not let him explain. I slew him without reason, and I am tired of slaying, and of the sword, and of life." Neq faced Vara. "Come, widow. Strike. I will not lift weapon against you."

"If you strike him thus," Tyl said to her, "you become guilty of the same crime you avenge. Knowingly."

"Nevertheless," she said.

"Understand him first—only then are you justified. Learn what he is, what he contemplates."

"What can he be, what can he plan, that will repay what he has stolen from me!" she cried.

"Nevertheless."

She cried, she cursed in Chinese, she threw her sticks at the ground; but she was already committed. As was Neq.

CHAPTER FOURTEEN

"Melt that?" the smithy cried incredulously. "That's Ancient-technology steel! My forge won't touch it!"

"Then sever it," Neq said.

"You don't understand. It would take a diamond drill to dent that metal. I just don't have the equipment."

No doubt an exaggeration, for Helicon had made the weapon. But these northerners were closer to the past wonders than were the nomads, having houses and heaters and even a few operating machines, and so they stood in greater awe of the Ancients. Neq himself stood in awe, after learning what had been done at Helicon. Perhaps this smithy was superstitious; at any rate, he would not do the job.

"I must be rid of it," Neq said. As long as his sword remained, he was a killer. Who would fall next—Vara? Tyl? Dr. Jones? The sword had to go.

The smithy shook his head. "You have to cut off your arm at the elbow. And that would probably kill you, because we don't have medical facilities in this town for such an operation. Find the man who put that sword on you; let him get it off again."

"He is three thousand miles away."

"Then you'll just have to wear it a while longer."

Neq looked at his sword-arm, frustrated. The shining blade had become an anathema to him, for while he wore it he was inseparable from his guilt.

He looked about the shop, unwilling to give up so readily. Metal hung from all the walls—horse shoes, plow-shares (so *that* was what the crazies had suggested he make his sword into, facetiously!) axes, bags of nails. All

the products of the smithy's art. The man was evidently competent; he must make a good living, in the fashion of these people who worked for recompense. In one corner dangled a curved piece of metal with a row of little panels mounted along a center strand. Neq could envision no possible use for it.

The smithy followed his gaze. "Don't you nomads believe in music?"

"A harp!" Neq exclaimed. "You made a harp!"

"Not I," the man said, laughing. He took it down fondly. "This is no harp; it has no strings. But it *is* a musical instrument. A glockenspiel. See—these are chimes—fourteen plates of graduated size, each a different note. I traded a hundred pounds of topgrade building spikes for this. I'm no musician, but I know fine metalwork! I've no idea who made it, or when—before the Blast, maybe. You play it with a hammer. Listen."

The smithy had become quite animate as he described his treasure. He fetched a little wooden hammer and struck lightly on the plates. The sound was like bells, seldom heard in the crazy demesnes. Every tone was clear yet lingering, and quite lovely.

Neq was entranced. This evoked old and pleasant memories. There had been a time when he was known for his voice as well as his sword . . . before the fall of the empire and horrors thereafter. He had sung to Neqa. . . .

He could not make his sword into a plowshare, obviously, but it gave him an idea. He did not have to cut off his weapon; he merely had to nullify it. To make it impossible for him to fight.

"The glock and spiel—fasten it to this sword so it won't come off," he said.

"To the sword! A marvelous instrument like this?" The smithy's horror was genuine.

"I have things to barter. What do you require for it?"

"I would not sell this glockenspiel for barter or for money! Not when it is only going to be destroyed by a barbarian with no appreciation for culture. Don't you understand? *This is a musical instrument!*"

"I know music. Let me have your little hammer."

"I won't let you close to an antique like this! Get out of my shop!"

Neq started to raise his sword, but caught himself. This was the very reaction he sought to quell: sword before reason. He had to *convince* the smithy, not intimidate him.

He looked about again. There was a barrel of water near the great anvil, and he was thirsty. He had walked all day with Tyl and Vara, and come into this village on sudden inspiration when he saw the smithy shop. If the man could only be made to understand. . . .

> All day I faced the barren waste
> > without the taste of water—
> Cool, clear, water!
> Dan and I with throats burned dry
> > and souls that cry for water—
> Cool, clear, water!

The smithy stared at him, astonished. "You can sing! I never heard a finer voice!"

Neq had not known he was going to sing. The need had arisen, the mood fit—and a silence of six years had been broken. "I know music," he said.

The man hesitated. Then he pushed the glockenspiel forward. "Try it with this."

Neq took the manner awkwardly in his pincers and tapped a note. The sound thrilled him, more perfect than any voice could be. He shifted key to match, striking the same note steadily to make a beat.

> The nights are cool and I'm a fool
> > each star's a pool of water—
> Cool, clear, water!

The smithy considered. "I would not have believed it! You want this to play?"

Neq nodded.

"Price was not my objection. I see you would have trouble playing the glockenspiel in the wilderness, unless it were attached. Yes. It *could* be done . . . I would have to coat the blade with an adhesive . . . but you would never be able to fight again. Do you realize that?"

They bargained, and it was done. He became Neq the Glockenspiel.

"A *what*?" Vara demanded, surprised and suspicious. "You have beaten your sword into a *what*?"

"A glockenspiel. A percussion instrument. My sword was too bloody."

She faced away angrily. Tyl smiled.

They traveled south and east. Tyl and Neq were returning to make their report to Dr. Jones. Vara, though she did not see it that way, *was* that report. She was the only one remaining who could answer the necessary questions about the nature of Helicon's demise. But she thought she was coming to have her vengeance on Neq; she did not mean to let him escape.

Tyl did not start any conversations. Neq hardly felt like talking himself, and Vara remained sullen. They had about three thousand miles to go: between three and four months at their swift pace. It was not likely to be a pleasant trip.

But they had to work together, for the natives were generally unfriendly and the old hostels no longer existed even in the formal crazy demesnes. They were cutting across what had been known as western Canada, intending to skirt the southern boundaries of a series of large lakes, and the northern boundaries of the worst badlands. Tyl had a crazy map; it claimed such a route existed.

Someone had to forage each day for food; someone had to stand guard each night; someone had to get them safely through outlaw territories. Tyl did most of it at first. Then Vara, shamed, began to help.

Neq, stripped of his sword, could neither fight nor forage effectively. He was dependent on the other two, and mortified by the situation. It was hard to give up a weapon, and not merely in the circle! All he could do was keep watch—and for that he had to stay awake. That was not easy after a twelve hour hike, each day.

One night as they camped by a river, Neq consoled himself by striking the tip of his pincers against the bells of his glockenspiel. He had not tried to play it since leaving the smithy's shop. But the sound was not proper; metal on metal annoyed him. He took the little wooden

hammer and tapped the notes experimentally, regaining the feel of the music. Soon he was running through the scales, improving his competence while the others slept. It was possible to play entire melodies with no more than the hammer! He began to hum, measuring his voice against the clear tones of the instrument. It was there in him yet: the joy of music.

Finally he unstopped the voice that had been dormant during the entire time of killing, and that had emerged only when his sword was buried. He sang, accompanying himself carefully on the glockenspiel:

> Then only say that you'll be mine
> And our love will happy be
> Down beside some water flow
> By the banks of the O-hi-o.

He sang all of it, though this was not that river and his voice, despite the smithy's compliment, was imperfect now, a creaky shadow of its prime. But the instrument gave him a certainty of key he had not had before, and the spirit of the melody suffused him with its odd rapture.

As he sang, he rocked to the lovely, tortured vision of it: the young woman taking a walk by the river strand, refusing to marry the suiter, being threatened by his knife at her breast, and finally drowned. An ugly story but a beautiful song—one of his favorites, before he had come too close to living it. There were tears in his eyes, making his watch difficult.

"Your wife—did you kill her too?"

He was not startled to find Vara awake. He had known he could not sing aloud without arousing her curiosity or ire. "I must have."

"I ask only because I have to," she said bitterly. "Tyl balked me, on pain I should know you. Before I kill you. I saw you had no bracelet."

"She was a crazy," he said, not caring what she might think about Neqa.

"A crazy! What have you to do with them?"

"I thought to rebuild Helicon."

"You lie!" she cried, clutching at her sticks, which were always with her, warrior-style.

Neq looked at her tiredly. "I *kill*. I do not *lie*."

She turned away. "I may not kill you yet."

"You want the mountain dead?"

"No!"

"Then tell me: what is Helicon to you? Were you not kept prisoner there, and betrayed at the end? Don't you hate it yet?"

"Helicon was my home! I loved it!"

He studied her in the moonlight, perplexed. "Do you want it restored, then, as I do?"

"No! Yes!" she cried, crying.

Neq let it be. He knew what grief was, and the burning for revenge. And futility. Vara was in the throes of it all, as he had been when Neqa died. As he was still. It might be months, years before she made sense to others or to herself, and she would not be so pretty, then.

He tapped the flat metal bells of the glockenspiel again, picking out a new tune. Then he sang, and Vara did not protest.

> "I know my love by her way of walking
> And I know my love by her way of talking . . ."

Tyl slept on, though their conversation was not quiet.

"When I first saw Var," Vara said, "he was standing on the plateau of Mt. Muse, looking down from the rim. He could have dropped a rock on me, but he didn't, because he wasn't the kind to take advantage."

"Why should anyone drop a rock on you?" Neq demanded, disliking this reference to the dead man.

"We were meeting in single combat. You know that."

"Why did Bob send a child?" Was the truth at last within reach?

"And after we fought, it was cold, and he held me so I would not shiver. He gave me his heat, for he was always generous."

They were working at cross purposes.

"Would you warm your enemy if he were cold?" she asked him.

"No."

"You see. Var was a giver of life, not of death."

She had meant to hurt him, and she had succeeded.

How could he return to this bitter girl what he had taken from her?

"Ambush," Tyl murmured. "Well-laid; I saw it too late. You two break while I cover the retreat."

Neither Neq or Vara reacted openly; both were too well versed in tactics. They exchanged a glance of chagrin, for neither had been aware of the situation. But if Tyl said there was an ambush, there was an ambush, though the forest seemed deserted.

Vara turned nonchalantly and started back. Neq shrugged and followed, while Tyl whistled idly and moved toward a tree as though for a call of nature. But it was too late; the trap sprung, and they were neatly in it.

From front, back and sides armed men appeared and converged. They carried clubs and staffs and sticks. No blades, oddly. Now Neq understood how the three had walked into the trap: the ambushers came out of holes in the ground! The trapdoors were flush with the forest floor and covered with leaves so that nothing showed until they opened.

But this was a great deal of trouble for a mere ambush! And no sharp weapons! Why?

Tyl and Vera had run together the moment the men appeared. Now they stood back to back, sticks in each hand. Neq remained where he was; his first abortive motion to uncover his sword had reminded him that he was no longer armed. If he joined the other two he would only hamper them.

The men closed in. Neq remembered the similar maneuver of a tribe six years before, closing in on a truck. If he could have known in time to save Neqa . . . !

"Yield," the leader of the ambush said.

No one answered. They were too wise in the ways of outlawism to doubt that death would be cleanest in battle. Such elaborate preparations would not have been made merely to recruit tribesmen!

"Yield or die!" the leader said. A ring formed about the two stickers, and another around Neq. "Who are you?"

"Tyl of Two Weapons."

"Vara—the Stick."

The ambusher considered. "Only one Tyl of Two

Weapons I know of, and this is pretty far out of his territory."

Tyl didn't bother to answer. His sticks remained ready; his sword hung at his side.

"If it *is* him, we won't take him alive," the leader said. "*Or* his woman."

Vara didn't deign to correct him. Her sticks were ready too.

"Why would he travel without his tribe?" another man inquired. "And with a girl young enough to be his daughter?"

"*That's* why, maybe," the leader said. He came over to Neq. "But this one doesn't talk, and he covers his weapon. Who are you?"

Slowly Neq raised his left arm. The loose sleeve fell away and the metal pincers came into view.

There was a murmur in the group. The leader stepped back. "I have heard of a man who had his hands cut off. So he had his sword grafted on, and—"

Neq nodded. "They were ambushers."

The circle about him widened as the men edged away.

"We have a gun," the leader said. "We do not want to kill you, but if you move—"

"We only pass through," Neq said. "We have no business with you." He was now talking to distract attention from Tyl, who might then get out his own gun unobserved. There were enough men here to overcome the little party, though that would not have been the case had Neq's blade been in place and Tyl's gun ready. The outlaw's gun was not the advantage they supposed.

"You *have* business with us," the leader said. "We require a service from you. Perform it and you shall go free with the wealth of our tribe on your shoulders. Fail it, and you shall die."

Neq ached with fury to be addressed in this manner, as though any threat by any straggling outlaw could move him. He had destroyed a tribe of such arrogance before. But he had given up the sword. Now he would live or die without it. "What is your service?"

"Walk the haunted forest at night."

Neq stifled a laugh. "You fear ghosts?"

"With reason. By day the forest harms no one, and

stands athwart our richest hunting-grounds, just a few miles down this trail. But the ghosts strike those who enter at night. First the blades, then the dull weapons. Banish our spook: walk it at night and live. We will reward you richly for breaking the spell. Our food, our equipment, our women——"

"Keep your trifles! Feed us today; tonight we challenge your ghost. Together. Not for your sake, but because it crosses our route."

"You will keep your sword covered in our camp?"

"I keep my arm covered if no man annoys me."

"And you?" the leader called to Tyl.

"And I," Tyl agreed, and Vara also nodded.

Slowly the encircling men lowered their weapons.

As the sun descended they were ushered to the edge of the haunted forest. It seemed normal—mixed birch, beech and ash, some pine, with pockets of pasture heavily grown. Rabbits scooted away from the party. Good hunting, certainly!

"Are there radiation markers near here?" Tyl inquired.

"Some. But that danger is over. We have a click-box; the kill-rays are gone."

"Yet men still die," Tyl murmured.

"Only by night."

That certainly didn't sound like radiation. It didn't come and go; it faded slowly, and was not affected by daylight.

"If Var were here——" Vara began. And caught herself.

"It is about ten miles," the tribe leader said. "We have a smaller digging downstream. Sometimes we need to travel between the two at night—but we must hike twice as far, over the mountain. No one passes the valley by night."

"The river looks clean," Tyl observed. "Your footpath is open?"

"Throughout. There are no natural pitfalls, no killer-animals here. Once there were shrews, but we exterminated them. Now there are deer, rabbits, game-birds. No hunting animals."

"You have found bodies?"

"Always. Some without marking. Some mutilated. Some

dead fighting. We never send a man alone or unarmed, yet all perish."

So they ambushed innocent travelers to send here, Neq thought. Very neat, but none too clever. Hadn't it occurred to them that whoever conquered the haunted forest might have second thoughts about the manner he had been introduced to it? He might decide on a bit of vengeance. In that case, solution of the forest riddle could be disastrous for the tribe.

Tyl began to walk. Neq and Vara followed quickly. It was not dark yet, but night would set in long before they got through the forest. A ten mile hike by night, rested and fed—routine, except for ghosts!

When they were well away from the tribesmen, they split, ducking down out of sight on either side of the trail. No word was spoken; all three were conversant with such technique. The greatest danger might be from the men behind, not the supposed ghosts in front. Strangers might be deliberately killed in the forest to sustain the notoriety of the region, for surely the tribesmen could not be entirely ignorant of the nature of the threat, whatever it was.

But no one was following. Cautiously the three proceeded, Tyl flanking the forest side of the trail, Vara following the river side, and Neq, who could not fight, moving cautiously down the center. He held a thin stick in his pincers, probing for deadfalls, and he walked hunched to avoid a potential trip-wire or hanging noose. He expected to encounter something deadly, and not a ghost!

In an hour they had covered less than two miles. Their extreme caution seemed to have been wasted; no threat of any kind materialized. But eight miles remained, and eight hours of darkness. The fear of the tribesmen had been genuine; perhaps they delved underground because of a lingering terror of the forest surface.

The way was beautiful, even at night. The somber trees overhung the path to the west, highlighted by the full moon, and the river coursed slowly on the east side, and great vines covered with night-blooming flowers lay along the ground. The heavy fragrance surrounded them increasingly, musky and refreshing in the slight breeze.

Neq recalled his childhood. It had been nice, then,

with his family and his sister. All the subsequent glory and ruin of empire could not compare with that early security. Why had he left it?

Hig the Stick! The man had cast his lustful gaze on Nemi, Neq's young twin sister! Neq clenched his sword-hand in reminiscent fury and bravado—and remembered he had no hand. Yod the Outlaw had taken it—

Time twisted about. It was dark, but Neq could see well enough in the diffused moonlight. A shape was coming at him, and it was the shape of Yod. Yod, whose foul loin had—

Neq whipped up his gleaming sword and launched himself at the enemy. A head would ride the stake tonight!

Contact! But his sword did not handle properly. It clanged, a discordant jangle.

Shocked, he remembered. No sword! This was the glockenspiel, for making music.

He peered more carefully at his opponent. "Tyl! Do you raise your sword to me in anger?"

Startled, Tyl stepped back. "Neq! I mistook you for—someone else. But he is dead. I must be overtired. I do not raise my sword to you."

Mutually shaken, they retreated from each other. How could such a confusion have come about? Had the glockenspiel not sounded, they might easily have fought, and Tyl could have slain him unwittingly. What irony, when they had not yet even encountered the menace of the forest!

Another shape approached him, stealthily. But Neq was far too experienced to be caught unawares. This was not Tyl—it was not even male!

Neqa! Blonde Miss Smith, the crazy woman! He ran to embrace her.

"Minos!" she cried. She was naked; her bosom heaved in outline as she brought up her sticks.

Sticks? That could not be Neqa! It had to be—Vara. Coming to kill him. Coming for her vengeance.

But she dropped her weapon again. "I may not resist you, Minos. Come, spit me on your monstrous member. Only let Var go." And she spread her arms in a kind of invitation.

What was happening to her, to him, to Tyl? Neq had

fancied Neqa before him; now Vara fancied Var. Or Minos, whoever *he* was. And Tyl had attacked. . . .

Neq retreated, trying to straighten it out, but confused images continued to spin in his brain. The standing trees seemed menacing, the river was a giant snake, the darkness itself was suffocating. He felt the urge to fight, to kill, to destroy.

Now Tyl was coming again, bearing his sticks. Vara too. Neq got out of the way with almost pusillanimous haste, not liking this situation at all. Tyl might have his grudges and Vara might have reason to kill him, but this was not proper and certainly not normal for either.

Tyl met Vara. "Get out of my camp, you slut!" Tyl cried, raising his sticks.

"No, Bob, no!" she screamed, retreating but keeping her face to him. "Touch me and I kill you!"

They were about to fight each other—and Neq's status was not the issue! They were like demons, prowling about each other in the night, too cautious to strike until the blow could be lethal. Like outlaws, killers of Neqa. . . .

Neq charged, his sword whistling. Death to them both! But he did what he never did: snagged his foot in a ground-vine and crashed down ignominiously. The dirt and leaves of the forest floor ground into his face, and the glockenspiel jangled again—an incongruous burst of sound.

Neq rolled over and spat out mud. His body had been humbled, but for the moment his mind was clear. *These were the ghosts!* These maddened people, seeing visions and attacking each other! That was the death that lurked in this forest!

The fragrance of the night-bloomers came again. anesthetizing his nostrils with its splendor. Like alcohol, the fumes altered his perspective, made the real unreal, the unreal real. . . .

There was killing to be done. The spooks were almost upon him. Neq lurched up, flung himself down the steep bank, into the black water of the river. The shock of cold brought his brain to full clarity again.

There was death here, all right. Death from the spirits. Vapor spirits—windblown alcohol that evoked the kill-passions. A gaseous murderer who left no footprint, no scar. The haunt of the forest. He knew it for what it was,

now—yet it could not be avoided. A man had to breathe!
Physical shocks could abate it only temporarily; already
that insidious fragrance was seeping through his nose and
into his lung and on to his brain, modifying his percep-
tion. substituting more evocative images. . . .

The sword could not battle this! Only an unarmed
man, alone, could hope to survive. And what man would
enter this forest that way?

Neq looked at his glistening glockenspiel, the metal
glowing faintly in the moonlight. Already it was wavering into the sword again. But it was a ghost sword; his
real sword was dead. The ghost-sword could deliver him
only into death, for he would be weaponless without believing it.

Suddenly he felt lonely. His existence had never seemed
so futile.

He tapped the sword, finding the bells of the glockenspiel by touch and sound. That was one way to keep
reminding himself that what he saw was false. He began
to pick out a tune, there in the water—the water that
seemed like rich warm blood—and the notes were lovely
and clear. They expanded to form a melody, each note
bearing its private animation but the theme expanding to
encompass the world. The tune was marching; each beat
was a bright foot. He saw them treading into the sky.

He sang:

> "You must walk this lonesome valley
> You have to walk it by yourself!
> Oh, nobody else can walk it for you . . ."

The melody took hold of him compellingly, carried him
up out of the river, gave him a glorious and sad strength.

> "We must walk this lonesome valley—"

Shapes came at him, male and female . . . but the
music daunted them. Like a cordon of warriors, the band
of notes swept back the opposition, softened its determination. He sang and sang, more wonderfully than ever
before.

"We have to walk it by ourselves
Oh, nobody else can walk it for us . . ."

Then, hesitatingly, the shapes joined in.

"We have to walk it by ourselves . . ."

With burgeoning confidence Neq started another sequence, marching down along the path while his body dripped wet water and the others followed.

"Takes a worried man
To sing a worried song!"

and the ghost-echo agreed, and they sang together, louder.

"It takes a worried man
To sing a worried song!
I'm worried now,
But I won't be worried long!"

Victoriously, Neq continued, throwing new forces of song and music into the fray as the old troops lost their potency against the ghost-fragrance. On down the path, through the dark forest, singlemindedly dispelling the insidious fumes with voice and instrument, leading the captive shapes out of the lonesome valley.

Then it was done. Embarrassed, Neq broke off his singing, finding his voice hoarse. They had walked and sang for hours. Tyl and Vara were there, shaking their heads as though waking from nightmare.

Dawn was coming.

CHAPTER FIFTEEN

"Stay clear of the tribesmen," Tyl said. "Let them think we are dead, or they may kill us to preserve their secret. We'll sleep in the forest today."

"The haunted forest?" Vara demanded nervously.

"It is safe by day. We shall want to visit it again by night."

Again!" Neq was incredulous. "We nearly killed each other there! The ghosts—"

"You spared us that," Tyl said. "Your weapon vanquished them and brought us out. But our conquest is not complete until we know what causes the effect, and why the outlaw tribe chooses to sacrifice ignorant strangers to it. Surely they know; they can not be so stupid as to spend their lives adjacent to it and not fathom the mystery. I have never fled from an enemy—or left a potential enemy behind me."

He was right. An enemy neglected was doubly dangerous. "The flowers," Neq said. "Night bloomers."

Tyl removed his weapons. "Sticks to you," he said to Vara. "Sword to you, Neq."

Neq could not hold the sword effectively in his claw, but he understood what Tyl was doing.

Tyl went to a hanging vine and plucked a closed bud. He pulled it open and put it to his nose. He sniffed. "Faint—not the same." He sniffed again, deeply. Then a third time.

His manner changed. His eyes widened, then narrowed. His hand went for his sword.

Then he grinned and dropped the flower. "This is it!"

he cried. "I'm high on it now—but I know what it is. Don't come near me—"

They knew what he meant. The weak, temporary daylight effect of one bud might not overcome a forewarned man, any more than an ounce of alcohol would. But the massed fragrance of thousands of blooms, in the flush of their strength, building up all night long—that would be another matter.

"I don't think we'd better stay the night," Vara said. "It fuels our passions. . . ."

Yes. And there was already a matter of death-vengeance between them.

Tyl went down to the river and dunked his head. He came back dripping but triumphant. "We know the haunt now!"

"We still have to breathe at night," Neq said, returning the sword. "We got through once, but it would be foolhardy to risk it again."

Tyl considered. "Yes. I knew what it was doing to me, just now, but I didn't care. If I had had my weapons—"

"It was the same with me last night," Neq admitted. "But all I had was song."

"The *flower* is the weapon," Tyl said. "One that would bring down a tribe. If others knew of it, it would be planted everywhere. We must make it ours."

Vara rubbed her eyes. None of them had slept yet, and the tribesmen could soon appear. Tyl was probably correct: the tribe had more interest in maintaining the secret of the forest than in exposing it. Dead men would spread its reputation, and prevent other tribes from moving in on the good hunting preserve. Naturally only strangers would be sacrificed. It was time to hide and sleep.

Tyl nodded. "We'll make a baffle by the water, under the bank, and sleep together without posting guard. If they find us, we'll stall until dusk—or dive into the river."

The tribesmen were either too confident or too stupid to search thoroughly. No one found them. Refreshed, the three walked to the southern fringe as the blooms opened. No tribesmen stood guard, understandably.

"If light makes them close . . ." Tyl murmured.

Neq jumped. Tyl was leading the way directly to a

large group of the opening flowers! "Careful—moonlight didn't stop them last night."

"Maybe it *did*," Vara said. "Maybe that's why we got through. We got only part of the effect. . . ."

"Stand upwind," Tyl said. He brought out his light. It was a small kerosene lantern with a circular wick and adjustable mantle, and it had a spark-striker attachment. It had been cumbersome to carry, and Tyl had seldom used it before, preferring his own night vision. He had never been one to travel unprepared, however.

He ignited the lantern, adjusted it for maximum brilliance, and brought it near the vine. There was a reflector, so that a surprising amount of illumination was concentrated in that vicinity.

Slowly the flowers closed.

"If light seals them, darkness must open them," Tyl said. "If we carried a vine with us—"

"It would die," Neq said, leary of the notion.

"A growing vine, with its earth. Set in a box with this light."

"A weapon!" Vara exclaimed, catching on. "Cover it by day, leave it among enemies. . . ."

Tyl nodded. "Pick it up when they are dead. Turn on the light. Travel on."

"A counter-ambush," Vara finished, her eyes seeming to glow in the night.

More killing, Neq thought. No end to it, whether with sword or flower. Yet the plan had merit. "This is a fringe zone. Will it grow beyond this forest?"

"Delicate mutation," Vara said excitedly. "Needs the right temperature, water, soil, shade—"

"We'll find out," Tyl said. "Man has tamed plants before."

The two of them hastened to dig up an appropriate sample and fix its enclosure. Neq had qualms, however. Any oversight, and the flowers could wipe out their little party. This was an uncertain ally.

"Var was self-sacrificing," Vara said. "He always helped me, even when I was pretending to be a boy. When we slept in the snows and I was stung by a badlands worm, he carried me back to the only hostel though his own

ankle had been turned. And he fought to preserve my rest, though he was not then fit for the circle. He was exhausted and his foot was swollen—"

Neq had to listen. This was the man he had killed. He could not restore what he had taken without first comprehending her loss. He understood what she was doing: Tyl had stopped her from attacking him with the sticks, so now she turned to words. Her voiced memories were terrible because they brought a dead man back to life, multiplying Var's greatness and the agony of his demise.

Her verbal campaign was calculated, and he knew it, but still it hurt him. He had no legitimate defense. He had killed her husband, the man who should have been his friend, and now could never be.

Sometimes when she said Var he heard Neqa. Neq himself had become Yod: slayer of the innocent.

It worked. The vine prospered under Tyl's care, and a minimum flame in the lantern kept the narcotic flowers closed. But normally they set the plant down some distance from their night camp and let it bloom, so that its natural cycle would not be unduly disrupted. They had no concern about animals bothering it; the fragrance was defense enough. A mile's separation seemed more than sufficient—less than a mile when the wind was sure—though upon occasion they smelled the faint perfume and felt a token enhancement of animal passion.

They did encounter another ambush, as such things were too common in this post-crazy world. They managed to barricade themselves defensively for an hour, using Tyl's gun to keep the outlaws at bay, while the covered vine slowly opened its flowers and poured its essence forth through vents in the box. Neq sang and played his glockenspiel when he felt the effect, confining himself to songs of solidarity and justice while the fragrance wafted into the afternoon air. Tyl and Vara joined him, laying their weapons on the ground under their feet, out of sight of the enemy. The ambushers laughed, thinking the whole show ludicrous.

Then the enemy warriors fell to quarreling among themselves. The fumes had spread. They were not strong, but the ambushers were aggressive and unsuspecting. Tyl un-

covered the vine to let in daylight, for they had to be free of the effect themselves before moving out. They were on guard against their own raw emotions, but there was no sense taking chances.

The ambushers were in disarray, not comprehending the reason. The strong passions of men driven to outlawry had been sufficient. Once the conflict started, it fed on itself.

Neq made the mistake of singing a love song. He became acutely conscious of Vara next to him, almost sixteen and at the height of her womanhood. He became sexually excited, not caring what else had passed between them. But Tyl was there, and in the sudden fierce resentment of the man's interfering presence Neq realized the danger and forced himself to shift songs. Love Vara? Safer to kiss a badlands kill-moth!

It was time to move out. "Onward Christian Soldiers!" Neq sang. The words were incomprehensible, but the tune and spirit were apt.

They marched singing through a wilderness of carnage. Only occasionally did they have to defend themselves from attack. Some pairs were locked in combat, some in amour, for the women had been drawn into the activity. A man and a woman snarled and bit at each other in the midst of copulation. Children were fighting as viciously as adults, and some were already dead.

The passion would pass, but the tribe would never quite recover.

Vara's campaign continued. Neq learned how Var had saved her from a monster machine in a tunnel—the same tunnel Neq had lacked the courage to enter—and from a hive of wasp-women, and how he had interposed his body to take arrows intended for her. He had fought the god-animal Minos to save her from a fate almost as bad as death.

Var had evidently had a short but full life. The documentation of that life was sufficient to cover more than a month of travel, at any rate. The climate became warmer as they moved south and east and further into spring, but the girl's language never ameliorated.

When she finally ran out of Var's virtues, she started on Var's faults.

"My husband was not pretty," Vara said. "He was hairy, and his back was hunched, and his hands and feet were deformed, and his skin was mottled." Neq knew that, for he had fought the man. "His voice was so hoarse it was hard to understand him." Yes. With clever enunciation, Neq might have understood enough in time to withhold his thrust. "He could not sing at all. I love him yet."

Gradually Neq got the thrust of this new attack. Neq himself was handsome, apart from the lattice of scars he had from years of combat and the mutilation of his hands. His voice was smooth and controlled. He could sing well. Vara held his very assets against him, making him ashamed of them.

It was like the vine narcotic. Neq knew what she was doing, but was powerless to oppose it. He had to listen, had to respond, had to hate himself as she hated him. He was a killer, worse than the man who had killed his own mate.

Tyl did not interfere.

In the next month of their travel, Vara grew especially sullen. Her campaign was not working, for Neq only accepted her taunts. "I had everything!" she exclaimed in frustration. "Now I have nothing. Not even vengeance."

She was learning.

She was silent for a week. Then: "Not even his child."

For Var had been sterile. Her father Sol had been castrate; she had been conceived on his bracelet by Sos the Rope, who later gave his own bracelet to Sosa at Helicon. So her husband, like her father, had had no child.

Neq knew that twisted story, now, and understood why the Weaponless, who had been Sos, had pursued Var. Vengeance, again! But Var had been hard to catch, for his discolored skin had been sensitive to radiation, a marvelous advantage near the badlands. But that ability had come at the cost of fertility.

"And my mother Sosa was barren," Vara cried. "Am I to be barren too?"

Tyl looked meaningfully at Neq.

Var had been naive. Neq was not. That had been estab-

lished and reestablished in the past two months, to his inevitable discredit. But this shocked him. The meaning of Tyl's original stricture had suddenly come clear.

Vara wanted a baby. . . .

She didn't seem to realize what she had said, or to comprehend why Tyl had stopped her from attacking Neq at the outset.

Yet what was in Tyl's mind? If he thought it important that Vara have her baby, there were other ways. As many ways as there were men in the world. Why this? Why Neq, Vara's enemy? Why dishonor?

There was an answer. Vara did not want just a baby— she wanted a child to Var. Any infant she bore would be Vari, the line of Var. Just as she herself had been born Soli, child of the castrate Sol. The bracelet, not the man, determined parentage in the eyes of the nomads. And what man would abuse Var's bracelet and his own honor by contributing to such adultery, however attractive the girl might be?

What man indeed—except one already shed of his bracelet, and so hopelessly sullied by his own crimes that violation of another bracelet could hardly make a difference? What man, except one bound by oath to return a life taken?

What man but Neq!

CHAPTER SIXTEEN

Now it was Tyl's turn to advance his cause, and Neq's to stand aside. The trek continued into the third month, interrupted by strategies and combats and natural hazards, but the important interaction was between Tyl and Vara. Vara's initial fury had been spent, and she was now vulnerable.

It started subtly. One day Tyl would ask her a question, seemingly innocuous, but whose answer forced her to consider her own motivations. Another day he would question Neq, bringing out some minor aspect of his background. In this way Tyl established that Vara's closest ties were to Sol, not her biological father, and to Sosa, not her natural mother, and that Sol and Sosa had lived together in deliberate violation of both their bracelets, making a family for Soli/Vara.

"It's different in Helicon," she said defensively. "There are no real marriages there. There aren't enough women. All the men share all the women, no matter who wears the bracelets. It wouldn't be fair, otherwise." She spoke as though Helicon still existed, though she knew the truth.

"Did Sosa share with all the men, then?" Tyl inquired as though merely clarifying a point of confusion. "Even those she disliked?"

"No, there was no point. She couldn't conceive. Oh, I suppose she took a turn once in a while, if someone insisted—she's quite attractive, you know. But it didn't mean anything. Sex is just sex, in Helicon. What counts is that women have babies."

Similarly true in the nomad society, Neq thought.

"Suppose you had stayed there?" Tyl asked.

"Why should I be different? I was only eight when I left, but already—" She stopped.

Tyl didn't speak, but after a while she felt compelled to explain. "One of the men—there's no age limit, you know. He liked them young, I suppose, and there weren't many girls anyway. But I wasn't ready. So I hit him with the sticks. That was all. I never told Sol—there would have been trouble."

There certainly would have been! Neq remembered something she had cried in the flower-forest, when the visions were strong. A threat to some attacking man.

"But if you had been older—" Tyl said.

"I would have gone with him, I guess. That's the way it is, in Helicon. Preference has nothing to do with it."

"But when you married Var—would you have returned to the mountain then?"

"That was where we were going!" Then she had to explain again. "Var would have understood. I would have kept his bracelet."

But she shared some of Var's naivete, for she still didn't comprehend where Tyl was leading her.

Neq's turn as subject, then, in similar fashion. Day by day, as they marched and fought and slept. He didn't want to cooperate, but Tyl was too clever for him, phrasing questions he had to answer openly or by default. Gradually the outline of Neq's service in the empire came out, and his extreme proficiency with the sword, and the code by which he had lived. Yes, he had killed many times as a subtribe leader, but never outside the circle and never without reason. Much of it had been done at Sol's direction; none on order of the Weaponless, who had not tried to expand the empire.

Vara remained grim, not liking this seeming alignment of character.

Then Tyl came at Neq's post-empire activity. "Why did you seek the crazies?"

"The empire was falling apart, and so was the nomad society, and outlaws were ravaging the hostels. There was no food, no supplies, no good weapons. I tried to learn why the crazies had retreated."

"Why *had* they retreated?"

"They depended on supplies from Helicon, and their trucks weren't getting through. So I said I'd take a look."

Then the description of what he had found at the mountain. Vara's impassivity crumbled; tears streamed down her cheeks. "I knew it was gone," she cried. "My two fathers did it, and Var and I helped. But we didn't know it was that awful. . . ."

Thus Tyl had somehow cast Neq as the upholder of civilized values, while Sol and the Weaponless and even Var were its destroyers. What a turnabout for Vara's assumptions!

They marched a few more days. Then Tyl resumed. "Did you go alone to Helicon?"

Neq would not answer, for the memories remained raw despite the years and he did not want this part of it discussed.

Surprisingly, it was Vara who pursued the questioning now. "You married a crazy! I remember, you admitted it. Did she go with you?"

Still Neq was silent. But Tyl answered. "Yes."

"Who was she? Why did she go?" Vara demanded.

"She was called Miss Smith," Tyl said. "She was secretary to Doctor Jones, the crazy chief. She went to show the way, and to write a report. They drove in a crazy truck, all the way across America. That's the Ancient name for the crazy demesnes—America."

"I know," she said shortly. And another day: "Was she fair?"

"She was," Tyl said. "Fair as only the civilized are fair."

"*I'm* fair!"

"Perhaps you too are civilized."

She winced at the implications. "Literate?"

"Of course." Few nomads could read, but most crazies had the ability. Vara herself was literate, but neither Tyl nor Neq.

Another day: "Was she a—a real woman?"

"She turned down the Weaponless, because he wouldn't stay with the crazies."

Neq winced this time. Neqa had put it another way.

"The Weaponless was my father!" Vara flared. Then: "My natural one. Not my real one."

"Nevertheless."

"And she loved Neq?" she demanded distastefully.

"What do you think?" Tyl asked in return, with a hint of impatience.

Another day: "How could a literate, civilized woman love *him*?"

"She must have known something we do not," Tyl said with gentle irony.

Finally: "How did she die?"

Neq left them then, afraid to discover how much Tyl knew. The man was embarrassingly well versed in Neq's private life, though he had given no hint of this before.

Neq ran through the forest until he was gasping for breath, then threw himself down in the dry leaves and sobbed. This merciless reopening of the old, deep wound; this sheer indignity of public analysis!

He lay there some time, and perhaps he slept. As darkness came he saw again the bloody forest floor, felt again the fire of severed hands. Six years had become as six hours, in the agony of Neqa's loss.

What use was it to practice vengeance, when every tribe was as savage as the one he had destroyed. Any one of those outlaw tribes could have done the same. The only answer was to ignore the problem—or to abolish them all. Or at least to abolish their savagery. To strike at the root. To rebuild Helicon.

Yet here he was, after having tried his best to organize that reconstruction, subject to the bitterness of a girl who saw him as the same kind of savage. With reason. How could a savage eliminate savagery?

It was all useless. None of it could recover the woman he had loved. The body lay there, tormenting him, mocking his efforts to reform. The musky perfume of the vine-lotus enhanced its horror. He didn't care.

After a time he rose to bury the corpse. *He* was a savage, but Dr. Jones was civilized. Neq could not help himself, but he could help the crazies. He had loved one of them—this one. To that extent he loved them all. He bent to touch the body, knowing his hand would strike something else, whatever it was that was really there. A stone, perhaps.

The flesh was there, and it was warm. It was a woman. "Neqa!" he cried, wild hope surging.

Then he knew. "Vara," he muttered, turning away in disgust. What preposterous deceit!

She scrambled up and came after him, circling her arms about his waist. "Tyl told me—told me why you killed. I would have killed too! I blamed you falsely!"

"No," he said, prying ineffectively at her arms with the heel of his pincers. "What I did was useless, only making more grief. And I did kill Var." The fumes were stronger. She looked like Neqa.

"Yes!" she screamed, clinging as he moved. "I hate you for that! But now I understand! I understand how it happened."

"Then kill me now." As so many had begged *him*, when he stalked Yod's tribe. "You have honored Tyl's stricture."

"But *you* haven't!" Her grip on him tightened.

"The vine is here. I smell it. Let me go before—before I forget."

"I brought the vine! So there would be truth between us!"

He batted at her arms with the closed pincers. "There can be no truth between us! Tyl would have us defile our bracelets—"

"I know! I know! I know!" she cried. "Be done with it, Minos! Set me free!" She climbed him, reaching for his face with her mouth. She was naked; she had been that way when he first touched her, as she played corpse.

The flower drug sang complex melodies within his brain, making him overreact on an animal level to this female provocation. He crushed her to him within the living portion of his embrace, joining his lips to hers.

It was savagely sweet.

She relaxed, fitting more neatly within the circle of his arms. The glockenspiel jangled against the pincers, jolting him into momentary awareness of their situation. In that moment he wrenched away from her. His body was aflame with lust, but his mind screamed dishonor! He ran.

She ran too, fleetly. "I hate you!" she panted. "I hate your handsome face! I hate your wonderful voice! I hate your fertile penis! But I have to do it!"

In the dark he smashed into brush and spun about, trying to avoid the tangle. She dived for him again. He fended her off with the claw, trying not to hurt her but determined to keep her at bay until the narcotic wore off. As long as she was desirable to him, he had to balk her ardor.

Now *she* was fighting *him*. She had fetched a stick along the way, a branch of a tree, and she struck him about the shoulders with it, hard enough to hurt. He knocked it away, then caught it in the pincers and wrenched it loose by superior strength. But her hands remained busy, striking him on nerves so that the pain was excruciating. She had the combat art of the Weaponless, all right!

Yet muscle and experience counted heavily, and they both knew that Neq could subdue her at any time merely by striking her hard enough with his claw. She was not really trying to defeat him; her intent was to maintain physical contact until her sexuality became irresistible.

But they had left the vine behind. The air was clear, here, and so was his head. Neq saw no more visions, and reacted normally. He had won.

Realizing this, Vara stopped abruptly. "So it didn't work," she said, as though she had merely stubbed her toe. "But I tried, didn't I?"

"Yes." How was it possible to comprehend her thought processes!

"So now it's real."

"Yes." He started to get up.

She was crying, with real tears. "You monster! You denied me my love, you denied me my vengeance, you even denied me my rationale. Are you going to deny me my humiliation too?"

Hers no more than his! "Yes."

She flung herself on him again, kissing him with her teary face, bearing him back against the brush. There was blood on her body where the branches and thorns had scraped her. "I call you by your name! Neq. Neq the Sword! No artifice between us. No deceit."

"No humiliation!" he said.

"No humiliation! Do you take me now as a woman—or do I take you as a man? *It shall be!*"

It had been a long time, she was highly desirable, and there were limits. Neq sighed. He, too, had tried. "It shall be."

They made love quickly, she doing more than he because he could not use his hands.

"I never completed the act with her," he said, both satisfied and bitter. "She was afraid. . . ."

"I know," Vara said. "As were you." Then: "Now we have done it. Now there is no onus. Stay if you wish."

"It is only sex. I do not want to love you."

"You have loved me for a month," she said. "As I have you. Stay."

Neq stayed. It was the first time he had completed the act with *any* woman, and she must have known that too, but she did not show it. Gradually they explored each other, letting down the physical and emotional barriers. They did not talk; it was no longer necessary.

The second time it was much better. Vara showed him some of what she knew, and she seemed to be as experienced in this respect as he was in battle. But mostly it was love, unfettered.

CHAPTER SEVENTEEN

The trip was done. The three reported to Dr. Jones at the crazy building. Tyl, the tacit leader, did the talking, summarizing Neq's search for missing people, Tyl's own trek with Neq, their encounter with Var and Vara, and their journey back—except for the dialogue and romance.

"Neq has renounced his sword," Tyl concluded. "He wears the glockenspiel now. Yet he retains the capacity for leadership."

Dr. Jones nodded as though something significant had been said. "The others will no doubt take the matter under advisement."

Tyl and the crazy leader went to round up the "others." Neq and Vara took the vine outside where there was more light. They settled under a spreading tree.

"Tyl will be master of Helicon," Vara said. "See how close he is to the crazies."

Neq agreed. "He brings people together."

"You and I came together inevitably," she said with feminine certainty. "Helicon was your idea. You should be master."

"With this?" He uncovered the glockenspiel.

"You could change it back. The sword is still there, underneath."

It was too complicated to explain that he never had been considered for the Helicon office. "If I wore the sword again, you would have to kill me."

She frowned, surprised. "I suppose I would."

A little boy about four years old wandered by, spotting them. "Who are you?" he asked boldly.

"Neq the Glockenspiel."

"Vara the Stick."

"I'm Jimi. You have funny hands."

"They are metal hands," Neq said, surprised that the boy had not been frightened. "To make music."

"My daddy Jim has metal guns. They make bangs."

"Music is better."

"It is not!"

"Listen." And Neq lifted the glockenspiel, took the little hammer in his pincers, and began to play. Then he sang:

> A farmer one day was a traveling to town
> Hey! Boom-fa-le-la,
>   sing fa-le-la,
>   boom fa-le-la lay!
> Saw a crow in a fir tree way up in the crown
> Hey! Boom fa-le-la,
>   sing fa-le-la,
>   boom fa-le-la lay!

"What's a town?" the boy inquired, impressed.

"A nomad camp with crazy buildings."

"I know what a boom falela is! A gun."

Vara laughed. "I want one like him," she murmured.

"Find Jim the Gun, then."

"After this one," she said, patting her abdomen.

Neq, startled, sang another verse for the boy.

> Then the gun from his shoulder
>   he quickly brought down . . .
> And he shot that black crow
>   and it fell to the ground . . .

"I told you guns were better!"

> The feathers were made
>   into featherbeds neat . . .
> And pitchforks were made
>   from the legs and the feet . . .

"How big was that crow?" Jimi inquired, fascinated. Neq struck a loud note. "About that size."

"Oh," the boy said, satisfied. "What's that thing?"

"A flower vine."

"It is not!"

"The flowers only open in the dark. Then they smell funny, and people do funny things."

"Like crows with pitchforks?"

Vara laughed again. "Just about," she said.

Tyl emerged from the building. "They're ready."

Vara picked up the vine-pot and they went inside. Jimi followed. "He has funny hands," he informed Tyl. "But he's fun."

They were all there: the group of odd-named oldsters he had rounded up, along with Dick the Surgeon, and Sola, and several more he did not know. Apparently Dr. Jones had located more of the people on the list during Neq's absence. Some were nomads, male and female. Jimi went to one of these, evidently Jim the Gun.

Vara, poised until this moment, took Neq's covered arm. "Who's that?" she whispered, nodding specifically.

"Sola," he replied before realizing the significance of her identity. The woman had recovered more than a suggestion of her former splendor.

Vara clutched his arm as though terrified. It was entirely uncharacteristic of her.

Tyl stepped in and performed the introduction. "Sola ... Vara. You have known each other."

Sola did not make the connection, for she had not known of Var's marriage. But the others saw the resemblance as the two women stood together. "Mother and daughter ..." Dick said.

"Widows, both," Tyl said. The words seemed cruel, but they were not, for this clarified a prime source of concern and confusion at once. No further questions about that matter would be asked. That meant in turn that the more devious and less honorable relationships would not be exposed.

Yet it was awkward. Sola and Vara had parted perhaps thirteen years ago, when Vara was hardly more than a baby. What was there to say?

Once more Tyl interceded. "You both knew Var well. And Sol. And the Weaponless. As I did. Soon we must talk together of great men."

"Yes," Sola said, and Vara agreed.

"In your absence," Dr. Jones said to Neq, "we located a few more volunteers, as you see. We have screened them as well as we could, and believe they represent a viable unit. Provided suitable leadership develops."

"There are leaders here," Neq said. Did the crazy want him to affirm his support for the leader already chosen?

"The destruction of the prior Helicon suggests that its leadership was inadequate," Dr. Jones said. "We have been obliged to make certain restrictions."

Neq pondered that. Apparently he was being asked not only to support, but to nominate the leader! "You won't work with just anybody. But you can work with Tyl—"

"I return shortly to my tribe," Tyl said. "My job is done. I am not of this group. I would not leave the nomad culture or take my family under the mountain."

Neq was amazed. So Tyl, too, had been merely supporting the effort, not directing it!

"I know of Jim the Gun," Neq said. "He armed the empire for the assault on—"

"I made a mistake!" Jim broke in. "I shall not make another. I know better than to command what I once destroyed."

Apparently Dr. Jones had not set things up so neatly after all! "What are your requirements?" Neq asked the crazy. "Literacy? Helicon experience? What?"

"We would have preferred such things," Dr. Jones admitted. "We would have liked very much to have found the Weaponless. But other qualities are more important now, and we must work with what we have."

"Why not Neq?" Vara asked.

Neq laughed uncomfortably. "My leadership has become a song. I shall not kill again."

"That is one of our requirements," Dr. Jones said. "There has been too much shedding of blood."

"Then you require the impossible," Neq said grimly. "Helicon was built on blood."

"But it shall not be *rebuilt* on blood!" Dr. Jones exclaimed with unseemly vehemence for one of his character. "History has clarified the folly of violence and deceit."

Many of the people in the room were nodding agree-

ment. But Neq thought of the way the outlaws would have to be tamed, and knew the dream of nonviolent civilization was untenable.

"Neq the Sword," Sola said after a pause. "We know your history. We do not condemn you. You say you shall not kill again. How can we believe you, when your whole way of life has been based on vengeance by the sword?"

Neq shrugged. He saw already that no man who could give the absolute assurance of pacifism they demanded could be an effective leader of Helicon. He could not kill by his own arm, but he had agreed to the indirect slaughter of the flower vine during the trek here. His stance against killing had been hypocritical.

"Take him as your leader!" Vara exclaimed. "All of you are here because of him!"

"Yes," one thin old crazy agreed. "This man lifted an outlaw siege against my post, and took a message for me that brought rescue. I trust him, whatever else he has done."

Jim the Gun spoke. He was a little old nomad with curly yellow hair. "We do not question Neq's capacity. We question his judgment under pressure. I myself was ready to shoot somebody when I learned how my brother had died in Helicon—but I did not. A man who would go berserk for weeks at a time, whatever the provocation—"

"I like him," Jimi said. "He has music hands."

Startled, Jim looked at his son. "That man is Neq the Sword!"

"He says music is better'n guns. But I like him."

"We share your vision," Sola said to Neq. "But we must have a leader of inflexible temperament. A man like the Weaponless."

"The Weaponless destroyed Helicon!" Vara flared. "Can anybody even count how many men died because of him? Yet you say no killing, and you want—"

Sola looked at her sadly. "He was your father."

"*That's* why he did it! He thought I was dead. You talk about a few weeks berserk—He planned it for *years*, then he followed Var for years. *Nothing had happened to me*! And you—you sent Var to kill the man who might harm me, when no one *had*. Who are you to judge? But Neq saw his wife—Dr. Jones' own secretary, a beautiful and

literate woman—Neq saw her raped by fifty men, and then they cut off his hands and dumped him in the forest with her corpse. He should have died then—but he brought that tribe to justice. Now he wants to stop *all* outlaws by rebuilding Helicon. And you hypocrites quibble about the past!"

"Where is Var the Stick?" Sola asked quietly.

Vara couldn't answer.

"I slew him," Neq said.

Their faces told the story. Many of these people had known Var, and more had heard of him. They were hardly ready to accept his killer as their leader. And why should they?

"It was an accident," Tyl said. "Neq thought Var had killed Soli in her childhood, as we all thought. He reacted as we all did. Before he learned the truth, Var was dead. Because of that error, Neq put aside the sword. Now I speak for his sincerity—and so does Vara."

"So we noticed," Jim said, in a tone that made Vara flush furiously.

Jimi was looking at the vine.

"Show your weapons," Tyl said to Neq.

Neq unveiled the glockenspiel. There was a murmur of amazement, for none of them had seen it before.

"Use it," Tyl said.

Neq looked about. The faces were grim and sad—grim for him, sad for Vara, who was crying without shame. These people evidently shared his vision of a new Helicon, but the example of the prior one frightened them. It frightened him too, for he had seen it in ruins.

Perhaps Helicon could not function without bloodshed, direct or indirect. Perhaps there was no way to restore the old society. But it had to be tried, and now was the time, and this was the group. He could not let it all slide away just because of the confused scruples of the moment.

They needed a leader. If he did not assume command, no one would. He was far from ideal, but there was no one else.

Neq turned to Dr. Jones. "You asked me to find out why Helicon perished, so that we could prevent it from happening again. How did the leadership fail? I do not

know. Perhaps it will fail again. Perhaps Helicon is doomed. But this is a risk that must be taken."

Dr. Jones did not respond.

Neq looked for his little hammer, but couldn't find it. So he tapped out a melody slowly with the pincers, touching the glockenspiel lightly so as to avoid the unpleasant metallic effect. Then he sang.

> If I had a hammer,
>   I'd hammer in the morning.
> I'd hammer in the evening
>   all over this land.
> I'd hammer out danger,
>   I'd hammer out warning!

As he sang, he looked first at one person, then another. The song had special meaning for him, as every song did, and while the melody was venting itself through his lung and mouth and instrument he believed it. Its pre-Blast originators could not have honored its precepts—but he was hammering out warning.

It was as though he were meeting each man in the circle and conquering him with his syncopation. And each woman was vulnerable to the sincerity of the song, the vibrant emotion of it. While his voice and hammer were in harness Neq the Glockenspiel was potent even in the face of their unified distrust.

> I'd hammer out love
>   between all my brothers
>   all over this land!

He finished that song, and sang another, and then another. It was as though he were marching out of the haunted forest again, and in a way he was, for there was nothing but song to do the job that had to be done. Vara began harmonizing with him, the way Neqa had done long ago, and slowly the others formed into a circle about him, compelled to echo the words.

He sang. The very room wavered and flowed, shaping itself into an ugly badlands mountainside girt by tangled

metal palisades, irregular stone battlements, a tunnel under the awful mountain, a vast cavern filled with ashes. Helicon formed, and Helicon's promise infused the group. From death came life—the mountain of death that meant life for the finest elements in man. The dream became tangible, thrilling, eternal; a force that no living man could deny.

At last he stopped. They were his, now, he knew. His dream had met their caution and prevailed, however illogically. Helicon would live again.

Then he saw the vine-box. Jimi had covered it, so that the flowers had opened in their darkness, and the narcotic had seeped into the room while Neq was singing.

Tyl must have seen it happen, and let it be, for Tyl was gone.

CHAPTER EIGHTEEN

Fifty strong, they unloaded at devastated Helicon. The mountain appeared much the same from the outside—a looming, forbidding mound of refuse.

"We shall not need to kill in Helicon's defense," Neq said. "We will accept those who climb to the snow line. If they are unsuitable, we will send them far away. No one who comes to us must be allowed to return to the nomad world."

The others nodded. They all knew the mischief such returns had made in the past. Had Helicon truly kept to itself, instead of dabbling in nomad politics, the original society of the crazy demesnes would have survived unbroken. It had been a lesson—one that Neq himself had learned most harshly of all.

The nomads were the real future of mankind. The crazies were only caretakers, preserving what they could of the civilization the nomads would one day draw upon. Helicon was the supplier for the crazies. But Helicon and the crazies could not make the civilization themselves, for that would be identical to the system of the past.

The past that had made the Blast. The most colossal failure in man's history.

Yet by the same token the nomads had to be prevented from assuming command of Helicon, either to destroy it or to absorb its technology directly. There must not be a forced choice between barbarism and the Blast. The caretaker order had to be maintained for centuries, perhaps millennia, until the nomads, in their own time, outgrew it. Then the new order would truly prevail, shed of the liabilities of the old.

That, at least, was Dr. Jones' theory. Neq only knew that they had a job to do. Perhaps the others understood it better than he did, for even the scattered children in the group were subdued.

"To many of you, the interior will be strange," Neq said. "Think of it as a larger crazy building, gutted at the moment but about to be restored by our effort. Each person will have his area of responsibility. Dick the Surgeon will be in charge of group health, as he was before; he will check the perimeters with the radiation counter—the crazy click-box—and set the limits of safety by posting warners. Only with his permission—and mine—will anyone go beyond these. The mountain is a badlands; the kill-spirits still lurk.

"Jim the Gun will be in charge of mechanical operations; restoring electric power, making the machinery functional. Most of us will work under his direction for as long as it takes. A year, perhaps. Without the machinery Helicon can not live; it will bring in air and water and keep the temperature even and make our night and day. Some of you are—*were*—crazies; you know more about electricity than Jim does. He's in charge because he's a leader and you are not. Had there been leadership among the crazies, Helicon might never have fallen, and would certainly have been rebuilt before this."

They nodded somberly. Leaders existed among the nomads, but the crazies didn't operate the same way. In time the new Helicon would amalgamate its disparate elements and rear its own leaders and technicians and be a complete society in itself. Right now everything had to be makeshift.

Neq continued announcing assignments while the others stared at the mountain. Cooking, explorations, foraging, supply, cleanup—he had worked this out carefully in consultation with literate crazy advisers during the truck journey here, and he wanted each person to know his place in the scheme as he viewed the interior for the first time. He put Vara in charge of defense, for the time being: she would cultivate the vines, and clear rooms for the flowers to occupy, and set up an effective system of lights and vents so that no one could penetrate Helicon by

stealth without passing through that narcotic atmosphere. The mountain would never be taken by storm! Sola was in charge of boarding; she had to assign a private room to each man, and provide for some recreational facilities.

"What about rooms for the women?" someone asked.

"We have no rooms," Sola said. "We will share with the men—a different room each night on strict rotation. That is the way it has to be, since we have only eight women within the nubile range, and forty men. There is no marriage here, and bracelets are only sentiment. You all knew that before you enlisted."

Then Vara described the history of Helicon, for the majority of this group was aware of only portions of it. She told how the Ancients, who had been like crazies with nomad passions, had filled the world with people they could not feed and had built machines whose action they could not control, and had finally blown themselves up in desperation. That was the Blast—the holocaust that had created the contemporary landscape.

Not all the people had died at once. More were killed by radiation than in the physical blast—actually a massive series of blasts—and that had taken time. There were desperation efforts to salvage civilization, most of which came to nothing. But one group in America assembled an army of construction equipment and bulldozed a mountain from the refuse of one of the former cities. It was the largest structure ever made by man, and probably the ugliest—but within its depths, shielded from further fallout, was the complex of Helicon: an enclave of preserved civilization and technology. Only a tiny portion of this labyrinth was residential. A larger section consisted of workshops and hydroponics, and one wing contained the atomic pile that generated virtually unlimited power.

"Dr. Jones assures us that's still functional," Vara said. "It's completely automatic, designed to operate for centuries. It made the first century, anyway. All we have to do is reconnect the wiring at our end."

The name Helicon had been borrowed from a myth of the Ancients: it was the mountain home of the muses, who were the nine daughters of the gods Zeus and Mnemosyne, and were themselves the goddesses of memory

and art and science. Poetry, history, tragedy, song—it all reflected the spirit of Helicon as originally conceived. The virtues of civilization were to have been remembered here.

But Helicon had lacked self-sufficiency in one vital respect: personnel. The people who first stocked it had been the elite of the devastated world: the scientists, the highly skilled technicians, the ranking professionals. Most were men, and most were not young. The few women, children of the elite, could hardly replenish the enclave in a generation without dangerous inbreeding—and they had substantial scruples about trying.

So it was necessary to allow limited immigration from the outside world. The prospect was appalling to the founders, for it meant admitting the very barbarians that Helicon was on guard against, but they had no choice. Without enough children to educate in the traditions and technology of civilization, Helicon would slowly die.

They were fortunate, for some elements of civilization had survived outside. People who later came to be known as the "crazies" because their idealistic mode of operation made no sense to the majority, were quick to appreciate the potential benefits of collaboration. They provided some new blood for Helicon, and pointed out that many barbarians could be safely recruited if they were made to understand that there was absolutely no return. Thus Helicon became the mountain of death—an honorable demise for those with courage. And regular, secret trade was instituted, with Helicon adapting a portion of its enormous technical resources to the manufacture of tools and machinery, while the crazies provided wood and surface produce that was much preferable to the hydroponic food turned out by less-than-expert chemists.

The crazies' vision turned out to be larger than that of the founders of Helicon, for the crazies were in touch with the real world and were necessarily pragmatic about nomad relations, despite the nomads' opinion. They ordered weapons from the Helicon machine shops—not modern ones, but simple nomad implements. Swords and daggers; clubs and quarterstaffs. They issued these to the nomads in return for a certain docility: the weapons were to be used only in formal combat, with noncombatants inviolate, and no person could be denied personal freedom.

Enforcement was indirect but effective: the crazies cut off the supply to any regions that failed to conform. Since the metal weapons were vastly superior to the homemade ones, the "crazy demesnes" spread rapidly as far as their supply lines were able to go. Their services expanded to include medicine and boarding, with hostels being assembled from prefabricated sections produced in Helicon. There was nothing the crazies could return in direct payment for Helicon's full-scale help—but the improvement in the local level of civilization was such that many more recruits were available for both the crazies and Helicon. All three parties to this enterprise profited.

But Helicon remained the key. Only there could high-quality items be mass-produced.

Then Helicon had been destroyed. And the crazy demesnes had collapsed.

"And ours was the best system in the world," Vara concluded. "There are other Helicons in other parts of the world, but they were never as good as ours and they don't have much effect. Var and I discovered that in the years we traveled. To the north they have guns and electricity, but they are not nice people. In Asia they have trucks and ships and buildings, but they—well, for us, our way is best. So now we are going to rebuild Helicon . . ."

Neq took them inside by way of the passage from the hostel. "This will be our secret," he said. "Converts will have to try the mountain. But the crazies can't send trucks up there, so they will bring supplies for trade to this point. This hostel is seldom used by nomads in the normal course, since it is an end station, not a travel station."

The tunnel curved into its darkness. The lift is on hostel power," Neq explained, reminded again of Neqa and her explanations to him so long ago. "Once we restore Helicon power . . . but lanterns will do for now."

When they were gathered in the storage room, he opened the panel to reveal the subway tracks. A wheeled cart was there; he had brought it up when he finished the long grisly cleanup job. Only a few of the party could ride it at a time, and it had to be pushed by hand, but it was still quicker to ferry them this way than to make them all walk.

The nomad converts in particular were nervous about these depths.

When all were assembled on the platform at the other end, he guided them up the ramp for the grand tour. The nomads were awed, the crazies impressed, and the Helicon survivors subdued. Everything was bare and clean—no doubt quite a contrast to what the former underworlders remembered.

At the dining hall he paused, feeling a chill himself. He remembered the way he had left it, after removing the bodies and cleaning out the charred furniture. He had stacked the salvageable items in one corner, and had left a cache of durable staples in the kitchen area.

One of the tables had been moved. Some of his dried beans had been used. Someone had been here.

Neq concealed his dismay by continuing the tour. "I don't know the purpose of all the rooms, and certainly not the equipment," he said. "We'll be drawing heavily on the experience of those of you who were here before."

Inwardly he was chagrined. He and the crazies had searched for every possible surviving member of Helicon. Compared experiences and his body-count suggested that very few were unaccounted for. Was the intruder from outside? Most of the tribesmen were terrified of this region, and would never enter the mountain even if they could find their way in.

Of course Tyl and his army had forced entry here during the conquest of the mountain, so those men could penetrate Helicon again if they chose. But Neq had sealed over the invasion apertures as well as he could and none of them seemed to have been reopened, and no damage had been done.

Someone had come without fear, looked about, had a bite to eat, and departed. That person could come again.

CHAPTER NINETEEN

"Yes, she is pregnant," Dick the Surgeon said. "I think under the circumstances she should be excused from, er, circulation. Our children will be our most important asset for some time, for they will be raised in the atmosphere of civilization. . . ."

It was Neq's decision to make, and it would set a precedent, but he was aware of his own bias. Intellectually he knew that the women had to be shared; emotionally he couldn't share Vara. "It's a matter of health," he said. "That's your department."

So Vara did not circulate. Actually the system had not been fully implemented yet; people needed time to settle in to it. There was some problem about the women's arrangements, for they required more privacy than the men's rooms provided, sexual aspects aside. Finally they were assigned rooms of their own, but were expected to make their rounds on schedule.

If the social system functioned with hesitation, at least the reconstruction didn't. The restoration of electric power was much simpler than anticipated. A few cables replaced, a few circuit-breakers closed, a few fixtures tinkered with, a few parts substituted, and there was light and heat and circulating air and sanitary facilities in operation. Helicon had been beautifully designed; they were not building or even rebuilding it. They were merely implementing a system that had been temporarily interrupted. In a month they were ready to tackle the peripheral machinery: the subway to the hostel, the manufacturing machines. In two months the first weapons were produced:

quarterstaffs cut from an endless metal pole extruded from an automatic smelter-processor. There was ore from the monstrous metallic refuse of the mountain—enough for a century's such operations.

Neq realized with a certain surprise that it was working! Helicon was coming back to life, beginning to function again. That simple, significant success had almost been obscured behind the minutiae of daily projects and crises! Actually, Helicon was an entity in itself, performing on its own fashion; the hiatus of years and the change of personnel seemed almost irrelevant to its giant personality.

The signal alarm woke Neq during the night cycle. Night was artificial here, as was day, but they maintained the same rhythm as above. The recently renovated television screen was on.

"We've netted something," Jim the Gun said tersely. "It didn't pass through any of the entrances we know, but it's inside now. I thought you'd want to be on hand."

"Yes!" Neq shrugged into his special open-sleeve robe and hurried through the half-lighted halls to Jim's laboratory. He remembered the mysterious visitor. Had he come again?

"I thought it was one of the fringe beasts," Jim said. "They keep finding new places. . . ." Neq knew what he meant. There were strange creatures in the radiation-soaked outer tunnels of the mountain—mutation-spawned monsters who had shaped their own grotesque ecology. Helicon proper had been sealed off from such sections, but the seal was imperfect, and sometimes rodents and amphibians got through. Once a dead toothy froglike thing had popped out of a flush toilet, and Jim had had to trace the sewer pipes to discover the entry point. It had been hopeless; Helicon's water came from a vast subterranean conduit and departed the same way after passing through a waste-recycling plant. It was too complex to unravel, and dangerous to tamper with, for the water was hot—so hot that live steam burst periodically from vents and filled the maintenance passages. Jim had had to settle for a filter in the main drinking-water pipe. Sometimes eerie noises penetrated the walls, as of alien creatures hunting or struggling. The increasing hum of functioning machinery drowned much of this out, and that was a blessing. It was

too easy for the nomads to believe in haunts—since, of course, there *were* haunts.

Jim had rigged an alarm system designed to spot the emergence of any such creatures, so that the holes could be located and plugged. "It's a big one this time," he said, leading Neq to a storeroom as yet unused. The back wall here seemed solid, but Jim had traced skuff-marks in the dust of the floor to a removable panel constructed to resemble stone. "Human or near-human, obviously," Jim said. "He came in from the other side—it seems to be a half-collapsed tunnel with some radiation—and pushed out the panel, then replaced it perfectly. Then on through the room and out to the hall—which is where he tripped my electric-eye system. He was gone by the time I got here, of course—but at least we know how he did it."

Neq felt the chill again. "But he's inside Helicon—right now!" Had he come for beans again—or something more?

Jim nodded. "He passed the eye half an hour ago. I can't tell from the signal whether it's a mouse or an elephant—uh, that's an extremely large animal that existed before the Blast. Elephant. I get several of these each night—"

"The Elephants?"

"Alarms. And I don't know anything until I check personally. Half the time it's one of our own personnel, on some unscheduled business. Or a couple of them. Quite a bit of out-of-turn trysting in these back rooms, you know. I have to be very cautious about checking. The girls share, but they want to get pregnant by particular men . . ."

Neq knew. He had never cracked down on it because he felt the same way himself. It was *his* baby Vara carried, whatever name it was to bear.

"So we're late starting, but we can run him down. Block off this exit and flood the halls with flower-narcotic—"

Neq didn't like it. "There are *people* going about," he pointed out. "We keep a limited night shift going now, and some are on the machines. A whiff of the flower, and equipment could be wrecked. The amount that gets around by accident is bad enough! No, we'll do it by hand. How could a stranger come, and not be seen?"

"He would have to know Helicon," Jim said. "Where to hide, where to step aside—"

"And how to bluff his way through when he *did* meet people," Neq said. "That makes him dangerous. We don't know his motive."

"It has to be a former member of Helicon," Jim said. "One of our retreads should be able to recognize him?"

"Helicon is open to the old members. Why hasn't he contacted us?"

"Maybe he's trying to."

"All he has to do is yell or bang on the wall."

"Let's go to my lab," Jim said. "If he keeps ducking out of sight, he'll have to trip other alarms."

They were in luck. The intruder tripped several alarms, ducking out of the way as others used the hall. Jim kept no eye-beams set in the main passages, since that would lead to hopeless confusion. It was coincidental, but his emplacements were ideally suited to this type of chase.

"He's going somewhere," Jim said. "See that pattern. I think he's literate—a couple of those dodges were near the dining room bulletin board. Now he knows what he wants. When we figure it out too, we'll be able to intercept him. Catch him by surprise, so he can't hurt anyone."

"Toward the sleeping quarters!" Neq exclaimed, looking at the chart of Helicon on which Jim had set his markers.

"Oh-oh. I don't have them bugged, for the obvious reason. We'll lose him."

"I'll post emergency guards." And Neq went about the matter quietly, using the underground intercom system to wake those on call. Soon armed men would stand at strategic points in all the halls of that section.

But *soon* was not *now*. A horrible picture formed in Neq's mind. The person who would have known Helicon best was its former leader, Bob. He would have escaped if anyone had. Neq used his office now, and was reminded of the man more than he liked. There were little things about the setup, such as the way the metal desk faced the only door, and the gun in that desk, and the wiring for intercom connections to every part of Helicon, and the spotlights set in the ceiling. That office was a little fortress. There had been scorch-marks in it, as in the rest of Helicon—but no corpse. Sol could have caught Bob elsewhere and killed him, of course—but there was

no proof of that. Bob might have survived, somehow—and now he could be returning, determined to be avenged on the child who had rejected his perverted advances. . . .

Abruptly something else came clear. *That was why Bob had sent Soli to her presumed death!* Vengeance for the embarrassment she had caused him! Instead of submitting, she had driven him off with her sticks . . . and at any time she could have told Sol. She had had to be eliminated —and what better way than by besieging nomads, Sol's kind?

And therein lay Bob's fatal mistake. He had not acted for the best interests of Helicon, but to avenge and cover his own mistake with Soli. He had let personal factors interfere with his duty.

"What?" Vara exclaimed as Neq entered. "Oh, it's you."

Just as Neq was letting his own involvement with the same girl interfere with his own duty. "There's a stranger in the halls, coming this way. For you, I think. There wasn't time to set guards—"

"Oh!" she said, going for her sticks.

He pushed her down on the bed again. She was heavy and her breasts were huge as he touched her in the dark. "No action for you! That's why I'm here. If he enters—"

"But I have no enemies, do I?" she asked. "Except maybe you, when I empty my belly and start sharing in a few months."

He laughed, but the remark cut him. How could he enforce the system for others, unless he honored it himself? No wonder the social system had not been working well.

Bob's mistake. . . .

"It is over between us," he said. "I love you, but I am master of Helicon. I must be objective. Do you understand?"

"Yes, you are right," she said, and it hurt him that she could agree so readily. "It has to be that way."

He knew then that it *was* over. She was a child of Helicon; she understood the sharing system emotionally as well as intellectually. She had never been his to keep.

A few minutes later they both heard it. Quick furtive steps in the hall, coming near.

The door opened. Neq raised his claw to strike, wishing for his sword. He nudged the light switch with his elbow. Brilliance erupted.

Vara screamed.

Momentarily blinded, the stranger stood with tousled hair and arms lifted on guard. A woman. Naked.

Pretty face, rather shapely figure, lithe legs, well formed breasts—had he had his sword, he would have cut her down before he realized.

"Sosa!" Vara cried, scrambling from the bed.

The two women embraced while Neq stood with claw frozen. Of all the developments!

"Oh, mother, I'm so glad!" Vara sobbed. "I *knew* you were alive . . ."

Sosa: the woman Vara considered her real mother, in preference to Sola. Naturally she had returned to join her daughter. Naturally she didn't care about anyone else. Or to meet anyone else, in her silent nudity. She just wanted to visit Vara and perhaps take her away, staying clear of other entanglements. She had probably had to swim through some of the fringe-cavern waterways, avoiding radiation. The mystery had been solved.

Now the two women were reunited, and oblivious to him. Neq left quietly, knowing he would not be missed.

Vara did not leave. Sosa stayed. She merged with the group so smoothly that it seemed she had always been there. She assumed Vara's duties including the sharing, and though she was of Neq's generation the men were very glad to participate with her. She was a small, active woman in very good condition and easy to get along with. Her immediate past was a mystery; she had disappeared when Helicon was destroyed, and reappeared now that it lived again, and she confessed her troubles to no one.

If Neq had doubted Vara's need for him before, now there was no question. Vara needed nobody but Sosa. It was good that such comfort was available in her period of stress, but it cast Neq loose without even the excuse of jealousy.

Jim's call on the newly-renovated television network awakened Neq again. Another routine emergency!

"Someone in the subway," Jim said. "Going, not coming. Seems to be female."

Vara, he thought, horrified. Sosa had finally talked her into leaving, so that the baby would not be subject to Helicon! "I'll check it myself," he said.

Jim nodded in the screen, perhaps understanding Neq's concern. It was a matter to handle privately.

Someone was certainly in the subway, but not using the cars. Neq let out the breath he held when passing through the flower-chambers and smelled the other faint perfume, the kind the women liked to wear. Of course she would not use one of the cars; such a drain on Helicon power would immediately alert the monitor. Few people knew about Jim's *other* monitors, as a matter of policy and security. Increasingly Neq appreciated the various mechanisms of his predecessor, Bob; it *was* necessary to know what was going on, without having to share that information with others.

There was no dust on the tracks now, for the subway was regularly used. He could not trace her visually. But when he put one ear to the metal he heard some faint brushing or knocking. Someone was walking along the track, headed for the hostel. Someone heavy, a bit clumsy . . . like a woman large with child.

He followed into the dark tunnel, running silently. Soon he could hear her directly, and he slowed to make sure he would not be prematurely detected. He wanted to catch her before she could do anything rash. Vara could be a difficult handful at the best of times. . . .

She was picking her way along as though afraid of the dark, making slow progress. One person, not two.

Why wasn't Sosa with her? Sosa was catlike in the dark, and she had other routes—but she would not leave her adopted daughter to stumble alone. Actually, Vara herself was a competent night marcher; pregnancy should not change that completely.

He came up behind her and spoke. "Go no farther."

"Oh!" It was a shriek of surprise, and something dropped.

The voice gave her away: Sola. She had been carrying her belongings in a bundle in her arms, together with

what must be a fair amount of food and water. No wonder she lumbered!

"What are you doing here?" he demanded, perversely angry at her for not being Vara.

"I'm leaving!"

Obviously. "No one leaves Helicon. You know that better than anyone."

"Then kill me!" she cried, hysterically defiant. "I won't stay with *her*!"

Why did everyone associate him with killing, still? "Vara? But she needs you more than ever now—"

"Sosa!" The name was hissed.

Belatedly, he made the connection. If *he* resented Sosa's captivity of Vara's affection, how much more should Vara's natural mother resent being shunted aside at the very time she had expected to be closest to her daughter? He had been narrow to view Sosa's impact only as it applied to himself. He had overlooked the natural reactions of others—just as Bob had, before. Was he fated to make all the same mistakes, until the same end came?

"You have other responsibilities," he said, somewhat lamely. "You can't run away just because one thing isn't right." Yet he had been feeling an increasing temptation to do just that himself, for administration bored and annoyed him as it had when he was a leader in the nomad empire, and without Vara he had little to brighten his outlook. "Here in Helicon there are no mates, no parents, no children—only jobs to do."

"I know it!" she cried. "That's the trouble! I have no mate, no child!"

"Every man is your mate. You described the policy of Helicon yourself. Sharing."

She laughed bitterly. "I'm an old woman. Men don't share with me."

Neq saw that she had more than one grudge against the underworld. Had he been doing his own job properly, he would have been aware of this problem long since. He had to do something now, or admit he was less a leader than Bob had been. Yet it was impossible to restore to her the sexual attraction she had had a generation ago.

Deprived of both sexuality and motherhood in a situation where both were doubly important—no wonder Sola

was miserable! "We need you in Helicon," he said. "I shall not let you go. There is no life for you outside."

"Sosa can do my job; talk to *her*."

"No! Sosa has a different temperament. She——" Then he had it. "She can't bear children!"

"Do you think *I* can?" Sola snapped. "I'm thirty-three years old!"

"You bore Vara! Then you lived with a castrate, and then a sterile man. When you tried with Var, he was sterile too. *They* could not make life; *you* could. And you can still! And Helicon must have that life! Children are our most important——"

"Childbirth would kill me at this age. I'm almost a grandmother." Yet he knew by her tone that she wanted to be convinced.

"Not with Dick the Surgeon attending. He made the Weaponless what he was——"

"Sterile!" she put in.

"That was an accident! Look what he did for these hands of mine! No one else could have restored me like that, and he didn't make *me* sterile! He can save life; he can save yours no matter how many babies you might bear, no matter how old. And if——it won't happen, but if—— if you *do* die—*what difference does it make*? You'll die anyway in the wilderness!"

That bit of cruelty brought a perverse glimmer of hope to her face, but it passed. "No man will touch me," she said sullenly.

"*Every* man will touch you!" he cried. "This is Helicon, and I am master! I'll send——" he broke off, realizing this was the wrong approach. He was saying in effect that men had to be forced, and she would never go along with that.

"You see? *You* don't travel; you know what I mean."

He did know. Now he saw his duty. "When I first saw you, you were sixteen. You were beautiful—more lovely than any. I used to dream about you—lewd dreams."

"Did you?" She seemed genuinely flattered.

"You're older now—but so am I. You're bitter—and so am I. Yet we can do anything the youngsters can. I will give you your baby—one no one can take away from you."

"You've done your duty already by my daughter," she said, the hint of a chuckle in her voice.

"That's over. The baby will not bear my name. I had to give her what I had taken from her. She will share hereafter—as will I. And you. You have beauty yet."

"Do I?" It was a little-girl query, plaintive.

There on the tracks he took her. And in the dark he found that he had spoken truly, and there was a lot of Vara in her, and it was better than he had expected.

CHAPTER TWENTY

It was just a faint whiff, but it brought a rash of strange feelings. Neq followed his nose.

There was a tiny crack in the wall he hadn't noticed before. From a distance it looked like an imperfection in the finish, but now he discovered that it was deep. Had Bob had a secret compartment in his office, along with all the rest?

He inserted the corner of a sheet of paper into it and probed. The paper disappeared—and now he had lost his weapons-production statistics for the past month! There was space in there, all right—and the odor was jetting out, a very small current of air.

He fetched a dagger and maneuvered it into the crack with his pincers. He pried. Something snapped, and a section of the wall swung in. There was a passage here— one he had missed, and might never have found, except for the little smell.

He peered in. It was dark, of course, and there was a warm draft. The odor was much stronger.

It was a man-hewn tunnel into the unexplored subterranean wilderness of Mt. Helicon. Anything at all could lie within, and the chances were more than even that it was deadly. This called for an armed party.

Neq shrugged and entered, alone. The stimulating breath of fragrance washed down along the corridor, lightening his step, and the stone and metal walls seemed to widen. This was Bob's escape route—and he had been right, a man needed such an exit from the tedium of leadership.

Vara had borne a fine boy and named him Vari. She had spent a reasonable period recovering and tending the

baby, then begun sharing. Sosa spent considerable time with the baby also, and already it seemed as though Vari were hers. Three months after the first birth, Vara was pregnant again, and not by Neq.

Sola, too, conceived, and her joy transformed her. The two women became closer, not as mother and daughter but as sister-expectants, comparing notes and talking about plans for the Helicon nursery facilities and schooling of children. They were fine examples for the others, and the problems of the sharing system were diminishing.

Neq walked on, in a daze of memory despite the danger of exploring the unknown alone. He had a flashlight, for he never could anticipate when he might need light in Helicon, and he used it to pick out his path through the expanding passage. Now there was no metal, and the rock bore mosslike growths and was convoluted into treelike formations.

Jim the Gun had completed his initial renovation of the equipment and instituted a training program for operation and maintenance so that the work could carry on without him. "I'm not leaving," he said. "I like it here. Machines are my thing, and these are wondrous! But accidents happen, and I am aging."

As the machinery of Helicon moved toward capacity production—the capacity of the human attendants, not the machines—the exports to the crazies increased. The old trucks were renovated, for Helicon produced motors and tires and gasoline and gears, and the six trucks the crazies had been able to maintain became twenty, then fifty. Nomads had to be recruited as drivers and guards, being paid in food and good weapons and medicine. The trucks always traveled in convoys: one for the payload, another filled with warriors armed and spoiling for battle, the third carrying gasoline and replacement parts and food and similar staples. A new tribe formed: the trucker tribe, dedicated to this service. The existence and function of Helicon was no longer secret, of course, but the conditions of admittance remained stringent. The Truckers felt they had the best of it: Helicon provisions, a rambling nomad life. Many died in the actions against greedy outlaws, but this was the nomad way. Heroism.

The trail wandered between the overhanging trees,

tunnel-like. Neq walked faster, eager to get where he was going.

He had wanted to have a crew lay down a telephone cable from Helicon to the main crazy outpost. But the expenditure in manpower would have been prohibitive, since they would have had either to raise the wire out of the casual reach of the outlaws, or bury it where it could not be found. There were mountains and rivers and badlands along the route. He had to settle for continuous radio contact, which would soon become television contact.

Dick the Surgeon started a hospital where nomads could receive medical attention and such drugs as required. But this posed another problem: either he had to leave Helicon, or nomads had to be admitted on a temporary basis. The old guidelines were inadequate. Neq dispensed with them. A portion of the underworld was blocked off from the rest, and a separate entrance opened. Dick began training those nomads who were interested in the potentials of medicine, though most of these were illiterate and ignorant. He had to devise simplified picture-codes for prescriptions: a circle with a jagged arrow through it representing a headache for aspirin; the outline of a tooth for novocaine; a squiggle representing a germ for antibiotics. He made sure no dangerous drugs were available without his supervision, and the system worked well enough. The nomad trainees were not stupid; they merely had to learn.

But Neq declared that the children of Helicon should be literate. He set the example by attending classes himself, painstakingly mastering the words: MAN, ROOM, FOOD, HONOR. There was an enormous amount to be learned from the old books, and the new generation would not be able to improve on the past without understanding it. The present generation was too busy to practice reading, and Neq had to graduate after building a vocabulary of twenty words, but he knew that once Helicon was thoroughly established the priorities would change.

Yes, it was all going well. Neq was as successful in running Helicon as he had been in running his own tribe for the empire.

This region was familiar. The contour of the route, the type of forest—there was a dead-spoked giant pine he

remembered. The memories were at once poignant and horrible, but he had to go on.

Vara's love had proved fickle. It was apparent that her affair with him had been the swing of the pendulum, compensation for her prior abuse of him. And his love for her—it had never compared to the sublime passion he had had for Neqa. He had succumbed to the lure of young flesh, thinking the experience more meaningful than it was. Vara had merely started sharing early, that Helicon might be repopulated.

Neqa: there was the meaning of it all. He had done what he had done to bring back the world that sponsored her kind—but he had not brought *her* back. This was where Yod's barricade had been set across the trail, balking their truck. Yod's tribe was gone now, of course, and even the staring skulls on poles were gone. Vengeance. . . .

It was time to make camp, for he had come far. Neq bared his sword to cut down saplings for a temporary lean-to. The gleaming steel reminded him: had he demonstrated just a bit of his sworder-skill and agreed to join Yod's outlaw tribe, he could have saved his hands and Neqa's life. Were he in the same situation today, he would do it. She would have had to share—but would that have been so very different from Vara's sharing at Helicon, after bearing the child of her husband's murderer? Would Neqa have been unworthy of his love after bearing Yod's child? She could have borne fifty children by other men, if that were the price of preserving her life! With greater circumspection he could have bided his time and eventually assumed the mastery of the tribe and recovered his woman. He had acted impetuously—and paid a grievous price.

Dusk—and someone was coming!

Neq's blade lifted, ready. He did not wish to kill—but this place was in its way sacred to him, and the man who abused his privacy would be in trouble.

In the gloom of evening beneath the dense forest, Neq paced the man more by sound than sight. The tread was light yet not furtive.

Now he saw the figure: small, very small, with no visible weapon.

"Neq!"

By the voice he knew her: Sosa.

"What are you doing here?" he demanded, knowing she had followed him all the way from the mountain: several days swift march. Did she seek to bring him back as he had brought Sola back?

"I smelled the flowers," she said. "I tend them now, and I thought it was a leak, but it wasn't. So I traced it to your office . . . I'm almost immune, after these months with the vine. But you—"

Neq stepped toward her, lifting the sword. But even in the worst of his vengeance he had not attacked women.

"I was afraid of that," she murmured. "I'll have to watch you, until I can locate the plants and shut them off."

She walked by him, passing quite close, and he was aware of her athletic surprisingly attractive body. Women didn't *have* to fade as they aged! Bemused, he followed her, not certain what she intended or what he desired.

Then he recognized her destination. "Stay clear of that grave!" he cried.

"Grave? That's your real wound, isn't it?" she said. "Ah, I think this is it. The passage is blocked, but there's an updraft—"

She began to scrape away the leaves and twigs that covered the site of Neqa's grave, exposing the rich earth beneath. "This is garbage!" she exclaimed.

Neq raised the sword again. "Stop, or surely you must die!"

"I'm doing this for you," she said, continuing. "The draft is bringing the fumes straight out. The flowers must be just beyond this refuse."

"I would not slay a woman," Neq said, his blade poised above her body. "But if I must—"

"In a moment I'll have it," she said. "Meanwhile, please don't threaten me with that thing. If you knew how many times I have been widowed, you would see that your sorrow is hardly unique. I don't care what you think you see; I have a job to do here."

He saw that she would not stop. But he could not allow Neqa's bones to be defiled.

He spread his arms so that the sword would not strike

her and moved forward, shoving her aside with his body. His own torso would guard the sacred earth!

But Sosa's dirt-caked hands came up, striking him across the neck so that he choked. She got her little shoulder under him and somehow threw him back. "Please stay clear," she said quietly. "There may be danger, and I have to get this junk out."

Now he remembered what Vara had said about this woman. She was skilled, circle-skilled, with her bare hands! She had taught the Weaponless his art. It was folly to attempt to wrestle with her.

Numbly, he watched the hole deepen. It was not mere bones she was searching out. He had no idea whether anything at all remained of Neqa after all these years. It was the associations of Neqa—the manner she had died, the way he had acted then. The nightmare portion of his nomad dream, that he had tried to put aside. Rape, murder, anguish, vengeance, futility. . . .

She struck solidity. Horrified, Neq shone the light as she reached down, grasped, and hauled up—

A hooflike foot.

Appalled, Neq stumbled back. This was the cairn of Var the Stick—the other nightmare!

The foot stirred, the gross blunted toes twitching. Earth showered off as the hairy leg kicked out of the ground.

"Oh-oh," Sosa said. "I didn't expect *this*!" She scrambled away from the hole.

An arm came up, levering against the surface. The body heaved. The corpse sat up.

The shock of it sobered Neq momentarily, and he realized that he was under the influence of the narcotic vine-flowers, as Sosa had tried to tell him. They must have seeded here, for the fumes were actually pollen, and there had been some leakages. If there were earth here, and moisture, and occasional light, the vines could have sprouted and bloomed.

The corpse was neither Neqa nor Var, but some living thing climbing out of the partially stopped passage. Something manlike—but *what*? Already his vision was becoming distorted again, for the fumes were heavy in this semi-confined space.

Neq tapped on the glockenspiel with his pincers, but could not think of a suitable song for the occasion.

"I thought you were dead!" Sosa cried at the shape.

A grotesquely formless head swiveled to cover her. "Hel-Helicon dead!" it growled.

"Helicon *lives*!" Neq cried, discovering suddenly loyalty after his recent, drug-strengthened doubts. He brought up his sword—and hesitated, knowing that so long as he saw it as a sword, the narcotic was ruling his mind. "Stop those flowers!" he cried at Sosa. "Use my flashlight—"

She came immediately and took it from him. She could use it far more effectively than he could with the pincers. She flashed it into the hole, searching for the vines that had to be near.

Neq faced the creature. "Who are you?" he demanded.

"Dead!" the thing repeated. It stood near the hole, as tall as a man, but with a scarred, hairless head.

"It's Bob," Sosa said. "Master of Helicon."

The former master! So he *had* escaped Sol's vengeance!

"I am master now," Neq said. "You and I must settle."

"Get out of here, Neq!" Sosa cried. "He's a *real* killer, and you're under the influence of the—"

"This way," Bob said. His voice was barely intelligible, as though it had not been used for years.

"Don't go there!" Sosa cried. "He's mad!"

The men ignored her. Bob descended into the grave and Neq followed, feeling with his pincers to locate the perimeters. He crawled along on elbows and knees, keeping his sword clear of the rubble. Sosa did not follow.

They emerged into a palatial cavern whose floor angled down into a steaming river: the Helicon water supply. It was hot here, and there was light: electric light from bulbs set in the ceiling.

"You've had power here—the whole time?"

"Certainly." Bob's voice was clearer now that he was in his own territory, and the flower fragrance was fading. "I prepared this refuge well, in case of need. There's a vent to the summit of the mountain, with a ladder and escape hatch."

"Why did you stay here, then?"

"It's cold up there." That was an understatement. The

top of the mounatin was always covered with snow, and death lurked in the form of countless cliffs and crevasses and avalanches. Mighty storms spun off the glaciers, feeding the melt-rivers of the snowline whose waters plunged into these atomically heated interior caverns. It would take a desperate man indeed to leave comfort like this to endure that.

"You are alone?" It was hard to believe that any man could endure seven years in complete isolation.

"Of course not. I have a most obliging and disciplined tribe. Come—you must see. I have no envy of your position." He showed the way along the river to a series of offshoot caverns.

There were animals here—mutant badlands creatures of diverse shapes and sizes. Some slunk away as the men approached, but others seemed to be tame. "These?" Neq asked.

"This is part of it. These are workers and gatherers— illiterate, of course. They do an excellent job of tending and harvesting the hydroponics, but they aren't very intelligent."

Neq saw that the ratlike individuals were nipping bits of fungus from crevices and carrying them away. "Hydroponics," he agreed.

"You really must meet my wife," Bob said expansively. "One thing about the life of the Helicon master: no woman to yourself."

"I know." So one of the women had come there too!

"That forced objectivity, when there are constant decisions of life and death, and no personal life—it isn't Helicon you've inherited, it's Hell."

Neq had learned about Hell through his songs. The parallel seemed apt enough. "I saw your traces in the dining room. I wondered who had visited."

"Traces? Not mine. I blocked up the passage with refuse and never used it, until you started burrowing from the other side just now. I had to investigate that commotion, of course."

Refuse—and the vine-flower spores had rooted there, downwind from Bob's caverns but upwind from Helicon. They had grown and blossomed, betraying the secret.

Sosa had not been excavating Neqa's grave or Var's cairn, but Bob's refuge.

"Why did you try to kill the child Soli?" Neq asked as though it were a matter of mere curiosity. Once he had a clear answer coinciding with what he already knew of the matter, he could consider his action. This time he would make no precipitous mistake!

"I never tried to kill her. I tried to save Helicon."

"You failed."

"The failure was not mine. I knew that no nomad would kill either a woman or a child, especially one as fetching as little Soli. I knew that the barbarian warrior, meeting her in the secrecy of the mesa, would either allow her the victory or hide her unharmed and claim the victory himself. In either case, Helicon was safe."

Bob, sealed in these caverns, could not have known the story of Var and Soli. He had calculated correctly— except for the human factor within Helicon. "Safe?"

"If she had the victory, the nomads were honor-bound to lift the siege. If she were announced dead, my revelation of her identity would neutralize the nomad leader and have the same effect. Sos knew how to put pressure on the mountain; he was a superb military tactician, and he had studied our defenses from inside. He might have won—but no other nomad would have had either the motive or the ability."

Somehow it made sense—except that it had failed. "Why didn't you tell the others your strategy?"

"A leader never tips his hand in advance. Surely you know that. I had to make it work, then explain it or not, as seemed best. Premature information could have been disastrous."

Neq wondered how well his song and flower gambit would have worked, had the group known what he was doing before he assumed the leadership. He knew the answer. Bob was right. Except: "But Sol fired Helicon!"

Bob glanced at him. "That barbarian? He lacked the wit. *I* fired Helicon."

Amazed, Neq said nothing.

"Somehow the fool librarian got hold of some of the information and the word spread before I was ready to

explain. Sol charged toward my office intending to attack me personally, and I saw in the monitors that the others actually sided with the fool. I have no tolerance for such short-sightedness. So I pushed the DESTRUCT button on my desk and came here. I never cared to return; it would have been messy."

"Vengeance?" Neq asked softly, muscles taut.

"There is no profit in vengeance; you'll learn that one day," Bob said condescendingly. "It was merely practicality. When discipline deteriorates, the organization is defunct. It is kinder to terminate it outright."

"But the entire nomad society collapsed!"

Bob shrugged. "One must accept the consequence of one's mistakes."

It was plausible. Bob had known what he was doing. When others had tried to interfere, he had acted most effectively to suppress the mutiny. This was true leadership. Had Bob been in Neq's situation seven years ago, he would have arranged to kill Yod before Neqa ever was threatened. Neq knew that next to this man he was an innocent; he lacked the fortitude to do what was necessary. Neq had blundered through life, either prevailing extemporaneously or suffering harshly.

They came to another large cavern. "Ah, here she is," Bob said. "A fine, loyal woman who embodies the very principles of obedience and trust and discretion I require. Had the functionaries of Helicon only been similar . . ."

A shaggy, bearlike creature with aquatic flipper-feet shuffled up: another fringe mutant. "Pleased to meet you, Boba," Neq said.

"Not Boba—that's decadent nomad nomenclature," Bob corrected him. "*Mrs.* Bob."

Neq nodded gravely. "Now I understand."

They met him the other side of the grave-dump. "What happened?" Jim demanded. "Did you kill him?"

"Of course not," Neq said, walking briskly on. "There is no profit in vengeance."

"But Bob was responsible for all the——" Sosa began.

"He has accepted the consequence of his mistake," Neq said. "As have I. Seal off the passage, and don't worry about the vines there; they make no difference." The

fragrance was strong here, and he wanted to get out of it before his judgment was distorted again.

"Almost forgot," Jim said. "Someone's been trying to reach us on the radio—not the crazies. I had it switched to your office, but—"

In moments Neq was there. The voice emerging from the speaker was foreign. He strode out of the tunnel and touched his broadcast button. "Speak English!" he snapped. "This is Helicon." Too bad the narcotic didn't make all things intelligible!

After a brief delay another voice came through, accented. "This is the Andes station. We have been trying to reach you. There has been no contact for seven years—"

"Merely an interruption," Neq said.

"But we sent an envoy by helicopter two years ago, and he reported that your premises were deserted—"

So that was the mysterious visitor! "There has been a change in personnel. We regret that our former leader, Robert, has had to retire. I am Neq. You may deal with me henceforth."

The voice sounded worried. "We dealt many years with Robert. How did he die?"

"Please, Andes!" Neq said, affecting shock. "Helicon is civilized! Bob left his position in order to devote his full energies to his wife—a charming creature. Send your representative again and we'll introduce him."

There was a pause. Then: "That will not be necessary. Are you in normal operation again? Do you need assistance?"

"How is your supply of young women?" Neq asked.

"How is your supply of electronic equipment?"

Neq smiled. He had a job to do, and suddenly he liked it.